PORTRAIT OF DESIRE

"Patience, Jennifer. Patience," Nicholas said, fidgeting with the gathers of her green satin dress, then letting his fingers move on upward, touching her waist, then most boldly putting his fingers to the bodice of her dress, feeling sweat prickling on his brow as he pretended to rearrange the lace that lay across the fullness of her breasts.

Jennifer's eyes widened, looking downward, watching. She seemed to stop breathing as his fingers continued to touch her there . . . where her heart then began to pound in unison with a strange throbbing deep down, inside her, between her thighs. It was an ache of sorts . . . but an ache that felt good.

"Nicholas, what are you—?" she began, and then their eyes met in a rapturous gaze. . . .

Books by Cassie Edwards

HER FORBIDDEN PIRATE

BELOVED EMBRACE

DESIRE'S BLOSSOM

ELUSIVE ECSTASY

ENCHANTED ENEMY

EUGENIA'S EMBRACE

FORBIDDEN EMBRACE

PASSION'S FIRE

PORTRAIT OF DESIRE

RAPTURE'S RENDEZVOUS

SAVAGE HEART

SAVAGE INNOCENCE

SAVAGE PARADISE

SAVAGE OBSESSION

SAVAGE TORMENT

SILKEN RAPTURE

Published by Kensington Publishing Corporation

Portrait of Desire

Cassie Edwards

ZEBRA BOOKS
KENSINGTON PUBLISHING CORP.
http://www.kensingtonbooks.com

ZEBRA BOOKS are published by

Kensington Publishing Corp.
119 West 40th Street
New York, NY 10018

All Kensington titles, imprints, and distributed lines are available at special quantity discounts for bulk purchases for sales pro-
motion, premiums, fund-raising, educational, or institutional use.

Special book excerpts or customized printings can also be created to fit specific needs. For details, write or phone the office
of the Kensington Special Sales Manager: Attn.: Special Sales
Department. Kensington Publishing Corp., 119 West 40th Street,
New York, NY 10018. Phone: 1-800-221-2647.

Zebra and the Z logo Reg. U.S. Pat. & TM Off.

ISBN-13: 978-1-4201-1958-9
ISBN-10: 1-4201-1958-3

First Printing: June 1982
10 9 8 7 6 5

Printed in the United States of America

The desire of the moth for the star . . .
Of the night for the morrow . . .
The devotion to something afar
From the sphere of our sorrow.

—SHELLEY

Part One

Seattle

Chapter One

August 1892

The midmorning sun played through the stained glass windows of the Seattle General Baptist Church like several miniature rainbows, settling on the faces of the choir members who sat, passive, behind the figure of Reverend Frank Brewster.

Jennifer Lynn Brewster sat in the fifth pew, attired in her long white eyelet dress, watching her father. When he finally sat back down on a high-backed chair, Jennifer breathed more easily. But when she saw his hand reach inside his suit jacket, to clutch at his heart, fear surged through her. She had worried that her father was trying to carry on "as usual" too soon after the loss of his wife. Now Jennifer was sure of it.

Even though her father had kept trying to reassure Jennifer that the Lord was with them . . . that He would show them the way . . . it hadn't kept Jennifer from puzzling over the why's of her mother's death. If the Lord showed people the way . . . then why had He led her mother to die in such a horrible fashion? Had her mother really been dead now . . . for two . . . full weeks? It didn't seem possible.

Jennifer couldn't help but wonder if she would ever be able to accept or understand her mother's death.

The stirrings of the congregation around her and the jingling of money made Jennifer sit more to attention, waiting for the church deacon to arrive at her pew to hand her the collection plate, for her to pass on down to the long row of people sitting beside her. While waiting, Jennifer tried to concentrate on the church music being played softly by both organ and piano in unison, but some whisperings from behind drew her keen attention. She stiffened and leaned further back against the seat when she realized that the whispers were about her. She soon recognized the voices—two of the known church gossips: Betty Sherman and Clara Rawlings.

"Do you think poor Jennifer even knows that it was Robert Harbison who was seeing her mother?"

"Harumph. Jennifer is fifteen. You know children these days. They make it their business to know everything."

"Shh. Here he comes."

"Can you imagine the gall of that man? Staying on here as a deacon of all things, after what he caused Camille to do?"

"Reverend Brewster ought to run him off."

"You know he's too kind and gentle to do such a thing."

"Shhh."

"No one can hear. The music's too loud. Now I want you to watch that Robert Harbison when he hands Jennifer the collection plate. I've seen it before. When he looks at Jennifer . . . he's seein' somethin' of Camille in her. Maybe it's the blue of her eyes or the gold of her long hair. What do you think, Clara?"

"Shh, Betty. Someone's bound to hear."

But Betty persisted. "Just watch him. He'll probably even try to touch Jennifer's hand when he hands her the plate."

"Betty, you're sinful. And here in church. Tsk. Tsk."

"There he is. Right beside her. . . ."

Jennifer could feel a blush rising upward from her neck, making her face feel suddenly hot. What were those women talking about? What had they meant when they said Robert

Harbison had been seeing her mother? And what had this man caused her mother to do? No. It ... couldn't ... have been because ... of ... this ... man. ...

A rustling of feet next to Jennifer, and the shine reflecting in her eyes from the silver platter being offered to her made her heart skip a few beats. She knew that this Robert Harbison was standing beside her ... and that his hands were holding this platter.

Dare she look upward to see him, to see which of her father's many deacons the women had been speaking so freely about? And if she should reach for the collection plate, which she had no choice but to do, would this man truly try to touch her hand?

With one quick movement, Jennifer grabbed the platter, making sure that he had no chance to touch her, and hurriedly passed it to the next person. She tried to focus her eyes on an object straight ahead, but she felt eyes burning through her, so she slowly turned her head and looked upward into dark, smoldering eyes.

Jennifer squirmed uneasily on the seat, feeling a bit of electricity flowing between her and this man. It was a strangeness between her thighs that confused her even more than his continuing look of intimacy in her direction, a look that lifted the corner of his lips in a soft mockery, making Jennifer suddenly cast her eyes downward. Shame flowed through her for having such feelings for this man ... for any man ... especially in her father's sacred house of worship.

But Robert Harbison appeared to be a man capable of doing this to most women. He had that look of having lived life to the fullest ... and possibly with whichever woman he would choose. ...

Had Jennifer's mother truly been among these women?

Jennifer was relieved when he took two steps and was standing at the end of the pew in front of her going through the same motion of passing the collection plate back and forth among these quietly seated people.

The strangeness stirred inside Jennifer once again when she let her gaze settle on the massiveness of this man attired in an impeccable brown woolen suit. She knew that he was her father's age, because of the traces of gray at his temples and the pencil-lined wrinkles in his face. But he was still a virile, quite handsome man.

Guilt flowed through her again for having such sinful thoughts—and in her father's church of all places. And suddenly, remembering the words of those two women, Jennifer knew that she would be asking her Aunt Minnie many questions this afternoon after their usual Sunday meal of roast beef. The truth of her mother's suicide had been kept from her long enough. If women of the church were making it casual gossip, then was Jennifer possibly the only one who hadn't been told?

As Robert Harbison began to make his way back up the aisle toward the back of the church, with a collection plate filled with loose, green bills and a few shining coins tossed throughout, his gaze settled on Jennifer, and he let a small smile play upon his thick, full lips.

Trying to hide her uneasiness, Jennifer scooted further down onto her seat. But she found it hard to focus her attention on her father and the sermon he was beginning to work his way through. The women's accusing words and Robert Harbison's staring at her had placed too much in her mind for her to be able to cast any of it aside so easily. Now she could hardly wait for the final Amen of the morning to be spoken.

Finally, forcing herself, she watched her father's lips moving slowly, but determinedly. It was a familiar sermon to Jennifer . . . about the woman who was taken to stand before God and openly accused of adultery.

Yes, Jennifer had heard it so often . . . when her father again this morning had read a scripture from the Bible. "He that is without sin among you, let him first cast a stone at her. . . ." Then he read further, "Neither do I condemn thee . . . go and sin no more. I am the light of the world: he that followeth me shall not walk in darkness, but shall have the light of life."

Something grabbed at Jennifer's heart when she saw a trace of tears in the corner of her father's eyes and heard his voice crack as he continued to preach. This particular passage hadn't so visibly disturbed him before. Why would it . . . now? Was it because . . . ? No. She wouldn't let herself think about it. She mainly had her father to worry about. He's truly too pale, she thought to herself. He's got to rest when he gets home. She was afraid of losing her father. Oh, how could she stand it if she lost first her mother . . . and then her father?

Finally he was finished. With a closed Bible and bowed head, Jennifer's father took his chair behind the pulpit. He kept his head bowed and clasped his hands together before him, in silent prayer.

Swallowing back a lump in her throat, Jennifer pulled the hymnal onto her lap and flipped the pages to the song to be sung for the invitational. She knew that her father always counted on new converts to step forward each Sunday, but even knowing this, Jennifer hoped that this was one Sunday when no one would feel the calling of the Lord. She wanted her father to be able to finish his morning's duties, because of his obvious need to get to the privacy of his home, and because of her own selfish reason of needing to speak in private with Aunt Minnie.

Sighing deeply, Jennifer was glad to hear the piano and organ begin playing "The Old Rugged Cross." The choir leader stepped forward, attired in a long black robe. She lifted her arms, urging all church members to stand while they sang.

Jennifer pushed herself upward and straightened her back, and hardly breathing, crossed her fingers, still hoping no one would go forward. She knew that the devil had to be guiding her thoughts, but nothing could make her think differently.

When the last stanza had been sung and her father still stood alone, ready to say the final prayer, he looked even more distraught because his sermon hadn't moved any souls to eternal salvation this day. Jennifer suddenly felt guilty for surely having hexed her father's sermon because of all her evil thoughts of that morning.

She closed her eyes and said her own silent prayer, asking forgiveness, but knowing that even this was useless, for her heart was elsewhere.

Low murmurings of "Amen" trembled on lips around Jennifer, making her aware that church was finally over. She opened her eyes, searching around her, as the congregation began to exchange gossip while they moved between the seats.

Jennifer pulled her white gloves on, smoothing them onto her fingers, then her lace-trimmed straw hat, tying the pink satin ribbon beneath her chin. She stood poised, forcing a smile, until everyone but her father had left the building.

A shuffling of feet at the far end of the auditorium made Jennifer turn with a start. It was her father, closing the last of the windows, then placing a few hymnals in place before walking toward Jennifer. His eyes looked empty and his walk was listless, a mere shadow now of what he had been even a year earlier.

"Hi, honey," he said, moving to pull Jennifer into his arms. "Kind of a bad day for your father. No converts means possibly one less person to have the chance to enter into the Kingdom of Heaven."

Jennifer's eyes gazed upward. Oh, how she had always adored him. And now . . . she felt responsible for having caused him an added heartache. She would never wish for no converts again. Never. "It's not your fault, Father," she murmured. "It really isn't. Don't you know that?"

"There was no one else on that pulpit but me, Jennifer," he said. "That means my sermon just wasn't given with enough strength."

"Father, you worry too much. You expect too much of yourself."

"Come. Let's go home," he said, guiding her outside to the waiting carriage. "No matter what you say, I know I must have spoken weakly, or chosen the wrong sermon. Do you think . . . I chose the wrong sermon? That maybe the congregation is tired of hearing that . . . one sermon . . . ?"

Jennifer leaned into his hand as he helped her up onto the carriage. "I don't believe so," she said quietly. "All your sermons are beautiful, Father." But she remembered too well the subject of this sermon and did have to wonder . . . why?

He walked to the other side of the carriage and climbed

upward, settling back against the padded seat. He lifted the reins and clucked to the horses. "Maybe tonight," he sighed. "Maybe at least one person will step forward tonight."

"Why is it so important to you, Father?"

"It's my job, honey. It's what God called me to do. And I want to think that I do it in the best way possible."

"But you can't expect to have conversions every time you preach."

"I guess I'm a bit like that mountain we see in the distance on the clearest days of spring," he said, guiding the carriage from the narrow drive next to the church.

"The . . . mountain . . . ?"

"Yes."

"Why, how could you compare yourself with a mountain?"

He sighed heavily. "Some days the mountain appears serene, with its white-capped peaks glowing orange beneath the sun . . . and other days, with the clouds swirling and weaving in and around it . . . it appears restless and unhappy. I guess that's the best way to describe myself. I was serene before your mother's death . . . and I've been restless . . . and unhappy . . . since."

Jennifer choked on a sob. She now knew why it was so important for her father to see as many people converted as possible. He thought he had surely failed his own wife. No true Christian would have taken her own life. Yes. He surely must hold himself responsible. She covered one of his hands with hers. "Oh, Father," she said. "I'm so sorry."

"I know. I know."

Her father chuckled a bit. "And do you think Aunt Minnie will have her usual roast beef ready and waiting for us, honey?"

The mention of Aunt Minnie reminded Jennifer of other disturbing matters. "I'm sure she will have," she said quietly.

Her father's mood grew somber again. "I worry about her, Jennifer."

"Aunt Minnie's strong, Father," she answered.

"But she's been ailin' a bit too much since Camille's passing."

"But it is only arthritis, Father. Please don't worry yourself so about it."

"Her eyes spoke more than that."

Jennifer turned her eyes from her father. She didn't want to think . . . or worry about Aunt Minnie's feelings. Aunt Minnie was the only one who could reveal all truths to her, no matter how bad she was feeling herself. Jennifer just couldn't wait any longer.

"Maybe she'll be able to attend church tonight, Father," she finally blurted.

"It would help release her inner torments. I'm sure of it."

The warm August air smelled sweetly of honeysuckle. The horses pranced proudly before the carriage . . . but Jennifer was all trembly inside. The closer she came to her house . . . the closer she was to maybe hearing what might even be too unbearable for her. . . .

She squeezed her father's hand and smiled reassuringly toward him when he glanced her way. He would never know that she had heard such gossip in his beloved church . . . *never.*

The aromas of roast beef, potatoes and carrots still clung to the spaces in the large dining room. Jennifer smoothed the lace tablecloth over the dining table and carefully arranged a bouquet of different colored snapdragons in the center. She stood back and admired her handiwork, then slowly slipped her apron off. The time had come. Aunt Minnie would soon have the dishes put away in the cupboard, then would be settling down in front of a small fire in the parlor. August had brought much cooler temperatures. The aroma of apple wood burning in the fireplace was welcome. It made for much more coziness, it seemed.

It was now time to proceed with her plans. Quietly, she tiptoed to her father's study and checked to see what he was doing. She sighed resolutely. She could see that his mind was fully occupied, already rehearsing silently to himself the sermon for the coming evening's service.

She stood and watched him, seeing again the look of despair

in his eyes, even though he was arranged comfortably in his usual rocking chair in front of the fireplace. She let guilt slow her progress of the moment. She didn't like the way he was in deep thought . . . with note pad and pencil in hand. She knew that it was safe enough to get to talk to Aunt Minnie in private . . . but yet . . . she again thought uneasily that her father needed rest more than study. She moved toward him, watching the shadows from the fire dancing around and onto him. It gave him an almost ghostly appearance . . . making a shudder tremble through Jennifer. She went and settled down onto the floor in front of him, slowly removing the pencil from between his fingers.

"What are you doing, Jennifer?" he asked, puzzlement lighting his eyes.

"It is now rest time for you, Father," she said, smiling upward at him.

"And since when does my own daughter dictate to me?"

Jennifer batted her thick lashes nervously. "I'm not dictating, Father," she said. "I'm merely worrying out loud. You need your rest. A short nap right now could do you wonders. Don't you think?"

He studied the tablet and what he had written, then looked toward Jennifer once again. "Yes, maybe you're right," he said. "It seems I'm repeating myself on paper again. What I need is a fresh mind to be able to come up with fresh material."

"Then you will go lie down for a while?"

He laughed nervously. "I'm afraid I will look like an old man, honey."

"Just because you've never allowed yourself such luxuries before doesn't mean you will be accused of being an old man if you do so now."

He shook his head in affirmation. "Yes. I guess maybe you are right."

Jennifer pushed herself up from the floor and reached a hand toward her father. "Then let me walk you to your room, Father," she said quietly.

"And what will you do the rest of the afternoon, young

lady?'' he asked, as he rose from the chair, gladly taking her hand in his.

A slight flush rose upward from Jennifer's neck. She swallowed hard, then answered, ''Just sit by the fire with Aunt Minnie.''

''I hear the apples in the orchards are ready to be picked,'' he said. ''You're always anxious to be one of the first to pick the reddest you can find. Maybe you should do that instead of sit by the fire. The fresh air can put more roses in your cheeks.''

''I shall. Maybe later in the day,'' she said softly. ''But . . . I do believe I will . . . keep Aunt Minnie company. For a while, at least.''

When they arrived at his bedroom door, Jennifer stood on tiptoe and kissed her father's cheek. ''And you? You get that rest, do you hear?''

''Anything my pretty little thing asks,'' he chuckled, then turned and closed the door between Jennifer and himself.

Feeling a slight apprehension, Jennifer moved on toward the parlor, fearful, yet anxious to know. . . .

Chapter Two

September 1898

Attired in a black velveteen hooded cape, Jennifer hurried from the fresh grave, carrying a lone long-stemmed rose. Her remorsefulness over her father's death wasn't as deep as her determination now to seek vengeance for her mother's.

"Wait up, hon," her Aunt Minnie said, from close behind her. "The dampness of this cemetery lawn keeps capturing my heels in the mud."

Jennifer turned and smiled in patient affection toward her aunt, who had been a substitute mother for Jennifer, since Jennifer's mother's death of now six years ago. And this day, from the way Aunt Minnie was dressed, with a black veil covering her aging features and her full dress of black, one would think her to be the widow of the deceased, instead of the mourning sister-in-law.

"Here, Auntie. Let me help you," Jennifer said, reaching to take her aunt's right hand in hers. The touch sent shivers through Jennifer. Its coldness reminded her of the last time she had touched her father.

"So many people came to the funeral, hon," Aunt Minnie said, sniffling. "Seems the whole congregation showed up. Just as though they expected your father to be there still alive, giving another of his sermons. The silence around the casket was almost too much for me to bear."

Jennifer looked toward the gravel lane that led away from the cemetery. Surreys and black buggies were moving slowly away, beneath clustered Douglas Firs and western cedar trees. The only sounds that could be heard were those of the horses' hooves, jingling bridles, and the clattering of iron wheels. "I know, Auntie. I know," Jennifer comforted in a soothing tone, but with thoughts elsewhere. One face had most definitely been missing in the crowd of mourners. That of Robert Harbison. It had been six full years now since Aunt Minnie had revealed the truth to Jennifer about Robert Harbison and Jennifer's mother. And now Jennifer would become acquainted with him. She had her own plans. . . .

The day was gray, and the cool and damp September wind whipped the cape around Jennifer's legs, so that she was glad to have finally reached her carriage. She went to her aunt's side, to assist her upward.

But Aunt Minnie hesitated for a moment, looking back toward the grave that was now covered with a mound of fresh flowers. "I sure do hate leaving Frank here all alone in the cold," she said, almost choking on the words.

"Auntie, please climb aboard the carriage. Father isn't alone. Remember that mother is lying beside him. They're together again. For eternity."

Aunt Minnie finally accepted the assistance of Jennifer's hand on her elbow, and pulled herself on up to arrange herself on the cushioned seat. She clasped her doubled fists together tightly in her lap. "Yes. Jennifer, I'm sure you're right," she said sullenly. "But who would've believed this could happen? Both your mother and father gone at your young age of twenty-one? And, oh, my sweet sister Camille. This day just brings to mind so much I can hardly bear to think about."

Jennifer rushed around to her side of the carriage and pulled herself up onto the seat. "Yes, who would have thought it," she murmured, not only blaming Robert Harbison for her mother's death, but also for the eventual fatal heart attack of her father. She lifted her cape up a bit from around her ankles, grabbed and flicked the reins, and clucked to the sleek black horse that always seemed to be patiently awaiting her commands.

When she would arrive at her house, which she had now inherited from her father, she would see to it that things would change . . . but quickly. Her father had been wrong to neglect the house since Jennifer's mother's death. In a sense, it had become a tomb . . . cold and unloved, no matter how much Aunt Minnie had tried to fill it with her colorful personality. Jennifer's father hadn't allowed the house to be used as it normally should have been.

The carriage quickly left the cemetery behind and moved along the plank-covered streets of Seattle. Even though Washington had been named the forty-second state, Seattle's streets had not yet been paved, except with boards. And those streets that hadn't yet been granted even this special privilege stayed deep in mud, because of Seattle's damp, rainy days.

Jennifer guided the horse left, onto Union Avenue, and felt the strain of the carriage as its wheels struggled with the steepness of the hill, where, located at its highest point, the Brewster house sat. She had at an earlier age silently cursed this hill, but when the big fire of 1889 had raged through the streets of Seattle, destroying most of its buildings and many of its homes, it was this hill that had saved Reverend Brewster's house and his church, only one block away, nestled deeply beneath pine and spruce trees. The fire had raged at lower levels, leaving those who lived up on the sides of Seattle's hills to watch in horror as the flames had washed like orange waves from building to building. But now, Seattle had been rebuilt, and only in brick and concrete.

Only a few feet up Union Avenue, Jennifer slowed the pace of the horse, to look toward a store that had been built on the side of this hill, squeezed in between many others on each side of it.

Jennifer continued to stare at the store, peering through the window on which HARBISON'S PAWNSHOP had been painted in bold, black print across the front. Hanging displayed behind the large plate glass window was an assortment of musical instruments, jewelry, guns and various other things that could draw a bargain hunter's attention. . . .

"Jennifer Lynn. Please," Aunt Minnie said, clearing her throat nervously.

Feeling a blush rising, Jennifer slapped the horse with the reins and commanded it to move on upward, past a few more buildings, and then past neatly painted white frame houses. Jennifer could remember so well how amazed she had been upon her first arrival in Seattle at the age of eight. The townspeople hadn't seemed to be aware that paint existed. Most of the houses had been colorless and weatherbeaten. But slowly, one by one, paint began to be applied. Jennifer had wondered if it was because Reverend Brewster's house, church, and church parsonage had stood out so beautifully with their fresh coats of paint. . . .

"It'll do you good getting back to college," Aunt Minnie said, lifting her veil. "It'll make it easier for you to forget all this unhappiness. But, honey, why don't you transfer from that small college in Portland to the Territorial University right here in Seattle? Now that your father's gone. . . ."

Jennifer set her jaw determinedly and interrupted her aunt. "I'm not going back to school, Auntie," she said, gripping more securely onto the horse's reins.

Aunt Minnie leaned forward and eyed Jennifer more closely. There was more than sadness in the depths of Jennifer's blue eyes. And the stubborn set of her jaw wasn't like Jennifer. It made her less pretty, somehow. It made her usual delicate features take on a hardness. No. It wasn't a bit like her Jennifer. "Oh, you mean you need a few more days alone before returning to the hustle and bustle of school activities," she said, reaching over to pat Jennifer's hand. "I understand, dear. I understand."

Jennifer shot Aunt Minnie a look of defiance. "No, Auntie.

That's not what I mean at all," she said. "And will you please quit patting my hand as though I'm a child? I'm an adult. Please treat me as such."

Withdrawing, Aunt Minnie clutched onto the edge of the seat, feeling a hurt deep inside. She had feared that with the death of Frank, things could change for her. Had she been right? She hated the thought of living alone . . . or returning to teaching . . . only for the companionship that it gave her.

She glanced over at Jennifer once again, trying to see in her what she had always seen when Jennifer had been a child . . . a girl full of laughter, always joking with her mother and father, almost in a too obvious attempt to make up for the fact that she was the only child. Her personality had always been bubbly, as though, when she entered a room, she wasn't only one person, but many.

But with the death of her mother, Jennifer had changed. She had become a bit withdrawn, and in her eyes there always seemed to be a restlessness . . . as though she was biding time . . . waiting . . . but for what?

"Then what do you mean, Jennifer?" Aunt Minnie murmured, all of this becoming just a bit too much for her this day. First the funeral . . . and now Jennifer's acting so . . . strangely. "You know you only have two semesters and another full year and you'll have your degree."

Guiding the horse into a narrow drive, Jennifer glanced quickly toward her aunt. "I can tell I've upset you, Auntie," she said, softly. "I'm sorry. But I've plans of my own . . . something I have a need to do."

"But your father wouldn't want you to quit college," Aunt Minnie said. Oh, how hard Frank had worked at raising his only child. And he had done well. But now? Whatever on earth was on Jennifer's mind?

"Auntie, I didn't want to go in the first place. Especially as far away as Portland," Jennifer said. But she had known why her father had arranged for that. It was because of that man . . . Robert Harbison. Her father hadn't wanted Jennifer to hear the gossip that she had already heard. She just hadn't confessed such an upsetting truth to her father.

"Jennifer, college is so important today. You know that."

"Not for me it isn't," Jennifer said sternly. "It's not needed for what I have in mind." She could feel her aunt's eyes still on her, puzzling, when she pulled the horse and carriage to a halt in front of a two-storied white frame house. Its design was a carryover from her earlier childhood days in San Francisco. It was Victorian, bristling with turrets and bay windows. Its details were elaborated by the addition of rich gingerbread moldings, and even the persistent damp weather of Seattle hadn't yet taken from its appearance.

Jennifer's father had been born during the California gold rush era. His parents had traveled from Boston shortly after their marriage, searching for a better life in California, where, they had heard, gold sparkled from all streams and mountainsides.

Joshua Brewster had found that gold. His wife Kathryn gave birth to two sons, Thadeus and Frank, and brought them into a world of luxury.

When the two brothers grew into adulthood, Thadeus had used his portion of the Brewster wealth to become a shipping magnate . . . and Frank, feeling the calling to become a minister of the Lord, had traveled with his beautiful wife Camille and his young daughter Jennifer to Seattle . . . a city that had been said to have been carved out of a primeval forest . . . a city thriving in evil ways.

Joshua and Kathryn had long since returned to the more quiet ways of Boston, where they still remained, basking in their wealth. They were still in good health in their old age.

"Come on inside, Auntie, and I'll tell you what I must do," Jennifer added now. She climbed from the carriage and secured the reins to a hitching post, then hurried around to help her aunt, whose arthritic knees and ankles worsened on the most damp and chilly days.

With the veil now removed from her aunt's face, Jennifer could once again see how typically old-maidish she was in appearance. She in no way resembled her dead sister Camille. The broadness of her nose and the pointed, stubble-covered chin had kept men from courting her, so she had chosen the life of a schoolteacher until her brother-in-law had needed her.

"Watch the icy patches of the walk and steps," Jennifer urged. "It seems the temperatures have dropped more than they were supposed to. But the snow has arrived already on the peaks of Mount Rainier, so I guess we can expect most anything now." She took a more firm hold on her aunt's elbow. "Careful now. We wouldn't want you falling and breaking a hip."

Aunt Minnie laughed. "Yes. Heaven forbid."

The parlor smelled of smoldering embers, so Jennifer went to the fireplace and arranged some fresh logs on the grate, wadded some day-old newspapers, and stuffed them, along with small pieces of kindling, around the logs, then struck a match to it and watched the fire take hold.

"There. That'll have this room cozy in no time flat," Jennifer said, removing her cape, tossing it across a high-backed chair. She avoided looking at the rocker that sat vacant in front of the fireplace. She knew that its padded arms would show wear where her father's arms had rested as he had sat in the rocker so many evenings, alone in front of the fire, after the passing of his wife.

The rest of the room was filled with comfortable upholstered chairs and one large divan covered with green crushed velvet, also arranged in front of the fireplace, with polished mahogany tables at each end. Pale green brocade draperies were opened to cast afternoon shadows on a long wall of bookshelves filled with mostly religious tabloids and novels.

"Now what's it on your mind, Jennifer," Aunt Minnie said, slipping her own coat off and attempting to straighten the lines on her basic, black, floor-length woolen dress that seemed to blend in so well with the gray hair that circled her head in a tight bun.

Jennifer stood, still looking around her. "Well, first thing, we're going to open all the doors to the upstairs rooms, air them out, and have them papered fresh and new carpets laid.''

''But . . . your . . . father,'' Aunt Minnie gasped, wide-eyed, leaning into Jennifer's face.

''Father is no longer here,'' Jennifer said flatly. ''This house is now mine and there will be some changes made.''

Jennifer went out and stood in the foyer, and looked up the steep staircase. It gave her chills remembering the night her father had locked each of the doors on the second floor and decreed that all the living would be done on the first floor of the house—where enough bedrooms and even two separate bathrooms made this possible.

Jennifer hadn't been allowed to enter any of these rooms for six years now. She went to her purse and pulled a heavy ring of keys from it and clutched possessively onto them. Then she felt a lump rise in her throat. She went back into the parlor to sit by the fire. She wasn't quite ready to enter those rooms yet . . . especially the bathroom . . . where her mother had died.

Kicking her shoes off, Jennifer tucked her feet beneath her, circling the fullness of her black woolen skirt to cover her toes. The fire's shadows reflected onto her high-necked white shirtwaist blouse, upward onto the fairness of her skin, giving her a more healthy coloring, and the slight slant to her heavy-lashed eyes gave her an almost wicked appearance, except that the gentle curve of her mouth showed the true side of her nature.

''For so long I've planned it, Auntie,'' she said, remembering the nights when she had lain sleepless in bed, replaying it over and over again in her mind, knowing that the time would come when she would be old enough . . . and possibly even free enough of family bonds . . . to get her planned revenge.

''Glory be, child,'' Aunt Minnie said, sighing with impatience. ''Don't keep me waiting forever. Whatever is it you are conjuring up in that brain of yours?''

Scooting more down onto the chair, Jennifer looked toward the fireplace and watched the flames caressing the logs. It was like watching strips of golden velvet smoothing out as the flames continued to curve up and around the logs. "Do you remember the day I insisted on being told everything about my mother's death?" she asked softly, remembering how she had argued and argued the point, insisting that age fifteen was old enough to be told all, threatening that she would go find out the truth from someone else . . . even that busybody Clara Rawlings, if it became necessary.

"Yes, dear. I remember," Aunt Minnie murmured, settling back in the chair she was trying so hard to relax against. Oh, how she hated having to rehash the past. Especially on the very day of this second funeral. And she knew that soon people would be coming calling, with their covered dishes and forced cheerfulness . . . the usual gathering after a funeral. . . . "Why on earth would you ever want to speak of it again?" she added hastily, frowning.

"The man who got my mother pregnant," Jennifer continued, feeling the renewed hate settling around her heart. having to mention his name once again. But she knew that she had to get used to his name. It would be with her now for days to come . . . possibly weeks. "Robert Harbison," she finally blurted. She hadn't seen much of him these past years. Since she had been sent from Seattle for her education, first the private girl's school, then an elite college of her father's choosing, she just hadn't returned home on that many Sundays to have seen Robert Harbison . . . always looking so innocent as he passed the communion and collection plates. . . .

Aunt Minnie felt her throat grow dry. "Yes. But what about him?"

"My hate for that man has grown in intensity through the years," Jennifer said quietly. "After knowing my mother killed herself because of the unsuccessful abortion of that man's child, I couldn't help but hate him."

"It isn't Christian to hold hate in the heart, honey," Aunt Minnie said, without conviction, knowing that her own hate was just as strong.

"That doesn't really matter, Auntie," Jennifer said, rising. She went and leaned her right elbow against the fireplace mantel, then rested her chin in her hand. "What matters now is getting my plans in motion now that father is gone. I don't believe I could have gone through with it while he was still alive. It would have hurt him to find out what I will in the end be guilty of."

Color drained from Aunt Minnie's face. She rose and went to Jennifer and grabbed her hand. "Jennifer, I don't know what's on your mind, but whatever it is, it's wrong. It's sinful. You must let bygones be bygones."

"Never," Jennifer said, stubbornly. "All I have to remember is my mother lying in a pool of her own blood from a botched-up abortion and sliced wrists, to know that what I'm planning has to be right."

"Oh, Christ, child," Aunt Minnie said, sighing heavily. "I just knew I shouldn't have told you the whole darn mess."

"Aunt Minnie, you know me well enough to know that I would have found out on my own."

"Yes. That's exactly why I did tell you. I didn't want you probing and asking questions of anyone else. Especially those biddies at the church."

"I remember my mother being so sweet and quiet—the man *had* to have raped her. I can't believe my mother would have gone to bed willingly with another man besides my father, especially since my father was so kind . . . and . . . a minister of the Lord."

"Love does strange things, Jennifer."

Jennifer swung around, glaring. "My mother loved only my father. I just know it."

Aunt Minnie slouched down onto a chair again. She felt drawn . . . tense . . . so very, very old. "All right, maybe she did," she said. "But it's all in the past. You've got to forget. Get on with your own life."

Jennifer's eyes flashed. "And that's exactly what I plan to do," she said. "Get on with my life."

"So, what are these plans you keep speaking of?" Aunt Minnie said, feeling defeated. She knew it did no good trying to talk sense into Jennifer. Jennifer had a mind of her own . . . and a stubborn one, at that.

"I can't explain it all, Auntie," Jennifer answered. "It would take too long. But I plan to get my revenge in my own way."

"Revenge?" Aunt Minnie gasped, clutching at her throat. "What . . . sort . . . of . . . revenge?"

"Only I can know the details," Jennifer said stubbornly, bending to slip back into her shoes. "But you will have to go along with some changes in my appearance. That's a necessary first step of my plan."

"What . . . sort . . . of changes?"

Jennifer's fingers combed through her hair. "I will get my hair dyed a dark brown. That will get me started," she said. She knew that if she left her hair its natural color of gold, Robert Harbison might recognize her. But now that she had matured, now that her face had filled out, as well as her bust, he could possibly not recognize her. And only in changing her hair coloring so drastically could she be assured of not being her mother's double.

Aunt Minnie paled even more. "Child, only harlots who work in brothels on First Avenue get their hair dyed. . . ."

Jennifer set her jaw firmly and interrupted her aunt. "Just let me finish, Auntie," she said. "After my hair is a different color, I will purchase myself a new wardrobe. Dresses of the latest fashions and no longer those that you have picked out for me with the high necklines. I will buy the most daring ones I can find." She paused for a moment when her aunt let out another gasp of disbelief, then continued. "Then I shall make my residence in a boarding house across from Robert Harbison's pawnshop, to watch his habits for awhile, then proceed with my plan, full speed ahead."

"Why on earth would you do such things?" Aunt Minnie sighed. "You're too sweet to do what I think you're planning to do . . . and it's so unchristian in nature."

"I do what I have to do . . . because it's all necessary."

"But you have this big, beautiful house, and I'm here. Why would you even think to move into one of those boarding houses downtown? You know they are roach infested. And what will people think?'' And she hadn't told Jennifer that Robert Harbison's mother's funeral had only been a week ago, and that his mother had been his only reason for having been in town in the first place . . . to please his mother in the last what he had thought at first would be months of her life on this earth. But his mother had been strong-willed and had clung to life, like a shriveled, brown leaf clinging stubbornly to an oak tree in winter.

Surprising to all, Robert Harbison had been the type of son who had tried to please his mother in every way . . . by running her small pawnshop for her, and even by attending church with her. It confused Aunt Minnie, knowing this side of him. And now that his mother was dead, Aunt Minnie wasn't sure what Robert Harbison had done. Had he stayed in Seattle, or returned to San Francisco, where he had been known to have owned a large business of some sort?

Aunt Minnie wondered if she should tell Jennifer, but she decided not to; she would not let herself be pulled into such a devious plot in any way whatsoever.

"Again. I repeat. It's necessary," Jennifer said. "And I've been away for so long, no one will even recognize me. Wearing the hooded cape at the funeral, and keeping it down around my face, assured me that no one got too good a look at me.''

"Oh, glory be," her aunt sighed again. "And what will you do when the church group arrives soon to serve us with a prepared meal . . . you know how they do after a funeral?''

"I shall be gone already," Jennifer said, then looked more closely at her aunt and suddenly saw something in her aunt's eyes that she should have recognized earlier. Her aunt wasn't only worrying about Jennifer, but also about being left alone. . . .

Jennifer went to her aunt and sat down on the floor in front of her and rested her elbows on her aunt's knees and then her chin in her hands. "And, Auntie, I have a more pleasant side to my plans that I will tell you about that includes you and your future.''

Aunt Minnie pushed a strand of loose hair away from Jennifer's forehead and let her fingers linger for awhile on the softness of her skin. "Pleasant news? About me? And my future?" she said. But nothing could erase the fear she was feeling for Jennifer. Jennifer had changed. But . . . maybe college changed all children these days. It just wasn't that way when *she* had attended school. . . .

"Yes, Auntie," Jennifer said eagerly, with eyes wide. "You know that now that father is gone, a new minister will be brought in."

"Yes, I know," Aunt Minnie sighed softly. "But what does that have to do with me?"

Jennifer flipped her hair back away from her face and around her shoulders and wet her lips with her tongue. She was feeling more relaxed now, being able to talk about something more pleasant. Something constructive . . . not destructive. She wasn't even sure if she could play out the script that she had written for herself. She wondered what Uncle Thadeus would think of how she had planned this play—in which she was to play the lead role. She laughed to herself, thinking about her uncle. Knowing him so well, through their steady correspondence, she guessed that he would probably eagerly arrive by one of his steamships to even direct and produce her every action.

Uncle Thadeus was known to be a restless man who needed more than to sit back and run his shipping empire. He had begun to invest his money in motion pictures . . . ever since Thomas Edison had made such a big hit with his films, which had been shown on a screen at Koster and Bial's Music Hall in New York City. It had even shown William McKinley during his campaign for the presidency!

Uncle Thadeus was studying all aspects of this film business, what kind of future it had—and he could even see himself actually hiring people to act out scenes that would be later shown on a screen. He was already writing scripts, getting ready for the big day.

The chiming of the clock on the fireplace mantel brought

Jennifer back to the present. She looked up into patient gray eyes. ''Auntie, if a new minister is brought in, that means the parsonage will have to be offered to him and his family.''

Aunt Minnie's hand went to her throat and her face drained of color once again. ''Glory be, Jennifer,'' she gasped. ''In my mournings for your father, I hadn't even thought about all those old folk in the parsonage. What will become of them?''

''I think I have an idea,'' Jennifer said, getting up to sit on the couch. ''It was the kindest of all Father's deeds when he didn't accept the use of the parsonage when we moved to town, knowing he had the money to pay for his own house. At first, some of the congregation thought it was for snobbish reasons, since the parsonage isn't as grand a house as this one father chose for us. They thought that he thought he was too good to live in the parsonage. But when he told the true reason, it sure did shut up some mouths.''

''Yes. I remember the day well,'' Aunt Minnie said. ''When your father stood tall and erect behind the pulpit and asked for the okay from the church congregation to use the parsonage for a home for the elderly, I don't believe there was a dry eye beneath that church roof.''

Jennifer swallowed hard, not wanting to remember too much of family this day. She didn't want to become soft inside . . . mellow. She didn't want to change her mind about Robert Harbison. ''Aunt Minnie, we shall bring all the old folks here,'' she blurted, scooting to the edge of the couch, feeling like a small child again, having been given a new toy to play with. But this time it was . . . life. ''You shall call the paper hangers tomorrow, the painters, have new draperies made for the rooms and new carpets laid and then we shall invite those lovely people here . . . to live.'' She watched her aunt's facial features soften, lessening the tension and worry lines around her eyes and mouth.

''Jennifer, you'd do that? Give up your house in such a way?''

''Yes!'' Jennifer exclaimed. She had a selfish reason, of course. Doing this for the elderly would help to ease her mind about the evil she was scheming elsewhere. Her father's sermons hadn't been unheeded by her. "That is, if you want to. Would it be too much for you? With the money father left us, we can do anything we wish. I'd be sure to have the same private nurses, round the clock, as father has paid for all along, while this has been an active thing at the parsonage. I truly believe all you'd be responsible for would be the sharing of your colorful personality with those who need it most. We'd bring the same cooks here. Everything. What do you think, Auntie?"

Aunt Minnie bent her head, covered her eyes and began to weep. "Jennifer, my sweet child," she sobbed. "You are an angel from heaven. I'm sorry I doubted your goodness for even one moment."

"Then you'll agree to this?"

Aunt Minnie wiped her eyes with the back of her hand. "Yes, my dear," she answered. "And I think your father would be very proud of you and what you're planning to do for these lonely people."

Jennifer rose, knowing she had to take the trip upstairs now, to see the rooms and the way they had been left on that fateful night. "I even think father would understand my other thought-out plans," she murmured softly to herself, then said aloud, "Auntie, I've much to do myself. I'll leave all this in your hands, if you truly don't mind."

Aunt Minnie rose and embraced Jennifer. "Don't you worry about a thing, honey," she said, patting Jennifer on the back. "Ol' Aunt Minnie's here to help." And, deep down, she too understood Jennifer's other plans, even though they were quite on the wicked side. . . .

"I'm so glad you understand me, Aunt Minnie," Jennifer said, returning her aunt's hug most affectionately. Then she turned and without another word went to the staircase and began the slow ascent. The closer she came to the upstairs landing, the more her heart throbbed. She suddenly felt like a schoolgirl . . . ready to commit a dark, evil sin. How often had she been told no by her father when she had asked to move back upstairs into her own bedroom? In life she hadn't ever defied him. In death, she was hoping . . . he would understand. . . .

Her heart pounded in unison with each footstep taken closer to the locked bedroom door. She had not even had the opportunity of removing her most personal possessions from her room. There had been her stack of letters from Uncle Thadeus. She had always treasured them. She had kept them in a nightstand drawer with a yellow satin bow tied around them.

Then there was her diary, which had held her most intimate of secrets . . . and the phonograph that Uncle Thadeus had shipped to her.

But all these things had been kept from her by a father who had let his remorsefulness guide him into the quickest and most wrong decisions. Before Jennifer had had a chance to rummage through her treasures to take them to her newly assigned bedroom, her father had closed and locked all the upstairs rooms. . . . "For eternity, if need be," he had mumbled with a heavy heart.

An air of mustiness filtered upward into Jennifer's nose. Now she almost feared opening the door. The room hadn't ever been cleaned or aired out. What she might find there might be even too unpleasant to bear. Which of her things would have been ruined by dust, or the damp days and nights of Seattle?

Half holding her breath, Jennifer turned the key, then pushed the door open. Tears burned at the corner of her eyes as she stepped into her past. As she stopped to look slowly around her, she felt as though time had stood still. It brought so much to mind that made her strength wane a bit. The child that was still such a big part of her wanted to go and pick up the doll that lay on her bed . . . to coddle it and explain to it why it hadn't had loving arms to rock it for so long.

Her gaze moved on around her, seeing her dressing table that held choice bottles of cologne that her mother had given her as gifts on special occasions. The nightstand beside her bed held her diary and a young-adult novel. A bookmark showed from the top, at the page where she had stopped reading it.

An oval braided rug muffled her steps as she went to pick up the diary and with a bit of hesitation turned to her last entry. She began to read it slowly, with tears blurring her eyes . . . wondering if she would read a clue about how her mother had been acting on the day prior to her death. She read:

Dear Diary:

I was allowed to go choose a few school clothes by myself today. I love to feel the freedom of going to the fancy dress emporiums to shop. I can hardly wait until I am an adult and can do this every day.

A new school year is only weeks away. I am very excited. I have missed seeing my friends. Most live too far from my house to keep in touch through the summer months.

Mother looked so beautiful today. It seems she is even radiant. I wish I knew her secret.

Jennifer swallowed hard and slammed the diary shut. She now knew why her mother had looked radiant. She had been pregnant. She had heard whispers that a pregnancy, even an unwanted one, had such an effect on a woman.

She wondered again about her last entry. There had been no mention of her mother's acting peculiar or looking sad. . . .

Placing the diary back in place, Jennifer moved on around the room, touching everything, beginning to doubt if she was strong enough . . . truly strong enough . . . to see her plans carried out to the end. Being in her bedroom, she felt the loneliness of what life had become closing in on her. She was still in mourning. The death of her father had left such a deep void in her life. To leave his house would almost be the same as leaving him and all that his life had stood for.

And would she even be branded as a loose woman if she set out on her own? Women had not yet acquired the rights that men had. It angered her to know that men reserved special rights and privileges . . . even, whenever possible, banned ladies from voting booths, clubs, and even some restaurants.

Remembering these things made her determination return

with strength. She was doing what she felt was right and she no longer would let herself care what anyone thought. She had been planning this for way too long to let fear of gossip stand in her way.

The sound of carriage wheels drew Jennifer's attention to the window. She went and pulled the curtain aside and saw the first arrival of church members. As a woman was aided from the carriage, Jennifer saw a large crock being held up before her as she headed for the house.

Jennifer shuddered. She thought it so barbaric to serve food . . . as though on a picnic . . . after a respected citizen's funeral. She would not be a part of it. Never. She would busy herself with her plans for the many days ahead. . . .

Chapter Three

The best Jennifer had been able to do for herself was to get established in a small room that was located above Seattle Hardware Store, across from Harbison's Pawnshop. Because of the gold rush in the Klondike, people were arriving in Seattle by the thousands. Hotels were putting extra cots in rooms and in the corridors. Livery stables were even renting sleeping space. Swelling crowds were squeezing through narrowing alleyways between storefronts and piled-up goods. Dawson was the capital of the Yukon gold country, and Dawson was the goal, making Seattle an ideal stopover point for all those following their dreams.

Jennifer had paid well for her room. She had bribed a young man who had just arrived from Illinois. She had said that she would only be there for a few days and that he could have it back if he would just be patient. He slept, even now, in the hallway, right outside her door, waiting.

Looking around her, Jennifer frowned. She hated this room that smelled of rat poison. The only furnishings were a cot to sleep on, one lone chair, and a chest of drawers. But she would only be there a short time. Surely, once she knew Robert's daily schedule, she would be able to get established in a more attractive setting to use . . . for trapping him.

But it had been three days now and Jennifer hadn't seen anyone who even resembled Robert Harbison coming or going from Harbison's Pawnshop. Her eyes were burning from watching so closely, and she was tired of being alone. She hadn't mentioned the name Robert Harbison to anyone, for fear that someone might reveal a knowingness in the depths of their eyes . . . the recognition that she was Jennifer Brewster, the daughter of Camille Brewster who had killed herself because of this man. . . .

The rattling of the pipes next to where Jennifer stood made her sigh with relief. She had been freezing this entire day, and now, finally, the coal furnace in the basement had heated up enough to push some steam upward into the radiator.

Jennifer had had plenty of time to contemplate these circumstances she had set up for herself. She was pleased with her hair coloring. She had managed to get a bottle of hair dye from a shop and had done quite well applying the color of dark auburn through her usual gold tresses. She ran her fingers through her hair. She had found that this darkness of coloring had made her complexion of ivory more pronounced, and the blue of her eyes more fresh and true. And, somehow, she had managed to look older than her age of twenty-one . . . the end result she had strived for.

This day, she had chosen to wear a mauve satin dress with a bodice cut low to show off her magnificent bosom. A look downward, at the cleavage so visible to the eye, and she felt a blush rising. She had never worn a dress so revealing. She had never even thought much about how well endowed she was in front. Until now, that fact had remained unimportant. But to get a man, a woman had to show off her better qualities . . . and Jennifer now knew that her breasts were made to be looked at. And . . . by men. Not only by herself in the privacy of her room.

Placing her hands on her hips, she was pleased to see how the dress dipped in at the waistline to show the smallness of her waist. From that point on, the dress hung long, and very full. She had chosen to wear a thin strand of pearls from around her neck, and one tiny pearl earring in each ear.

Smiling, she knew that, yes, she was quite beautiful, and ready for this, her first attempt to enter Harbison's Pawnshop, to actually confront him for that very first time. . . .

A roach rushed beneath the chair beside her, making Jennifer shudder as she threw her beige mink-trimmed cape around her shoulders, and then a small mink hat to sit a bit sideways on her head.

Taking in a deep breath, to try and restore her confidence, she decided that she was ready to cross the street and perform act one on Robert Harbison. If she couldn't watch and follow him, to learn his habits, she would just have to approach him more directly. Her patience had worn thin. She had waited too long already. . . .

Grabbing her purse, Jennifer stepped out into the hallway, stopping to look down upon the young man who still slept soundly. It seemed the long trip from Illinois had completely exhausted him. Instead of being out among the other gold seekers preparing for their long journey to the Yukon, he had remained by her door.

She couldn't tell much by his appearance, because he wore a stocking hat of sorts most of the time, pulled down, revealing only the bluest of eyes and a weather-tanned face, but Jennifer did know that he had to be near her own age.

She had noticed that in his possession was an easel and a case that appeared to be material used by a painter. But why did he linger? Why hadn't he made plans for something besides waiting for this room? It confused Jennifer. If he was headed for the Yukon, a room wouldn't even be needed. He could go on his way, since he had apparently had sufficient rest now.

Shrugging her shoulders, Jennifer moved on down the hallway, and made her way down its narrowness, brushing against other sleeping men sprawled out along the walls. She hadn't felt all that safe these past few days, with so many men around. But she had kept the doors secured. At all times.

She rushed on down the narrow staircase and stepped out into the blustery winds of September. Holding on to her hat, she pushed her way through the crowds of people. A war with Spain was going on, but it hadn't seemed to get in the way of the gold rush. In the Seattle papers even the news of Dewey's victory at Manila had been somewhat cramped by Alaska steamship advertisements that shared the same page.

Having taken the time to read of this victory, Jennifer had felt a keen pride at being able to boast of being an American. Admiral Dewey had gone to the Philippine Islands and had destroyed the Spanish fleet without the loss of even one American life. Yes, these were exciting times, Jennifer thought to herself, feeling her heart pumping faster as she now stood in front of Harbison's Pawnshop. She hesitated, then determinedly walked on inside.

The aroma was of mustiness and the air felt stifling, almost to the point of choking Jennifer, so that she had to drape her cape more off her shoulders. A quick look around showed that she was alone in the room. She began to walk around the shop, wondering when he would step from behind the pale golden velveteen gathered curtain that was being used to separate the business quarters from whatever quarters were kept hidden from the public eye.

Probably where he seduces his latest conquests, Jennifer thought to herself, wishing a feeling of dread wouldn't envelop her every time she thought of their first meeting. Wasn't it . . . only . . . moments away?

Hearing heavy footsteps moving toward her from behind the curtain, Jennifer swallowed hard and busied herself by picking up an antique clock, turning it from side to side.

"Well, young lady," a voice spoke from behind her. "Interested in clocks, eh?"

Jennifer clutched tightly onto the tarnished, gold-clustered clock, then let her gaze settle on a man . . . who . . . wasn't whom she had expected to see. Her eyes widened and she didn't know quite what to say. This wasn't how she had planned it. . . .

This man was short, paunchy, and his shirt was gaping open at the front, revealing a thick crop of black chest hair that sparkled on the tips with perspiration. He wiped his balding head and flushed cheeks with a handkerchief and questioned her further. "Hey, ma'am," he grumbled. "I'm here to buy, trade, or sell. What can I interest you in doin'?"

With trembling fingers, Jennifer replaced the clock on the counter top, then moved on further down the narrow space left between the many displayed articles for sale, and found herself looking downward, through a glass case, eyeing a pearl-handled gun. Something inside her made her point to it. "I'd like to see that gun, please," she said, not knowing, even herself, what had truly compelled her to ask to see such a device of violence.

The man shuffled over behind the counter, bent down and unlocked the case, slid the glass door aside and lifted the gun out to hand to her.

"Mighty nice piece," he said, wiping his brow again, watching her closely. There was something familiar about this customer, but he just didn't know. "Jist right for a lady your size. Mighty easy to pull the trigger, if'n the need arises."

Jennifer felt a strangeness surge through her as the coldness of the steel rested in the palm of her right hand. She studied it carefully. It was so small, it didn't even fill out the full size of her hand, and the pearl handle had a chip out of its corner. "How much?" she asked, still unbelieving that she would even be considering purchasing a gun. Her father had preached against gun possession and the violence that could be prevented in the city of Seattle if guns weren't so readily available.

"What'd you offer for it?" the man said, tilting a brow.

Jennifer placed the gun in her other hand, amazed at how little it weighed, considering the havoc it could bring to even a whole community. "Sir, I have no idea," she said, then looked toward the curtain that led to the back, trying to see between where it was pulled almost shut in the middle. "Maybe ... if you would ask Mr. Harbison to step out here a minute, maybe I can bargain with him." She could feel a weakness in her knees, not believing she had actually had the nerve to ask to see Robert.

"Mr. Harbison?" the man said, scratching his head. "Why Mr. Harbison, ma'am?"

Jennifer swallowed hard. "Isn't he the . . . uh . . . owner of this shop?" she stammered, placing the gun back on the counter.

"No, ma'am. He ain't."

Jennifer grew a bit impatient, feeling her courage returning. "Is your name Harbison? The window reads Harbison's Pawnshop," she said. "And Robert Harbison is known to be the owner of this shop. Now. May I please . . . see . . . him about this purchase?"

The man leaned over the counter and into Jennifer's face. "Lady, you don't hear so well," he said flatly. "But I guess the best way to put this to you is *I'm* now the owner of this shop. If'n any tradin' is done, I'm the one to argue with."

The color drained from Jennifer's face. She leaned against the counter, feeling a bit lightheaded, thinking about the exactness of her plans . . . all gone . . . awry. And . . . so soon? She had waited so long . . . and now to be backed against the wall?

"You're . . . the . . . proprietor of this shop?" she whispered, now feeling a bit ridiculous, having taken a rat hole of a room, watching this shop that . . . wasn't . . . even owned by the man she hated?

"Mr. Harbison's headed back to California now that his mother has passed away," the man said, pulling a cigar from his front shirt pocket. He licked its tip, then stuck it into his mouth and lit it.

"To . . . California?"

"Hell, yes. He only came back to mingle with us little folk 'cause of his ailin' ma. He had her plumb fooled, he did, takin' her to church in her wheelchair each Sunday and all."

"His . . . mother . . . ?"

"Few years back, his mother was discovered to be dyin' of consumption, or somethin' like that, so she begged her son to spend 'er last months with 'er, so's to help 'er with this shop," the man said, then guffawed, slapping a leg. "But she hung on. For way too long accordin' to everybody. So did her son. Glad he's got the hell outta here since his ma's funeral. Couldn't stand the stuffed-shirt son of a bitch. But he sold me this place good'n cheap, though. Can say that 'bout him.''

Jennifer was feeling torn now over her feelings for this man. Could a man who had helped his mother be all that bad? But still . . . Jennifer had to remember *her* mother. ''Where in California did he go?'' she asked, casting her eyes downward. She knew that this man would soon be wondering about her most evident interest in this Robert Harbison.

''San Francisco,'' he said, taking the gun, checking it over himself. ''Owner of some large corporation out there. Don't know how the hell he could leave it for so long to stay here with his ma. But rich folks can do things we poor folk cain't.'' He paused for a minute, then held the gun toward Jennifer once again. ''But no more talk about that son of a bitch. Do you want this gun . . . or don't ya? I'll trade it for those pearls hangin' from round yore neck. Huh? Whatcha think? They are genuine pearls, ain't they?''

Jennifer's fingers went to the necklace. It didn't have any sentimental value . . . she had purchased it especially for this dress she now wore . . . so . . . yes . . . she could part with it. ''Why, yes. They are quite real,'' she said. And she had to travel to San Francisco now. This had to be an added part to her plans. She'd feel more secure if she did own a hand gun. She hadn't been on such a trip alone; she would need protection . . . even if she was to travel on one of her uncle's steamships.

''Wanna trade? Huh?'' the man persisted, taking deep puffs from his cigar, watching her closely.

Jennifer reached behind her neck and unclasped the necklace and handed it toward him. In turn, he handed her the gun.

''You'll have to sign a papa statin' you bought it, ma'am.''

Jennifer's eyes widened and her mouth grew dry. ''I'll have to do what?'' she gasped.

''For the authorities. That damn Reverend Brewster is the one who's responsible for the sheriff jumpin' down my throat for tradin' so many guns across the counter like I do and all.

You know. He convinced the sheriff that the many strangers rushin' into our city has made the streets kinda dangerous. Well, Reverend Brewster got his way 'fore he died, but now that he's dead, things'll go back the way they were.''

Jennifer clenched her fists with anger and felt a burning of the eyes, wanting so badly to defend her father's name. But she couldn't. This wasn't the time or the place. And if she hadn't felt that she would need protection on the long trip ahead of her, she would have just thrown the gun back at this horrible man.

But, instead, she thrust the gun inside her purse and said, ''Fine. I don't mind.'' Names . . . different names rushed through her brain. She couldn't sign her true name. She couldn't let this man see or let gossip get around that the late Reverend Brewster's daughter had purchased a gun.

When she signed Priscilla Blankenship, she felt criminal . . . and knew that her face had become flushed. She also knew that if this man asked for identification, she was in a lot of trouble. While handing the man's pencil back to him, Jennifer held her breath waiting.

''Need some bullets?'' the man asked, putting the signed list of names on the counter top.

Feeling even more criminal, Jennifer shook her head yes in response. Four closed, small boxes were placed before her. ''The earrings could pay for those okay,'' he grumbled, flicking ashes from his cigar on the floor below him.

Jennifer's eyes flashed. She knew the worth of her earrings, but not wanting to draw any more attention to herself, she frowned and plucked each from her ears and thrust them in his direction.

''Enjoy the gun,'' the man said, eyeing the pearls beneath a bright light.

''Enjoy . . . ?'' Jennifer whispered, placing the bullets also inside her purse, then added, ''Sir, what corporation does . . . Mr. Harbison . . . own?'' It had come out so easily she hadn't been sure if she *could* ask . . . she knew how curious this bulgyeyed man was already. She could see it in the depths of his colorless eyes.

"Roberto's," he answered. "In some section of town near the waterfront. Handles designin' of clothes. Somethin' like that." He leaned into Jennifer's face again. "Jist have to ask. What's so damn important about Harbison that you'd ask further 'bout him?"

"No reason," she murmured. "No reason." She turned and rushed from the shop, now wondering what she truly was going to do. Could she really go to San Francisco? Would Aunt Minnie truly understand? Tears came to her eyes. She knew all the answers already. Nothing would stop her planned vengeance. She hadn't anticipated anything being easy about this . . . she just had to accept what setbacks she would run into. . . .

Chapter Four

Seattle's waterfront was a mass of energy as throngs of people rushed around, almost in a frenzy. In their eyes, Jennifer could see a glint of anticipation . . . and she knew that the reason for this was the gold that they were even risking their lives to go in search of. Tales of lost people, even entire families, were being told each day, tales of snowslides, or even people just freezing to death on the treacherous routes that led to the Yukon gold country.

But Jennifer's interests lay in the opposite direction. She was headed for San Francisco.

"Jennifer Lynn, this is absolute foolishness," Aunt Minnie argued, sidling closer to Jennifer. She hated the pushing and shouting of the men who surrounded her. The waterfront was not a decent place for a Christian lady to be standing. "You must change your mind and return home with me. This instant. Do you hear me?" She pulled her black woolen cape more around her and set her jaw firmly, then stuck her nose up into the air when a man lugging a bag winked at her.

Jennifer saw this and giggled. She arranged her own brown velveteen hooded cape to be less binding. "Auntie, you know my mind is made up. And Uncle Thad will meet the ship's arrival. I will be staying with him. No need to fret so," she said. She knew she was doing the right thing. And eagerness to begin her adventure flowed through her veins. She continued to watch the people unloading from the *Madrona*. Would there ever be an end?

"If you could wait for two more weeks, Thad said that his most comfortable vessel, the *Elite* would be arriving again in Seattle," Aunt Minnie argued further. "If you must make this trip, at least wait and travel in some form of luxury. In Thad's wire, he warned of the complete antiqueness of the *Madrona* . . . that it is supposed to only be used for shipping of cargo. It wasn't built for passengers."

"Haven't you even noticed the passengers leaving the *Madrona?*" Jennifer said impatiently. "If there was room for that many people on the trip to Seattle, there most assuredly will be room for *me* to go to San Francisco."

"Yes. I know. But you don't know the conditions under which these people have traveled. Without proper cabins, I can just imagine what it must have been like."

"Uncle Thad also said in his wire that he would see to it that I would get the use of the one other cabin that's next to the captain's. That extra cabin was built for Uncle Thad, in case he ever chose to travel on this ship himself. I'm sure it will be quite adequate."

"Then, there's no changing your mind, Jennifer?"

"No. I am going. And you have plenty to do to busy your mind. Remember. You are needed by the elderly."

"It will not be enough to keep my mind free of worries about you," Aunt Minnie sighed.

Jennifer put her arms around her aunt and hugged her tightly. "You worry too much. I'm very capable of taking care of myself."

A different sort of clamor began aboard the *Madrona*. After the last passenger disappeared into the crowd, crates and all sorts of cargo began to be rushed on deck of this squat steamer. Smoke began to spiral upward from the round smokestack of the ship, blackening the sky, soot particles settling back down onto the ship's deck. The crash of water against the ship and the creak of ropes were soon drowned out, as the rumble of the boilers began in earnest.

"I feel I must board now, Auntie," Jennifer said. She couldn't help but feel a bit sad, having to say goodbye to her aunt, whom she had grown so close to. But her heartbeats were counting out the minutes . . . the hours . . . the days . . . that stood between her . . . and her revenge.

"Must you so soon?" Aunt Minnie said, silent pleading in her eyes. "Stay a bit longer. It'll take them some time to get the ship ready for travel."

"I feel the need to get settled before the ship departs, Auntie."

"But will you . . . truly . . . be safe?"

"Uncle Thad assured me that all his captains are fine navigators."

"Will you be sure and dress warmly . . . and not get a chill?" Aunt Minnie asked, still in shock over the daring, low-cut dresses she had seen Jennifer pack into her trunks. Would her sweet Jennifer actually wear such revealing dresses in front of a man? Oh, that Robert Harbison! He was still tearing the Brewster family apart. Would it ever end? She eyed Jennifer questionably. What on earth could Jennifer be planning? Oh, it was almost too much to bear.

"Auntie, I will wear my warmest dresses at all times," Jennifer said. And on deck she *would* wear her usual, high-necked dresses. They would assure her warmth . . . and privacy from the wandering eyes of the ship's crew. She had worried a bit about this. But one thing that her aunt wasn't aware of was Jennifer's pearl-handled pistol which she planned to keep on hand at all times for whatever protection she might need. Her gaze lighted on some trunks now being carried on deck and she recognized them to be her own. She now knew she must say goodbye to her aunt. She wanted to see to it that her trunks reached her cabin safely and didn't get lost among the many other crates being so roughly tossed about.

"Auntie, I must really go," she said, kissing her aunt swiftly on the cheek. The taste of salt from her aunt's tears made her own eyes begin to burn from the urge to weep. But she couldn't board ship with any trace of red, swollen eyes. She was the niece of this ship's owner and she wanted to show the strong side to her character, that she also was a Brewster, a name that was spoken with pride.

Aunt Minnie touched Jennifer's cheek softly. "I'll pray for you, Jennifer Lynn," she murmured. "I'll pray for you every day."

Jennifer swallowed back a lump in her throat. "Thank you, Auntie," she said, then picked the skirt of her dress and the tail end of her cape up into her arms and rushed toward the ship and boarded it. She didn't pause to look back toward her aunt, for if she had she knew that she would witness such a look of grief, that she too might break down and rush back into her aunt's arms. Wasn't there a security in her aunt's embrace that she wouldn't find elsewhere? But no. She had to move onward to find her own way in the world. Auntie chose her way of life at age twenty-one . . . so shall I, Jennifer thought stubbornly to herself.

"Jennifer Brewster? Is this Thad's niece I've heard so much about?" a voice boomed loudly from beside her.

Startled, Jennifer stopped to see who it might be who would know of her and Uncle Thadeus. "Yes," she said softly. "I am Jennifer. And who, may I ask, are you?" The man now standing before her was of a burly sort with rough facial features. He was hatless and dressed in all black, matching his thick head of black hair, and held a pipe between his thin line of lips. He extended a pudgy hand toward Jennifer. "Captain Klein at your service, ma'am," he drawled. "Only someone dressed in velvet boardin' this ship could be Thad's niece. You see, I ain't used to anything but riffraff since this ain't no passenger ship."

"Oh, I see," Jennifer said, accepting his handshake. She looked quickly around her. There were very few passengers.

No one, it seemed, wanted to head south. All the gold had been claimed there.

"We do make exceptions, though," he continued, removing his hand from her grasp, to thrust both hands in his rear breeches' pockets. "With this gold rush thing in the Yukon, your uncle's addin' to his already accumulated fortune by these foolhardy people. Then the trip back, we always make room for those who've tried their luck and failed. Even give free board to those who've lost all their belongings in the Yukon."

"That's very kind of you, sir."

"Just call me captain. Sometime I think I was born with that as my proper name," he laughed hoarsely. "Been called captain so long, can hardly recall the name my ma give me at birth, may God rest her soul in heaven."

"Uncle Thad said that I would have a cabin of my own. May I be directed to it now? I want to be assured that my trunks have arrived there safely."

"Saw to it myself. Watched for the name Brewster as the trunks were carried aboard. They're safe and sound," he said. "But come ahead. I'll show you where you'll be spendin' the next few days. Ain't the best. But better'n sleepin' out on deck like everyone else'll be doin'."

Captain Klein offered Jennifer an arm, which she gladly accepted. They were now walking through strewn debris that had been left by the earlier passengers. There were rotting food, fish bones, human excrement, and the strong aroma of urine and vomit. Jennifer's nostrils flared and she choked back nausea as she tried to watch carefully where she stepped. She couldn't understand how the captain of any ship could let such things as this remain on deck. But surely, before the ship took to the sea, the crew would have to scrub the decks, to make them more sanitary. If not, she would realize what a mistake she had made to not wait for the ship *Elite* to arrive.

"And here 'tis." Captain Klein stooped and opened a door, then stood aside for Jennifer to enter. "Your cabin. I hope you'll be comfortable."

"I'm sure I will, thank you," Jennifer said, tensing, afraid to see where she would be sleeping and eating. If this cabin was filthy like the rest of the ship, she would still have time to change her mind.

"I've many things to attend to," Captain Klein said, bowing stiffly. "Just step on inside and if there's ever a need, just you holler. I won't ever be too far away."

"I'll remember that. Thank you, captain." She watched as he walked away from her, hands clasped behind him and eyes straight ahead, still obviously uncaring about the condition of his ship's deck.

Sighing resolutely, Jennifer leaned down and stepped over a threshold into the small cabin. Once inside, she straightened her back and began to slowly look around. The cabin was somewhat crude, paneled in a colorless wood. A skylight of stained glass was reflecting many colors of the rainbow downward onto furnishings that consisted of a lone bunk on which one would most obviously not rest comfortably, a built-in rolltop desk, and a table that sat against the opposite wall. A basin was attached to another wall, with a chamber pot placed beneath it. And on each wall, a whale oil lamp had been lighted, flickering, making ghostly figures on the ceiling above them.

Jennifer's three trunks had been placed in the middle of the cabin's floor. She went and sat down on one of them, feeling a bit disillusioned about this sea voyage that she had so looked forward to. When she and her parents had made such a voyage many years ago, it had been on one of her uncle's better ships. She could remember having the most comfortable of cabins and the best of meals, which couldn't have even been matched in the finest restaurants of San Francisco. But this? She shuddered . . . thinking of the several days of sea ahead of her. Hadn't her aunt warned her? If her determination to seek revenge wasn't so strong, how easy it would be to turn back. . . .

Loud shouts and the shrieking of a whistle drew Jennifer back to her feet. She could feel a sudden vibration in the flooring and realized that the engine was picking up more steam. A straining and rattling of chains met her ears and she recognized this to be the anchor being pulled up, and she knew that the ship would soon be moving away from the wharves. Feeling a last tinge of small regret, she rushed from the cabin and went to cling to the ship's rail. Her eyes hurried through the crowd that was fast being left behind, then found Aunt Minnie with handkerchief to her nose, yet managing to wave, almost frantically.

Jennifer waved back, then watched the shoreline move farther and farther away. And the further away the ship took Jennifer, the more she wanted to see. If she looked hard enough, she could even see the two-storied Brewster house at the topmost part of Union Avenue, that was only one street among the many in this city of Seattle that led straight upward from the bay. A city of hills. A city of wild roses and green ferns, everywhere you looked. And now, the green mountainous shores were being left behind, as though they had only been a dream.

Wiping her face of a wild spray of sea water, Jennifer looked to the east and saw Mount Rainier in its vastness, with its white peak thrusting upward into the sky. Smoky clouds swirled around its base, like ghosts protecting the mountain from intruders . . . maybe even Indian ancestors, lingering, just the wind, making one almost hear a chanting. . . .

The damp chill of the air made Jennifer clasp her arms around her. Suddenly she felt as though she was being observed. She could feel the penetration of eyes from behind her, so she turned to see who . . . and she saw a man's face half hidden behind an easel, halfway across the width of the ship.

Curiously, Jennifer made her way toward him. Stepping up beside the easel, she gasped when she recognized the face. "Why, it's you," she said, in a near whisper. She hadn't paid much attention yet to those others who had boarded. She most certainly wouldn't have expected to see *this* person. . . .

Nicholas Oglesby wiped a brush with a cloth and slipped it into a tin can of many other brushes that were of all sizes and shapes. "Do you like what I've just painted?" he said, eyeing his painting, then the mountain that was quickly turning into what seemed a mirage as a dense fog began to rise upward from the water.

Nicholas hadn't planned for Jennifer to see him so soon on this trip . . . but he hadn't expected that there would be so few passengers, either. There were no crowds to mingle with. So this had been his best approach to meeting Jennifer again. His paintings were often a way of communicating.

Jennifer looked downward at the painting of black and white, and she gasped anew. The mountain stood as a backdrop for a young lady standing at the rail's edge, but whose hair was flowing into the wind, not hidden beneath the hood of a cape like Jennifer's was. Her pulse began to race, knowing this was a painting of herself . . . for there was no other lady standing at the rail. . . .

"I'm sure you would feel more free with the hood off your head," he said, lifting his hand to gently push the hood back and away, revealing glossy dark hair hanging long and loose around her shoulders. "Yes. As I remember seeing it." His heart raced, being so near to her once again. And in the brightness of this day, wasn't she even more beautiful? The slant of her eyes gave her a quality of mystery . . . and hadn't all her actions since the day they had first met been that of intrigue? Why had a woman dressed in such expensive clothes lived in such non-luxury for those few days?

And he would find out what was behind her trip to the pawnshop. He had noted the absence of her necklace and earrings when she had finished with her business there.

Even now, he could remember how close she had come to seeing him following her that day. If not for the crowded streets. . . .

Feeling somewhat embarrassed, Jennifer brushed his hand aside. "What are you doing on this ship?" she asked. "I believe you've made a mistake. This ship is headed south. Not north." All the while Nicholas had been sleeping outside her door, in the hallway, waiting for her rented room, Jennifer hadn't ever really gotten a good look at him. He now stood, tall and lean, and the tightness of his shirt and breeches revealed heavily muscled legs and arms. He had discarded his toboggan hat and was letting his blond wavy hair blow gently in the sea breeze.

"No. No mistake, Jennifer," he said. He had also followed her on *this* day to make sure they would board the same ship.

Jennifer observed how his blue eyes seemed always to display a sparkle, giving a hint of a pleasant personality, as did the always present half-smile playing on his lips when he spoke. "But why?" she asked. They had made their formal introductions to one another on Jennifer's last day in her dreary room. He had seemed eager enough to take the room. She had seen how his weather-tanned, smooth face had lit up when she had said that he could have the room . . . that she was headed for San Francisco. Her eyes widened. Why hadn't he mentioned at that time his plans to travel to San Francisco . . . and not the Yukon? But it had been none of her business . . . as her business was none of his.

"I told you I was from Illinois?" he said, dismantling his easel.

"Yes. I remember."

"I've worked the Illinois farmland since I was a small lad," he said. "I painted in the evenings, before the sun set, or by candlelight. Then, only a few months ago, I heard about all this excitement in Seattle and in the Yukon, about the gold and all, and I wanted to get in on it. For some adventure, before I grew to be an old man."

"And you did arrive in Seattle. Wasn't it adventuresome enough for you?"

"Damn too much excitement for a quiet farmer boy like myself," he chuckled. "Damn. Never dreamed a town could be so filled with people and problems. And when I heard about people dying . . . even starvin' to death in the Yukon, I said to hell with that. I don't need gold to make me happy. I've got my painting."

"But why did you choose to go to San Francisco?" Jennifer persisted. "I'm sure you know that it's a much larger city even than Seattle. What makes you think you'll like it any better?"

"I have my reasons," he answered, smiling sheepishly in

her direction. "And you? Why are you heading for San Francisco?" he added, squatting down on the deck, looking upward at her.

"I have my own reasons also," she said flatly.

"Secrets, huh?" he laughed.

"My own personal business."

"Oh. I see," he said. "And what're you going to do to pleasure yourself with, the next several days? A sea voyage can get mighty boring and lonesome."

Feeling a sudden need to flee to the privacy of her cabin, to get away from Nicholas's persistent questions, Jennifer placed the hood back on her head and began to walk away.

"I'd like to paint your portrait," he yelled after her.

She hesitated, eyes wide, then moved onward. A rushing of feet brought him to her side once again. "I'm serious," he said. "You're beautiful. I'd love to paint your portrait. How about it?" The words had come so easily, words he hadn't spoken before to any woman . . . that . . . she was beautiful. . . .

Jennifer felt her heart pumping at a faster rate of speed than usual and the penetration of his blue eyes gave her the most unusual of sensations between her thighs and at the pit of her stomach. She could remember feeling this way at only one other time in her life—when Robert Harbison had looked at her so intimately that day in church, when she had been only fifteen.

She set her jaw firmly and said a flat no, and rushed on into her cabin and closed and bolt-locked the door. She leaned heavily against it, breathing hard, but suddenly feeling ashamed of herself. Nicholas was only being kind, and here she was being so rude. And his eyes. They were like magnets, making her not want to take her eyes off him. Wasn't he ever so handsome and polite? And couldn't it be exciting to pose for a portrait? The painting he had just shown her represented much artistic talent!

Turning swiftly, she unbolted the door and opened it, feeling lucky that he was still standing there, as though he had known she would change her mind.

"I'm sorry I was so rude," she said, casting her eyes downward. "Please come into my cabin and we can discuss doing the painting."

"I'm so glad you've changed your mind," he said, feeling a deep relief wash over him. Damn. He *had* to capture her on canvas. The urge to paint a particular subject hadn't ever been so strong before. But he hadn't met anyone like her before. She was the first woman he deeply desired to possess . . . not only on canvas . . . but wholly. He so longed to pull her into his arms and taste the sweetness of her lips. . . .

"Please leave the door open, though," Jennifer urged. "To make it look proper. You know."

"Yes. I know," he said, smiling. He stooped and stepped on into the cabin and squatted on the floor as Jennifer removed her cape and sat down on the edge of the cot.

"You really do think I could be a good subject for a painting?" she asked, sitting stiffly erect, very aware of these two blue eyes studying her so closely. Again, she felt foreign stirrings inside herself. And this was only the beginning of the voyage. Was this really happening?

"I've never painted anyone as beautiful as you," Nicholas said, wrapping his arms around his knees.

"You're embarrassing me," she murmured, casting her eyes downward once again.

"I don't mean to," he said. "I'm an artist and I'm most truthful in my assessments of what beauty truly is. Now, I have to ask. Do you have a dress that's . . . uh. . . how can I put this . . . a bit more revealing . . . in front?" He already knew the answer to this question. When she had left the pawnshop that day, her cape had been draped only over her shoulders, revealing the greatness of her bosom in her beautiful satin dress.

He also wanted to possess this part of her anatomy. But not only on canvas. Just a touch of such soft mounds would set his loins afire.

Jennifer's hand went to her throat. "What?" she whispered.

"To paint you, I would want you in a magnificent dress that

reveals your shoulders and a bit . . . of . . . your . . . uh . . . cleavage.'' The dress she now wore, with its stiff, high white collar, had to go. Again, he was confused by her. First to dress so boldly . . . and now so conservatively. Yes, he was quite eager to find out who this Jennifer truly was. There were reasons for all that she was doing . . . hidden truths . . . that could prove quite interesting to him.

''Nicholas . . . why . . . I never. . . .''

''You do have such a dress in one of your three trunks?''

''Why . . . yes. . . .''

''Would you mind wearing it for the portrait's sake?''

''Well . . . I guess it could be arranged.''

''That would be perfect,'' he said. ''Would you like to begin today . . . or wait until first thing in the morning?''

''Where do you plan to do this? I can't do it for all the ship's crew to see.''

''Could you let me do it here in the privacy of your cabin? With the skylight and four lamps, the lighting would be sufficient to paint by.''

''There would be talk. I'm afraid it could be a bit awkward.''

Nicholas laughed. ''Only envious talk because I'll be sharing all these hours alone with you.''

''But what if my Uncle Thad or Aunt Minnie would find out?''

''I won't even bother to ask who they are. All I can say is, let's make this trip pass more quickly by enjoying ourselves by working on this painting. What can it truly hurt?''

Jennifer rose and went to stand beside Nicholas who was now standing, fumbling with the bolt lock on the door. ''I think it can be fun, Nicholas. Sure. Let's do it. Tomorrow we shall begin.''

Suddenly, the ship lurched and Jennifer was in his arms, but only briefly, as he gave her a quick kiss, then hurried from her cabin. . . .

''My word,'' she gasped, putting her fingers to her lips. She still tasted his kiss, and it had left her breathless . . . wondering.

A tingling was surging through her, an inner excitement, this being the first kiss ... ever ... from a man.

Stepping to the doorway, she peered out, searching for him, and when she saw him, she couldn't understand the thumping of her heart.

Chapter Five

The ship rose, fell, and rolled, making it hard for Jennifer to sit poised in the middle of the cabin. The fullness of her dress was draped around below her, to hide the fact that she was sitting on one of her closed trunks. At this moment, she wanted to place her hands across her stomach, because it seemed to be lurching, as the ship also kept doing. She just hoped she wouldn't become ill to her stomach. From her opened door, she had seen an elderly man retching, to add more filth to the ship's deck. She would most certainly report the conditions of this horrible ship to her Uncle Thad!

"Keep your back straight, Jennifer," Nicholas said, cursing silently to himself. The damn ship. Why couldn't it ride the waves more peacefully? Just as he was ready to add another stroke of paint to the canvas, he would find his hand jerked in a different direction. And the easel! Even after he had nailed its legs to the flooring, it still continued to bounce unmercifully.

But nothing would stop him from painting . . . except, maybe, a touch from the lips of his model. His gaze fell to her heaving bosom. "And I must rearrange the dress," he added quickly, feeling his pulse beat quicken, knowing what he was planning to do in only moments. . . .

"Oh, Nicholas," Jennifer argued, pouting. "Can't you just get on with it? My back is aching so. I'm not used to sitting in one position for so long."

"Patience, Jennifer. Patience," Nicholas said, fidgeting with the gathers of her green satin dress, then letting his fingers move on upward, touching her waist, then most boldly putting his fingers to the bodice of her dress, feeling sweat prickling on his brow as he pretended to rearrange the lace that lay across the fullness of her breasts.

Jennifer's eyes widened, looking downward, watching. She seemed to stop breathing as his fingers continued to touch her there . . . where her heart then began to pound in unison with a strange throbbing deep down, inside her, between her thighs. It was an ache of sorts . . . but an ache that felt good.

"Nicholas, what . . . are . . . you. . . ?" she began, and then their eyes met in a rapturous gaze.

His fingers moved on upward and touched the velvet softness of her flesh, making Jennifer gasp and close her eyes. When his fingers continued to explore, now inside her gown, circling each nipple, desire awakened inside Jennifer . . . but also shame. She suddenly remembered who she was. A minister's daughter, having never been with a man before . . . and she couldn't . . . not . . . now. . . . She opened her eyes widely, all flushed, and immediately shoved Nicholas away from her.

She arose and went to the other side of the cabin, and stood with her back to him. "How could you have taken . . . such . . . liberties with my body?" she whispered, biting her lower lip. She knew that she couldn't accuse him fully . . . because she had let him. She even now wanted him to touch her further. She had liked the excitement he had stirred inside her. But she felt so utterly wicked! What would her Aunt Minnie think of her now? And had Aunt Minnie been right? Did wearing such revealing dresses bring out the devil in both a woman and a man? She stiffened when she felt Nicholas's presence by her side. She was afraid he might touch her again. If he did . . .

could she say no to whatever he asked of her? She now knew that she was falling in love with this Illinois farmer whom she had only known such a short time. And couldn't love even get in the way of her plans . . . ?

She swung around, trying to appear angry . . . hurt. "And what *do* you have to say for yourself, Nicholas? Are we to do only a painting here, or shall I have to ask you to leave?" Her heart melted, seeing the apology in the depths of his blue eyes. She so wanted to put her fingers to his lips, to touch them. . . .

"I'm awful sorry, Jennifer," Nicholas said, with hands tucked in his rear breeches pockets. "I don't know what possessed me to do such a thing. I only meant . . . to rearrange the dress. Make it lie just perfect for the painting." Damn it. Now he most surely would never be able to pull her into his arms and kiss her. He had rushed into it too soon.

Jennifer set her jaw firmly and straightened her back. "If there's to be any rearranging done, just tell me what's to be done . . . and I shall do it myself."

"That sounds fine to me."

"Then you will . . . keep your . . . hands . . . to . . . yourself?"

"It's a promise. Cross my heart and hope to die."

Jennifer felt herself loosening into a laugh. She hadn't heard that particular saying since she was a child. "Cross your heart and hope to die?" she said, not only loving Nicholas . . . but liking him as a person. He was a genuine, likable sort.

Nicholas could feel a blush rising and walked back toward his easel. He picked up a brush, watching her. How lucky he had been to have found her. She was becoming more precious to him than all the gold in the Yukon. "Shall we get back to it, before the sun sets behind the horizon?" he asked, looking upward through the skylight. Two days gone at sea, and only five to go. Could he complete the portrait in so little time . . . and could he capture her love . . . also in so little time?

Jennifer rearranged herself on the trunk in the usual pose and sat quietly as Nicholas began to make slow strokes on the canvas. As she continued to watch him, she felt her feelings for him growing. She hadn't ever experienced anything like this before. It was a restlessness that his continued studying of her aroused. She batted her lashes nervously and tried to continue smiling, wondering if he could see the difference in her expression.

"Wine and fried salmon for the two lovebirds," Captain Klein said, suddenly filling the room with his presence and the aroma of grease-soaked fish.

"Lovebirds?" Jennifer gasped, putting her hand to her throat. Did the captain and the crew think . . . ? But, no. The cabin door had been left open at all times. Oh, no, she thought further. Had they just seen what had happened? She cast her eyes downward and climbed from the trunk.

"Thanks for the grub," Nicholas said. Then he laughed. "And even wine? Hmm. First-class treatment on board this fine ship. Thank you, kind sir."

Jennifer strolled to her bunk and sat down upon it, worrying about what the captain might have seen . . . and would he . . . tell Uncle Thad? She was relieved to see the captain hurry on from the cabin.

"Here. Let's eat our meal and drink some wine and forget the painting until tomorrow," Nicholas said, sitting down beside her.

Jennifer turned her face from him. "I'm suddenly not hungry," she murmured. She flinched when she felt the warmth of his hand as he turned her face back to him.

"It was what the captain called us, wasn't it?" he asked tenderly.

Jennifer swallowed hard. "Well, yes," she said, watching him with wide eyes.

"He was only teasing us, Jennifer. You know. Us being alone and all in . . . your . . . cabin."

"That's what I mean," she gulped. "Because we *are* alone in the cabin. If we hadn't been alone, *that* wouldn't have happened awhile ago."

"I said I was sorry."

"I know."

"Shall I pour you some wine?"

"I've never drank wine before."

"If you want to be able to not taste that ghastly salmon that's been served to us, I suggest you force yourself to take a few swallows of wine."

"All right. If you truly feel it's best."

"Believe me. It's best."

Taking tin cups from the serving platters, Nicholas poured the red wine into each. He handed one toward Jennifer. "Here. Now, only sip on it. You'll like it. It'll be refreshing after breathing in the stench of this ship and salt water all day."

With her hands on each side of the cup, she tipped it upward and sipped very slightly from it. The tartness curled her tongue, yet it was refreshing. The ship's water tasted of boiled mud. She tilted the cup more and took a deep swallow, which caused her to cough and her eyes to burn.

Nicholas roared with laughter. "It's not like drinking tea. You must remember that," he said, handing her the platter of fried salmon.

The aroma rising from the fish made Jennifer turn her nose from it, but she was hungry, and she knew that she had no choice but to eat it. Salmon appeared to be the only thing served on this miserable ship. Oh, how she hated it.

"Go ahead. Eat," Nicholas urged. "You don't want to lose your strength, do you?"

"No," she murmured. "I don't." She forced herself to take a bite, then quickly washed it down with another drink of wine. She was surprised how much more easy each drink of this red liquid became, the more she drank. It was even helping to warm her insides against the fast approaching chill of the night air. She forced the last bite of the salmon into her mouth, then quickly thrust the empty platter away from her, placing it on the floor.

Nicholas stretched his long, lean legs out in front of him and slouched more down onto the bunk. "You must admit, it does make one more relaxed to have food in the stomach," he said, noticing the flush of Jennifer's cheeks. He smiled to himself as she took another sip of her wine. Apparently, she wasn't aware of how much she had already consumed. Then he looked upward at the skylight, noticing no light showing through it now. Night had fallen in the utter blackness that seemed to characterize night at sea.

The whale oil lamps flickered in pale goldens onto the ceiling and wall, resembling a panorama of paintings in ever changing forms.

A loud banging made Nicholas jump with a start, but he smiled even more to himself when he discovered that it had only been the door to the cabin jarring shut from another lurch of the ship.

Looking toward Jennifer, Nicholas felt the renewed heat in his loins, but saw that she was lying in a swoon across the other end of the bunk. Disappointed, he bent down over her. "Jennifer? Jennifer," he said. But he soon realized that it was the wine that had caused her to fall fast asleep.

"There's always tomorrow, my love," he whispered, scooting from the bunk himself, to make room for the full length of her body. He arranged her, as though she was a rag doll, then gently covered her with a brown, woolen blanket. His eyes took in the slow heaving of her bosom, and he couldn't resist leaning down to place a kiss upon one of her breasts.

Then, standing, he took one last look and tiptoed around the room, snuffing the life from the whale oil lamps, then hurried from her cabin.

Jennifer's eyes fluttered open. She smiled mischievously. She had done quite well in her pretense at being asleep. But had she not, she knew that he would have soon tried to approach her again. There was something pulling them together. And would she be able to continue in his presence without giving in to the strong urgings pulsating throughout her body? Her body was trying to tell her that she was a woman . . . with womanly desires.

With the slightest touch of her fingers, Jennifer brushed against the breast which his lips had so gently kissed . . . then she closed her eyes and fell into a deep sleep . . . unashamedly dreaming of him.

A nearby creaking of the floor awakened Jennifer with a start. Pulling the blanket more beneath her chin, she tried to focus her eyes to the darkness of the room, to search around her. But it was impossible. There weren't even any shadows to see this night. She wished now that Nicholas had not turned the lamps off.

As she strained to listen more closely, the night noises of the ship became more pronounced. The continuing rumbling of the boiler was ever present, as was the splash of the water against the ship's side. The timbers strained and creaked both day and night also, but she again heard another creaking, and it was in her room.

Her heart began to pound and her mouth went dry. "Who's there?" she asked, trembling. Then she could hear someone's uneven breathing and she knew she was no longer alone in her cabin.

"Nicholas, is that you?" she further asked, rising to lean against the ship's wall.

A rumble of quiet laughter was the reply and she suddenly felt the roughness of hands groping for her in the darkness, touching her face and then . . . much lower. She gasped and pulled away, but she couldn't manage to jump from the cot to get free.

"No, my fine lady. This ain't no baby-faced Nicholas," the stranger finally said in a low, throaty voice. "But I be jist as good in bed and prob'ly better'n him. Ah'll give you a chance to be the judge o' tha' question."

"Please. Get away from me, whoever you are," she pleaded, feeling lightheaded from fear. The feel of those hands again on her body made Jennifer gag with disgust. If only she had placed her gun beneath the pillow! Now she had no way to defend herself.

"Where are those beauties?" the stranger continued, then jerked the blanket from Jennifer and soon found her breasts.

"Oh, no. You mustn't," Jennifer sobbed, pulling and twisting, trying to set herself free, but this man had already positioned himself atop her and was pressing down against her with all his might.

"No fightin' will set ya free, fine lady," the stranger hissed, then captured her lips beneath his and sought to probe inside her mouth with his tongue as a hand worked at freeing a breast from the tight confines of her satin dress, which she so neglectfully had kept on in her stupor from the wine she had drunk with her supper. "Pure silk. That's whut yore skin is. Pure silk," he mumbled as he then moved his mouth to cover the now exposed breast.

"Please, don't," Jennifer continued. She was afraid to scream. She had felt something cold in his left hand and wasn't sure if it was a gun or a knife. Disgust was flowing through her veins. The man smelled of cheap whiskey and tobacco and his clothes reeked of dried perspiration. She again tried to push him away from her, but felt his body as a piece of brute steel, unable to be moved.

"And now, fine lady, whut lies hidden much lower?" the stranger said, reaching his hand down to lift the gathered skirts of her dress and many petticoats upward.

"You just can't do this to me. My uncle owns this ship," Jennifer continued to sob. "You shall be hanged. You shall."

But the one hand continued to move up the inside of her left thigh until he had reached the most intimate of undergarments. With one swift stroke, he had this torn from her body and his fingers were pinching and exploring her, where no other man's fingers had ever been before.

"Cain't say that don' feel good," the man leered, then kissed her again, forcefully, wetly, until Jennifer could feel the spinning of her head and knew she was near to fainting from the disgust of the moment. Then her eyes widened and her breathing seemed to stop when she heard him fumbling with his breeches, from which he had quickly loosened his manhood to search for her.

Not caring any longer if it was a knife or gun next to her throat, Jennifer began to scream and bite and fight, until a rush of feet in the cabin pulled the intruder from atop her.

"Wha' the hell?" the stranger shouted, then let out a gurgling sound as he fell to the floor.

"Who's . . . who's . . . there?" Jennifer sobbed, pulling the skirt of her dress down, trying again to see through the darkness, but seeing only the dim lighting from a small lantern being held by—"Oh, thank goodness. It's you," she quickly added, sobbing almost hysterically, as her eyes adjusted to the room around her.

"It's me. Captain Klein, ma'am," the captain boomed. "Damn. Damn sorry, 'bout this. But he won't be botherin' you or any other woman again."

"Did you . . . ?"

"I thrust my knife in him. If that's what you be a askin'."

"Oh, good Lord," Jennifer blurted, sobbing anew.

Another rush of feet brough Nicholas to her bunk as Captain Klein lit a whale oil lamp, to reveal the disarray of Jennifer's clothing and the dead sailor lying face down on the floor next to the bunk.

"Jennifer. My God, sweet Jennifer. Are you all right?" Nicholas asked, pulling her into his arms.

She clung to him, sobbing, turning her eyes from the ugliness lying on the floor. "It was so horrible, Nicholas," she said. "He tried . . . to . . . he almost. . . ."

"Shh. Don't say anymore," he whispered, caressing her back. Then he turned to the captain. "Well, don't just stand there," he said. "Get that goddamned thing out of this cabin. And see to it we have some sherry sent in here right away for Jennifer."

"Sure thing, lad," the captain grumbled, then pulled the body away, leaving Jennifer and Nicholas alone.

"Oh, Nicholas, I feel so dirty," Jennifer said, pulling away from him. She looked down, and most embarrassingly, saw the still exposed breast. She could still feel this stranger's hands and lips exploring. Blushing, she hurriedly pulled her dress into place. Then she saw the circle of blood on the floor. She gagged and turned her eyes away.

"I'll see that it's covered until morning. Then someone will clean it up. Bright and early."

"What kind of man would force himself on a woman?" she said, bringing Robert Harbison to mind . . . and how he more than likely had put her mother through something like this. Oh, how even more she hated him! "And doesn't my uncle choose a crew carefully?" she quickly added.

"Some men you can't tell about. This one? Just wanted to test his luck. I guess he thought you'd be worth the chance of getting caught."

Jennifer scooted more close to Nicholas, feeling an achiness slowly encompassing her. "Hold me, Nicholas," she whispered. "Please hold me."

"My love, I shall never let you go," he said, then held her again, until the captain stepped back into the cabin with a bottle of sherry and two wine glasses. The captain cleared his throat nervously.

"Ma'am, lad, here's the sherry, and I've brought you two crystal glasses instead of the usual tin cups. Maybe as an apology again for what happened here."

"Thank you," Jennifer whispered, pulling free of Nicholas's embrace, running her fingers through her hair.

Nicholas took the wine and glasses. "And what might you have to cover this soiled floor?" he said firmly. But before the captain had a chance to answer, a rushing of feet brought another sailor, all ready with a pail of water and stiff brush.

"Ah'll have this up in no time flat, sir," the sailor mumbled, then stooped to his knees and began scrubbing.

"That should take care of everything, ma'am," Captain Klein said. "Again, my apologies."

"Apologies accepted," Jennifer said and watched heavy-lidded as he rushed from the room.

"Hurry on with you," Nicholas ordered the sailor.

"Yes, sir," the sailor said and left with his pail and brush.

"There'll always be a stain there. You'll have to just get used to it, Jennifer."

Jennifer shuddered. "It shall always be a reminder."

"Yes, I know," Nicholas said, then poured the sherry and handed a glass to Jennifer. He took a sip from his own glass, then laughed softly. "One good thing, that damn bastard didn't walk into the easel while groping through the dark of the room. Damn. If he would've, he'd have torn the painting for sure."

Jennifer took a swallow of the sherry and felt it trickle down her throat, relaxing her. "Yes. At least something good we can say about this terrible thing."

"Jennifer, I refuse to leave you alone anymore at night while on this ship."

"What do you mean?"

"I shall stay here in the cabin with you. I'll sleep on the floor. I won't risk something like this happening again."

"But it wouldn't look proper."

"I don't give a damn. And do you, really, after this?"

"Not if you could mention the reason to the captain," she said softly.

"Then you really think it would be all right?"

"I doubt if I'd ever be able to sleep again on this trip if you didn't."

"Then I shall leave momentarily, so you can clean up a bit and get into proper night things and I shall return with my own travel bag soon."

"Okay," she said softly. She set her glass down and went to bolt lock the door behind him. If she had only done that earlier in the evening—but the wine had made her careless.

Hurrying, she removed her dress and soiled undergarments. She briskly scrubbed her body, to remove all signs of the man's touches, then slipped her long-sleeved cotton nightgown over her head, already feeling a bit relieved. And wasn't she even anxious now for the return of Nicholas? And was she truly being wise . . . to have him so close for the rest of the trip? She sighed deeply. At least this stranger's attack hadn't spoiled her feelings for all men. She desired Nicholas now . . . even more than before; for even though the stranger's touches had disgusted her, the thought of Nicholas doing the same made her mind spin with a hungry desire for him.

A tapping at the door made her swirl around and rush to it. She unbolted it and opened it, to smile sheepishly toward Nicholas, who stood with his arms filled with his own bags and sleeping paraphernalia.

His eyes took in the full figure of her, standing so angelic in her long, white gown, with her dark hair flowing around her shoulders. He now wished he could have been the one to have plunged the knife into the man who had touched this innocence standing before him.

"Can I truly come in?" he asked, bending, to speak more in her face, so no one else on deck could hear.

"Yes. Please do," she whispered, knowing that her face was flushed scarlet.

She let him step on in, then very confidently bolt locked the door behind her. She watched as he quietly spread blankets on the floor on which to sleep. Then she walked over to her bunk. "Want another glass of sherry?" she asked.

"I really don't believe so," he answered.

"Then I guess I'll say good night," she said quietly.

"I shall dim the whale light, but only to its lowest point."

"Yes. Please do."

Jennifer stretched out on the bunk, with her back to Nicholas, but she could feel his eyes on her. Her heart began to pump more quickly. "Nicholas?" she said, trembling.

"Yes?"

"Would it hurt if you just lay next to me? To hold me? But nothing more?"

He didn't respond. He just went to her and pulled her around to face him, then pulled her into his arms. He knew that it would be hard to lie so close without taking her completely . . . but this wasn't the time . . . the near rape was too fresh in her mind.

"Nicholas?"

"Yes?"

"I do believe I'm in love with you."

"And I . . . you. . . ."

Jennifer snuggled closer to him . . . knowing her body ached for more from him . . . but not now. And was this truly going to get in the way of her so carefully schemed plans waiting in San Francisco?

   She couldn't think about it now. Now her mind was too full of Nicholas and how it felt to lie so close to him. . . .

Chapter Six

The sea was surprisingly calm this day, but there were the continuing shreds of mist in the air, settling on Jennifer's face as she stood, clinging to the ship's rail.

She was quite aware of Nicholas at her side and felt a bit of embarrassment, realizing the ship's gossip was all about Nicholas and herself. For the past two nights they had shared her cabin, but that had been all they had shared. By the knowing stares from the ship's crew, indicated clearly to Jennifer what had to be in their thoughts.

"Jennifer, the dampness of the air is going to droop your hair," Nicholas said, interrupting her train of thought. "Can't we just return to the cabin and continue with the portrait?"

Jennifer pulled the hood of her cape closer around her face. "Just give me a few more minutes, Nicholas," she answered. "I needed some fresh air. That's all. We spend too much time in that cabin." She looked into his blue eyes and again felt the sweet, harsh pain of young love. Oh, what was she to do? She didn't want any of this to get in her way . . . and wasn't San Francisco ever so close?

Nicholas leaned down, resting his elbows on the ship's railing. "Darling, is it really so terrible . . . being alone with me so much?" he asked, his usual half-smile playing on his lips.

Jerking her head around to stare out at the horizon of blues meeting blues, almost a velvet backdrop for her thoughts, Jennifer's heart filled with palpitations. Nicholas had just called her "darling."

"No. Not really," she finally answered demurely, pulling her hand away when he tried to clasp onto it. "Nicholas. Please don't," she quickly added. She was afraid of where his touch would lead. It always seemed to awaken her insides to such a trembling warmth . . . something she didn't seem to have any control over.

"If you're worried about Captain Klein and what he might think, don't," Nicholas scolded. "He would think us strange, indeed, if we didn't show affection for one another. And haven't you caught a glimpse of the beauty he has stowed away in his own cabin? Damn. I wonder where he even found her."

Jennifer's eyes widened and she felt a blush rising. She turned her gaze to meet Nicholas's and saw the dancing of his eyes. "Are you telling me . . . that . . . Captain Klein . . . ?" she whispered.

"Yep. The one and only. Why are you so surprised?"

"Well . . . I . . . uh . . . don't know."

Nicholas leaned closer. "Darling, this is a part of life," he said softly. "Man and woman? Together? That's what life is all about."

"Nicholas," Jennifer stated flatly, then flipped the tail of her cape around and headed for her cabin. She knew that her face was flushed crimson, but she held her chin proudly high, not wanting to care about what anyone thought. But she was the niece of this ship's owner . . . she had to care.

The creaking of timber and splashing of water seemed to be all around her as she made a turn on deck, now so close to the captain's cabin she couldn't help but stare toward it, wondering if there truly was a woman sharing his quarters. If so, why hadn't she let herself be seen by anyone else?

The door of the captain's cabin swung suddenly open, startling Jennifer. She jumped and batted her lashes nervously as Captain Klein stepped out on deck, stretching and yawning. He was attired only in a gray-stained T-shirt and loose-fitted dark breeches. His hair was mussed as though he had just awakened from a long night's sleep . . . even though it was only growing dusk.

"Oh, hello there, Jennifer," he grumbled, snapping his suspenders as he let out a deep breath of air. "Nice evenin', ain't it?" he quickly added.

"Why . . . uh . . . yes. Very," she replied, and stole a fast look around him and indeed saw a dark-skinned girl standing half-nude in the far corner of his cabin. Jennifer swallowed hard and looked quickly away as this girl's gaze met hers in an utter boldness, making Jennifer feel guilty for having been so rude as to search this man's private cabin with wandering eyes.

A rumble of laughter surfaced from deep inside Captain Klein. His eyes gleamed, having seen Jennifer looking for his wench. "Got someone I'd like ya to meet," he said, then turned and yelled into the cabin. "Make yoreself presentable, Lil. Got company comin' in."

"I don't know," Jennifer mumbled, looking desperately from side to side. She now wished that she had listened to Nicholas's urgings and had gone back to her own cabin much sooner. Then she wouldn't have met the captain under such embarrassing circumstances.

A strong hand gripped her right elbow and guided her on inside the cabin. "Lil, I want you to meet Jennifer Brewster. Thad's niece. Jennifer . . . Lil. . . ."

Jennifer was stunned, to the point of being wordless. Captain Klein's Lil was a Negro. Jennifer hadn't ever known of any white man actually consorting with . . . a. . . . But wasn't Lil so beautiful, with her sleek, shiny black skin, wide, red lips and flashing eyes?

"So, you're Thad's blood relation, are you?" Lil said, extending a hand. "Interesting. Very interesting."

Jennifer's brow lifted. How did this girl know her Uncle

Thad . . . and why did she find it so interesting to meet one of Thad's relations? She felt the solid grip of a hand and tried to not let her gaze lower to the mostly exposed, great bosom of the girl, who appeared to be only in her late teens. The sheer chemise was draped loosely, to show the petiteness of her hips and waist.

"Yes. Thad's my uncle," Jennifer answered, pulling her hand away.

The girl flipped her long, black hair from around her shoulders and eased herself down onto the captain's bunk, crossing her bare legs beneath her. She smiled wickedly up at Jennifer. "I know your uncle," she said. "Quite well."

"You . . . do . . . ?" Jennifer gasped. She understood the restlessness of her uncle, but was he this restless?

"Yes. Captain here introduced us. I think Thad's going to try and put me in his motion pictures. That's what he tells me, anyway."

"Really?" Jennifer gasped.

"Damn interestin' project Thad's workin' on. Could make him quite famous," Captain Klein said, pulling a black woolen shirt on and buttoning it up the front. "Yeah. Might be a future for those movin' pictures on a screen."

"Yes. I'm sure," Jennifer said softly, then turned and eyed the open door. "I really must be on my way," she added, turning to smile awkwardly at Lil and then Captain Klein.

Captain Klein took her by the elbow once again. "Here. Let me help you," he said.

"Nice making your acquaintance, Jennifer," Lil said.

"And yours also," Jennifer replied, then was relieved to be out on the open deck once again.

"You seemed uncomfortable in Lil's presence." Captain Klein laughed throatily as he continued to walk beside Jennifer. "She's pleasant company for an old salt like myself, but she don't get on too well with womenfolk."

"I found her pleasant enough," Jennifer replied, feeling a need to lie. She couldn't shake the wonder from her mind . . .

the wonder that this white man . . . and colored girl . . . and the fact that this colored girl . . . even knew . . . Uncle Thad?

"I hope you also have found the improved conditions of the ship pleasant enough," Captain Klein said, taking on a serious note. "I still feel damn bad 'bout the other night. That damn crazy sailor and all. Made me aware of my neglects. Now I keep the crew busy day and night. To busy their minds and hands."

"Yes. I have noticed," Jennifer said, looking around at the spotlessness of the deck. Each morning now it was scrubbed down, and an improvement had even been made in the meals served to the few passengers on board. She stopped at her cabin door and turned to face Captain Klein.

"And you won't tell Thad 'bout anything that happened here?" Captain Klein said in a near whisper as he leaned down into Jennifer's face. His eyes showed a weariness. Or was it a bit of fright? Was he afraid of losing his job?

"But Uncle Thad will have to know of the sailor's death, won't he?"

"I do the firin' and hirin' of the crew. He never counts heads."

"I just don't know, captain."

"It'd by *my* head if ya tell, young lady," he said more firmly.

Jennifer cast her eyes downward, not really wanting to relive the experience anyway, which she, in truth, would be doing, if she had to tell anyone about that horrible night. Her gaze shot upward. "Captain, I won't tell Uncle Thad about anything that happened on your ship, if you'll promise to not tell him about my relationship with Nicholas," she quickly blurted, not believing she was actually bargaining with this man for his silence.

Captain Klein laughed boisterously. "Damn if it ain't a deal, Jennifer," he said.

"And your . . . uh . . . woman friend . . . Lil? Will you make sure she is also made to not tell . . . since she confesses to knowing my uncle so well?"

Another deep chuckle rumbled inside Captain Klein's chest

as a sparkle lit up his eyes. "Good as done," he said. "No need worryin' yore pretty head 'bout that. Lil wouldn't even want Thad knowin' of her presence on this ship."

Jennifer's brows lifted in confusion. "Oh?" she murmured. "She . . . wouldn't . . . ?" She wanted to go further to ask the why's of this statement, but Nicholas opened the cabin door and stepped outside to stand beside her.

"I was getting worried about you, Jennifer," he said with a furrowed brow. "Where did you disappear to?"

Jennifer looked from Nicholas to Captain Klein, blushing slightly. "I met Captain Klein's . . . uh . . . companion," she stammered.

"Oh?" Nicholas said, raising a brow.

"You'll have to come meet my Lil also, lad. She might even pose for a portrait for ya. A beautiful subject she'd be."

Jennifer began to push Nicholas back inside the cabin. "Captain, I believe it will take the rest of the trip for Nicholas to complete *my* portrait," she said, with a set jaw. "Isn't that so, Nicholas?" She looked up at him with blazing eyes.

He laughed amusedly. "Yeah. Sure," he said, then half saluted Captain Klein. "I guess I've got some work to do here. Be talking to you later."

"Sure, lad. Sure," Captain Klein said, laughing harshly as he turned and headed back toward his own cabin.

"Did I see fire in your eyes, or was I imagining things?" Nicholas said, helping Jennifer with the removal of her cape.

"I imagine you see what you want to see," she snapped, hating the thought of Nicholas's being introduced to Lil. Lil was black . . . but she was beautiful . . . and could possibly be the making of an interesting portrait.

"I like it when you show anger," Nicholas said, circling her waist to pull her into his arms. He had managed to control his desire for her since her near rape, but now, he could hardly resist. Jealousy had caused her anger, which showed the deepness of her feelings for him. But she pushed against his chest and soon had herself free of his grasp.

"The sun is setting, Nicholas," she said. She worked with

her hair to straighten it, then poised herself atop the same trunk, waiting. "You wanted to return to the cabin to paint, so get on with it. You know the light will soon be gone." She held her back straight and tried to control her uneven breathing. She had so desired to cling to him, to let his mouth capture hers, but doubts had begun to assail her. Would she every truly be able to give herself wholly to Nicholas . . . or any man . . . no matter how deeply she wanted it? Her upbringing had taught her differently. To give in to a man before wedlock was known to be sinful . . . but . . . who would know if she did? Being away from family . . . home . . . and church had sparked a keen sense of freedom in her . . . and oh, how she wanted this feeling to include Nicholas.

Nicholas was adding stroke after stroke to the painting, squinting as the sunset played in reds through the open door. "Yes, we must get this portrait done before the journey's end," he said, barely audible. His heart raced with each dab of blue he added to the eyes of the portrait. Damn it. He wasn't blind. He could see the desire in the depths of Jennifer's blue eyes. He would capture this look and would title this painting "Portrait of Desire." It would always have a special meaning for him and he hoped it eventually would for her also. And this night . . . he would nurture that desire in her, but now he had to put his thoughts elsewhere.

"I recognize the dress you're wearing from a day in Seattle," he said, watching her, testing her. There weren't that many days left on board this ship. If he was to find out some hidden facts about her he had to begin probing, but in a way that wouldn't offend her.

"Why haven't you mentioned this earlier, Nicholas? I've worn this same dress for the portrait . . . since . . . the day after that . . . filthy man mussed my other one."

"My mind has been too occupied."

"Tell me which day you are speaking of? Before boarding this ship, I only saw you sleeping in the hallway of that horrid building, except for my last day, and even then we only spoke briefly."

"It was that day. I saw you entering and leaving a pawnshop also that day. Did you have to pawn your jewelry for tickets to board this ship?"

"My . . . jewelry . . . ?" she gasped. "How did you know . . . unless . . . you . . ."

"Yes. Unless I followed you."

"But, why?"

"A beautiful lady all alone in the city with all the men roaming the streets? I wanted to be sure you were safe."

"Is that why you were always outside my door? Not just because you were waiting for my room, but because you were . . . watching . . . me . . . ?"

"Love at first sight."

"Nicholas. No."

"Yes, Jennifer."

"And boarding the same ship as I?"

"No accident."

"But if you followed me, you must have also seen me return to my house to gather my belongings?"

"I saw you enter that one large house, but I thought it might belong to a relative. I saw a woman embrace you on the day you returned there."

"That was my Aunt Minnie."

"Then that was your Aunt Minnie's house?"

Jennifer felt her throat grow dry. Should she tell him all? Could his knowing disrupt her plans in San Francisco? But surely not. Whenever she chose to set herself free from him, she would tell him so and he would have no choice but to do as she requested. And wouldn't it be a relief to talk about home to somebody . . . especially to Nicholas?

"No. That is my house," she answered, tilting her chin up a bit more, proud to be the owner of such a grand house . . . and feeling a wave of sadness for her father as she remembered how he had handpicked that particular house for his family those many years ago.

Nicholas began to wipe his brush with a cloth, now even more confused. "That was truly your house?" he stammered.

"Then why the room . . . the pawnshop . . . ? It doesn't make any sense."

"Nicholas, I can't really reveal my personal life to you to the extent you wish me to," she said, moving from the trunk. She knew that he was quitting for the evening when he began to clean his brushes. "But I can tell you that my father passed away only a short time ago and that is the reason for the house now belonging to me."

"I'm sorry about your father, Jennifer."

Jennifer swung the long gathers of her dress around and went to sit on the bunk, feeling a deep sadness for her father. Thinking about him gave her such an empty, almost helpless feeling inside. "My father was the most kindest, gentlest of men," she murmured, feeling her eyes burning with the need to weep. "His ministry will always be remembered by the people of Seattle."

Nicholas' heart skipped a beat. "Your father . . . was a minister?"

"Yes. The best."

"I . . . didn't . . . know," Nicholas said, remembering how he had so boldly touched Jennifer's breasts that one time . . . and how he had so wanted to seduce her. Had he known she was a minister's daughter. . . .

Jennifer could see the desperation in Nicholas's eyes. All her life, she had been made to feel as though she was different . . . untouchable . . . because she was a minister's daughter. She could now see the change in attitude toward her that Nicholas was undergoing. She quickly arose and took one of his hands in hers.

"Please, Nicholas. Don't treat me differently now that you know. I don't think I could bear it."

"But . . . you are a minister's daughter."

"Does that truly make me so different?"

"No. Not different. But just a bit special."

"And why must that be so?"

"Because you were brought up being taught the right values

of life. I'm sure you feel much different about life than, let's say, for example, Captain Klein's wench.''

Remembering Lil and the way she was so scantily dressed, Jennifer walked away from Nicholas. "I cannot understand how a white man . . . can . . . you know . . . with a girl like her,'' she said softly.

"Her being black? Is that what you mean?''

Jennifer swung around and faced Nicholas with a set jaw. "Yes. She's of a different color and upbringing. Why, you'd never, would you, Nicholas?''

Nicholas placed the last cleaned brush in a tin can and went to Jennifer and pulled her into his arms. He held her close to him, smelling the fragrance of her hair. It was similar to the aroma of jasmine. "Jennifer, I'm in love with a minister's daughter,'' he said. "You know that, now don't you?'' You should. I've admitted that to you already. I could even go so far as to say I want to marry you. Even as soon as we arrive at San Francisco.''

A weakness lay where Jennifer's heart normally beat, having heard a proposal from a man she so dearly loved but had known for so short a time. "Marry?'' she whispered. "Did you . . . marry . . . ?''

Nicholas held her at arm's length. The thickness of her lashes cast heavy shadows over the soft pink of her cheeks. Had she ever been so lovely as at this moment? "Yes. Marry. You're alone . . . I'm alone. We belong together. You can't say you don't feel the same about me as I do about you.''

"But . . . Nicholas . . .'' she murmured, stunned, not knowing what to say. Marriage was the furthest thing from her mind. And how could Nicholas have thought up such an idea so quickly? Was it because she had told him she was a preacher's daughter . . . making him want to make his desires legal? Or could he possibly think he would be marrying into wealth, since she had told him of the house she had inherited from her father? Or did he possibly . . . truly . . . love her enough to want to marry her for love, and for that reason only? She had yet to tell him about Uncle Thadeus and the wealth he possessed . . .

"No buts, Jennifer," he said, kissing her fingertips. "I cannot even imagine you being set loose, alone, in San Francisco. I want you to marry me, so I can take care of you. Watch over you. You are so gentle and sweet, you need someone to care for you."

"Nicholas, I shan't be alone in San Francisco. My Uncle Thadeus is to meet me there upon my arrival."

Nicholas's blue eyes wavered and his weathered, tan, youthful face, creased with the first signs of doubt. He went to his brushes and began to pull them, one by one, from the tin can, in an effort to busy his fingers, by wiping them each anew on a dampened cloth. "So you have kin in San Francisco? You never mentioned any."

"I don't remember you asking."

"And if I had, would you have even told me?"

"I'm not so sure, Nicholas."

Nicholas hung his head, to hide his displeasure over this new bit of news. "And who might this Uncle Thadeus be?" he asked, rearranging his brushes back into the tin can.

"Uncle Thadeus? He's my father's brother."

"How is it that he is in San Francisco and you and your family were in Seattle?"

"I was born in San Francisco. My father and mother and myself moved to Seattle when my father got a calling from the Lord to take his ministry to Seattle."

After shutting the cabin door and securing the bolt lock, Nicholas went and sat beside Jennifer. Locking the door at dusk had become a habit.

"And what does your Uncle Thadeus do for a living?" Nicholas asked, touching the softness of her satin dress. It reminded him of the touch of her breasts. He ached to secure this touch once again. But now would he ever succeed? She seemed a bit distant at the moment. Damn. Maybe he had plied her with too many questions . . . when the important thing was to be able to stretch out atop her and guide his throbbing hardness inside the soft sweetness of her.

Jennifer watched the long lankiness of his fingers. The hands of an artist. They were now caressing the skirt of her dress as though they were touching her flesh. Her gaze moved upward to meet his. She could see the passion in his eyes . . . smoldering . . . setting small flames burning inside her. "My Uncle Thad?" she whispered. "He . . . owns many ships. He even owns this very ship that we are sailing on."

"Well, my God," Nicholas exclaimed. "I should've guessed. Why else would you be given this cabin while all else sleep on open deck?"

"Yes. That is the reason why."

"There's one person you've failed to elaborate on through all this."

"And who is that?"

"Your mother."

Jennifer stood up abruptly, biting her lower lip. She could feel an emptiness at the pit of her stomach, aching, gnawing. "My mother is also dead," she said softly.

Nicholas could see how distraught Jennifer had become at the mention of her mother. He went to her and took a hand. "I'm sorry, darling," he murmured.

"Just don't ever ask . . . how . . . my mother died," she said, almost choking on the words.

"I won't. I promise," he said, then pulled her next to him and lifted her chin so his mouth could cover hers softly. "I want to kiss away the hurt my questions have caused you," he added. "May I, Jennifer? May I hold and kiss you? Make you want to be mine, even though you haven't agreed to marry me?"

The emptiness at the pit of Jennifer's stomach slowly began to be filled with a thrilling warmth. Her lashes fluttered nervously. She now knew that she could no longer refuse him, for to refuse him was also to . . . refuse . . . herself . . . and the growing ache between her thighs needed to be quieted, or else she might burst inside from want. She looked up into his eyes.

She could see how anxiously he waited for her answer. She reached upward and stroked the smoothness of his face, then the trembling of his perfectly formed lips. "My love, I am waiting. Please kiss me and hold me," she whispered. "I need you. I am yours. Fully. If you want me." She watched the glowing of his eyes, showing the increased anxiety he was feeling.

"Are you really sure?" he asked, admiring the swell of her bosom that lay so temptingly close to him. But he couldn't forget her strict upbringing. He didn't want to defile her. He wanted her to say it again . . . to assure him that it was all right . . . so it could be a true union of love. . . .

The thought of what she was agreeing to frightened and further excited Jennifer. She could so well remember the filthy sailor and what he had tried with her. Oh, how he had repelled her. But the ever clinging thoughts since then of Nicholas doing these same things to her had left her breathless at times and in a near swoon, experiencing unexplainable surgings through her body. And that continuing dull ache plaguing her between her thighs at night had made her feel so strangely unnerved. When she lay awake, with Nicholas so close by, asleep on his make-shift bed on the floor, all this had begun to leave her with an unfulfilled longing.

"Oh, yes. I am sure, Nicholas," she finally answered, feeling a sense of euphoria as his hands brushed her hair from her shoulders, then traced the line of her chin, tilting her face up to kiss her again. And, oh, ever so gently. Jennifer's body became a thousand heartbeats as his fingers never ceased to move over the bareness of her shoulders and her back, and then slowly began to unbutton the small mother of pearl buttons that held her dress together in the back.

Jennifer began to utter a soft protest, then relaxed and let him have his way with her. She tried to convince herself that by letting him do so, he wouldn't try to encourage her to marry him, if a sexual encounter was what he needed from her to quell his passions for her. She couldn't marry yet. She still had to settle things with Robert Harbison . . . .

Her breath quickened and her heart raced as he continued to ply her with kisses . . . first on the lips . . . her cheeks . . . eyes . . . the hollow of her throat . . . then her breasts, making her head swim with an even deeper ache for him.

"Nicholas, my Nicholas," she said, putting her fingers to his hair, pushing his head into the thickness between her breasts. "I do love you so much," she murmured further, not letting guilt rise to the surface. Suddenly Nicholas had become a part of her plans but plans that held only pleasure for her. And she wouldn't let herself think this to be wicked. She loved Nicholas too much . . . and oh, how intoxicated she was at this moment . . . and not because she had consumed any wine this time. She was being consumed by the magic of his lips . . . his hands. . .

The sweet smell of her was almost too much for Nicholas to bear. He had the need to force himself on her now, this moment, to aid in the release of the heat of his throbbing manhood. But he wanted her to respect him not accuse him of being a rogue. So he must go slowly make sure she enjoyed it as much as he so she would want to participate in it again maybe even truly consider marrying him. San Francisco could be such a lonely place for a painter who knew no other skills besides farming . . . or making love.

His fingers slowly began to lower her gown and let it drop to lie in a mass around her feet. "Your undergarments also, darling," he said, beginning to remove his own clothes. He had waited so long and now it was becoming a reality.

Jennifer felt the hotness of her face and her eyes as she shivered from both anticipation and exposure to the watchful eyes before her. She cast her eyes downward as she stepped out of her many petticoats, then continued to look downward as she saw Nicholas's breeches being stepped out of. She had never seen a man nude before . . . not even the sailor who had come so close to taking her virginity from her. That night, the room had been bathed in total darkness. But now? The room was well lighted by the golden flickerings from the whale oil lamps.

She still wouldn't look his way when his hand clasped onto

hers and led her toward the bunk. She knew that his eyes were upon her, studying her, as though he was going to paint her in the nude. This made her face flush even more.

"You are more beautiful nude than in clothes," he said thickly, guiding her downward onto the bunk, careful to not yet touch her on the sensitive areas of her body. He had to take it slow . . . easy . . . so as not to frighten her. She just couldn't be frightened into changing her mind. No. He had to have her. And . . . this night. "And what do you think of me since I've disrobed in front of you?" he asked, needing her to look at him, to prepare her for what was to come. Oh, God. He knew that she was a virgin. Only a virgin would be acting so timid . . . so shy . . . around a nude male. Was he to be the one to remove her virginity . . . and her being a preacher's daughter? But, Jesus. He was beyond any point of stopping now. He felt as though he might burst if he didn't get a satisfied release soon. The nights of watching her sleep so close to him had been the most difficult of his life. Only after she had fallen asleep had he been able to release some of his tensions by the aid of his own hand, which in no way was ever satisfactory, to his way of thinking.

Jennifer shut her eyes, refusing to look, embarrassed that she was acting so much like a child. She only wished he would lie down beside her, so she wouldn't have to see . . . that . . . part . . . of him.

"Jennifer, please look. It will make you less tense. Please believe me."

Swallowing hard, she opened her eyes and did look toward him, first only into his eyes, then much lower, to see his erect, throbbing manhood that he was slowly caressing with one hand. She suddenly became frightened. How could she go through with this? How could he . . . insert that . . . huge . . . thing inside her without tearing her apart?

"I just don't know," she whispered.

Nicholas sat down on the bunk next to her. "Here. Touch it," he insisted.

She withdrew, shuddering. "I can't," she whined.

Nicholas then stretched out beside her and let his manhood touch her leg.

"You're . . . uh . . . so . . . hot there," she said, then hushed when his lips covered hers and his hands began to explore, setting small fires on her flesh with each fresh touch. Mesmerized by the added touches and his continuing, long kiss, Jennifer seemed to melt into the bunk, aching for the sweet satisfaction that might possibly be only moments away.

She was no longer afraid. She placed her arms around his neck as he eased himself atop her, now leaning down to capture a breast between his lips, sucking until a sharp peak rose against his tongue. Gently, his one hand wandered lower until he found the secret spot between her legs and began to caress her there, gently . . . softly . . . until Jennifer shut her eyes and began to moan, not ever having experienced anything so delicious . . . not even in her wildest fantasies that had awakened her in the middle of the night with a pounding heart and sweat on the brow.

"I don't want to hurt you," Nicholas said, probing further with his fingers, hoping this would make it easier for her when he truly entered her.

"Oh, Nicholas. None of this is hurting me. It's only the most beautiful experience so far in my life. It's making my mind leave me, it's so marvelous."

With a knee, he spread her legs apart and slowly guided his manhood toward her, feeling her grow tense when it touched her there. "Slowly, ever so slowly, my love," he whispered, stroking a breast again, kissing her so gently, as her head continued to swim.

Then he thrust deeply inside her, feeling the wall break, and a gush of blood rush over him, making his passion go wild as he began to thrust in and outward, as he panted and could feel the sweat forming, making their stomachs slip and slide together.

The pain was only one brief instant, then Jennifer felt the lust of desire flooding her brain. She clung to him, arching her body upward, so aroused, the rest of the world was forgotten to her. She could only feel expanding waves of pleasure washing over her . . . taking her to heights . . . to pressures . . . soon to be released inside her . . . a sudden loss of memory to be replaced by a vibration of many different warm colors inside her brain.

Suddenly Nicholas gripped her more fiercely, stiffening, and began to pound harder inside her until his whole body seemed to be wracked with spasms, accompanied by moaning and groaning like her own.

After his body slowed, he continued to lie atop her, panting, sweating, but still searching her body with his hands. Oh God, could he ever let her go? He wanted to make love to her. Over and over again. In his youthful adventures, he had had many young ladies, but none ever to compare with Jennifer. He now knew that life without her would be no life at all. "Please marry me, Jennifer," he pleaded, kissing a breast ever so gently. "We could have a lifetime of tonights. Can you think of a better way to spend your life?"

Jennifer trembled, leaning her breast closer to his touch, never having known a man and a woman together could create such feelings of pleasurable release. But she could not marry Nicholas. Even he couldn't make her forget her planned revenge. She had to find Robert Harbison. "Please don't ask this of me," she said, touching his cheek, then running her fingers through the thick blond curls of his chest.

"And why not?"

"I've things to do."

"In San Francisco? Is that why you're going there?"

"Yes, Nicholas."

"Is it something to do with your Uncle Thadeus?"

"Nothing whatsoever."

"Then what the hell could it be?"

Jennifer sat up, pulling from his touch, trembling as she did so. "Nicholas, I cannot tell you, nor anyone. It's just something I have to do."

He leaned up on an elbow beside her. "But maybe I could help."

Jennifer shook her hair around her shoulders, narrowing her eyes. "No. Only I can accomplish it," she snapped.

"Will it put you in any danger?"

She laughed bitterly. "No. Not myself. But maybe someone else," she said, with a set jaw.

Nicholas jumped from the bunk and pulled his breeches on. "Damn it, Jennifer. I don't like the sounds of this."

"I can take care of myself."

"Are you so sure of that?"

Jennifer's face flushed, seeing his eyes roaming over her still nude body. She pulled a blanket up to cover herself. "Yes. I'm sure."

"Are you planning to stay with your Uncle Thadeus?"

"For a while."

"What the hell does that mean?" Nicholas said, almost shouting. "Where else would you be staying? I want to be sure to be able to see you . . . take you out . . . court you . . . if that's what you require before marriage."

Jennifer sighed deeply. "Nicholas, you'll just have to be patient with me. Please?"

"Oh, damn it," he grumbled.

Jennifer batted her lashes toward Nicholas "Nicholas, please come and sit beside me again. Please?"

Feeling the desire making his manhood rise anew, he did as she asked. She unashamedly traced his chest hair, circling each nipple, then let her fingers lower to where she could feel the hardness of his manhood beneath the tight confines of his breeches. She smiled at him sheepishly, wondering about this mystery of a man, then let her blanket drop from around her as he took her roughly into his arms and pressed her breasts against his own chest and sought inside her mouth with his tongue, making her senses begin to reel all over again. . . .

No longer could she be treated as "different" because she was born a minister's daughter. Most of the secrets of life had been unfolded to her this night . . . and now she had only one more secret left to seek out and the answer would be found in

San Francisco but only away from the watchful eye of Uncle Thadeus and now Nicholas.

Sighing with a deep contentment, Jennifer awakened. She turned on her side and gazed rapturously toward Nicholas. How much of a child he appeared to be this morning with his hair strewn around and beneath his head. He was breathing slow and quiet; he was also at peace with the world.

Jennifer reached over and touched the flesh of his back, laughing softly when the skin rippled with reflex. She wanted to kiss the spot . . . even move her lips on around to search out his lips, to see how he would react to being awakened in such a manner. But a sudden sound of waves thrashing against the sides of the ship and the lurch of the ship made an uneasy fear grip Jennifer, as though someone had placed their hands around her throat slowly squeezing.

Moving to an upright position, she tensed even more, hearing loud crashes, creaks, and the slaps of high winds as the ship was being pulled further into rougher waters of the sea.

She had become acquainted with the different temperaments of the sea, but this day, its mood had turned even more ugly.

All loose objects in the cabin suddenly became airborne, even the portrait.

"Nicholas! Nicholas!" Jennifer screamed, shaking him.

Nicholas pushed himself up with a start, looking anxiously around. "My God! What the hell's happening?" He wiped his hair back from his eyes, now awake enough to see and hear for himself. Damn. He had thought the waters had been too calm. He had expected something like this . . . but even sooner.

His first thoughts were of Jennifer. He turned to her and secured his arm around her. "It'll be all right," he mumbled. "Most ships have this battle. I'm sure this same ship has gone through this many times."

Jennifer trembled, even though his arms were warm and tight. "But hear how the ship is suddenly creaking," she said. "It sounds as though it might split in half at any moment now."

Nicholas pulled a blanket up and wrapped its rough brown material around Jennifer. "Now hold that tightly around you," he said. His gaze moved around him, seeing the portrait of Jennifer shimmying across the floor. His guts twisted. He had to rescue the portrait. It meant more to him than only another piece of decorated canvas.

Quickly, in one stroke it seemed, he had his breeches pulled on and buttoned. Then he bent and reached for the portrait, only to see it crash against a far wall. The sea seemed to breathe a heavy sigh as the ship plunged and rolled along, at times even bucking like a horse.

Once again, Nicholas reached for the portrait, only to be knocked down when the ship plunged at an even different, dangerous angle.

"Nicholas," Jennifer screamed, jumping from the bunk to go to him. She fell to her knees, reaching, when another crash hit the side of the ship, to be followed by the sound of what sounded like large marbles plummeting the ship's roof overhead.

Nicholas crawled to Jennifer on all fours. "Damn it, Jennifer," he grumbled. "I told you to stay on the bunk. I can take care of myself." He lifted her up into his arms and took her to the bunk and replaced the blanket around her. He laughed. "But I must say, you did make an erotic picture . . . sitting there on that floor without a stitch of clothes on."

Jennifer's face reddened. She cast her eyes downward, clutching the blanket snugly beneath her chin. "Nicholas, please," she replied.

"Now I'm going to get that portrait if it's the last thing I do," he growled, turning, moving in jerks until he finally was able to reach and secure the portrait in his hands.

"What can you do to protect it if the storm even worsens?" Jennifer asked, trembling from the chill she had received from jumping from the bunk without any protective clothing on. Clothes had been the furthest thing from her mind after Nicholas had made love to her. She had felt a bit wicked lying next to him ... feeling flesh against flesh all night long. But she had never slept so peacefully in weeks ... even months.

"The storm has worsened," Nicholas said, moving back toward her. "Don't you hear the hailstones attacking the ship?"

Jennifer listened more closely. She cringed. Not only was she hearing the thundering of hailstones against the roof of the cabin ... but also the screams and wails of passengers out on open deck. Each cry seemed to pierce her heart even a bit deeper.

"Here. Place the portrait between you and the wall," Nicholas ordered. "That way, it won't have a chance to go flying off into the air."

More screams and crashing of what was probably trunks and derelict ship equipment met Jennifer's ears. "Nicholas, it's as though we've just made entrance into hell," she cried. "Is there anything we can do for those ... those ... poor people out on open deck?"

Nicholas turned his head toward the door, to see if the lock was in place, then sat down next to Jennifer, holding onto the side of the bunk, thankful that it had been secured to the wall by long, strong bolts. His brows sagged heavily as he then looked toward Jennifer. "Honey, to open that door now would be to enter into hell," he mumbled. "Everyone out there would be like crazed lions, ready to do anything and everything to get in here where it's dry and safe. No. We can't take that chance. We don't have room. How would one choose which ones to invite in and which ones to stay out to fight the stormy waves?" He reached up and touched her gently on the lips. "You see, my darling, don't you?"

Tears wetted her cheeks. "But it is so horrible," she cried. "Some may even be washed overboard."

"That is Captain Klein's concern. Not yours, Jennifer."

"But I feel ... guilty ... sitting here where the waves cannot reach us!"

"Jennifer—" Nicholas began, but was stopped by the sound of loud bangs on the door. Nicholas stiffened. He reached for Jennifer, placing an arm around her. "Who's there?" he yelled.

"Captain Klein. Lad, we need your muscles out here or this ship may plunge to its grave 'fore you know it."

Jennifer's eyes widened. She grabbed for Nicholas, desperate. "No," she screamed. "You cannot, Nicholas."

Captain Klein yelled again. "Lad? Can I depend on you?"

Nicholas's pulsebeat raced. He no longer could say it was only Captain Klein's battle. He had been invited to be a part of it. He was pulled between the need to protect Jennifer and the need to show that he wasn't a coward.

"Nicholas, you can't," Jennifer urged once again.

Nicholas pushed himself from the bunk and made his way to the door, leaning with the ship, first one way then another. He was about to do what he had told Jennifer would possibly be a thing of disaster. But he had to open the door.

With a quick flick of the wrist, he pushed the bolt lock aside and readied himself with doubled fists in case anyone else chose to rush through the door. "Come on in, Captain," he shouted . . . posed . . . ready . . . .

When the door swung aside, a crash of water slapped into Nicholas, sending him sprawling onto the floor. Captain Klein slammed the door shut again and reached down to offer a helping hand to Nicholas. "Damn sorry 'bout that, lad," he grumbled.

Nicholas sputtered and spit and felt his feet slippery beneath him when he rose up. "How are conditions out there, captain?" he asked, coughing and wiping his face with the back of his hand. When his eyes were clear, he could see a drenched man standing before him, with water glistening in his full beard and hair. His clothes clung to him and his eyes showed a desperation Nicholas had never seen before. Fear trembled up and down his spine.

"No fatalities yet," Captain Klein grumbled, looking toward Jennifer, seeing her sitting on the bunk beneath a blanket, wide-eyed, and visibly shuddering. He knew what his responsibility was in getting her safely to San Francisco's shores. If he didn't, he could count on possibly being shot or hung by Thad.

"And now what do you propose to do?" Nicholas asked, pulling a shirt on, then shoes.

"Right now we've got to toss some of the cargo over the sides to relieve the strain on the ship."

"It's that bad, huh?"

"You might say the ship's on the verge of breakin' up," Captain Klein growled, lowering his eyes.

"Oh, no," Jennifer moaned. She hadn't feared anything like this. She had thought that the main things to fear lay ahead . . . on San Francisco's shores.

"Then I can see where my help might indeed be needed," Nicholas said. He eyed Jennifer with a throbbing heart. In truth, this might even be the last time he would see her. The possibilities were strong that even he might be tossed from the ship by those angry fingers of the sea. He hurried to her and fell to his knees. "Whatever you do, don't open the door to strangers," he said. "You must lock the door. As soon as we leave. Please. Do as I ask."

"I will," she sobbed, wanting to fall into his arms. But with only a blanket hiding her nudity, she had to stay huddled.

"Then I shall take my leave, darling," Nicholas said, leaning, kissing her swiftly on the lips.

The wind howled and the water beat like drums against the side of the ship as Jennifer watched Nicholas walk through the door. Remembering what he said, she let the blanket drop from around her and rushed to the door and got it bolt locked just as she heard someone's low cursing on the other side. Her heart palpitated. Someone had been . . . that close . . . to rushing on into the cabin. She felt faint thinking of what could have even then happened. She still remembered vividly the night of the near rape.

Biting her lower lip, she went to a trunk and pulled a dress from inside it and hurriedly dressed, all the while watching first the door . . . then the portrait that had fallen. "At least I can take care of the portrait for Nicholas," she whispered, rushing back to the bunk. "It will be almost the same as guarding him,'' she whispered further, pulling the portrait into her arms, hugging it to her.

''Nothing can happen to him ... nothing,'' she kept repeating, rocking back and forth, staring into the open spaces of the cabin.

The wind had finally deserted the *Madrona* altogether now and Jennifer busied herself picking up all that had been tossed about in her cabin. She worked, almost breathlessly, waiting anxiously to hear Nicholas's voice from behind the closed door. The nightmare wouldn't be over until he was safe in her arms.

After managing to get Nicholas's easel back in place in the middle of the room, Jennifer gingerly placed the portrait back on it. She stepped back to study it, to see if any damage had been inflicted. ''No. None,'' she whispered, clasping her hands together, sighing deeply.

Stooping, she scooped all of Nicholas's brushes back into his tin can, then sat the tin can and his paints beside the portrait, knowing how happy Nicholas would be to see his equipment safe and sound.

Then her heart thundered against her chest when she heard his voice. She rushed to the door and swung it aside, then giggled when she saw him standing there ... so pitiful ... like a wet puppy ... smiling and winking at her. ''Nicholas, oh, Nicholas,'' she said, rushing into his arms.

''You're going to get just as wet as me,'' he said, holding her tightly.

''Do you really think I care?''

''It would even be fun to be wet together in the privacy of our cabin,'' he said, covering her face with hungry kisses.

She leaned back, searching his face now even closer. ''You are all right, aren't you, darling?'' she whispered.

''A bit worn out ... but yes ... all right.''

Jennifer took his hand and guided him into the cabin, closing and locking the door behind them. ''Was it really so terrible, Nicholas?'' she asked, unbuttoning his shirt for him, hardly believing he was truly with her again. She had feared the worst, the more the waves had thrashed the ship about. But he was with her in one piece. She hungered for more touches from him, to make it even more real . . . .

"I wouldn't expect any more wine on this trip," he laughed, now unbuttoning his breeches.

"And why is that?"

"It's at the bottom of the ocean. Maybe getting a few fish drunk."

"And what else had to be tossed overboard?"

"Most all that could be lifted over the rails."

"And the passengers?"

"Not one loss," he answered, drying himself with a towel. "Drowned as field rats, but no worse."

Jennifer plopped down onto the bunk, now realizing how mentally drained she was from the ordeal. She had come close to losing Nicholas. No doubt about that. It would now even be harder to say goodbye to him when they reached San Francisco. She now knew how important he was to her. Could she even say goodbye to him? Could she? But yes! She had to! Oh, God, she still knew that she had to! She was driven. She had to succeed!

Nicholas sat down beside her, flaunting his nudity. "I'm not too tired, if you aren't?" he whispered, reaching down inside her bodice to capture a breast.

She blinked her lashes nervously toward him, acting the innocent she had been until they had met. "Too tired for what?" she purred.

"You vixen," he grumbled, pushing her down and stretching out beside her.

"You'll muss my dress, Mr. Oglesby," she teased.

"Damn the dress," he said, helping her off with it.

Her body arched upward to meet his first thrust inside her. "Nicholas, I was so afraid for you," she whispered, clinging.

"But now I'm here. Don't you see now that we should never ever part again? Didn't the anger of the storm make you realize how short life might even be?'' His body kept moving, making Jennifer's senses reel in colors of ambers and goldens.

''Let's not think about it,'' she sighed. ''Let's just enjoy this moment. Let's try to make it last forever . . . and ever. . . .''

Part Two

San Francisco

Chapter Seven

The fog lay heavy, like a white velvet shroud, as the ship moved into the harbor. Shivering from the damp chill, Jennifer hurried to the ship's railing, wanting to catch a glimpse of this city of San Francisco where she had been born. But the darkness of night and the fog made what lay ahead a hidden mystery.

Sighing, Jennifer turned and moved back toward the cabin, thinking. When she had departed San Francisco at age eight, she had done so with a deep inner sadness. Leaving this city had also meant leaving behind Uncle Thadeus who, since her birth, had managed to weave a strong bond between the two of them. Jennifer had never wondered much about the why's of this . . . always having thought it to be because her uncle had chosen to not take a bride for himself and had thus been left without children of his own to coddle and spoil. His brother's child had in a sense become his own. And, oh how Jennifer had missed him.

She wondered now how the years might have changed him. Would he still be as handsome, with his smooth, regular features and eyes so pale gray they seemed bottomless? Or had he aged as quickly as her father had before his untimely death? But no.

Surely not. Uncle Thad led a much different sort of life. Even though Thad was a successful businessman, he seemed to have a life without worries. And because it had all come so easily for him, couldn't such a life keep a man young?

The activity all around her now made Jennifer keenly aware that in a very short time the ship would be mooring and she would be seeing her uncle. She rushed on into her cabin and checked to see if she had secured all her belongings inside her trunks, and then slowly looked around her. In this cabin, she had been awakened to the wonders of love . . . a love that she knew would never die. Even now, she could feel a growing ache in the deepest part of herself, with that same burning desire all over again at the mere thought of Nicholas and what his fingers and mouth had aroused in her. . . .

"Darling?"

Jennifer swung the long tail of her velvet cape around and found Nicholas standing in the shadows behind her. Her pulse-beat quickened, knowing their goodbye was only moments away. Could she truly walk away from him and what they had found together? But she had no choice. She was driven. She had to finish what she had begun.

"Nicholas? I didn't see you standing there. I thought you had gone to speak with Captain Klein about when we might be ready to leave the ship." Jennifer had only hoped that Nicholas wouldn't see Lil while there. Jennifer would never forget the beauty of that young black girl. And once she left Nicholas alone on the waterfront, going off with Uncle Thad, might Nicholas seek out another woman to get pleasure from? And would . . . he . . . with such a girl as Lil? Her face flushed with such thoughts as these. Her thoughts were definitely no longer those of a preacher's daughter. But this being so, didn't she feel, oh, so much more alive?

Wearing the same brightly colored knit hat that he had been wearing the first time Jennifer had seen him, Nicholas moved to capture her in his arms. "We'll be parting soon, Jennifer," he said gruffly. "The fog has slowed the ship's progress some. But in a blink of an eye, it will seem, you will just become as a beautiful dream I have had. You musn't let it be that way. You must say you'll stay with me. Be mine. Marry me. We mustn't separate. We may never see one another again.''

Jennifer could feel the trembling of his hands as they caressed her back. Her eyes became hot with tears wanting to surface. She didn't want to say goodbye either. But he would one day understand her reasons why. One day she would reveal it all to him.

She lifted her eyes to his. "I've plans of my own to carry out, Nicholas. You know that,'' she said quietly. "You must understand how important this is to me. And if you love me, you'll tell me you understand.''

"But when will I see you again?''

She cast her eyes downward. "I don't know,'' she whispered.

"You don't know?'' he uttered, then stepped away from her, pouting.

"Nicholas, I love you,'' she said, going to cling to him, only to be brushed aside.

"Hah! Love. You must not know the true meaning,'' he scoffed.

Yes, I know the meaning, she thought to herself. More than you can ever realize. But to Jennifer there were different types of love. And the love for her dead mother and father was still too strong to deny herself this thing she had to do . . . in the name of this love.

A clanking of chains and the shaking of the ship's flooring were true indications that the anchor had just been dropped into the deepest waters of the bay. The shrieking of the ship's whistle and the loud boisterous shouts of glee from the ship's crew drew Jennifer's attention from the troubled face of Nicholas. Her heart was thumping with the anticipation of seeing her uncle . . . but a part of her heart suddenly lurched when she saw Nicholas rush from the cabin without even a last goodbye.

"Oh, Nicholas. I *do* love you,'' she whispered, already feeling his absence. But they would meet again. She would make it so. And didn't he have the portrait to complete? Their last two days and nights at sea had been filled with lovemaking instead of painting making Jennifer blush anew to realize how wanton she had become. . . .

"Can I help you with anything, Miss Brewster?" Captain Klein asked, abruptly stepping at the cabin's door.

"My trunks, sir," she said, straightening the hood of her cape.

"They'll be seen to properly. Later. I'll see to it myself that they be delivered at Thad's door," he said. "But now let me help you off the ship. I noticed your young man friend already takin' off, disappearin' into the fog. Have a spat? Huh?"

Jennifer set her jaw firmly and lifted her chin. "That isn't any of your concern, captain," she murmured petulantly.

Captain Klein laughed harshly. "I see. I see," he said, offering an arm, which Jennifer accepted. She gazed sideways at him, thinking he blended in well enough with the dark of the night, being attired in dark clothing and with his face covered with a fresh growth of whiskers. A billed hat covered the thickness of his dark hair, but his eyes danced as Jennifer found them peering at her. "And no word of the ship's condition or the loss of life on my ship to Thad, eh?" he burst forth in a sudden grumbling.

Jennifer smiled weakly. "No. None. None whatsoever," she answered. Much had happened to remove that one unfortunate night from her mind. But now, being reminded of it, she did know that she owed Captain Klein her loyalty . . . and she hoped that he would also show her such loyalty, by not speaking of Nicholas to her Uncle Thad. But then there was Lil. Could she truly be trusted to keep her silence?

Jennifer's eyes searched the dark corners around her . . . wondering about Lil and where she might be. Would Lil continue with Captain Klein on his further journey? Or would she be set free to be a part of this large city also? Jennifer hoped for the former.

"I'm to direct you to Thad's carriage, Jennifer," Captain Klein said further, guiding Jennifer from the ship onto the damp, loose, boards of the pier.

Trunks and baggage were being unloaded and stacked on all

sides of Jennifer, and the few other passengers who had also been on the ship rushed into the darkness of the night.

The lateness of night was reason for the inactivity of the waterfront, and the sound of a foghorn in the distance broke through the fog in an almost haunting wail.

"Thad's carriage should be close by," Captain Klein said, helping to guide Jennifer around a tall stack of baggages. "Ah, there it be."

Jennifer squinted her eyes, searching through the swirling, rolling damp mist in the air, and finally saw the flickering of lamps that flanked the perch on each side of a great, black carriage. The aroma of fish from the splashing water on the one side of her flared her nostrils, hastening her pace, until she stopped, almost breathless, at the carriage's side.

A liveried coachman, attired in black, jumped from the carriage seat and aided her inside, closing the door behind her. Jennifer leaned from the window and said, "I truly do thank you, Captain Klein, for all your assistance. I shall tell my uncle how well you have seen to my safety."

"You do that, young missus," he said. "You do that." He then turned and rushed back toward his ship.

The snapping of the whip and a cry from the coachman made Jennifer's blood surge with excitement, knowing that Uncle Thad's mansion on Nob Hill was only a few horses' hoofbeats away.

The carriage lurched and began to jolt over the cobblestones of the street, but Jennifer sank back in luxury on the soft velvet seats and rested her head against a plump soft cushion. But one thing was missing. Uncle Thadeus. Why hadn't he met her himself? Didn't he care enough? Or did his business ventures keep him occupied even to way late into the night? Or . . . was it the company of a female . . . who had waylaid him?

She sighed, toying with a fringed swag at the window, knowing that it didn't matter. She would be seeing him soon enough. The delayed meeting gave her even more time in which to prepare herself for the explanations of her actions of the days to come.

Would he persist in questioning her? Or would he leave her be and let her proceed at her own discretion? To reveal all the reasons behind her sudden visit to San Francisco would be to reveal her hidden, tormented thoughts of the past six years.

Feeling the sudden strain of the carriage, Jennifer knew that the two black mares were now struggling up the steep grade of street that San Francisco was well known for. As in Seattle, the houses and buildings had been built to cling to the sides of the steep hills, but from Jennifer's remembrances, the houses were much more elaborate and eye-catching in San Francisco.

She wished she could see now, but there was only the continuing billowing fog that not only hid the houses and buildings behind it, but all the meanness that nightfall brought to this growing city.

Jennifer's thoughts went to Nicholas . . . wondering where he might be . . . where he might spend the night. Had he made sure to carry the unfinished portrait with him? Or did he hate her so much now that he might have even possibly thrown the portrait into the bay . . . for the rats to feast upon?

Shivers ran through her, then she caught the breath in her throat when she felt the carriage being pulled to a halt. Straining her neck, she leaned out the window and felt the hastening of her heartbeat when she recognized the house. As a child, she had spent so many evenings there, sitting by the hearth, being told spine-chilling ghostly tales by her Uncle Thad. And there had been other evenings when he had worked with her at the piano, playing simple songs with her, laughing at her childish awkwardness, then embracing her before she would be taken by his fancy carriage the several blocks to her parents' house.

The white, delicate gingerbread trimming still looked as delicious to her as icing on a cake, and lights flickered gaily from many cantilevered windows, on both the first and second floors of this great Victorian house.

Swallowing hard, Jennifer didn't wait for the coachman to open the door. She swung it wide open herself and rushed up the steep front steps of the house, not even stopping to knock with the heavy brass knocker to announce her presence.

With a racing heart, she stepped on inside to the warmth of the parlor, and stood wide-eyed as she took in the familiarity of all this now surrounding her. It didn't appear to be the house of an unmarried man. It showed feminine touches, but from the presence of several maids and a live-in housekeeper, with its lemon-oiled aroma of furniture polish and gleaming hardwood floors that trimmed a thick oriental rug that lay in its splendor in front of a roaring fire on the hearth. Gas wall sconces were highly lit, casting shadowed images onto the red velveteen draperies that hung long and smooth along the corniced windows.

Wondering where Uncle Thad might be, Jennifer moved slowly around the room, touching the thickly cushioned, gilt-trimmed chairs and the smoothness of the redwood furniture. There was a combination of comfortable seating covered in French flower prints with a bright green background against the red walls, and the stacking of framed pictures on the walls made this house indeed Victorian. Yes, this house reflected the best in comfort, with its flower-bedecked wallcoverings and fabrics in this rich, red, two-storied living room. A gallery with a brass railing overlooked the living room; it contained the Brewster library, which was filled with works of the most famous authors and poets.

At the far end of the room, Jennifer spied the sleek, shining, black baby grand piano. How many hours had she sat there . . . mesmerized by her uncle's presence next to her. . . .

With brisk steps, she hurried to the piano, and just as she began to peck out a familiar tune, she heard a sudden rush of feet into the room. She turned and saw him . . . no older, it seemed . . . and just as handsome as she remembered him.

"Jennifer? Honey? Is it really you?" Thad said, holding his arms out before him, inviting her into them.

"Uncle Thad. Oh, Uncle Thad," she cried and rushed with anxious heart and fell into his embrace. She hugged him tightly to her, smelling a mixture of aromas on his clothing . . . a bit of tobacco . . . possibly some whiskey . . . and a faint odor of cologne. Could it even have been from a female he had just set free from his back door . . . ?

He held her at arm's length, eyeing her warmly with his pale gray eyes. "You've grown into a woman all right," he murmured. God. *How* she had grown into a woman. And if he had seen her on the street, wouldn't he have even . . . possibly . . . taken her for her mother Camille? Didn't she have the same sensuous lips and soft curve of the jaw? But her eyes. Damn her eyes. Slanted, so like his own . . . but they were as blue as Camille's . . . like looking into the depths of the clearest ocean.

"And you. Don't you ever age, Uncle Thad?" Jennifer giggled. Only a few lines creased his face around his eyes and mouth. But other than that he would have passed for forty instead of fifty. And wasn't he a picture of wealth with his black frock coat filling out his wide, rigid shoulders, and with his tight matching trousers? His gray silk cravat displayed a diamond stickpin that sparkled in many colors of the rainbow beneath the rays of the many gaslights in the room.

"Remove your cloak, Jennifer. Let me take a better look at you," Thad said with a sweep of the hand, pushing the hood from around her hair and face. His eyes grew large and he gasped noisily. "My Lord! What have you done with your hair? Where are the beautiful locks of gold I so well remember? Damn it, Jennifer. An explanation is in order, wouldn't you say?"

Unbuttoning the only button at the hollow of her throat, Jennifer pulled her cape from around her shoulders. Trembling, she placed it gently across the back of a velveteen settee and went and stood before the fire, watching the flames continually changing forms before her eyes, like elves dancing, even possibly weaving to unheard music. Suddenly she felt Thad's presence at her side.

"I'll ask you again. Why? Jennifer?" he persisted. He had eagerly awaited her arrival . . . for *many* reasons. But the hair color change had shattered many of his hidden dreams about her. Why would she destroy her innocent beauty by covering up her hair of gold, like spun silk? Why?

Jennifer was glad that she had chosen to wear her simple attire—a plain, white shirtwaist blouse and black, serge skirt. If she had worn one of her newest dresses with its plunging neckline, then Uncle Thad's brows would have tilted even more. The questioning was what she had been dreading the most about this trip to San Francisco. She wanted to keep Uncle Thad's trust . . . .

With heavy lashes casting shadows over her eyes, Jennifer turned to her uncle and spoke in a forced innocent manner. "Why, Uncle Thad," she said demurely. "I thought you would like my hair. In Seattle, it's the latest rave of the women to use some of the new dyes for hair being sold on the market. I feel I look more mature. Now I'm disappointed. I only did it to surprise you." She could feel a flush rising upward from her neck, so unaccustomed was she to lying. But she was fast learning the craft . . . and how necessary it was . . . to be able to succeed in her plans.

Thad's pale gray eyes took on flecks of black as he continued to glare down at her from his six-foot-four-inch height. "Well, I don't approve," he said harshly. "You were quite wrong in doing it."

The lining of Jennifer's skirt rustled as she whirled around and walked to a pale beige velveteen settee, where she arranged her skirt around her as she sat down. She touched a hand delicately to her forehead and wiped a strand of hair away. "It will grow out," she said stubbornly. She only hoped . . . not . . . too quickly. . . .

Thad clasped his hands behind him and rocked back and forth from toe to heel. "And how was the trip? Were you comfortable enough on my ship?"

Another blush. Oh, how Jennifer hated herself for such a weakness. "Yes, quite," she answered softly. And would she always blush when her thoughts wandered to Nicholas?

"And you didn't mind being met only by carriage?"

"It was quite adequate also," she said, watching him. She wished the strain between them would melt away into a smooth pleasantness. They had been apart for so many years. Didn't they have so much more to say to one another other than this small talk of nonsense?

Thad cleared his throat nervously. "I . . . uh . . . was detained at the last moment."

"I'm sure," Jennifer said, unable to keep a bubbly giggle from surfacing. Then she watched as her giggle became contagious as a small jerk at the corner of her uncle's mouth formed into a wide grin.

"Then you do understand?" he said, laughing softly, running a hand through his hair that was peppered with colors of rust and gray.

"Quite well," she said in return, laughing softly. She was glad when one wide stride brought him to sit beside her on the settee. He took her hand in his and squeezed it, showing a welcome amusement in his eyes.

"And, now, young lady. Tell me how the hell you talked Minnie into letting you come all the way from Seattle to San Francisco without a guardian? Either she's grown senile, or more trusting of men. The latter I would refuse to believe, knowing her dislike of them."

"Neither, Uncle Thad. Aunt Minnie didn't have any decision in this, one way or the other. I just told her I was coming. She had no choice but to agree."

"So you *have* grown into a woman. Not only in looks, but in mind," Thad said thickly. His eyes wavered. "It does become you, Jennifer. And I'm sure you have attracted many a young man to your doorstep with those eyes that make you to maybe appear a bit wicked . . . I've been told so often by some flippy women that mine also have had this effect on them."

"Yes, our eyes are the same, except in coloring," Jennifer said a bit quietly.

Thad pushed himself abruptly from the settee and went to a liquor cabinet. He opened the glass door and pulled from it a cut glass stoppered bottle, which showed the color of deep red through it. "May I pour you a glass of vintage port?" he asked hurriedly.

Jennifer wondered why he suddenly seemed unnerved once

again. When she was a young girl, they had always been so relaxed in each other's presence. Or had she been too much of a child to recognize the signs of tensions between two people? But why? It didn't make any sense to her. "Just a bit, Uncle Thad," she finally answered.

"So you do partake in spirits? I thought your . . . father . . . would have forbid it."

Jennifer had noticed the hesitation when Uncle Thad had spoken of her father. Except by wire, she hadn't yet spoken of her father's death to her uncle. She knew that it must have been a hard thing to have had to live through . . . knowing a brother was being buried . . . and Thad being too many days away by ship to be able to be a part of the grieving family of Brewsters at the graveside.

"My father kept many varieties of wine in the liquor storehouse in our basement in Seattle. He didn't let the congregation of his church know of his habit, but after my mother's death, my father spent many lonely evenings sipping on . . . many glasses . . . of wine."

Thad handed Jennifer a crystal goblet filled with the red, sparkling liquid. "Do you feel alone in the world now that both your mother . . . and . . . father are gone?" he asked, taking a sip of wine, then turning his back to Jennifer, to watch the flames on the hearth. A log had rolled from the grate and was turning from a shimmering orange to an ashen gray, flaking off, dropping to settle onto the hearth in even softer grays. As he always did, Thad felt the same emptiness at the pit of his stomach when he spoke of loneliness. But now, maybe Jennifer could fill the void in his life. . . .

Jennifer turned the glass in her hands, watching the gaslights reflecting onto the crystal. "I miss mother and father. Immensely," she murmured. "But I have Aunt Minnie . . . and always you," she added . . . and so wanted to speak the name Nicholas, to make him a reality once again. . . .

Thad turned, heavy-lidded, to face Jennifer. "Yes. You always have me," he said. "But now. Tell me the true reason you have popped in here on your favorite uncle."

"First, I want to hear of your exciting ventures, Uncle Thad," Jennifer encouraged him. She still didn't know how she could explain her reasons for being there. But she would have to think of something . . . and fast. This still was a part of her plan that hadn't come so easily to her. She knew her uncle's intelligence . . . and worried that he would see through her. . . .

"Like what?" he asked, pouring himself a bit more wine.

"Like the motion pictures. What's this I hear? You've invested in pictures that move on a screen? Please tell me more about it."

Thad settled himself opposite Jennifer on a high-backed chair. "I've kept you up to date in our correspondence. Not much new to tell, except that I've found that most of the motion picture industry is possibly going to be located in Los Angeles because of the many hundred of acres of natural scenery surrounding it."

"So what will you do? You won't leave this beautiful home to live there, will you?"

"It might be a possibility. But that's far into the future."

"But for now, what shall you do? Los Angeles is so far away. Wouldn't it take many days by carriage or even by boat to arrive there? How could you possibly carry on a successful business venture in this way?"

"The times are changing, honey," Thad said, stretching his legs out before him. "I've got my fingers in many pots. The horseless carriage? I have already ordered one. It's being made to my specifications. It will solve many problems for me."

"The horseless carriage? The contraption that's known to shake and tremble so badly? I've even read that they spat fire and smoke from their rear end."

Thad laughed gruffly. "Yes. I believe we're speaking of the same mode of transportation," he said. "But there is a future for it. Mark my word."

"You really believe so?"

"Yes, honey. I do. But until I get mine, I shall stick close to home. Right now I spend many of my free evenings devoting the time to writing stage or screenplays."

Jennifer's thoughts went to Lil . . . and how she had spoken so intimately of Thad. . . . "And . . . actresses?" she said softly, testing. "You've even chosen some actresses?"

He laughed. "I've got my eyes on a few. Why do you ask?"

She cast her eyes downward. "No particular reason. No. No particular reason."

"Okay. I've told you a bit of my plans, now you must open up to me."

"May I have some more wine, Uncle Thad?" she asked, hoping the strain didn't show in her voice.

"You sure you can handle it? I don't want my . . . uh . . . niece . . . intoxicated by the hand of her . . . uncle," he said, then laughed softly.

"Yes. Please?"

He stood and brought the bottle to her and poured her glass only half full. "And now, I believe you've evaded my question long enough. Or is there some reason you don't want to talk about why you've chosen to visit me at this time?" He sat down opposite her again . . . watching.

"I've come only for the adventure," she quickly blurted, but avoiding his eyes.

"Adventure? I hear there's much excitement in Seattle these days with the gold rush to the Klondike. Things here are boring in comparison, I'm sure."

"I just had to get away. My father's death . . ." she said.

"Oh, I'm beginning to understand. You felt his presence in the house even after he was gone. Yes. I can understand."

"So I would like to be able to enjoy my visit with you, Uncle Thad. And I won't get in your way. I have much exploring to do in your fine city." She couldn't tell him what kind of . . . exploring. She wasn't even yet quite sure how she was going to go about it.

"You get in my way? Never," he said, rising. "This house has been too quiet. For way too long. Of course it won't be the same as when you were a child . . . all giggling and mischievous. But your beauty alone will make the house appear as though the sun never sets."

"You are so sweet, Uncle Thad."

Shadows fell across his face as he frowned. "And, honey? While you're here, please drop the uncle before my name," he said. "Makes me sound a bit ancient, don't you think?" Through the years he had wanted to tell her, many times, to not call him uncle. He would so have preferred being called . . . His thoughts were interrupted by her lips suddenly brushing so softly against his.

"Thad it will be," she said, tiptoeing to be his same height. "My sweet Thad. Our time together will be such fun. You shall see."

He pulled her into his arms and embraced her tenderly. He buried his nose into the depths of her hair, feeling so many stirrings inside himself, even to the point of letting a tear drop from the corner of his eye. "Yes, Jennifer. Our time together shall be treasured."

She pulled from him, yawning and stretching. "But for now, I must get some rest. The hour is late for me. I'm not accustomed to it. Could you please show me my room?"

"Did Captain Klein assure you of the delivery of your trunks?"

"Yes. He said he would see to their safety himself."

"Well, it appears he's a bit slow. But no need to worry. I believe there's a spare chemise in the room that I've chosen to be yours."

"Oh?" she said, tilting a brow. And did she see a blush on Thad's face as he looked quickly away from her? She laughed to herself and walked next to him up a wide, plushly carpeted staircase. Then when they reached the narrow hallway that led to many bedrooms on each side, Jennifer was reminded once again of Nicholas, for on the hallway wall there hung a long row of ancestral portraits, which in a sense was a pictorial history of the Brewsters.

As they passed each portrait, Jennifer glanced at it quickly, but then stopped and stared more openly at the one that had yellowed and wrinkled with age. She could remember studying this one as a child, having been told this particular ancestor,

William Brewster, had actually arrived in America on the May-flower.

"Still making over another uncle I see," Thad laughed, stopping also. "I imagine this portrait could have even been responsible for setting my brother's mind to thinking about religion. Mother told Frank the same story, over and over again, about his ancestor uncle who had been the chief spiritual leader at Plymouth."

Jennifer studied the portrait even more closely. Something grabbed at her heart. This uncle so resembled her father, except for this man's long white hair and beard and full moustache. But it was the sadness in his pale-colored eyes and the thinness of his face, made to appear even more so by of the long, lean nose. She swallowed hard. "Didn't you once tell me that William Brewster was employed by one of Queen Elizabeth's ministers of state?"

"Yes. A Sir William Davison. William was supposed to have traveled to the Netherlands, but returned to Scrooby, Not-tinghamshire, in England, when Elizabeth unjustly imprisoned Davison for the beheading of Mary, Queen of Scots."

"And then he came to America?"

"Only after he began publishing religious books that dis-pleased King James I of England."

"A sort of rebel in his day, huh?"

"Just guided by strong convictions, as most Brewsters who followed after him."

So now Jennifer knew from whom she had acquired her determination. Not only from the present generation of Brew-sters, but from those who had even helped to found this great country.

Tomorrow. Yes, tomorrow she would meet Robert Harbison . . . face to face. But what if he should recognize her . . . ?

"Here's your room, honey," Thad was saying, opening a door. "My room is just next to yours in case you ever get frightened by anything. In fact, the rooms have adjoining doors. One cry from you will send me to running to your rescue."

Jennifer smiled warmly. "Thad, I don't frighten so easily.

Remember, I'm a grown woman now. Not a child afraid of the dark.'' She stepped on into the room and felt as though she was entering another parlor.

"Why, it's breathtaking," she said, going to touch the soft rose color of the settee that was arranged in front of another fire on a hearth. The brocade draperies were of a soft rose, as was the thick-piled carpet.

"The bedroom is in the adjoining room," Thad said.

Jennifer's eyes widened. "But I thought you said your bedroom adjoined."

"Our *bed*rooms adjoin," he said, laughing softly. "Not our sitting rooms."

"Oh, I see," she answered. Gaslights flickered cheerfully from wall sconces and a fragrance of jasmine filled the air. Then Jennifer spied the fresh bouquet of a mixture of autumn flowers in the midst of which circled a few sprigs of honeysuckle.

"For me?" she sighed, going to the flowers, touching the softness of the petals of many-colored chrysanthemums, dahlias, cockscombs, and even the gloriosa daisy.

"For my sweet Jennifer," Thad said, standing before the fire with his hands clasped tightly behind him. He was hoping that he was making her homecoming grand enough. Had it truly taken the deaths of both Camille and Frank to bring them together? But even now . . . how long could it last? Wouldn't some young man pull Jennifer away from him again? 'Oh, God,' he thought further. 'Give me some time with her. I know I've neglected my prayers, but please give me some time with Jennifer.' ''

"And the bedroom is through here?" she asked, pushing another door open, to find a huge canopied bed, with white eyelit trimming the canopy and the bedspread. A gilt-lined floor-length mirror reflected the room, making it appear as many rooms of pale rose satin drapes and carpet.

Flowers also spilled their sweet fragrance into the room, but these were more gentle and smooth, almost velvet in appearance: red roses with opening buds.

Jennifer gasped as she went and touched their softness and inhaled the heady aroma. "Thad. You're much too good to me. How can I repay you?" she asked as she rushed back into the sitting room.

"Just be yourself, honey. That's all I have ever wanted."

"You've missed me this much?"

"I've missed you that much."

Jennifer went to him and welcomed the circle of his arms as she leaned into his embrace. "You make me forget the loss of my father, because, in a sense, you've become he," she said, choking back tears. She looked quickly up when she heard him also swallowing back tears of emotion.

"I must leave so you can get some rest," he said, batting his lashes nervously. "You will find adequate night things in the closet. And tomorrow, I shall have your trunks brought up to you."

"Thanks, Thad. I'll always remember your kindness."

He went to the door, but stopped. "I'm here. Whenever you need me. Always."

"I shall remember." She blew a kiss toward him and watched him leave, then went to the closet and opened the door, shocked to find many styles and designs of lacy, sheer chemises to choose from. Even alone, her face flushed in embarrassment as she thought of herself attired in one of them. And whom had Thad purchased these for ... ? His many female friends ... ? Why, she had never. . . .

But her fingers couldn't refuse a quick touch of one. Ah, it was so soft. And wouldn't she feel so utterly wicked sleeping in such a skimpy outfit?

But who was to see her?

Giggling, she slipped one from a padded hanger and held it before her, imagining what she would look like if her thick, heavy garments were removed and she was to only wear ... this ... ?

She placed the chemise on the bed and hurriedly shed her clothing, blushing momentarily when she saw her full nude reflection in the mirror, then slipped the chemise over her head.

She sighed. Didn't it feel like a caress to her body? And didn't she look the part of a seductress with her breasts so highly visible beneath the sheerness of the cloth? Her hands went to her breasts and cupped them, shamelessly toying with the nipples, watching them hardening to stiff erectness.

Couldn't such actions drive a man wild if he was to watch? She was even stirring the desire in herself again by these devilish actions that she had never let herself do before to her own body.

But hearing footsteps so close by in the adjoining room made Jennifer aware of what wrong she was doing, and knowing that Uncle Thad would, indeed, be disappointed in her if he caught her in such evil actions, she hurried on into her private bathroom, where she found gold accessories everywhere she looked. Gold and marble. That's what this bathroom was made of.

Sighing, she drew her bath and removed the chemise to climb into the warmth of the water. She settled herself deeply beneath the suds and closed her eyes, planning the day ahead of her.

It saddened her that Nicholas wouldn't be a part of it . . . but one day . . . he surely could be again. . . .

Chapter Eight

This early morning's awakening was much different for Jennifer than the awakening of the past week. It even felt a bit awkward for her to not hear the constant movement of water beneath and beside where she had lain. But didn't she feel so secure without the constant swaying of the ship?

She snuggled more deeply into the softness of the feathered mattress, sighing. She would never forget the hardness of the bunk on which she had slept while on Thad's filthy, unkempt ship. But Nicholas's arms had been a welcome pillow for her head. Oh, how she missed him. This made the need to hasten and be done with her revenge of even more utmost importance in her mind. Only by doing what she had to do speedily, could she be free to welcome Nicholas into her embrace once again.

Hurriedly, she climbed from her bed, her head all aswirl with plans. What should she do first? But this wasn't hard to answer. She would have to evade Thad's further questionings and only hope that she could secure a carriage and dependable horse from him for this day's adventure. In no way did she want to tackle the hills of San Francisco by foot. Such hills could make an old woman of her way before her time.

Going to the window, Jennifer pushed the drapes aside and looked outward onto the beauty of the day awaiting her. She had left the cold, gray days of Seattle behind her and welcomed the bright, cheerful sunshine of San Francisco. All assortments of flowers in deep purples, reds and yellows lined this street on which Thad's house stood, and ivy-covered homes led straight downward to where the bay met land.

The clanging from a cable car moving downward along the tracks outside the window filled Jennifer with even more eagerness. Didn't the men on board this unique mode of transportation look most important in their twilled suits and derby hats? Could Robert Harbison even be aboard this cable car, on his way to Roberto's, his own place of business? And couldn't she have even been on the same cable car with Robert Harbison?

But no. A closer look revealed the lack of women on the cable car, which had to mean that the women were made to feel improper boarding them. Did it mean that a woman was thought to look more feminine in a horse-drawn carriage? It didn't seem right to Jennifer. But she shrugged her shoulders. This wasn't the time or place to argue politics. She had more important things on her mind. . . .

A light tapping on her sitting room door made Jennifer jump with a start. Her gaze quickly took in the skimpiness of her attire and she searched around her for something with which to cover herself. But nothing. Only her soiled travel skirt and blouse, and Jennifer had no desire to wear them again this day. Only the dresses she had chosen in Seattle would be appropriate.

Going into her sitting room, she sighed with relief. All three of her trunks had been delivered and had been placed in the middle of the room. When Jennifer noticed that one had been opened and half emptied, she began to be angry. But it was then that she saw the dresses that had been removed draped neatly over the back of the settee, each having been neatly pressed and made ready for wearing.

The light tapping persisted, then a soft voice spoke from behind the closed door. "Miss Jennifer? Miss Jennifer? It's

Carlita. Your assigned personal maid. Is there something I can help you with this morning?''

Rummaging quickly through the opened trunk, Jennifer pulled from inside it a flowing robe of old rose panne velvet, trimmed with gold cording and braid. She slipped into it and secured it in place with a matching velvet braided belt. ''Coming,'' she said, giving her hair a quick flip to hang away from her shoulders and more down her back.

Opening the door, Jennifer found a petite, dark-skinned woman standing patiently waiting. She was attired in a long, black, heavy-appearing cotton dress that was made to look more delicate with its white lace trimming at the collar and at the far end of its long sleeves.

Dark hair and skin were contrasted by the wide grin of white, straight teeth. ''Mr. Thadeus has assigned me to you, Miss Jennifer,'' Carlita said, her dark eyes snapping. ''Shall I bring you a breakfast tray or draw your early morning bath? I'm here to do as you command.''

''Carlita? Is that what you said your name was?'' Jennifer asked, noticing that Carlita was of Mexican descent, as were so many in San Francisco. Chinese and Mexicans were scattered throughout this city, whereas in Seattle many Chinese and Eskimos could be found settling in their own little corners of that city. The new railroads and the busy seaports were now constantly delivering immigrants from all over Asia and Europe.

''Yes, ma'am,'' Carlita answered eagerly, wringing her hands before her. A few lines on her face, mainly creasing her forehead, made Jennifer guess that Carlita might be in her early forties, even though she still had the figure of a younger woman maybe in her late twenties.

''I don't believe I'm hungry for anything right yet,'' Jennifer answered. ''And as for my bath, I'm in too big a rush to worry about that this morning.'' She cleared her throat nervously, leaning out a bit more into the hallway, to look toward the door that led into Thad's room. She moved closer to Carlita, whispering. ''What I do want, is to know when my uncle usually leaves for his place of business?''

Carlita smiled even more widely. "He's already gone, Miss Jennifer," she answered.

"Gone?"

"He usually rises with the sun. Leaves before anyone else is stirring in the house."

"My word," Jennifer declared. Had she been wrong about Thad's leading such a leisurely life? Did he truly run his shipping empire himself, when he had enough money to hire any number of assistants to do it for him?

But she did remember his restlessness. . . .

"Mr. Thadeus has left word that you are to have the finest horse and carriage at your disposal at all times," Carlita said. "I will tell Henry, the stable hand, whenever you desire to have the carriage readied for you."

"That would be just fine, Carlita," Jennifer answered, feeling almost smug as she turned to go back into her sitting room. Her one worry had been dispelled. At least she didn't have Uncle Thadeus to deal with before heading out on her own this morning. Maybe this time, she would finally succeed in finding Robert Harbison. Her failure to do so in Seattle still gnawed at her insides.

She stopped and motioned for Carlita to enter the room also. "And was it you who pressed my dresses so neatly?" she asked further.

"Yes, ma'am. And I will do the same for the rest of your wardrobe. This very day. I shall make you feel at home right away."

"I believe we are going to get along real well, Carlita," Jennifer said, smiling. "But now, I must rush. I have many things to do."

"Shall I brush your hair? Help you into your dress?"

"Carlita, you don't have to be *that* eager to please. I'm quite used to brushing my own hair and dressing myself."

Carlita's eyes cast downward. "Yes, Miss Jennifer," she uttered softly.

"And please drop the miss before my name. Please just call me Jennifer. I would feel more comfortable if you did."

"Yes, ma'am," Carlita said, then giggled, covering her mouth with a hand. "I mean Jennifer," she quickly added.

"I do need to rush now, Carlita. And you can go and inform Henry that I wish to have the horse and carriage ready for travel in one hour's time."

"I'll run and tell him now," Carlita said. "And by nightfall, your closet shall be filled with your freshly pressed garments."

Jennifer laughed throatily. "Anything you do for me will be greatly appreciated. And I do like my uncle's choice of maids."

Carlita's eyes were cast downward again, then she hurried from the room.

Jennifer shut the door, then swung around on her heel, feeling her heartbeats hastening. Was it really going to happen? After six long years, was she truly going to meet Robert Harbison face to face? She tried to envision him now and mainly remembered his dark, penetrating eyes that had seemed to burn through her, setting small fires inside her, even though she had only been fifteen at the time.

But that brief moment of desire for him had been changed to hate when she had found out what havoc he had wreaked on the Brewster household. . . .

Pulling her robe off and then the sheer, lacy chemise, Jennifer went to stand beside the window once again, letting her gaze travel from one building to another along the waterfront.

"Robert Harbison, which of those buildings is yours?" she murmured aloud. "Will I truly be able to find your Roberto's today? And when I do, can I refrain from spitting onto your face as I most deeply desire to do? Or will I be able to pretend. . . ."

She swung around to carefully choose a dress . . . one that would be proper to enter his place of business . . . one that would normally be worn by a business woman, but yet still be alluring. She had to capture his eye. Instantly. But her most provocative dresses would be worn in the evenings . . . when she and Robert Harbison would be . . . alone. . . .

"But my pretenses will be very short-lived, Robert Harbison," she hissed, holding a dress before her, studying it most carefully. "Yes, this will do," she said. It was a meticulously tucked silk dress of deep wine coloring, with a matching double-faced cape to be worn over it.

It wouldn't be long now, she thought, then hurriedly dressed. . . .

Chapter Nine

The sleek black stallion pranced proudly before the carriage, very skillfully maneuvering its way through the thickness of the morning traffic of other carriages and the ever annoying cable cars with their constant clangings and clatterings along the tracks.

Jennifer sat poised on the padded seat of her own carriage, clucking to the black stallion and handling the horse's reins, taking in the scenery. There was so much to recapture of what she remembered as a child of eight—but so much had truly changed. There were many more buildings of brick, and the streets had been expanded, and fancy gaslights had been placed at each street corner.

The street she was now on appeared to be that of the rich class of San Francisco. The pane glass windows on the buildings displayed the latest fashions on lined-up racks, and even the best of furnishings for Victorian mansions.

Women attired in different colors of cloaks and matching hats intermingled with fancily dressed businessmen hurrying to and from these buildings.

"Things have changed. Indeed they have," Jennifer murmured to herself. In her youth, she remembered mainly men walking these sidewalks. The women, even more then than now, had been made to feel their place was in the home . . . cooking, canning, slaving. . . .

She clucked to the horse and hurried onward, now watching the buildings more carefully. Surely she would soon see the sign that had haunted her for so long. The name Roberto's had to be displayed for all to see. She didn't want to have to stop to inquire about it. She wanted to find it all on her own . . . as she planned to handle this entire scheme of hers.

She swallowed hard, doubts assailing her. She was so close . . . . could she truly . . . ? It had never been in her as a child to be vindictive. Hadn't she been taught better by her minister father? But she had no time for further thoughts, for there before her eyes, in bold red letters, was the name her eyes had been straining to find.

Jennifer's body became one large heartbeat as she guided her horse to a hitching post before the large, three-story brick building. Its width stretched out a full city block, and at its rear the waters of the bay were visibly lapping at the shore.

Seagulls circled overhead, studying Jennifer with black, watchful eyes as she climbed from the carriage, rehearsing in her mind what she had to convince Robert of: She was a dress designer, having traveled from Los Angeles . . . when he would ask to see her sketches, she would demurely invite him to see them in the privacy of her hotel suite (which hotel she had yet to decide upon). She would tell him that she would let him know her hotel by messenger a bit later in the day . . . to arouse his curiosity even more by her air of mystery. . . .

"Ah, yes. He will catch the bait," she whispered to herself. "I will make it so. And when you arrive at the suite I establish myself in, what a surprise I will have for you, Robert Harbison."

But she did have to choose a hotel . . . one breathtaking enough in decor . . . one that would be appropriate for what she had in mind. And . . . how could she keep Thad from finding out . . . ?

Jennifer stopped momentarily, seeing the many other horse-drawn carriages waiting also outside this building. There were many people coming and going from this many-windowed establishment. Through some of the windows she could see racks and racks of women's wear hanging, and through others she could see women poised behind sewing machines, busy at work.

"I must hurry on," she said further to herself. But her fingers were trembling. How could she hide this from Robert? His first impression of her was most important. . . .

Swinging her dark hair around to hang in long waves across her maroon-colored cape, she tilted her chin upward and hurried on inside, finding many doors to choose from. She chose to step on inside a door that had been left ajar and found herself standing in a small cubicle of a room. Her gaze darted around her at the disarray of papers and catalogues piled high on the floor in corners. The sun's rays fell in streamers onto a desk also cluttered by papers and debris, and having at its center one of the newest inventions of the century, a late model Remington typewriter.

A secretary was sitting behind the desk, absorbed in trying to master her new skill at the moment, her fingers slowly searching out which key of the typewriter to place themselves on. But other than obviously being unlearned at how to work this gadget that Jennifer was also unacquainted with, the young girl looked the typical role of secretary, her hair tied securely in a bun atop her head and gold-framed spectacles perched on her long, thin nose. Her white shirtwaist blouse with a tied black bow tie at its collar completed the picture.

Jennifer shuffled her feet and cleared her throat noisily, her impatience making anger take the place of her heightened anxieties of the meeting now only moments away.

The girl lifted her head, gazing toward Jennifer with eyes that looked golden behind the thick-lensed eyeglasses. "Yes?" she asked in a deep voice, more like a man's than a woman's. "Can I help you with something?" she quickly added, rising to step from behind the desk.

Jennifer's eyes widened, seeing the length of this girl's

thickly pleated skirt. If not for the black lisle stockings, the girl's ankles would have been exposed to the eye. Was this a part of this autumn's fashion that hadn't been revealed to her by all those whom she had questioned in Seattle? Hadn't the dress designers she had interviewed known of this California way of dress? Now she wondered about the tablet of sketches that she had so carefully hidden at the bottom of one of her trunks. Would she in fact be able to fool Robert Harbison for even a brief moment before she set her further plans in motion . . . ? Doubts assailed her all over again. She again cleared her throat. "I would like to see Mr. Harbison please," she finally blurted, hating herself when her voice cracked.

The girl pushed her glasses back further on her nose and frowned. "You'd like to see whom?" she said.

"Mr. Harbison. Mr. Robert Harbison," Jennifer said nervously.

"I know of no Robert Harbison," the girl said, turning to walk away from Jennifer.

"Young lady," Jennifer snapped, feeling her face reddening, wondering how this girl could be hired to work at Roberto's and not even be aware of her employer's true name.

The girl stooped to pick up a catalogue, fully ignoring Jennifer's presence.

"Miss," Jennifer said more loudly. "I've asked to see Mr. Harbison. Now will you please see to it that this is arranged?"

The girl slammed the catalogue down on her desk with a twitch quivering her chin. "Listen, whoever you are. I think you've entered the wrong building. There is no Mr. Harbison here. Now I have things to do. Will you please leave?"

Jennifer's heart began to pound furiously. History was repeating itself, it seemed. She so vividly remembered the same argument at Harbison's Pawnshop in Seattle. But surely there was a mistake here. She only had to find someone, possibly even in the next room, who would be aware of Roberto's real name.

"May I see someone else who is in charge here? Possibly the personnel manager of Roberto's?" Jennifer said stiffly.

"You are a persistent one, aren't you?" the girl grumbled and rushed through a door at the rear of the room, shouting the name Gonzalez above the steady humming of sewing machines.

Jennifer began to pace the room nervously. She hadn't anticipated such difficulties as these. Couldn't it have been so easy . . . just asking . . . then being taken to Robert's office? But, no. There always had to be a complication, making this that she had dreaded for so long even more difficult for her. Somehow it just didn't seem fair. But maybe it was her father looking down from heaven causing this to happen. Was it truly meant for her to not meet Robert?

"Gonzalez here," a short, balding Mexican said, entering the small cubicle of the room. "I believe you're asking for Robert Harbison."

"Yes, I am," Jennifer murmured, thinking to be immediately taken to him. This elderly man seemed to be a person with authority. She could tell by the way he spoke the name that he did know Robert Harbison.

"He's no longer the owner of Roberto's," Gonzalez blurted with a smirk on his thick red lips.

There was an awkward silence following his disclosure. Jennifer was too stunned to speak. This just wasn't happening. What this short, squatty man said just couldn't be so. Her heart hammered against her chest and her palms had grown sweaty. "What do . . . you . . . mean?" she finally stammered, resting her weight against the edge of the desk.

"Robert Harbison had a bit of bad luck a few years back," Gonzalez said, pulling a pack of cigarettes from his front shirt pocket. "Cigarette?" he asked, offering the opened end to Jennifer.

Jennifer's face flushed with a mixture of confusion and embarrassment. "No, thank you," she said, putting a hand to her throat.

"Yeah. Bankrupt as hell," Gonzalez laughed, tapping a cigarette out onto the palm of his dark hand.

"Bankrupt?" Jennifer gasped, feeling suddenly lightheaded.

"You . . . surely . . . must be . . . wrong. Surely you must be wrong."

"Went bankrupt," Gonzalez repeated. "Sure's I'm standing here," he laughed again.

"But . . . then . . . where . . . ?"

"Where? He lives in a dive. Over on Front Street."

"In . . . a . . . dive . . . ?"

"Yeah. A joint where all losers end up. Skid row. You know what I mean?"

Tears burned at the corner of Jennifer's eyes. Now what was she to do? Wasn't this a dead end for her? Again? "How do you know all of this?" she asked, touching away a wetness at the corner of her right eye.

"I watched him work his way from the top to the bottom," Gonzalez said smoothly. "Now I'm on top . . . and he's on bottom."

"You . . . ?"

"Roberto's is now mine."

"Yours . . . ?"

"Mine."

Jennifer swung around, ready to rush from the room, then stopped with lowered eyes. "Could you give me the address of his residence, please?" she asked, barely audible.

"Why the hell would a lady like yourself want to even bother with Harbison?" Gonzalez asked, flipping ashes on the floor. "He ain't nothin' but trash. Filth."

"Never you mind about that," Jennifer forced herself to say. "Just the address please?"

"Sure. Two-oh-one West Front Street."

"Thank you," Jennifer said, then hurried outside, stopping momentarily to take a breath. Again she clutched at her throat, feeling a choking sensation. Her mind was such a mass of confusion, she didn't know which way to turn. Did she dare go in search any further for Robert Harbison? Couldn't doing so put her in danger . . . if it meant . . . having to travel alone to Skid Row?

"I have to," she said beneath her breath. "I *must.*" Lifting the tail of her cape and the skirt of her dress up into her arms, she climbed onto her carriage and yanked a bit too hard on the horse's reins, making the horse lurch suddenly forward, almost toppling Jennifer from the padded seat.

Gasping, she scooted back, to lean against the back of the seat. "I must calm down," she said. "Getting myself in a dither isn't going to help things. Not one bit." Then making sure the stallion moved onward at a more steady gallop, Jennifer tried to gain complete composure so she could think more clearly. So far none of her so carefully thought out plans had worked. Would she in fact even be able to think up another? And had she just discovered why Robert Harbison had pretended to be so kind and faithful to his mother? Hadn't he in truth just waited to get his hands on whatever money he could claim as his . . . once his mother was gone?

Anger surged through Jennifer, making her snap the reins a bit too harshly once again, and she found the carriage speeding around other carriages at a daring pace. Then she made a turn and found herself on the filthy tenement row of Front Street. She slowed her stallion and gazed unbelievingly around her. What lay before her eyes was much worse than she had ever seen on Skid Row in Seattle.

Horse dung lay in large, swirled piles covering most of the cobblestone street, and flies were buzzing freely in the air. Broken whiskey bottles lay sharp side up in various corners of the street, and men sat on barrels in the doorways of most of the establishments, attired in unwashed, tattered clothes. The blank looks in their eyes were evidence enough that they had failed in this thriving, competitive city.

Suddenly Jennifer didn't feel so afraid. No man even seemed to notice her. They were as if in a stupor, in their own little worlds . . . worlds of no longer caring. . . .

Something grabbed at her heart. Would it be the same for Robert Harbison? Had he lost so much, that he, too, would no longer be caring?

"No. It can't be" Jennifer whispered to herself. "It has to

be *my* doings that makes him no longer care. If it cannot be so, I will have failed at what I've set out to do.''

Determination made her jaw set firmly as she spied the brick building on which was marked with hardly visible numbers the evidence that she had just found 201 West Front Street.

Unable to control the tremors in her fingers, Jennifer guided her horse to a hitching post and sat for a moment studying this building, trying to muster up enough courage to enter.

As with most of the buildings along this street, there was more evidence of lack of caring from the tenants. Each window gracing the front three stories showed layer after layer of gray grime. Yellowed curtains hung on some, and on others, tattered and torn window shades, some pulled closed, and some hanging at precarious angles.

A shiver ran up and down Jennifer's spine, making even the nape of her neck grow tense, as an elderly man came stumbling from the front door of the building. He staggered a few feet, then slumped down with bowed head against the brick wall.

Jennifer watched as he pulled a brown bottle from inside his wrinkled jacket pocket, then tipped the bottle to his lips, only to thrust it inside his pocket once again, and then continue to sit there, his head bobbing up and down nervously. And when a mongrel dog came sniffing at the man's clothing, even then the man didn't show signs of awareness.

A deep sadness for this poor unfortunate fellow made Jennifer's heart ache, and she wondered where this man's family might be . . . and how a person could let himself get into such a depraved condition. If this had been Seattle, Jennifer could have guided the man to her house of old folks and possibly given him a bit of hope for the future.

But this wasn't Seattle. This was San Francisco. And she had to think of her own self now . . . which meant having to move past this creature of misfortune to find out which room Robert Harbison was making his residence in.

Securing the reins of her horse, Jennifer moved cautiously toward the door. The smell of the garbage lining the walks and the fish aroma blowing in from the bay made a terrible combination, almost too much for Jennifer, with her usual clean habits, to bear. It was even a relief to step inside the dreary darkness of the entranceway that led to a long row of rooms on each side of a steep staircase that led straight upward to the other two levels of the building.

Strewn yellowed newspapers and dust balls blew in circles around Jennifer's feet, making her hurriedly close the door behind her. The tension of the moment made her back stiffen as she began to make her way down the unlit hallway, looking from one door to another, now wondering how she might discover which closed door stood between herself and the man she loathed, but still not knowing how she would even approach him, once she did know which door to knock upon.

She continued to move onward, holding the tail of her dress and cape up away from the filth that surrounded her on the floor, and listening to the different sounds that met her from behind each separate closed door.

From behind one door came the hacking cough of one who might even be dying from pneumonia, as so many poor were wont to do these days. . . .

A baby's persistent crying was a sign of a mother's neglect. . . .

The rattling of pans and the aroma of vegetables possibly cooking in a brothy stew represented one who wasn't quite as hard up as maybe the next-door occupant. . . .

Then one of these doors swung widely open, revealing a frail lady possibly in her sixties, all bent and shaking from some sort of palsy. The emptiness in her eyes revealed the life she led. . . .

"Who be ye a lookin' for, missie?" the lady said in a flutey voice as she continued to stare openly at the richness of the fabric of Jennifer's cape and dress.

Jennifer put a hand lightly to her brow, smiling weakly. She looked from side to side, then leaned more down into the lady's face. "Robert Harbison, ma'am," she whispered. "Might you know which of these rooms is his?"

A bit of color rose on the lady's cheeks and her eyes seemed to come suddenly alive. She cackled throatily, looking up the staircase, pulling a moth-eaten shawl more closely around her scrawny self. "All ladies know where that gent lives," she said smugly. "A mighty good looker he be. Wished I wuz a bit younger meself. I'd go a knockin' on *his* door, I would."

Jennifer felt a blush rising and shifted her weight, to stand more erect. She now knew that she had succeeded. She was actually so close. . . . But what had the woman meant about all ladies knowing where Robert Harbison lived?

"Which room, ma'am?" she persisted, following the lady's gaze up the staircase, knowing that that was where she would be going in only a matter of moments.

"He be up the stairs apiece," the lady answered. "Room C. Cain't miss it. Ain't a bit surprised tah see a lady of yore class askin' to see him. He's nothin' but class himself, even though he's pertnere as poor as the next folk in this here buildin'."

"I sure do thank you for the information, ma'am," Jennifer said, looking on past the lady and into the room, seeing another person just as frail, a gentleman of about the same age, sitting beside a window in a rocker, rocking back and forth with hope erased from his eyes. Jennifer was suddenly reminded of her father and his last days on earth. Hadn't he looked as lost as he had sat rocking the lonely evenings away?

Then she couldn't help herself. She reached deep inside her cape pocket and pulled some folded crisp bills from it. "Here. Take this money for your trouble," she said warmly, thrusting the money into the lady's trembling hands.

Tears came to Jennifer's eyes as she watched the lady's mouth open in disbelief. And for only a moment the elderly lady stared at the money that had so generously been given to her, but then, and not to Jennifer's surprise, she quickly stuffed the money into an apron pocket and slammed the door in Jennifer's face. The identifiable sound of a bolt lock being latched made Jennifer aware of why no thanks had been handed her way for her gift. It was apparent that the lady had been afraid that even one instant of hesitation could have proven unwise for her . . . so obviously afraid that someone might rush by and snatch it from her, before she even had a chance to spend it on herself and her mate. . . .

"Sad. Oh, so sad," Jennifer said, swallowing back another lump in her throat. But she was already climbing the rickety stairs, feeling them give a bit beneath the weight of her body, making her grasp even more firmly on to the banister at her side. Her heartbeats quickened with each step, until she found herself standing in another hallway like the one that she had just left below her, with similar noises behind each door.

Slowly, but deliberately, Jennifer walked from one door to another until she was standing before Room C. Her breath caught in her throat when she moved closer and could hear movements from inside the room. She had finally found Robert Harbison . . . but she couldn't raise her hand to knock upon his door. She had suddenly realized that to do so surely would set him to questioning . . . and she didn't have the answers yet.

The door opposite to where she was standing flew open abruptly, startling Jennifer to feel a weakness in both her head and knees. She swung around and faced a short, paunchy man who was shirtless. The darkness of this upper hallway made it impossible for him to study her too closely, but he stepped toward her, eyeing her before shuffling his bare feet along the floor until he reached a door not too far from where Jennifer stood, at the end of the hallway.

Out of the corner of her eye, Jennifer continued to watch him, and then quickly looked away when she realized the man had just stepped inside a toilet. The sound of his urine splashing into the water of the toilet bowl embarrassed Jennifer, and she began to inch her way toward the staircase, but she was embarrassed even more when the door slammed open against the wall and the paunchy man came out, his fingers busy buttoning the fly of his breeches.

After spitting a wad of chewing tobacco on the floor before him, the man peered with keen interest toward Jennifer, who hadn't yet succeeded at taking that first step downward.

"I'm Andrews, the landlord of this here buildin'," he grumbled. "Are you lookin' for a room? I've got one that's cleaned up spankin' new for the likes of a lady like yoreself. Wanna see it? Huh? You can have it damn cheap."

Jennifer's eyes widened, glancing quickly around her once again, still hearing the clamor from room to room and smelling many unpleasant odors. She shuddered when her gaze settled on a large, set rat trap that sat in a corner, next to the door that led to the toilet.

Pulling her cape more snugly around her shoulders, she stammered, "Me? Are you asking me if I want. . . ." But she didn't complete her question. She now knew what her next move had to be. She put her hand to her throat and cleared it noisily. "Uh . . . yes. . . ." she murmured, tilting her chin upward, "I do believe I'd like to see the . . . uh . . . the room you have to let."

The man moved his tongue around inside his mouth, curled it, and spat again, wiping brown spittle from the corner of his mouth before stepping closer to Jennifer. He thrust his hands inside his breeches' pockets and squinted upward at her. "Yore man too? Huh? Or kids?"

Batting her lashes nervously, Jennifer moved back away from him. He smelled more offensive than anyone she had ever been near before. And was he now looking at her with a different kind of interest? Did he wish for more than money from her for payment of rent? The thought sickened her. But she had no choice but to tell him that she would be needing a room for only herself. No one would have knowledge of this room except for . . . Robert Harbison.

"Only myself, sir," she murmured, now most certainly seeing a glint in his dark eyes. But she would be sure to bring her pearl-handled pistol with her for protection. This man would never have a chance even to get near her. . . .

"Widowed?"

Yes," Jennifer said softly, casting her eyes downward.

"How?" he persisted.

"How . . . ?" she stammered, now watching an amused mockery in his eyes. "At sea," she said smoothly then, batting her heavy lashes nervously, touching the corner of an eye, feigning a tear. "Yes, my husband died at sea. Now may I see the room?"

"Glad to show it. Glad to," he grumbled, reaching inside a pocket to pull out a heavy ring of keys. He sorted through them and walked a few steps and stopped at the door that led to a room right next to Robert Harbison's.

"Room D. Like I said. All clean and proper for the likes of you."

Things were finally working out for Jennifer . . . even better than she had ever thought possible. To actually have a room . . . right next to where Robert Harbison lived? The filth of the building became a minor problem . . . until the room she was to be a part of was revealed to her.

She cringed as the door swung widely open. An aroma similar to wet dog hair tumbled out and clung to her as she stepped on into the room. A tarnished brass bed with a yellow covering thrown across the mattress filled most of the space in this room, and lined up around the room, against the wall, were all the necessities needed to exist. A small woodburning stove, black from collected soot, stood next to a basin that sat on four squatty legs, and next to that was an enamel-painted table and two chairs, with a kerosene lamp with its smoked black chimney placed in the middle. Shelves above the table displayed an assortment of chipped dishes and cooking utensils.

A nightstand with a small wall mirror hanging above it sat against the wall opposite these, and a lone, faded overstuffed chair with a table beside it provided the only semblance of comfort in this room of peeling, parched wallpaper.

The man went to the stove and kicked at it. "Serves as cookin' and heatin' for a person," he grumbled. "I supply the wood and even occasional lumps of coal if'n I kin ever git my hands on some. Goes like hot cakes, that coal." He roared with laughter at his own joke. "Git it? Like hot cakes? The coal?"

Jennifer laughed awkwardly, then went to the window and wiped at the collection of grime with a finger. How could this man call this place clean? She couldn't even see from the window. With a turn of a heel, she gazed toward the bed, wondering how many filthy bodies had slept on it. And wasn't the unpleasant aroma surfacing from the mattress for sure . . . that . . . of dried . . . urine . . . ?

"Well? Take it or leave it. I've got better things to do than stand here waitin' on a female to give me an answer to this sort of question," the man grumbled further. He went and sidled up next to Jennifer, lifting a brow. "You see, I'd much rather be waitin' for the answer to a more personal question," he said thickly, leering. "If'n you know what I mean," he quickly added, going to the bed, patting the mattress knowingly.

Jennifer felt rage building up inside herself. She wanted to flee. She didn't want to be near this filthy man or be a part of these terrible surroundings. But she had come too far to give up so easily. The sudden sound of a phonograph being played in the room adjoining hers . . . the room in which Robert Harbison was now throatily singing along with the recording . . . made Jennifer thrust her hand deeply inside her cape pocket once again. She pulled out more crisp bills. "How much?" she asked, feeling her pulse quickening as Robert's voice grew louder. And doesn't he sing beautifully? Jennifer wondered to herself, now being even more confused about this man of mystery. He seemed to have so many sides to his nature. . . .

"Ten big ones," the man growled, holding his sweaty palm outward.

"A . . . week . . . ?" Jennifer stammered.

"A month," he said. "But if'n you want tah pay that much a week, I'll gladly take it," he laughed, grabbing the money with one fast sweep of the hand.

Jennifer just frowned and set her jaw firmly, wanting to tell the filthy-minded man that she wouldn't even be there for a month. What she had to do, she wanted to do quickly, so she could go in search of the man she loved. Oh, if only she was letting a room . . . a beautiful, cheerful room for herself and Nicholas . . . with a wedding band on her finger to seal their union. . . .

"The toilet is at the end of the hall, if'n you ever require

the need of such a thing as that,'' the man scoffed, pushing
the money down into his breeches' pocket.

Jennifer's eyed widened. ''Is that . . . the . . . only . . . ?''

''For the whole damn buildin'. Plumbin' costin' whut it does
today, cain't afford more'n one a buildin'. You'll jist have to
make do, dearie,'' he answered. He slipped the key for this
room from his ring of keys and offered it to Jennifer.

''And now, since the room is paid for, sir,'' Jennifer said
sternly, going to open the door, gesturing with a nod of her
head for him to leave.

''You bet. You bet,'' he laughed, walking on past her. He
stopped and leaned toward her. ''But if'n ya ever git cold or
lonely, I've got just what you need to git you warm.''

''Oh!'' Jennifer snapped, stomping a foot, then slammed the
door in his face. With clenched fists, she began to move around
the room, shivering. Now she had done it. Made a positive
move. But was this truly the right thing to do? By doing so,
she had to change all the details of her earlier plans. Her new,
beautiful low-cut satin gowns could not be worn in surroundings
such as these, for to do so would be to create much suspicion.
And her tablet of autumn dress design sketches would have to
continue to lie hidden at the bottom of her trunk. Robert Harbison would have no need of them; therefore, neither would she.

Touching her fingers lightly along the furniture, she began
to make inventory in her mind of the things she would need
to purchase to take up housekeeping for the few days required.
First she would have to purchase many bars of soap with which
to clean this room, then an adequate amount of food that could
easily be prepared, since she didn't have much knowledge of
cooking, always having had someone else to do this chore for
her, in each Brewster house that she had been a part of.

And then . . . her wardrobe. Two or three cotton print dresses
would be sufficient, along with a simple knitted shawl to take
the place of her usual fancy capes.

''Yes, this is how it shall be,'' she said aloud, now hearing
only silence from the room adjoining hers. Deciding to go
shopping and then return to get all that was required for living

in the room in place before returning to her uncle's establishment for her last night there for many nights to come, she rushed from the room. Almost too much to think and plan on, she thought as she inched on past Robert's door. It was quite taxing to her brain.

She knew that her next entrance into this building would have to be made in a cotton dress . . . in case he opened his door to check out this new tenant who would be moving into the room right next to his.

"Oh, so ever close," Jennifer sighed to herself, feeling proud of being so near to succeeding. And *that* she *would* do. . . .

Chapter Ten

Already feeling triumphant, Jennifer whirled out of her bedroom and began to glide down the staircase in the dress she had chosen to wear just for her uncle. She had thought this dress to be a divine act of flattery the first time she had seen it hanging in Catherine's Dress Emporium in Seattle, from its smocked and ruffled neckline to the eighty hand-painted flowers and vines that skimmed the front. A sheer, lean, long line of creme silk fell away from the gathered skirt of the dress to a flutter of hem. Ah, Jennifer relished the feel of the silken material next to her skin, knowing that this would be the last time she would wear such fabrics for a while, having many days ahead of her of cotton dresses to make her appear as the poor widow she was to be acting out.

And hadn't the word ''widow'' been spoken so easily? She was still amazed at her skills at being able to plot so easily.

Before entering the parlor, Jennifer's fingers went to her hair, checking to see if it was still in place in the fancy pompadour that she had so skillfully arranged in deep curls and swirls at different angles on her head.

The soft music being played from the phonograph lured her on into the room where a roaring fire on the hearth and bright lighting from the many gaslights greeted her entrance. When she saw smoke sprialing upward from behind a high-backed chair, she imagined Thad to be sitting there, leisurely puffing on a good cigar. She laughed softly to herself, feeling mischievous. She suddenly felt like a child again, with everything finally falling into place for her.

Walking lightly across the oriental carpet, she stepped behind the chair, stopped, laughed to herself some more, then jumped around to the front, thinking to take her uncle by surprise. But it was Jennifer who received the surprise. Her heart palpitated and she gasped. "You! What are you . . . ?"

"What am I doing here?" Lil said smoothly, taking another drag from her long, thin cigarette. "Why, Jennifer darling. Are you trying to make me feel as though I shouldn't be in Thad's house?"

"I can't believe. . . ." Jennifer gasped again, realizing at this moment how little she did know and understand about her uncle. In thirteen years, much about him had changed. But why would he require the presence of Lil when he already had a house guest . . . his niece . . . of whom he had appeared to be so fond? Somehow, Jennifer no longer felt special in this mansion on Nob Hill.

With a racing pulse, she watched Lil rise from the chair. On the ship that one evening, attired in only a brief chemise, Lil had been beautiful. But now, fully clothed, she was many more things. She was chic, haughty, graceful and shatteringly pretty in her gold velvet, full-swept dress, with its touch of gold piping outlining its crisscrossed low-cut bodice, which made her delicious, brown breasts appear even more rounded and shapely than they were.

With a tilt of her pompadoured head, Lil went to stand at Jennifer's side, smelling of rich French cologne. "And, Jennifer," she hissed. "You had better not mention my presence on Thad's ship, or I will fill Thad's head with tales of a preacher's daughter whoring around for seven full days and nights. And with a poor farmer boy? Shame be upon you, Jennifer.''

Jennifer set her jaw firmly, anger almost blinding her. ''Why you,'' she whispered. ''How could my Uncle Thad . . . ?''

''He likes me because I'm young, black, and beautiful,'' Lil laughed, stepping gracefully to the hearth to flip her ashes into the flames.

''Where is my Uncle Thadeus?'' Jennifer asked coolly.

''He's gone to ask that a third plate be added to the dining table.''

''Then you weren't invited? Even Thad didn't know of your coming?''

''I'm always full of surprises, Jennifer darling.''

''Thad should have shut the door in your face.''

Lil laughed wickedly. ''Never. Don't you know I'm his plaything, both in bed and on the stage? He couldn't do without me.''

''You are disgusting,'' Jennifer snapped, feeling the need to rush from the room, to get away from the knowing eyes of Lil. At this moment, she almost hated Thad. She glanced quickly across the room as he entered. And wasn't he oh so handsome in his luxurious smoking jacket with its sky-blue herringbone pattern and black satin shawl lapels? His reddish hair was slicked down with pomade, but his eyes reflected the tensions he was presently feeling. He took long strides and was soon pulling Jennifer into his arms, giving her a brief kiss on the cheek.

''You look beautiful, honey,'' he whispered into her ear. He didn't quite know how to explain away Lil's presence. And why the hell had Lil chosen this evening, of all evenings, to come unannounced to his house? He glanced quickly toward her, feeling the blood rise in his loins. It had been two full weeks now since they had been together. And now that she had returned from Los Angeles, where she had told him that she had to go, to check out the possibilities of securing a role in a latest motion picture, they had much to discuss. But he had wanted to do a lot of this "discussing" on the softness of a bed. . . .

He then glanced toward Jennifer. God. He didn't know which was the more beautiful of these two women standing glaring at one another. But he did know that he couldn't let Lil leave his house this night without first thrusting his aching manhood inside her . . . even if it meant waiting until he was assured of Jennifer's being asleep . . . and even if it meant having to sneak, taking Lil to a lower-floor room that was not inhabited by any maids at present.

He continued to hold Jennifer around the waist, feeling the tenseness of her body. "Jennifer, this is Lillian Jones, a promising starlet for both stage and screen," he said, clearing his throat nervously. "And, Lillian, my niece Jennifer, of whom I've spoken so much."

Playing the role to the hilt, Lil extended her hand toward Jennifer, her dark eyes flashing. "Pleased to meet you," she said petulantly. "And just call me Lil, as Thad most normally does."

Jennifer pulled from Thad's embrace and turned her back to both Thad and Lil, refusing to take Lil's hand in hers. She didn't like being in the same room with Lil . . . let alone having to touch her sleek brown hand. She felt a disgust at the pit of her stomach, unable to brush from her mind the thought of Thad and Lil possibly embracing soon in the nude . . . and after Lil had just left Captain Klein's bed? Lil wasn't only black and too young for her uncle, but much too immoral for him.

"So. Shall we all sit and enjoy the fire and the music of Brahms?" Thad said nervously, going to a gold box to lift a cigar from it. He bit one tip off and spat it into the fire, then wet the other end with the quick curl of his tongue, before securing a burning twig from the fire with which to light it. He was worried about Jennifer's reaction to Lil. And wasn't Lil even acting a bit strangely in Jennifer's presence? Lil *knew* that Jennifer was his . . . he had told Lil that Jennifer was his . . . niece . . . nothing more. . . .

"Maybe I should return to my room, Thad," Jennifer said demurely, still refusing to look his way. She knew that her disappointment of him would show in her eyes, and she wasn't sure she could stand it if he was to realize that things had suddenly changed between the two of them.

"Jennifer Lynn Brewster," Thad said with sudden strength. "You are behaving like a child. Now come and sit down with your uncle and guest. Please do not be rude." He hated being so abrupt with her, but knew that he had no other choice but to do so. He had to gain control of this situation now if he was to ever succeed at explaining it all to Jennifer.

But . . . didn't Jennifer know of his interest in motion pictures? Shouldn't that be explanation enough?

Yes. He had to pretend that Lil was just a guest. No more or no less. He would then deal with Lil . . . later. Yes. He had his ways of dealing with her. He could already feel the skills of her tongue. . . .

Jennifer felt a flush rising from her neck, upward to her face. She swung around and saw the cruel mockery in Lil's eyes. And she was shocked all over again when Thad most politely aided with the lighting of another cigarette for Lil. Jennifer had always been taught that women did not practice such a crude habit as smoking. And hadn't some women actually even been jailed after being caught doing it?

She then eyed Thad more carefully. Her heart ached to see the side of him that she had always known. But she now knew that a veil of sorts had been pulled between them and that nothing would ever be the same again.

Swallowing back a lump in her throat, she did as he bade and gathered the skirt of her dress around her as she sat down on the sofa opposite to where Lil had positioned herself, her tilted chin showing a haughtiness that Jennifer had already learned to despise.

"And now, ladies. I'd like to hear about each of your adventures," Thad said, sitting down on the high-backed chair that was midway between Jennifer and Lil. He puffed nervously at his cigar, then hunched more down into the chair, crossing his long legs before him. "You first, Jennifer. How was your day? Did you find your carriage comfortable enough? And did you go shopping at some outrageous emporium for a whole new wardrobe?"

Jennifer's thick lashes were shadows over the blue of her eyes. But she still cast her eyes downward, toying with the edge of the sofa, no longer feeling any responsibility whatsoever to worry about what Thad would feel when he discovered her gone from his house the next day. He had already disappointed her more than she could ever possibly disappoint him. "Yes. The carriage was quite adequate," she murmured. "And, yes. I did enjoy shopping today." But he would never know that her shopping had been done on the waterfront . . . where the cheapest of cotton dresses were sold.

"The dress you are now wearing," he said, fitting his fingertips carefully in front of him. "Is that one that you chose? It is quite eye-catching."

"No. This dress I'm wearing is one I chose in Seattle."

His eyes drifted upward to her face. "But damn it all to hell," he said further. "I shall never understand why you colored your hair."

"I'm sure Jennifer is capable of doing many things you wouldn't understand, Thad," Lil said sharply, leaning forward to glare into Jennifer's eyes.

Jennifer's jaw squared with anger. "We women all have our own little secrets, don't we?" she snapped.

"God! What's going on here between the two of you?" Thad exclaimed. "You act as though you've already met and have some kind of grudge against one another. What the hell's the matter?"

Lil flipped her cigarette into the fire and leaned back against the chair once again, the whiteness of her teeth working nervously on her lower lip. "It's nothing, Thad. Nothing," she purred. "Just women talk. Honest. That's all it is."

"Jennifer? Have you anything to say?" Thad asked, chewing angrily on the tip of his cigar.

"Just like Lil says," she answered softly. "Nothing. I guess maybe it's the lateness of the hour. I didn't mean to snap at you, Lil. I apologize. " She knew that making Lil angry at her was indeed a dangerous game to play. Didn't Lil already know much too much she could tell Thad? And couldn't Lil even be wicked enough to spy on her and find out what she would be doing the next several days? No. Jennifer didn't need Lil as an enemy. . . .

Lil's dark eyes flashed. "And I to you," she said bluntly. "I could do with a drink, Thad," she quickly added.

"Some port coming up," he said, rising to go to his liquor cabinet. "And you also, Jennifer?"

"No, thank you," she answered. All she wished was to return to the privacy of her room. But she knew that she would have to continue her own little game of playacting, as Lil was doing, until the meal was consumed and it was then the proper thing to do to excuse oneself.

It wouldn't be much longer . . . and then she would even be in her own little world . . . in the small room she had let. Thinking of being alone there, so close to Robert Harbison, made her heart lurch. But she had to do it. Then she could seek out Nicholas and fall into his arms for all the comfort she now knew she would never find in the arms of her uncle. . . .

She watched Thad hand a sparkling glass of red wine to Lil, then sit back down, sipping on his own.

"And, now, Lil. Tell us of your adventures in Los Angeles? Did you secure a part?" Thad said, eyeing her warmly.

Lil's eyes wavered as she took another fast drink of wine. Jennifer was amused at the lie Lil was trying to cover up. Los Angeles indeed! On Thad's filthy ship the whole time . . . in the arms of the even more filthy Captain Klein.

"It was quite exciting, Thad," Lil began. "But, no. I didn't secure the part. A new name . . . Ethel Barrymore got the main role. They didn't have a part for . . . someone colored like . . . myself."

"I'm sorry to hear that," Thad said. His pale gray eyes had

grown moody. "One day your name will be heard from New York to San Francisco. You'll see. We will make it so."

Lil batted her lashes and tilted her chin a bit downward, drawing her lips into a pout. "I did try, Thad," she purred. "Honest I did."

"I'm sure you did, Lil," he answered. "I'm sure you did." He took another sip of wine, then a draw from his cigar. "And while there, did you hear word of the Chaplin family?"

Looking flustered, Lil stood up and went to face the fire. "No. I didn't," she said softly.

"I hear they are a fine combination of wit," Thad laughed. "It is the small child that makes the trio come to life. Charlie, I believe his name is. Charlie Chaplin. I'd like to see them sometime. Maybe we can drive to Los Angeles together when I get my horseless carriage. Sound okay to you, Lil?"

Lil still didn't turn to meet his gaze. "Sure, Thad. Sure," she said softly.

"And then you can introduce me to your connections," he said, tossing his cigar into the fire.

Jennifer smiled to herself, knowing that for Lil to go to Los Angeles would be for her to reveal all her nontruths to Thad. "It does sound exciting, doesn't it, Lil?" she encouraged, then wished she hadn't when Lil turned and glowered in her direction.

The rustling of feet behind them made Jennifer sigh with relief.

"Dinner is served Mr. Thadeus and Miss Jennifer," a house-servant said as she entered the room.

"Ah, good," Thad beamed. "Shall we girls?" he said, rising, offering each of them an arm.

Handsome sliding doors opened into the dining room. The table was set with Bavarian china and candles flickered in dancing goldens at each end. Jennifer knew that she soon could be free from this unbearable evening. She thanked Thad as he offered her a chair, hoping the strain would not be too thick in the air for her to be able to enjoy the food that was creating such tantalizing aromas as it was being carried from the kitchen into the dining room. She knew that the next few days would be quite a test for her endurance . . . not even knowing how to boil water for a decent cup of coffee. . . .

Chapter Eleven

Sleep wouldn't come for Jennifer. No matter which way she lay, her eyes just would not stay shut. She didn't know if it was from the anticipation of the excitement of the days to come ... or possibly even more from fear than excitement. Or was it because of the complete disillusionment she now felt about her uncle? She had seen it in his eyes the whole evening. The desire for that she devil Lil. Oh, how could he lower himself to such depths ... ?

Tired of tossing, she climbed from the bed and pulled a robe around her shoulders and then walked through her private sitting room. She slowly opened the door that led to the hallway. All was quiet and only a dim light continued to flicker at the foot of the stairs. "Maybe a glass of warm milk will help," she murmured, then tiptoed from her room, stopping only momentarily outside Thad's door, listening, sighing with relief when no noise surfaced from it.

"He must be asleep," she said further to herself, even though she hadn't heard him retiring for the night. But maybe she had slept momentarily and hadn't even been aware of it. Maybe then he had slipped into his room and had fallen into a sudden sleep . . . exhausted from his own long day's adventures . . . or from . . . having wrestled in bed with . . . Lil. . . .

Walking as lightfooted as possible, Jennifer moved on toward the stairs, then rushed on down and headed for the kitchen, having to pass many rooms before she reached it. A sudden noise from one of those rooms caught her attention: a female's giggling, and a male's deep voice, obviously filled with sexual pleasure.

Jennifer crept toward the room, seeing a partial opening of the door, not wanting to be guilty of voyeurism, but wondering who might be so openly coupling, for all to hear . . . and even see . . . if they so chose to do.

Cautiously, Jennifer stepped to the open door and peered inward. Something caught in her throat as the dim light revealed to her two bodies . . . both nude. One was her uncle . . . and the other . . . the dark, velvety one . . . was Lil.

"Oh, no," Jennifer gasped silently, feeling nausea rising. What was being acted out before her looked to be even more sinful than anything she could ever have dreamed of two people sharing so intimately together. Thad was stretched out across the bed with legs spread widely apart and eyes closed in rapture as Lil hovered over him with her mouth working on his erect manhood.

"I must get away from here," Jennifer said to herself, but she wasn't quite fast enough. Lil's gaze shot around and captured Jennifer standing there, but to Jennifer's surprise Lil didn't stop her manipulations. Instead, a glimmer came in the darkness of Lil's eyes as she began to move her mouth, assisted by her hands, in an even faster motion, until Jennifer stood terrified as she watched her uncle's body begin to tremble, then explode in a series of spasms. . . .

Feeling the burning of her eyes and throat, Jennifer turned and began to run, and she didn't stop until she had her bedroom door locked behind her. Again she replayed the scene in her mind, not believing her uncle could have participated in it. She had always thought of him to be so pure . . . so wholesome. But having never married had apparently turned him into some

sort of monster, having to seek depraved ways of sexual release
. . . and from the most wicked of women. . .

Jennifer was beside herself with both hurt and anger. Now
the next morning would not be soon enough to leave this house
of her uncle's. And once gone, could she ever return? She lit
a small gaslight and went to stare at her long row of gowns
that hung on padded hangers, and then to lift the lid of her
jewelry box. Even under the lighting of the gaslight, she could
see the diamonds sparkling. She was saddened even more; but,
yes, she would also have to leave these behind. When she
returned to Seattle, she could begin again. Her father had left
her well taken care of financially. And she now knew that she
would have to talk Nicholas into returning to Seattle also . . .
for she could not stay for long in this city . . . where her uncle
practiced his depraved ways.

With tears streaming down her face, Jennifer slipped out of
her nightclothes and pulled a simple cotton dress over her head,
buttoning its front with trembling fingers. Her head was aswirl
with worries. How could she get to the waterfront alone in this
late hour of the night . . . without falling into the hands of some
creature who might even do worse things to her than the sailor
had tried on her uncle's ship? She knew that she couldn't go
by horse and carriage. That would be a sure way for Thad to
trace her. And she also knew that an expensive carriage would
not be a proper conveyance for a poor, saddened widow. There
was only one way to go. And that was by foot. She had her
gun to protect her. One look at that weapon would most surely
set a stranger to running in another direction.

Now, how could she disguise herself in the darkness of night?
Surely there could be a way to do so. If she could be less
noticeable, then she would have a much better chance of arriving at Front Street safely.

Checking through her wardrobe once again, Jennifer quickly
pulled her black velveteen cape from a hanger. Hiding herself
beneath this would be almost the same as being a part of the
blackness of night herself. Couldn't she run through the streets
and possibly down alleys without even being noticed? Yes. It

was the only way. She would pull the hood of the cape so closely around her face that no one would even be able to see that she was a small, defenseless woman, running scared, and full of grief over what she had just witnessed, full of a scheming that had been a part of her life for way too long now.

Soon. Soon it would be over and she could return to her Christian ways of living once again. But now? Now she had to remove her small pearl-handled gun from its hiding place.

Going to the mattress of her bed, she lifted a corner and pulled the gun from beneath it, letting it rest in the palm of her hand as she also pulled free from their hiding place many small bullets. Fitting what bullets she could into the chamber of the gun, she dropped the loaded gun into her one inside cape pocket, then let the remaining bullets slide freely into a front pocket, making them easily accessible if she would possibly need them also.

"Could I even truly shoot a man?" she whispered as she slipped the cape over her shoulders and up around her face. "Could I truly?" How many sermons had she heard her father preach about taking another man's life? "But if it's for my own safety, Father?" she whispered further. "Truly that would not be a sin." And hadn't she already sinned in the eyes of the Lord? And wasn't she even planning to sin even more . . . very, very soon? Oh, the web she had already begun to weave for herself . . . could she ever truly get free from it all?

Her shoes now slipped into and securely snapped, she tiptoed to her door once again, slowly opening it to listen for any sounds that might prove that it would not be safe to leave just yet. But it was as before. Nothing. Not even a tick from a clock could be heard in this well-structured house of her uncle's.

Only the staircase stood between herself and her freedom. She now hoped for the rendezvous between Thad and Lil to not yet be complete . . . so they would be too occupied to hear the front door opening. Had Lil yet spoken to Thad of what she had seen? And had Lil purposely managed to leave that door open so she and Thad could be seen together . . . even possibly hoping that Jennifer would walk by . . . and see it herself?

"Oh. How I hate you, Lil," Jennifer whispered, clenching her fists tightly into two knots. "One day I hope to get my revenge. One day." But how? And when? Right now, Jennifer's mind was too full of this one revenge to even consider planning another. . . .

With light footsteps she walked downward, one step at a time, until she reached the foot of the staircase, stopping only momentarily to take one last look at this house that she had dreamed of so often in her growing-up years. A house that now would only hold unpleasant memories for her, once she had fled through the front door.

Turning, she crept on to the door and carefully, as quietly as possible, pulled it open, feeling the cold dampness of night circling around her exposed face. Feeling the hammering of her heart against her chest, she closed the door behind her and flew down the front steps, stopping to check all that was around her. As always, the fog lay in its heavy white shroud over everything. Only circles of purplish mists could be seen around the gaslights on each street corner, making the night even more terrifyingly dark for Jennifer. But she had to move on. She had several blocks to go before reaching her destination.

The steepness of the slope downward kept Jennifer moving at almost a running pace. She panted, continuing to watch all around her for any sudden movements in her direction. The eeriness of foghorns rising upward from the bay penetrated the heavy cloud of swirling fog, making shivers run up and down her spine. She had never felt so alone. And when a rat scurried past her, she muffled a scream and stopped to lean against a lamp post, near to tears once again.

She took a quick breath and decided to go on her way, seeing dim lighting ahead of her, not able to make out from which it was surfacing. But she hoped that it meant that she was drawing near to the buildings that lined the waterfront, knowing that this would mean that possible safety was finally near.

The sound of hoofbeats approached beside her on the cobblestone street, then passed on by her, making her sigh deeply with relief. Pulling the skirt of her dress and hem of her cape up into her arms, she stepped downward and crossed the street, feeling a sudden lurch of her heart when a stooped figure moved past her to disappear on ahead of her and into the darkness of an alley. The sound of a cat's meow unnerved her once again and the rattle of a can echoed around her, making her hurry her pace.

The familiar foul odor of Front Street finally met her nostrils as she made a turn and began to make her way down the shadowy walk. As during the day, she could see figures of men leaning against the buildings and sitting on barrels. And she could feel their eyes watching her as she passed on by them. So far no one had attempted to stall her flight to freedom . . . and only a few more footsteps to go and she would be entering the building where Robert Harbison unknowingly waited. . . .

Almost crying with relief, she opened the door to the stairs that led to the room that she had let. Fumbling, she secured its key between her fingers and rushed upward in the semidarkness, stopping momentarily at the top of the stairs as she heard a door opening somewhere along the long, narrow hallway. A whispering of voices made desperation seize Jennifer. She looked from side to side, knowing she had no place to hide. She had to get to her room before anyone could see her. But as she began to make her way down the hallway, her eyes widened. There was Robert Harbison leaning across the threshold, gently kissing a woman who appeared to be as richly dressed as Jennifer most generally was. This woman's cape of crimson satin hung loosely from around her, also revealing a dress of such rich fabric worn beneath it.

Jennifer tried to move past them, but she felt dark, penetrating eyes watching her. With a fast glance, she looked in his direction, seeing Robert standing shirtless and now openly watching her as she thrust her key into the lock. Feeling as though her heartbeats were going to drown her, she hurried on inside and locked the door behind her, wondering now how she would explain her own rich attire of velvet, and also wondering . . .

who might the woman have been whom he had been embracing in such a tender fashion. She had appeared to be too wealthy to be a part of this drab building.

Fumbling through the dark of the room, Jennifer felt her way to the only chair in the room and collapsed onto it, hanging her head in her hand. It was true. She had finally managed to find Robert Harbison. It had been him out there, so close to her in the hallway. But could the fact of Robert's already having a woman friend possibly stand in Jennifer's way? No. She just couldn't let it. Even though the woman did appear to have class and wealth, Jennifer would weave her wand of magic over him and make him fall in love with her. And then she would have her fun.

She became slowly aware of the pitch darkness in which she sat, so she pushed herself out of the chair and felt around her until she found the kerosene lamp that she had left on the nightstand beside the chair and bed. With the strike of a match, a soft yellow glow guided her hand to the chimney of the lamp, lifting it, then turned the wick up so one touch of a match could fill the room with the warm glow of light, which Jennifer needed at this moment to make her feel more comfortable in this room that was to be her home . . . but . . . for how . . . long? She shuddered . . . thinking of the days ahead.

She listened to the movement of feet in the room adjoining hers and wondered what Robert Harbison was doing. Surely the woman was now gone . . . and he was alone. Hurriedly, she removed her gun and the several bullets from the cape pocket and slipped them beneath the mattress of this bed, hoping that she would never have the need to use them. Then she swung her cape from her shoulders and hid it deeply inside the closet, arranging the few cotton dresses and nightclothes she had purchased earlier in the day in front of it.

Looking around, she felt a bit of pride in what she had succeeded at doing, also earlier in the day. The room was now spotless, and she had even placed delicate, lacy white curtains at the window, which she had also scrubbed, so that the water of the bay could now be seen as lights from ships twinkled down into it.

Fresh linens were stacked on shelves, alongside many canned foods, and the aroma of lemon oil filtered upward, making her feel as though the furniture wasn't too dirty to touch and be a part of.

She looked at the bed. It was the only thing remaining that still sent chills through her. Even though she had placed sparkling clean sheets over the mattress, and over this, an embroidered bedspread, purchased cheaply at a second hand store, she wasn't sure if she could arrange herself atop it to get a decent night's sleep. Nothing she did could erase its ugly smell. Even now, she could smell the same dried perspiration and aroma of urine. But, she knew that she had to tolerate all of this . . . to in the end succeed at what she had to do.

A light tapping on her door startled her. She tensed. Could it be . . . ? No. He wouldn't . . . who else . . . ? The landlord?

She hurried to the door and put her ear to it. "Yes? Who is it?" she asked, trembling anew.

"I couldn't help but see you a few minutes ago," the voice spoke deeply. "I don't believe we've ever met . . . miss . . . is it . . . ?"

"The hour is late, sir," she said, feeling the pulsebeat quicken in her throat. "I do not know you. Please leave."

"I have the adjoining room. You have nothing to fear from me," he persisted. "My name is Robert Harbison. I'm quite harmless. Believe me. I only wish to see to your comfort since you are new in this building."

Jennifer shut her eyes tightly and doubled her fists, knowing he was so close now . . . unbelievable . . . but oh, so close. Should she, so soon . . . ? Yes . . . yes . . . yes. . . . She turned the lock on the door and opened it, truly seeing him now after those many years ago. But didn't he appear to be even younger? Where was the gray in his hair? And why hadn't poverty taken its toll on his appearance? Here he stood, square-jawed and clean shaven, with the same dark, mocking eyes and dark skin, and the same rigid shoulders. Ah, wasn't he so handsome?

Those thick, black lashes . . . those dark, penetrating eyes . . . and his tight black breeches and beige shirt with buttons straining across his chest. . . .

She swallowed hard as her hands went to her throat. "And what is it you really want of me, sir?" she asked petulantly, wishing her heart would slow down. She didn't want this man to affect her in the strange manner he had when she had been a girl of fifteen.

"I know it may sound as a come on," he laughed gruffly, kneading his brow. "But I have the damnedest feeling I've seen you somewhere before. We haven't met, have we? This is why I had to knock on your door. It would've bugged the hell out of me all night if I hadn't."

Something grabbed at Jennifer's insides. Had he recognized her . . . even though her hair was now dark and she had aged six years? Did she still so resemble her dead mother . . . that he would see her in Jennifer? It couldn't be. No. It just couldn't be. Then her plans would be destroyed . . . before she even had a chance to carry them through.

"Sir, the first time I laid eyes on you was only a moment ago when you . . . were . . . that . . . lady," she stammered, knowing that a blush was rising. She hated having stumbled over her words so. She had to get hold of herself. She had to be able to handle things in a more quiet manner . . . not let him guess . . . if he hadn't already. . . .

The corner of his thick lips lifted in a smile. "Oh, you did see my lady friend," he laughed. "Theresa. That was her name. And now. May I ask yours?" He was watching her with intensity . . . Jennifer knew that he was seeing much in her . . . but maybe it was only the kind of interest she had *wanted* to stir in him . . . maybe he liked what he saw.

She had to think fast about a name. She had forgotten about that one little item while making plans. In no way could she speak her true name. Not even her first name. He would then know.

Now what was the name she had used earlier when she had been put in this same position . . . at Harbison's Pawnshop? It

had come so easily to her then. Was . . . it . . . ? Yes. It had
been . . . Priscilla. But what had been the last name? She could
remember the name Priscilla so well . . . because that had been
the name that she had given her first doll given to her by her
Uncle Thad. A pain in her heart made her cringe when she
thought of her uncle . . . remembering. . . .

"Priscilla," she quickly answered, fluttering her own heavy
lashes upward at him. She just wouldn't use a last name. She
would just tell him that was no concern of his. None whatsoever.
If he even chose to ask.

"Priscilla. Hmmm. That's a pretty name for a pretty lady,"
he said smoothly, making an approach to move on inside Jennifer's room.

Jennifer gasped . . . wondering . . . should she . . . ?

"Why, thank you, sir," she said, stepping aside, watching
him enter. She couldn't control the trembling in her knees as
he began to saunter around the room, taking in all that she
had managed to do to it. Had she been too meticulous? Was
everything too scrubbed and shining clean for someone so poor
and down on her luck? A widow . . . who had lost everything
in life with the downing of a ship at sea?

"Nice," he said. "Nice. And do you have a husband who
you are waiting for? Or are you alone . . . in these . . . uh,
surroundings?" He swung around and watched in obvious
amused mockery as she moved away from the door to stand
on the other side of the room from him.

"Sir, I am a widow," she said, casting her eyes downward.

"A girl named Priscilla, and a widow," he said thickly.
"And living next door to me? Interesting."

Jennifer's heartbeats hastened, knowing her plan was beginning to truly take shape for the first time. . . .

"But, damn it. I still see something in you," he blurted,
going to her, grabbing her by the shoulders to pull her to stand
before him in the light. Jennifer felt a strangeness stirring at
the pit of her stomach when she was forced to meet his gaze
with the lift of his forefinger.

Oh, my, she thought, feeling a spinning in her head. What

power does he have over a woman? I even now wish him to pull me into his arm to kiss me!

"It's the eyes. Damn it. It's the eyes," he shouted, setting her free from his grasp, walking away from her, kneading his brow once again. "I know I've seen those eyes. Somewhere."

Jennifer's heart skipped a few beats. She swallowed hard, then settled herself down onto the chair, knowing that her legs wouldn't hold her up any longer. She was a mixture of feelings now. Confusion . . . fear . . . and dread. "I don't have any idea of what you are speaking, sir," she whispered. "There are many women with the same eyes as mine, I am sure." But she herself had rarely seen such eyes as hers. The slant made them and her uncle's quite unique. But now it was the color Robert Harbison was speaking of. She knew it. The color of blue . . . so much like her mother's. The color also was unique—the deepest blue of any eyes she had ever seen—besides her mother's. So wasn't he remembering . . . Camille's . . . ?

"No matter," he said, swinging his body around. "Now that we've made acquaintance, maybe we can make one another's life a bit less lonely."

"Yes, I'm sure," she gulped, still watching, wondering.

He settled himself down on the edge of the bed and pulled a cigarette from his front shirt pocket. "Care if I smoke?" he asked, surprising Jennifer. Most men never asked. Just took their pleasure of those dreadful, burning things without even considering a woman's feelings.

"Please smoke if you like," she answered.

"Thanks," he said, lifting the chimney of the lamp, to lean his cigarette into the flame. Placing the chimney back in place, he continued to watch her. "And how did you become widowed? Or does it pain you too much to speak of it?"

"My husband . . . my . . . John . . . was drowned at sea. Only a short time ago," she said, casting her eyes downward once again, still amazed at herself and the ease with which she could lie. But it was necessary . . . as this all was. . . .

"That's really too bad," he said, taking a deep draw from

his cigarette. "And how did you happen to choose this flea bag of a building to settle in?"

"This is all I can afford," she answered. "And I hoped to find work near here. I even looked for a while today, but without any luck."

"What sort of work are you looking for?"

"Factory work. Maybe even a seamstress. I've heard tell of those new-fangled sewing machines. I'm sure I could learn to use one fast. But I can't find work. Anywhere." She watched his expression closely, knowing that the mention of sewing machines had hit a nerve. . . .

"A seamstress?" he said, scowling. "A few months ago, I could have aided you in your pursuit. But now? All I can do is give you a shoulder to cry upon."

"What do you mean you could have aided me . . . ?"

"I once held a . . . uh . . . high position but ran into some bad luck," he answered. "But I'm on my way back up. In time. . . ."

Jennifer pushed herself up out of the chair and began slowly pacing the room. "You're . . . on your way up? How?"

Robert laughed hoarsely and went to her, and stopped her by grabbing a hand. "Hmmm. Do I hear interest in your voice? A complete stranger actually caring?" he said, smiling.

She swallowed hard and glanced quickly downward at her captured hand. His touch was too warm . . . too electrifying. This wasn't suppose to happen. She hated him. She loathed him. "Please free my hand, sir," she said, angry at herself for letting her voice crack.

"Robert. The name's Robert. Robert Harbison."

"Please release my hand . . . ROBERT," she said more firmly, forcing herself to look into his face.

"Okay. No need to get angry," he exclaimed, moving away from her.

"Thank you," she said, wringing her hands, still feeling the impression of his hand in hers.

"Your family?" he asked, drawing on his cigarette again. "Where is your family? I can't believe a beautiful, young thing like yourself has been turned loose in this city of San Francisco. This city does have a way of swallowing up defenseless creatures like yourself.''

Jennifer's face turned to all shadows. ''My family?'' she murmured, turning her back to him. ''I have no fare to go back to my mother and father. ''

''Where might they be?''

''In . . . in . . . Boston,'' she blurted. I came from Boston . . . with my John. We were married there . . . a . . . a year ago.''

''Poor baby,'' he said smoothy, moving toward her again.

Having had enough of this game for one night, Jennifer hurried to the door and held it wide open. ''I really must retire now, Robert,'' she said demurely. ''It's been a long, tiring day for me.''

''There's always tomorrow, sweet thing,'' he said smoothly, running a finger across her nose, making her tingle instead of cringe, as she wished to do as a result of his touch.

''Tomorrow?''

''Breakfast. How about breakfast?''

''Where?''

''In my room. I'll do the honors,'' he said suavely, lifting the corner of his lips into a smile.

''You . . . ?''

He laughed hoarsely. ''Yes. Living alone, one has to learn to do many things for oneself.''

She cast her eyes downward again, being so continually unnerved by his penetrating, dark eyes. ''Yes, I'm sure,'' she murmured.

''Till then, sweet thing,'' he said, saluting with the flick of his wrist.

Almost in a state of shock, Jennifer watched him until he disappeared inside his own room. Then she shut and locked her door, leaning against it, unable to stop the tears from running down her cheeks. For the first time in her life, she uttered words of the devil. . . .

''Damn. Damn,'' she mumbled. ''Why? Oh, why has he

affected me this way? I hate him. I've always hated him.'' But he had left her with an unexplainable stirring inside herself. It was a need of sorts . . . something similar to how she had felt . . . and still did . . . about Nicholas, yet so much more powerful.

''Tomorrow. I will begin tomorrow,'' she hissed, reaching upward to unbutton her dress. ''I shall get my revenge. I shall.''

Chapter Twelve

"You don't mind if I shave in your presence, do you?"
Robert asked, as he peered into the tilt of the mirror that was
attached to his shaving cabinet. "After breakfast, this is my
usual second step of the day."

Jennifer laughed a bit nervously as she began to clear the
table of dishes. "No. I don't mind," she answered, still feeling
a bit awkward about being in a man's room so early in the
morning. She had spent many mornings with Nicholas . . . but
that had been with the man she loved . . . and on a ship.

"It's not every day I have the opportunity of sharing my
skills as a cook," Robert chuckled, working up a lather on his
face with a brush of soft badger hair. "Did you enjoy the eggs
and coffee?"

"Yes. Quite," she answered.

"You're not one for saying much," he said, placing his
brush back into a china shaving mug that was ornamented
with his personal insignia. He turned and stared at her, having
become a man with a white beard and moustache of shaving
suds applied carefully to his face. He lifted the corner of his
lips in mockery. "Not been with a man since your late John,

huh?'' he blurted, now holding a straight-edged razor with an
ivory handle in the air, ready to take its first-clean sweep of
soap and whiskers.

Jennifer's eyes lowered, more from the pressure of the contin-
uation of lies than from the sadness she was suppose to be
representing from the loss of a husband. ''None, sir,'' she
whispered, hurrying to the basin to run some water into a
teakettle, which she placed on the stove for heating water for
the soiled dishes.

Robert laughed harshly. ''Well, it's time you give up your
mourning, sweet thing,'' he said, turning to face the mirror
again. ''And I'm the man to help you do it.''

Jennifer swung around, now glaring at the back of his head.
''You're skilled at such things, are you, sir?'' she asked sharply.
She felt as though she was being made to feel that she had
spent the night with him instead of just the morning hours.

''The damn best,'' he bragged, then screwed his face sideways as he began to take wide strokes with his razor. He stopped
momentarily, to look at her from the mirror. ''And hell, sweet
thing, like I said before. Call me Robert? Okay? I don't like
ladies calling me sir. Makes me feel as though I'm old enough
to be their father . . . which . . . I . . . uh am not,'' he said,
furrowing a brow.

''All right, Robert,'' Jennifer murmured, trying to hold her
feelings intact. She knew his age. And she now knew the
darkness of his hair had the same source as the darkness of her
own. She had spied a bottle of hair dye carefully hidden behind
some canned foods in a cabinet. Yes, his gray had been skillfully
covered in an effort to preserve the youthful look that it seemed
all men desired . . . .

And, also, she knew of his ways with women. She knew,
oh, way too much about him. And soon he would know all
about her . . . about her father . . . and who her mother had
been. But not yet. Not yet.

Her gaze traveled around her, realizing there was still much
about him that she did not know. This room of Robert's was
the same small square of a room as Jennifer's but it was filled

with the most expensive of furnishings that the space would allow. A carved mahogany chair sat opposite a gold velvet settee, next to a bed with a great brass headboard. Kerosene lamps were smoking on both a mahogany table next to the bed and the small, round kitchen table. An icebox sat in grand style, along with all other accessories needed to stock a kitchen in the richest of styles. There was a polished, lemon-oiled cleanliness to the room, and even the windows were sparkling clean, as cut glass sparkles beneath the rays of the sun, with gold satin draperies hung long and smooth and open to reveal the activity of the piers on San Francisco Bay.

Where Robert stood, a red granite washstand was surrounded to capacity with a man's toilet items. A blue glass bottle was visible through the open door of the kind of small boxwood case where only the most expensive of men's colognes were usually kept. There were several other glass decanters filled with more cologne, and after shave was placed next to a jar of the pomade that was used to slick a man's hair.

The fresh, clean aroma of Robert now filled Jennifer's nostrils as he moved next to her. "Better, huh?" he asked, patting after shave onto the smoothness of his clean-shaven face.

"A bit," Jennifer laughed, glad to be rescued by the whistling of the teakettle. She swung around to lift it from the stove, but was stopped by Robert's hand grabbing her own.

"We've got to do something about you being so quiet," he said, pulling her into his arms. "If you persist at being so, we might as well get better acquainted in a different way. A way that requires no speaking."

Jennifer's pulse began to race as her blood surged in a sudden wild thrill. Through his tight, tan breeches, she could feel the hardness of his manhood pressing against her. Her flimsy cotton dress was in no way a barrier between two bodies of heated passion.

She looked upward onto his face and could now see the fine wrinkles around his eyes and mouth and rippling his forehead, but it was his eyes that again captured her full attention. They were dark . . . smoldering . . . setting her afire inside. She tried to force the memory of her mother and father to the front of her mind, but his lips on hers erased everything but a mysterious lust washing her mind clear of all but him and his closeness . . . .

Then a light tapping on the door brought Jennifer back to her senses. She pulled free from his hold and rushed across the room, trembling. "Sir! You must remember. I'm only recently widowed," she murmured, running her hand lightly across her lips.

"Damn. Is it 'sir' again?" he blurted, then stormed to the door and opened it. "Yeah? What is it?" he said darkly. Then he quickly added, "Oh. It's you. What the hell do you think you're doing disturbing a body so early in the morning?"

Trying to hear what the small boy was saying to Robert, Jennifer inched her way across the room. The boy looked as though he might be the age of twelve or thirteen, very dirty-faced, and also as dirty in his attire, and he was looking upward at Robert Harbison with fear filling his dark eyes. Was this child a messenger boy of sorts? He was handing an envelope to Robert. The name "Patricia" was murmured followed closely by the boy's rushing away, leaving Robert Harbison pulling a stack of green bills from the envelope. He thumbed through them, counting the money then laughed deeply as he swung around to slam the door shut behind him. Then his face became all shadows when his gaze crept across the room and settled on Jennifer.

Jennifer swallowed hard. It was quite apparent that he had forgotten her presence . . . until . . . now. He began to slap the money against the palm of his other hand and moved toward her.

"My pay," he mumbled.

"For . . . what . . . ?" she murmured.

"My own damn business," he said.

"But . . . it's so much . . . money," she stammered, looking around the room again, seeing the expensive way in which he lived. His air of mystery made Jennifer suddenly afraid.

"Well earned," he said, going to settle down on the settee. His fingers worked with the money, counting it all over again.

Jennifer went and sat down on the.chair opposite him, sitting stiffly erect with her hands clasped on her lap. "Gambling? Is that how you live? By gambling?" she inquired further. Only that made sense to her. How else could he acquire such a fortune when it was quite apparent that he didn't work anywhere? Her eyes searched around her once again. It still didn't add up. All these expensive furnishings in such a rat trap of a building . . . ?

"Yeah. Sure," he laughed throatily. "Gambling. The best kind around."

"Horses?" she persisted. "Or dog races? I hear there are races in San Francisco now. Or maybe . . . cock . . . fights?"

"Seems as though you've found your tongue," he said darkly. "First you don't have much to say and now that you do, it's all questions. What is this? You with Pinkerton? Huh?"

"Pinkerton?" Jennifer stammered. "Why would you think . . . ?"

A loud roll of laughter filled the room as Robert pushed himself off the settee. "God! You are a naive, sweet thing," he said, going to a poster of his bed. He began to screw the top off one end, watching her closely. "I was only kidding you, sweet thing. I was only kidding."

Jennifer's eyes widened as she watched him form the money into a round mass and stuff it down the insides of the brass leg.

"My own personal bank," he chuckled. "No way a person can go bankrupt if they have their own personal bank. Right?"

"I wouldn't know, Robert," Jennifer answered, rising. "I've never had enough money to even keep me from worrying from one day to the next how I'll make it to the next day." Lies . . . how easily they now flowed from her mouth . . . .

"Need a few bucks to tide you over?" he offered, pulling some money from its hiding place, handing it in her direction.

Feeling a blush rising, Jennifer hurried to the stove again to remove the teakettle that had ceased to sing long ago. "No, thank you," she said demurely. "I plan to make my own way. Somehow."

She heard quick footsteps and felt his hand pulling her from the stove once again. "Damn it. You do insist on washing the dishes, don't you?"

"I feel it's the least I can do. To pay for my breakfast you so kindly prepared for me."

"I can think of another way you can pay me," he said, tilting her chin up so their eyes could meet.

"Like . . . what . . . ?" she murmured, hating the trembling of her lips. What if he kissed her again? Could she refuse the needs of her body, even though she hated him so . . . ? And wasn't there Nicholas to consider? He was out there . . . somewhere . . . waiting for her . . . to fulfill both their needs. But this man's fingers now so boldly unbuttoning the front of her dress made Jennifer's body become like a million heartbeats.

"Like letting me kiss the softness of your breast, Priscilla," he said, reaching inside to fondle and squeeze.

But the spoken name "Priscilla" made a warning go off inside Jennifer's brain . . . remembering why she had even had to choose a name other than her own when she had met Robert Harbison face to face. "I really can't let you," she whispered, shoving him away from her.

"The circumstances aren't the best?" he said scowling. "You're not used to being bedded in broad daylight? Is that it?"

The boldness of his words unnerved Jennifer for a moment, then she hurriedly buttoned her dress. "I'm not used to being . . . bedded . . . as you have chosen to call it . . . by strangers, sir," she spat back at him. A feeling of power surged through her. She could see the desire for her in the depths of his dark eyes. She was succeeding at what she had set out to do. But now she had to conquer her own feelings . . . by refusing him.

Yes. She'd let him always get so close . . . and then she'd back away . . . after his passion had peaked. She would soon own him . . . then she would turn him aside.

He laughed hoarsely as he kneaded his brow. "Sweet thing, I'm going to change all that for you," he said. "You'll be begging for it. You'll see."

Jennifer's eyes wavered, doubts suddenly assailing her. Would it be truly in the end he who would hold power over her? No. She wouldn't let it happen. "I truly doubt that, Robert," she murmured, moving toward the door.

"Be that as it may," he said further, following her, "I'd like to take you some place special tonight."

Jennifer swung around, eyes wide. "You wish to take me out?" she asked softly.

"Yes. Get our relationship started all over again on a more solid footing. Are you game?"

"Where do you plan to go?" she asked, filled with an inner excitement, having the need for a change, even if it meant having to go with Robert Harbison.

"To a swinging place over on Market Street. A place called People's."

"What sort of a place is it?"

"Let that be my surprise."

Jennifer's fingers began to work with the cotton of her dress. "But all I have to wear is this simple dress," she whispered, longing for one of her new dresses that she had had to leave behind. But no. She had to put Thad and everything associated with him from her mind.

"No fear, sweet thing," Robert said, a smile playing on his lips. "I shall supply the dress." He studied her with a hand now kneading his chin. "Hmm. Size five. Am I right?"

Jennifer blushed. "Yes. That's what size I wear," she answered. "But, I can't . . . let . . . you . . . ." Wouldn't she then truly owe him a debt she never planned to pay?

"Yes you can, and you will," he said, stepping closer to her. "We shall step out in grand style tonight. Just the two of us. You won't be sorry."

Feeling the hastening of her heartbeats again, she batted her thick lashes nervously. "Well, all right. I guess just this once . . .'' she said, suddenly realizing that for him to see her best was a way to tease his sense even more.

"No. Not just this once. It's a beginning, sweet thing.''

When his lips searched her face, Jennifer felt as though her insides were melting, but she hurriedly opened the door to escape her feelings . . . if indeed she even could.

"Around seven tonight, Priscilla?'' he said, saluting her with the flick of wrist.

"Yes, tonight,'' she said, stepping out into the hallway. She swung the skirt of her dress around to go to her room, when she felt eyes other than Robert's on her.

A sudden chill raced through her when she found the short, squatty Mr. Andrews standing at his partially opened doorway, leering after her. One jaw was filled like a chipmunk's but became quickly emptied as he spat a wad of brown chewing tobacco out onto the hallway floor.

A smile creased his lips as he continued to watch her and Jennifer's breath caught in her throat when she saw his hand reach down to touch the large bulge in his breeches, then make obscene gestures with his free hand for Jennifer to openly see.

"My word,'' she gasped, turning her eyes, hoping to see that Robert had also seen this, also hoping for his possible protection of her, but she could tell that the angle in which he stood in his doorway prevented him from viewing the demonstration of filth from behind the other partially opened door.

Fumbling with the key to her room, Jennifer took another quick look toward where Mr. Andrews stood, and grew faint as she saw him now openly fondling his manhood as it protruded from his unbuttoned breeches.

Not seeing whether or not Robert was waiting for another goodbye from her lips, Jennifer rushed on into her room, shutting and bolt locking the door behind her. She felt suddenly quite ill to her stomach. But to rush to the toilet to release the bitterness circling in her throat would be to again expose herself to that twisted Mr. Andrews all over again. And might he even force his way into the toilet and do terrible things to her even there . . . ?

Hanging her head in her hands, Jennifer swallowed hard and walked across the room to stand beside the window. It was as though she was in prison . . . one that she had made for herself, and she felt . . . oh so alone.

"Can I continue with this?" she whispered, sobbing softly. "This is becoming more and more than I bargained for." Even with Robert Harbison, she could feel her defenses weakening. This had not been a part of the plan.

Her eyes moved to the door, feeling ill all over again. Nor had she planned on the likes of Mr. Andrews. How could he do such an evil thing for her eyes to see?

A phonograph playing soft music reverberated through the thin wall that separated Jennifer's and Robert's rooms. She held her breath to listen. In only a matter of moments, his voice filled the air, singing along with the music.

"You are indeed a man of mystery, Robert Harbison," she whispered, feeling a tingling inside her when she remembered his hand on her breast. She unbuttoned her dress, to reach inside to touch her breast herself, wondering why this part of her anatomy could create such dizziness inside her head whenever it was caressed . . . .

The nipple hardened between her fingers, making shame rush through her in torrents.

"I'm no better than that Mr. Andrews," she whispered, quickly securing her buttons again. But there was an ache between her thighs that confused her still. Was she becoming completely awakened sexually by all that surrounded her? Was she truly just as depraved as her uncle?

Or was she more like her mother? Had mother not been raped, but encouraged sex with Robert . . . as Jennifer now so deeply desired to do herself? Was she to become her mother's daughter in *that* sense . . . ?

"Oh, no, mother," she whispered. "I'm sorry. I didn't mean to think such vile things about you. I'm sorry. I truly am."

She went and threw herself across the bed, pounding her fists into the mattress.

"Aunt Minnie," she sobbed. "I should have listened to you. I should have stayed in Seattle. What is to become of me now . . . ?"

Chapter Thirteen

Jennifer ran her hands over the smoothness of the maroon velveteen dress that Robert had brought to her earlier in the day. It was a dress meant to be worn with the finest of jewels, and its low-cut bodice that came to a point in front, revealing her magnificent bosom, made her blush anew. Jennifer now knew how a "kept" woman might possibly feel, never having been given anything by a man before . . . and especially not a dress of such expensive taste as Robert Harbison had chosen to give to her.

"You do look quite breathtaking," Robert said, adjusting the sleeves of his white, lace-edged shirt. His black coat was worn over a black waistcoat, and his breeches were also black, and tight and revealing. "You do like my choice in dresses?" he added.

Upon his arrival to her room, Jennifer had noticed right away how handsome he was. And didn't the darkness of the suit accentuate even more the darkness of his hair, eyes, and even his skin . . . ? She had again hated having noticed. She tilted her chin upward, showing a planned haughtiness. She would not let him think any longer that she was the weak-minded, saddened person she had at first appeared. She was now in phase two of her revenge.

"It is quite lovely," she answered, flipping her hair to hang in long, dark curls down the ivory skin of her bare shoulders and back. She had begun to notice a trace of blonde at the roots of her hair and knew that her game would soon catch up with her if she didn't indeed bring it to a climax on her own . . . and soon.

"Then do you have a wrap of sorts?" he asked, smoothing his hair with his hand. "Do I recall a dark cape? One you had on the first night that I saw you? One of velvet . . . I do . . . believe . . . ?"

Feeling her defenses crumbling once again, Jennifer rushed to the closet and pulled her knitted shawl from a hanger. "No. You're mistaken," she said. "This is the only wrap I own. It will have to make do."

"If you say so, sweet thing," he said, lifting the corner of his lips in mockery. "For whatever reason you choose to hide your cape from me, I won't question it."

Jennifer's pulse quickened. "What?" she gasped. "What do you mean?" She pulled the shawl around her shoulders, wondering if he was smart enough to realize that she was indeed playing a game with him. She had tried to avoid his eyes this night, always seeing in their depths such a smoldering passion, just waiting to be released. But now, she had to see what lay hidden in their depths. Looking upward, her heart fluttered anew. He was looking at her . . . studying her with such intensity that she felt a weakness in her knees all over again.

"What I meant by that is of no importance at the moment," he said. "What is important is taking you out, to show off my good fortune at finding such a rose in this building of thorns."

Turning her head aside so that he wouldn't see another blush rising, she lifted the skirt of her dress up into her free arm, and left her room with him. She glanced momentarily toward Mr. Andrews's door. She sighed with relief when she saw that the door was closed, remembering quite vividly his performance earlier in the day. Would she be safe when left alone later this night? But she did have a bolt lock on her door . . . .

"Watch these damn steps," Robert encouraged. "You'd think that damn Andrews could do something about the lighting and the filth."

Jennifer wanted to ask Robert the why's of his choice of buildings, when it was so apparent that he had enough money to live anywhere of his choice. But she couldn't ask him this. She had plied him with too many questions earlier in the day and had already aroused his suspicions. Instead she asked, "Robert, where are you planning to go? And how shall we even get there? Do you own a horse and carriage?"

He laughed sardonically. "I'm taking you many places, sweet thing," he answered, opening the door that led to the street. "I'm going to show you some San Francisco night life. And, no, I don't own a horse and carriage, but I rented one earlier in the afternoon, just for this special occasion."

"How nice," Jennifer said, following along beside him into the darkness of the night. There were the usual lonely men standing alongside the building, but this night there was something else that caught Jennifer's sudden attention. Lying next to the cobblestone street was the elderly man she had seen on other occasions, but this time he was curled up in a fetal position, lying so still, grasping onto a half-emptied wine bottle.

"Damn wino," Robert growled, kicking at the man. "If this street isn't cluttered with enough filth, there has to be this adding to the stench." He kicked at the man again. "Get up, goddamn you," he shouted.

Jennifer gasped loudly. She yanked at Robert's arm. "Robert. Please don't do that," she said forcefully. She was seeing a side of Robert that she had always known existed, and her hate for him was renewed. It was such people as this unfortunate man lying helpless on the sidewalk that Jennifer and her father had aided in Seattle. One day, she would return and forget this time in her life.

"Oh, all right," Robert mumbled, guiding her toward a

stately horse and carriage. "Here. Let me help you in board-ing," he said, holding her by the waist as she stepped upward.

"Thank you," she murmured, still seething inside from his show of noncaring for the less fortunate. It was quite evident that Robert Harbison was first on Robert Harbison's list of caring. She watched him as he climbed onto the seat next to her, wondering what in life could have hardened him so. He was such a handsome, well-groomed man. Such a waste, she thought to herself.

Robert gave the reins a slap, causing the carriage to lurch forward. "Hahh!" he shouted, making the lone chestnut mare snort as she picked up speed.

Jennifer sank back against the padded seat, securing herself with one hand, and holding her freely blowing hair with the other, glad to be leaving Front Street behind.

The aroma and the dampness of the sea breeze caught in her throat and she shivered with its chill. But it was a bit too early for the foggy mist to have settled in its shroud, enabling Jennifer to see the increased traffic of horse-drawn carriages and cable cars as Robert directed the carriage onto a well-lighted street.

A cable car clattered past them and the noise from the many carriages and horses' hooves on the cobblestone street made an excitement grow inside Jennifer. She was seeing a side of city life that she hadn't ever seen before. Clusters of gaslights lined the street, lighting it as though it was broad daylight, and people were parading up and down the sidewalks in expensive evening attire, walking past a variety of well-lighted shops.

"You're about to see how the other half live, sweet thing," Robert drawled, pulling the carriage up to the curb, next to a horseless carriage . . . the first that Jennifer had ever been so close to.

"I'm going to own one of those one day," Robert said determinedly, seeing what had captured Jennifer's full attention.

Her head swung around. "You do plan to purchase one of those things?" she asked, wide-eyed.

"Ah, yes. I do," he said, studying the automobile. "Now I

may not choose that particular model. More than likely I shall choose an Olds.''

''Do you really think this piece of machinery will be more popular than the horse and carriage?'' she further inquired, remembering that Thad had said that he had already ordered one for himself. ''I feel that they lack charm. Grace. I find this contraption downright ugly. And they are so noisy.''

Robert laughed hoarsely. ''My dear, I believe all women feel as you do,'' he said. ''But the automobile is the thing of the future. I know enough of business ventures to know this to be a fact.''

Jennifer turned and studied the vehicle once again, frowning. ''All I see is a piece of steel. Nothing more.''

''Well, I see much more than that,'' Robert argued. ''But only a man is capable of knowing such arguments,'' he quickly added, climbing from the carriage, securing the reins to a hitching post.

''Why must you men always feel that we women are too dumb to discuss matters of the world?'' Jennifer said petulantly, as she let him aid her from the carriage. ''Myself? I've even attended . . . .'' she began to add, but caught herself before revealing that she had attended college. Her palms became sweaty, realizing how close she had come to revealing a truth about herself that Robert shouldn't discover . . . until the end . . . .

''You started to say? You've what?'' he asked, with a tilted, dark brow, as he guided her by the elbow onto the crowded sidewalk.

Jennifer had to think fast . . . but this was easily done when her gaze took in all that was around her. ''Oh, my. This is so exciting,'' she exclaimed, moving onward toward a colorful setting behind a paned-glass window, seeing a lady dressed in black sitting behind a table over which was draped a black covering.

Jennifer stepped back and looked at the picture that had been painted on the window. It was that of a large hand, on which was written in bold red print the words "past," "present," and "future."

Next to the hand were the words: "Palmistry, Read Skillfully by Madame Jewel."

"A fortune teller," Robert said, stopping to pause before the window also. "Want to have your fortune read? Could reveal some surprises in your future."

Jennifer snuggled closer to the window, laughing to herself, thinking Robert to be the one who was to receive a surprise in the near future. She watched closely now as this "Madame Jewel" leaned over the table to pull the palm of a petite lady into the light beneath the flickering of a red-shaded lantern. "What does she do?" Jennifer whispered.

"She's suppose to read the lines of the palm of a person's hand," Robert scoffed. "These palmists claim that they can tell a person's fortune and character by these lines."

"Amazing," Jennifer sighed. "Absolutely amazing."

"Hogwash. That's what it is," Robert said, guiding Jennifer on to the next window.

"My word," Jennifer said, placing her fingers to her cheek. "Why would a person do such a terrible thing to their body?"

"Tatooing?" Robert said, pulling a cigarette from an inner pocket to light it. "The Japanese think this to be a thing of beauty."

"Why . . . it's . . . ghastly," Jennifer said, looking in utter disbelief at a tiny Japanese woman who was sitting with her back to the lighted window for all to see, while a male Japanese tatoo artist was adding more designs to her already colorfully designed back. "I'm sure it has to hurt," she added quickly, visibly shuddering, seeing this man pricking small deep holes in the skin, then placing color in them.

"I wouldn't want to see your back scarred in such a manner," Robert said smoothly, moving on to the display in the next window. "And now. Care to go inside to watch a boxing match?"

"A . . . what . . . ?" Jennifer asked, peering into the window. At the far end of this room stood a crowd of shouting, boisterous men around a roped-off area, where two men were actively swinging their fists at one another. She turned her eyes away when she saw a mallet being applied to one of these men's heads.

"By God! Did you see that?" Robert shouted. "I'd heard that they did this to whomever was fighting the champ, but I didn't believe it."

"How could they?" she gagged.

"That large fella is the heavyweight boxer Josh McWilliams. He's supposed to knock the locals out in one round. I guess the mallet assures his win."

"It's disgusting. Disgraceful."

"I guess you've seen enough of this part of Market Street," he said, offering her his arm. "Let's head on to People's. I'm sure it's about time for the show to begin."

"Show? What sort of show?"

"You'll see. You'll see," Robert guffawed, flipping his cigarette onto the cobblestones of the street.

The atmosphere that surrounded them as they continued to push their way through the crowded walks was like that of a circus. But it didn't smell that way. Jennifer had recognized the different aromas of rich French perfume surfacing from the women she continued to pass by. And weren't they dressed so elegantly in their silks and satins? It gave Jennifer an air of importance, until she remembered her reason for even being on this street . . . and with whom she was walking. . . .

"Here 'tis," Robert teased. "People's. The new establishment of San Francisco. Let's give it a try, sweet thing."

Jennifer's gaze settled on the three-story building. In front of it had been built three white columned pillars, graced by a huge, sparkling chandelier, set all aglow by many gaslights. The door leading into the building was covered with a bright red velveteen fabric. "It is a beautiful building," she said, now engrossed by the throng of people waiting to enter.

Then Jennifer's attention was drawn elsewhere. It was a discordant blare from a brass band and out-of-tune voices singing hymns. "What is that?" she asked, turning her head in the direction of the racket. Then her eyes widened when she saw a large uniformed group, consisting of both men and women, moving down the middle of Market Street, carrying smoking and sputtering torches and flags waving in the breeze.

"Oh, my God," Robert moaned, urging Jennifer toward the door of People's. "It's that damned Salvation Army. Don't they ever give up?"

"What are they doing?"

"Preaching the glory of their God," he growled. "Trying to save all the lost souls of those who work in and frequent these establishments. Some damn preacher's idea of a joke, I've always thought."

Jennifer frowned at Robert's words, remembering her father and all those he had saved. Before returning to Seattle, she would make sure that she would look into this Salvation Army . . . maybe take some ideas back with her. Seattle had been in dire need of some salvation when she had left . . . and more than she and her Aunt Minnie could ever think of handling.

"Come on, Priscilla," Robert urged with a yank on her arm. "I've paid our fifty cents. Let's hurry on inside before the feature show begins."

"What type of show?" Jennifer said, catching her breath from the rushing.

"A stage show," he exclaimed. "Haven't you ever seen a stage show?"

She would have liked to have said, "No. Being a preacher's daughter, I have never even desired to see a stage show." But again . . . much too much would be revealed about herself by admitting such truths. Then something grabbed at the pit of her stomach. If a stage show was the popular place to be . . . would her Uncle Thad possibly be in the audience? His interests were now focused on this new aspect of life. She withdrew a bit, pulling her arm free from Robert's. He turned, glaring, in her direction.

"What the hell's the matter with you?" he spat angrily. "Come on. I want to get a seat up front."

"No. Maybe I'd better not," she murmured, turning to leave.

She couldn't take a chance that her Uncle Thad might be there. If he was . . . and he saw her . . . then everything would be lost.

"Hey! I don't get it," Robert said, grabbing her roughly by the arm. "I've bought you a dress just for this special occasion. You're not going to back out for whatever damn reason you've got in that head of yours."

Jennifer swung around and eyed him darkly with her blazing blue eyes. She wanted to lash out at him. Right then and there. Tell him of her hatred for him and why. But she couldn't. Not yet. And she now knew that she had to take a chance on seeing Thad. San Francisco was a big place. Most surely he wouldn't choose this particular establishment this particular night . . . this only night that she would be there. But she still had to be cautious. "I will only attend this stage show with you if you'll choose a table at the far back of the room," she said stubbornly, her jaw set.

"Oh, Christ," he mumbled. "Why the hell would you insist on sitting clear at the back?"

"Why? Because if you don't do as I ask, I shall turn right around and leave. That's why," she said, even more firmly.

"God! Women!" he grumbled with a jerk of the head. "Aw, all right. Come on," he added, taking her by the arm once again.

Feeling the tension in her back and neck, Jennifer proceeded beside him, looking quickly around at each cluster of people grouped at separate tables in the dimly lighted room. It was a saloon with a theater attached. Jennifer could feel a blush rising when her gaze fell upon the women scurrying from table to table serving alcholic drinks. These women wore dresses revealing *so* much . . . reaching nearly to the point above their knees, with stained and sweaty tights. Their bare arms and necks were uncovered over halfway to their waists, and some wore powdered wigs, with faces rouged and powdered.

Working their way on through the heavy cigarette and cigar smoke circling above their heads, they were motioned toward an empty table that sat almost hidden in a dark corner, with

only a small candle flickering inside a crystal decanter lighting
the bright red linen tablecloth spread neatly across the table.

"Sit down and relax, sweet thing," Robert encouraged as
he reached his hand up to get the attention of a waitress. "I
guess we can see the stage all right from here."

"Beer is five a glass, sir," a girl said, with wide, dark eyes.
"Two here? One for you and the lady?"

"No," Jennifer whispered hurriedly. "None for me, Robert." Her heart pounded. She was feeling quite out of place in
this house of the devil.

"A mug of beer for me and a glass of vintage port for my
sweet thing here," Robert ordered, winking at Jennifer. She
cringed a bit when she felt his hand creep under the table to
touch her knowingly on the knee.

She pulled her knee free, fuming inside. "I told you I didn't
want any, Robert," she hissed.

"A bit of wine will put more of a sparkle in your eye, sweet
thing," he said smoothly. Then he laughed. "Come on, relax.
You're supposed to be enjoying yourself. You look as though
you've signed your own death warrant. It's a stage show. Something grand. Damn. Even myself, I'd love to perform on the
stage."

"You . . . ?"

"I'd sing. I have a talent for it, but I'm afraid it's too soon
for the likes of a crowd who gathers here to accept a man on
the stage."

Jennifer's brows tilted, now remembering hearing him singing . . . and even more than once. Yes. He did confuse her. He
had many personalities behind that smooth facade.

The glass of wine and mug of beer were placed on their
table just as an individual began to hammer away at a piano
at the foot of the stage, which was brightly lighted by many
lanterns circling its edge.

"It's about time," Robert said, lighting a cigarette. "Just
wait til you see her."

"See who?"

"Little Egypt."

"Who is Little Egypt?"

"Ah, you are now to see," Robert purred, watching eagerly as the curtain was drawn to reveal a scantily clad maiden lying poised on a red velveteen carpet.

"My word," Jennifer gasped, feeling faint.

"She was arrested in New York for dancing nude at a stage party at Sherry's," Robert boasted, puffing more fiercely on his cigarette.

"She . . . was . . . what . . . ?"

Robert glanced toward Jennifer with amusement in his eyes. "She was acquitted. All she had to do was tell the judge that she just looked naked," he said, laughing hoarsely.

A bass drum began to pound out um pah pahs as the girl slithered upward from the stage with hands on hips, flaunting the full skimpiness of her attire. Her breasts were barely covered by a thin cloth stretched across them, revealing the erectness of her large, firm breasts. Her skirt hung down across her hips, emphasizing the flatness of her stomach and showing off her navel, which had a sequin popped inside it to sparkle as her stomach began to move.

"This is evil," Jennifer whispered, clasping her hands on her lap, but unable to take her eyes off this woman whose hips and stomach were gyrating to the continuing beats of the drum. As the beat accelerated, so did her hips, causing gasps to rise from the audience.

A smile played on the girl's wide red lips, knowing that she held her audience captive, and she flaunted her abilities to the utmost as her torso quivered and shook, until three final thrusts from her abdomen brought the act to a halt.

"My God, what a belly dancer," Robert shouted, clapping, as the curtain fell. He looked toward Jennifer, his eyes showing an increased passion for her. "How'd you like it? Did it get you hot?"

"Robert!" Jennifer exclaimed, understanding his insinuation. Was that why he had brought her here? To ply her with alcohol and with the wicked ways of the world, to whet her sexual appetite?

"Well? She *was* magnificent, wasn't she?" he insisted, still watching Jennifer.

"She's a shameless hussy. That's what she is," Jennifer hissed. But there was no denying that watching such a demonstration had unnerved her . . . and not only for the guilt of having witnessed it. It had made that same familiar ache between her thighs surface once again. She didn't understand why. But she did know that she didn't like this happening to her. She wanted to be in more control of her feelings. Only in this way could she succeed at what she had set out to do.

"You've just not been exposed to ways of the world," he said, drinking the last of the beer from his mug. "I guess marriage does that for a missus if she weds too young."

A rustling of feet beside her made Jennifer turn her head to see who might be entering, now that the main attraction was over. Her heart palpitated as she swung her head back around to hide her face. She wished to escape but knew that she was now in a trap . . . sinking deeper into the claws of deception. She felt the warmth of Robert's hand on hers.

"What is it, Priscilla?" he asked quickly. "I can tell that something besides Little Egypt has upset you."

Afraid that Thad or Lil might see her still, Jennifer refused to turn to face Robert. She instead took a sip of her wine, hoping to find solace in the thick, sweet liquid.

"Priscilla, what is it?" Robert insisted, turning her gaze to meet his with his forefinger. But her gaze didn't hold. It was following Thad and Lil to a table that sat closer to the stage than all other tables. Jennifer tensed even more when she glanced quickly toward Robert, finding that he had discovered what had become so important to her.

"Why would seeing Thadeus Brewster and his colored broad cause you to react in such a manner?" he asked slyly. "What are they to you?"

Jennifer's pulse quickened in the hollow of her throat. Even though seeing Thad had caused many different feelings to well up in her, she couldn't let Robert suspect any of them. Then her eyes moved back to Robert, suddenly realizing there was even more for her to worry about. Why hadn't it come to her immediately? It was there in Robert's eyes: a hatred. And now Jennifer had to wonder what had truly entered Robert's thoughts when he had seen Thadeus Brewster—the late Camille Brewster's brother-in-law. Surely Robert was aware of this relationship between the man across the room and the woman whose death he was responsible for.

"It's a white man . . . with a colored girl that sets my blood to boiling," she said hurriedly. "Isn't it so degrading?" She hoped that Robert couldn't see the wavering of her eyes as she turned them back to her uncle. It was all so vivid in her mind once again . . . the love that she had had for her uncle all those years . . . the loss of her mother and father . . . .

But she still had to pretend.

"Oh, is that all?" he said darkly, lighting a cigarette. "In San Francisco, you can see many things. Especially here on Market Street, as you already know."

"That doesn't make it right."

"Take that Thadeus Brewster," Robert said coolly. "He's rich. Can buy and sell almost anyone else in San Francisco. He's got a gold mine here at his People's Theatre."

Jennifer felt the color draining from her face. She gripped her wine glass more tightly. "This place belongs to . . . that . . . uh . . . that man?" she whispered. When Thad had mentioned an interest in the moving pictures and stage productions, Jennifer would never have thought it to mean . . . such a place as this.

"This and a Kinetscope Show House further up the Market Street strip."

"A Kinetscope?"

"It's the beginning of the moving picture era here in San Francisco."

"Would you please take me to see one?" Jennifer blurted, feeling the need to leave before Thad's eyes began to search around and found her.

"You'd really want to?" Robert said, glancing toward the stage as the um pah of the drum began again.

"Yes. Yes. And now?" Jennifer said, rising, watching the

curtain being drawn, slowly revealing the poised, waiting figure of Little Egypt again. Jennifer didn't want to have to sit through another such performance. And to think her Uncle Thad was responsible for such a distasteful show of flesh. It was hard for Jennifer to understand how two brothers could be so different. Thad with his immoral way . . . and her father . . . such a holy man of God.

"After we watch Little Egypt again," Robert argued.

"No. We must leave now," Jennifer said, placing her fingertips to her brow. "I feel faint, Robert. Truly I do. It must be the wine."

"Oh, God," Robert groaned, pushing himself up out of the chair. "Fifty cents wasted. God. A whole evening ahead of us and you grow faint? Jesus."

Jennifer moved toward the door, hearing Robert's continuing mumblings, making her smile. At least she had managed to ruin his evening thus far. Could she even further? She breathed a sigh of relief when she stepped out into the night air, glad to have left behind her all the noise, smoke, and . . . Thad.

"This way," Robert grumbled, taking her by the arm, guiding her through the crowded walk again. "Just a few buildings down this way."

Jennifer pulled her shawl more snugly around her shoulders, feeling the evening air increasing in its damp coolness. Traces of fog were settling around the gaslights in almost rainbowed circles, but a thickening crowd in front of a building drew Jennifer's attention. Lettered on the building she read: Brewster's Kinetscope Show. Shivers ran down her spine at seeing her own name on display for all to see.

"Another fifty cents," Robert grumbled, reaching into his front breeches' pocket. "Damn Brewster. Hate to give him any of *my* money."

Jennifer's heart skipped a beat. "What did you say?" she asked, holding a breath inward.

"Thadeus Brewster. I hate his guts. Hate to give him any of my hard-earned money."

A prickling sensation flowed through Jennifer. He did know,

for sure, of Thad's relationship with Camille Brewster . . . and what had Robert meant by his "hard-earned money"? He didn't have employment anywhere . . . but . . . there was all that money that had been handed him by the small delivery boy.

Jennifer now knew the source of this prickling sensation that seemed to be invading all her nerve endings. It was a fear . . . fear of the side of Robert Harbison she might soon discover— a side perhaps more evil than she had ever suspected.

"Now are you sure you won't grow faint after entering this establishment?" Robert asked, leaning down into her face. "Fifty cents is fifty cents. I don't want to pay, unless you're sure you'll see this thing through."

"Yes," she mumbled. "I do want to see a kinetscope show." She mainly wanted to see if this house of Thad's was one of depravity, like his People's Theater. She hoped that she wouldn't have reason *to* feel faint.

"All right," Robert said, paying for entrance, then guiding her inside the building by the elbow. They entered a large, semidark room, where people were lined up along each side, looking downward through peepholes on top of tall, narrow boxes.

"Well, here we are. Another nickel for each kinetscope. You choose one," Robert urged.

Jennifer pushed her way through the crowd, watching in disbelief at the chaos in the room. "It's quite interesting . . . amazing," she said. "Isn't it, Robert?"

"Not the best, but a beginning," he answered back, lighting a cigarette.

"This one," Jennifer said eagerly and watched Robert drop a nickel in a slot at the side of the box.

"Now put your eyes to that peephole and turn the knob on the side above the slot where I inserted the money."

"Then what?" Jennifer asked, wide-eyed.

"Turn the knob. You'll see a film that moves in a roll on spools."

Jennifer did as told and watched, almost spellbound, as Teddy Roosevelt appeared below her eyes, grinning, then William

Jennings Bryan shaking his long head of hair. Several women suddenly appeared, in jerky fashion, modeling the latest in evening gowns and bathing suits.

"Do you see everything clearly enough?"

"Yes. It's marvelous," she squealed. "Quite unique," she sighed even further, then felt a stirring next to her and tensed when she saw Thad and Lil moving behind her and Robert. Truly feeling faint this time, Jennifer clutched on to Robert's hand. "We must leave. I'm ill again," she whispered, feeling a tearing at the heart to be so close to Thad and not be able to touch him . . . and what if he was to look behind him . . . ?

"You what?" Robert growled, much too loudly, causing a stir in the room.

Jennifer turned her head away when Thad turned his head partially sideways, not seeing her because of the darkness of the room. Jennifer knew from her own experience that it took awhile for the eyes to adjust to the darkness after first entering. But she knew that her time was running out. Soon Thad or Lil could make out who it was standing so close.

Jennifer swirled around and moved past Robert and on out into the street, breathing hard. Had Robert seen Thad? If so, he could very easily guess the why's of Jennifer's two sudden fainting spells. She leaned against the building, fanning herself with the tail of her shawl when Robert burst from the doorway.

"I've never met anyone quite like you, Priscilla," he grumbled. "I think it's time to take you back to your room. That is, if you're not too faint to climb aboard the carriage," he added angrily, stomping away from her.

Smiling almost wickedly from the pleasure she was deriving from his added anger, Jennifer was able to brush her mixture of feelings for her uncle momentarily from her mind. She hurried to walk beside Robert, then let him help her up onto the carriage. She sat in silence as he readied the carriage for departure, then fell a bit sideways as he yelled a loud "Giddyup" and snapped the horse's reins much too severely.

The carriage swerved in and out of the traffic of other horses and carriages and then on past a cable car, until Market Street was left behind, and they were speeding down the cobblestones of Front Street.

"Did you see that damn Brewster?" Robert suddenly shouted. "He was making his rounds this evening. I guess he's counting the gold as it rolls in. I'm glad you grew faint when you did. I don't care to have to sit so close to a twerp such as that damn Brewster."

Jennifer's insides froze and her eyes widened as Robert continued to ramble. "Goddamned Brewster didn't come by his money by sweat on the brow. He was handed it in a silver platter from his father. Don't know why he's always acted so high and mighty. He's no better than me."

The fog now swirling in its thick white mist helped to dissipate some of the sting of Robert's words, but Jennifer couldn't shake the numbness that had invaded her body. Robert's hatred of her Uncle Thad was deep. Was that the reason Robert had pursued Camille Brewster . . . to do anything to get back at the Brewsters? But why? And what would Robert do when he found out who Jennifer truly was . . . another Brewster . . . ?

Suddenly Jennifer felt that maybe she shouldn't continue with her revenge . . . especially not alone. She was now more afraid of Robert than she had ever previously been.

Robert directed the carriage up next to the curb in front of their building, then jumped from the carriage to secure the reins. He reached up to help Jennifer, which she accepted. "Sorry about tonight," he said softly.

"You're sorry?" she asked, walking beside him as he pushed the door of the building open for her.

"Yeah. Seems I tried to push too much on you in one night."

Jennifer swallowed hard, seeing a different side of him once again. He was a person whose personality changed from one minute to the next. "I'm sorry if I disappointed you," she said, still finding the lies waiting to be spoken . . . so easily. She lifted the skirt of her dress up into her arms as she began to climb the darkened staircase, hearing an eerie silence all around her. But what else did these unfortunate people have to do but go to bed when darkness encompassed the city? Surely none of them had ever ventured down to Market Street.

"You could do something for me to help me forget any disappointment I may have felt," Robert said smoothly, pulling her next to him as they reached the second floor and began to walk down the dark, dingy hallway.

Jennifer's insides twisted as she felt his breath on her ear when he leaned even closer to her. "What do you mean?" she asked, glad, but yet afraid, when they reached her door.

"Let me come in for a while," he asked, feeling her waist through her dress in a caressing, even arousing fashion.

Jennifer's heart began to pound as his hand moved on around and onto a breast, cupping and kneading it, also through her dress. "Robert, please," she murmured, looking all around her, still remembering Mr. Andrews and his evil manipulations of his own body.

"If I remember correctly, your breast was as smooth as this velvet fabric," he whispered further into her ear, sending shivers of pleasure down her spine. But only moments ago, hadn't she even been afraid of him? Why could he touch her and make her forget so quickly?

"Come on, sweet thing," he quickly added, growing more bold with his fingers. "Open the door and let me join you. I'll show you a good time. Much better than what you've just left behind."

Hardly able to control her heartbeats, Jennifer thrust her key into its lock and turned it, eager to rush into the room to put the door between Robert and the feelings he was able to awaken in her. She had meant to capture his full attention, lure him into a lover's trap, then leave him to ache after her. But his advances were forceful, making her head swim with a hungry desire.

She pushed the door open and swung around to close it, but he stepped on inside the room and had her swept into his arms before she could even catch her breath. Regaining partial senses, she began to push at him, moving her lips from his, gasping for air. "Robert, please. You mustn't. Please leave," she said, panting. She was quite aware of her racing pulse and the dizziness she truly now felt . . . but a dizziness created by his lingering kiss and wandering hands. She ached to have his lips possess the pulsating nipples of her breasts and needed him to quell the throbbing of her love mound, which had swollen from her need for released passion.

Oh, Nicholas, she thought to herself. *Where are you now? What am I to do . . . and possibly only moments away? I am a woman . . . a woman with needs . . . with desires of the flesh. Robert is here. You are . . . not . . .*

"I will not leave, Priscilla," Robert said darkly, slamming the door shut behind them. Jennifer stood trembling as she heard the bolt lock crash in place. Then she waited, watching for him in the dark, when he struck a match and lit her kerosene lamp. "And I want to see you. All of you, my sweet thing," he purred, as he turned the wick of the lamp up to make a brighter light fill the room.

Jennifer stepped back away from him, seeing the light flicker of gold onto the darkness of his face. His eyes were even darker than usual. . . filled with passion, and his face was masked with desire as he slowly began to remove his clothing. "If you don't remove your dress, I shall do it for you," he said thickly, already undressed now to the waist. Jennifer's eyes lowered as he began to unbutton the front of his breeches, making room now for his throbbing sex to be set free before him. "As you see, I am more than ready," he added further, caressing himself with one hand, while the other busied itself at removing the rest of his clothes.

"Robert, I cannot let this happen," Jennifer said, swinging around to put her back to him. She thrust a knuckle between her teeth, so wanting to control this moment . . . to be able to turn him away . . . to laugh at his member thrusting so pointedly in front of himself. But it was this part of his anatomy that had completed the job of unnerving her . . . causing the wicked feelings and desires to erase all else from her mind again.

Her flesh burned where his hands now were touching her and she let out a whimper as he tore her dress from her in one fast movement of those roaming, eager hands. "You no longer have any say in the matter," he hissed, pulling her roughly by the wrist to shove her onto the bed.

She began to sob frantically, now realizing that what she had been feeling wasn't going to be fulfilled in the same gentle manner as with Nicholas—but by sheer, brutal force, making her fright return in hot, flashing waves of dread.

While she tried to fight him back, he continued to disrobe her until she lay sprawled and naked beneath him. His dark, smoldering eyes raked over her, raping her even before he touched her in her most private part of her body.

"The more you squirm, the more I'll enjoy it, sweet thing," he snarled, then sought her mouth with his with quick urgent hunger. When his hand moved downward and began to penetrate her, Jennifer's tears streamed down her face, while a low moan surfaced from somewhere inside her. She arched her body upward from animal instinct, her desire having returned. It was flaming, spreading, burning her insides . . . like a raging fire, even as she began to murmur, over and over again, "I hate you, Robert Harbison. Oh, how I hate you."

But his kiss continued to burn her lips, even more passionately than before, making her realize that she was fast forgetting how much she *did* despise this man . . . this rogue . . . who had consorted with her father's wife . . . .

"Oh, please leave me be," she pleaded once more, but it was much too late, as he entered her in crushing thrusts, over and over again, making their bodies fuse into one rising crescendo of climaxes . . . .

Jennifer turned her head from his as her climax turned into a body filled with more continued angry sobs. "If you knew how much I hated you," she cried, beating her fists against his chest. "You've had your fun. Now go!" She felt defeated. Her body and her mind had betrayed her. Now nothing could ever be the same for her. He had won. She had not.

"I remember only one other woman in my life who could make love as well," Robert said smoothly as he stepped from the bed. "Only one out of the many," he continued, making

Jennifer feel even more dirty and degraded. He made it a habit to possess women. Now he could add her to the list.

"And your eyes? I'd felt I'd seen them before," he went on, and then. "*She* had such blue eyes. . . ."

Jennifer jumped from the bed and began clawing at his body, not wanting him to speak the name Camille to her face. Jennifer knew now that he was seeing Camille in her . . . as everybody had until her hair color change. "I only want you out of here and out of my life," she screamed. "At once. Do you hear me?"

But his only answer was another crushing of his lips against hers . . . silencing all else in the room. Then he jerked from her, glaring. "I'll see you tomorrow . . . Priscilla," he hissed, then continued to dress before rushing from the room.

Half falling, she rushed to the door and hurriedly bolt locked it. She was in a state of shock. How could this all have gotten so out of hand?

She wiped her eyes with the back of her hand. "And does he even know who I am before I have a chance to tell him? Has my vengeance finally been brought to a halt?"

Trembling, she pulled a chemise over her head and went to bed, sobbing anew. . . .

Chapter Fourteen

The day was gray and gloomy, more like Seattle than San Francisco. Jennifer stood alone at her window, gazing at the moving ships on the horizon. To her it seemed that San Francisco Bay was a continuing panorama of movement, with ships both coming and going at all hours of the day and night.

She crossed her arms before her, shivering, wishing to be on one of those ships, to be returning to the tranquility of her Aunt Minnie's comforting embrace.

Had the whole thing really gotten so out of control for her? Had she actually let Robert . . . ?

"I must get out of here," she said, hurrying to the closet to pull her shawl from it. She didn't want to face Robert Harbison, if at all possible, never again. But she couldn't return to Thad's house. Her feelings were running too deep against him. The only thing to do now was to go check on a ship's departure and ready herself to leave, hopefully as early as the next morning . . . which would mean having to leave Nicholas behind.

"Nicholas, I have betrayed you with my body," she said aloud, speaking his name, making pains pierce her heart. "But I'll never love anyone but you. Never."

After pulling her hair back away from her face, to secure it with wooden combs on each side of her head, Jennifer tossed her shawl around her shoulders. She cautiously opened her door and peered outward, checking all around her, making sure neither Mr. Andrews or Robert was anywhere to be seen. The usual day noises of the building met her, but no one could be seen coming or going from any of the doors along the long, narrow hallway.

"I'm sure it is safe now," she whispered, swinging her door hurriedly shut, locking it behind her. She hadn't heard any sounds from Robert's room all morning, which surprised her. Why, she had even expected him to come knocking on her door, asking for more of what she had handed him the night before.

Now? It was all like a nightmare to her . . . one that she didn't wish to repeat. . . .

Silently creeping, she made it past Robert's door, then fled down the staircase, breathing a deep sigh of relief when she reached the bottom step. One quick glance toward the cobblestone street told her that Robert had already left, for the fancy carriage and horse were gone.

She stepped on outside, immediately seeing the elderly man who had been dozing on the sidewalk the night before. He was now leaning against the building with a fresh bottle of wine, sipping from it.

Jennifer smiled weakly toward him and hurried on her way. She didn't have far to go to reach the waterfront. But walking along this awful street would make it seem to be miles upon miles.

The usual damp chill wrapped itself around her, making her shiver even more as she stepped from the sidewalk to cross the street, watching the circling of seagulls, knowing that water was near . . . and where there was water . . . there were ships.

"But not your ships, Uncle Thadeus," she said firmly. "Never again on your ships. Surely there are more ships than yours making trips to Seattle. There just has to be."

Now entering a street that was lined on one side with piers,

Jennifer noticed the increased activity around her. It was as though she had stepped into another world. A world of fun and merriment, but much different than she had found on another street of San Francisco the previous evening. The attractions on the street she now walked along were more family-oriented . . . wholesome. . . .

She hurried along her way, anxious to mingle with the men and women and children who were enjoying the many outdoor vendors and what they were offering to each passer-by for only a few cents.

Many women, attired in simple cotton dresses such as Jennifer's, clung to the hands of small children, creating a picture of happiness and tranquility. The children appeared to be bubbling with contentment . . . some even displaying brightly colored balloons floating above their heads from tied strings that had been attached to their wrists.

Jennifer was reminded of her own childhood . . . the loneliness of being an only child. Balloons and dolls had never been enough to fill the gap in her life.

But not wanting to be reminded of "family" and how hers had been so torn apart by that rake Robert Harbison, she moved onward, looking into each open stall that had been built along the sidewalk for vendors to display their wares.

In one stall, Jennifer could smell the aroma of fish deep frying in lard, and she watched as a young man paid a few cents for a cup of these freshly cooked morsels. In the next stall bright red apples were being offered, reminding Jennifer of the apples for which Seattle was well known.

The next stall displayed row upon row of necklaces that had been made from beautiful seashells, and the next, a unique collection of butterflies. By someone's hand, they had been captured and killed, then pinned to many separate sheets of plywood, and each of these were now offered for sale to anyone who wouldn't feel saddened about the loss of life of such beautiful creatures, as Jennifer now felt.

She hurried on her way, and stopped to watch a juggling act. A juggler stood on one street corner, too young it seemed to be so talented, and when he chose three sharp knives to whirl simultaneously up into the air, Jennifer quickly turned her head away.

A crowd gathering at the far end of the street made Jennifer hurry onward again. She couldn't see what the attraction was, but she could tell that whoever was in the center of this crowd most surely had a way of holding an audience captive.

Being so petite in build, Jennifer was able to maneuver her way quite skillfully through the crowd—then she felt a dizziness sweeping over her when she saw who was standing behind an easel. "Nicholas," she whispered, putting her fingers to her forehead, then felt the breath catch in her throat when she looked further, to see who the model was. Lil was sitting poised on an overturned barrel, attired in a seductive, low-necked dress, with her dark skin glistening and her eyes absorbing the handsome, blue-eyed artist.

Jennifer turned to rush away, then felt the cold grip of a hand on hers. She swung around and found Captain Klein staring down into her face with amusement dancing in the depths of his dark eyes. "So I've found Thad's runaway, eh?" he drawled, tightening his hold even more.

"Let go of me," Jennifer hissed, jerking and squirming. She knew that rats roamed the dark passageways of the waterfront, but she had forgotten about Captain Klein and the she-devil Lil. And how could Lil? Did Lil spend days fornicating with Captain Klein when he was in port . . . and then her nights with Thad? Thinking of that possibility made her jerk even harder, but without success.

"Now what do ye think ye be a doin'? Where do ye think ye be a goin', Missie?" Captain Klein laughed throatily. "Why, Thad's payin' top dollar for Pinkerton's men to find ye. Hell, I might as well get the money meself, mightn' I?"

"You tell Thad about seeing me and I'll tell Thad many things about you," Jennifer said, with a jerk of her head.

"I'm sure Thad's seein' you would make anythin' you'd say 'bout me of less importance."

"You forget, Captain," Jennifer spat angrily. "I saw you

kill a man on my uncle's ship. I saw the filth of my uncle's ship, and I now see that you and Lil are playing a dangerous game with my uncle.''

"Eh?"

"You know what I mean,'' Jennifer said smugly. "I don't understand Thad's fascination with Lil, but fascinated he is. And he wouldn't like knowing that she leaves his bed and immediately goes to yours. It could be a bit unhealthy for you, Captain. Don't you think?''

"You're just like I remember your mother a bein','' Captain Klein grumbled, releasing his hold.

Jennifer's eyes widened as she rubbed her raw wrist. "My . . . mother?'' she whispered. "What . . . about my mother?''

Captain Klein's eyes wavered as he began kneading the whiskers of his now fully developed dark beard. "Jist forget I said that,'' he answered. "A slip of the tongue. That's whut it was. A slip of the tongue.''

"What about my mother?'' Jennifer demanded.

Captain Klein turned to leave, then looked in Jennifer's direction again. "Jist forget I said that,'' he said darkly. "If'n you know what's good for ye.''

Jennifer began to tremble. What *had* he meant? How had he even known her mother? But all was erased from her mind when Nicholas's gaze met hers. She wanted to run to him . . . to throw herself into his arms . . . but instead, seeing Lil rising, smoothing her beige silken dress, she stood still, feeling a sense of futility wash over her.

She began to push her way through the crowd once again, in an effort to escape. Even when Nicholas began to shout her name, she refused to stop. Lil had found her way to Nicholas's canvas . . . and next, it would be to his heart. Jennifer just knew this to be true. Lil used men. And she would find a way to use Nicholas.

"Jennifer. Please wait!'' Nicholas continued to yell.

Jennifer could hear his footsteps drawing nearer. And when she turned to hide between two buildings, he was suddenly there, grabbing her.

"Where have you been these past few days, Jennifer?" he asked, taking her by the shoulders, digging his fingers into her flesh. "I've been searching for you. Everywhere."

She gazed in renewed rapture up into his eyes. He was as she had remembered him to be at the time of their last goodbye—his weather-tanned face, so smooth and clear, and his golden, tousled hair, even more so now from the constant damp breeze from the bay . . . and that steady gaze from eyes almost as blue as her own. . . .

"You've been searching for me, Nicholas?" she asked, fluttering her thick lashes nervously. Oh, if only her heart would stop pounding so. Couldn't he even see it, through the thin cotton of her dress?

"I went to your uncle's house, to inquire about your safety, and he told me you had disappeared," Nicholas said, scowling. "Where in the hell have you been, Jennifer? Don't you know it's not safe for you to live alone?" His eyes traveled over the whole of her. Damn. She was still as beautiful as he had captured in the portrait. But there was something different in her eyes. A lack of luster . . . a lack of determination . . . and something else . . . he could not define it. He wanted so to love her . . . to again plead with her to marry him . . . but that would have to come at the proper time . . . in the perfect setting. . . .

"Nicholas, I told you I had things to do in San Francisco and that they didn't have anything to do with my uncle."

"But, hell, Jennifer. I didn't know you had planned to go running off on your own."

"I'm all right. You can see that I'm all right."

"I'm not so sure about that."

"What do you mean?" she asked softly. Could he tell by looking at her that she had slept with another man? Did such a thing show?

"I don't know what I mean," he grumbled, searching her face, hoping never to lose sight of her again.

"I see you have a new model," she said petulantly, looking at Lil who now stood staring back at Jennifer with her hands on her hips.

Nicholas released his hold and cast his eyes downward. "Only for the moment," he murmured, thrusting his hands in his rear pocket.

"What does that mean, Nicholas?"

"That means that I use several models. All day. Every day."

Jennifer's pulse began to race, hoping that she had been wrong about Lil and Nicholas. "How, Nicholas?"

"That's how I earn my living, darling."

A blush crept upward on Jennifer's face, hearing the familiarity with which he spoke the word "darling." "You paint each day for money?"

"As many portraits as people will pose for . . . and preferably women." He laughed and turned his head away.

"And Lil?"

"She just happened along today."

"Honestly? This is the first time you've seen her since those days on the ship?"

"No lie, Jennifer."

She sighed with relief. "And my portrait, Nicholas? Where is it now?"

His gleamed as he looked back in her direction. "It's where I can gaze upon it when I first wake up each morning," he said thickly. "When I look at the portrait and into the blue of your eyes, I see the desire, and I hunger for you all over again."

"Oh, Nicholas," Jennifer whispered, searching for his hand to touch it. "I've needed you. I *do* need you. I shall always and always desire you."

"Then will you return to my room where we can have some privacy . . . and . . . talk. . . ?"

With a pounding heart, Jennifer looked toward the waiting ships in the harbor. Which should she do? Secure passage on the next ship to Seattle . . . or . . . linger, and be with Nicholas for at least a little while? She didn't believe she was fit to be Nicholas's wife now . . . not since Robert. But she still could take some time to talk with him . . . maybe even encourage him to complete the portrait. There hadn't been that much left of it to do and hadn't it appeared to mean so much to him . . .

as it also did to her . . . since their love had been consummated at the time of its painting?

"Well, Jennifer? Will you return to my room with me? It's only a few footsteps away."

"It . . . is . . . ?" she stammered, realizing that all along he had been so close. . . .

"I needed to get residence close to this community, knowing this would be where I would be painting each day."

"And has it truly been profitable, Nicholas?"

"Enough. You see, it's not only the money. It's the enjoyment of the moment . . . when I add each fresh stroke to the canvas."

"You're such a special person, Nicholas talented . . . so nice. . . ."

He laughed, turning on his heel to look toward his easel that now sat alone on the walk, except for a glaring Lil and a pacing Captain Klein. "I think there are two people who might disagree with you," he said, pulling a rag from his front pocket. "I'll go and clean my brushes and get my easel; then we can leave this place."

Jennifer tiptoed and whispered into his ear. "Aren't you going to finish Lil's portrait?" she asked demurely.

"If she wants, she can return tomorrow."

"She won't like being done this way."

"Who the hell cares?"

Smiling wickedly, Jennifer strolled along beside Nicholas, watching Lil's expression changing from indifference to exasperation as Nicholas explained the delay of the completion of the portrait.

"But I cannot return tomorrow," Lil argued hotly, giving Jennifer a look of utter contempt.

"Then you can pay for an unfinished portrait, ma'am," Nicholas said smoothly, cleaning his brushes one by one.

"Why, I never," Lil hissed, then went to Jennifer and spoke into her face. "And as for you, I don't know where you've been hiding yourself, but I will now inform Thad of your whereabouts."

"I think not, Lil," Captain Klein said, taking her by the arm.

"And why the hell not?" she screamed, jerking from him. "I'd like for Thad to know that his kin is dressed and acting like a waterfront whore . . . just like she did on your ship with this . . . with this . . . farmer boy."

"You'll just keep yore goddamned mouth shut, Lil," Captain Klein grumbled further, pulling some green, crisp bills from his front breeches pocket. He went to Nicholas and thrust the money into Nicholas's tin can of brushes. "I think that'll be enough for the paintin', lad, he added, then grabbed the canvas in one hand and Lil's arm with the other and hurried along, continuing to grumble at Lil who was stumbling, protesting, at his side.

"Ready to go, darling?" Nicholas asked as he tucked the folded easel beneath one arm and carried his paints and brushes in the crook of the other, leaving his hand free to capture hers.

"Yes," she answered, swinging the skirt of her dress around to proudly walk beside him. "I'm ready. And suddenly it's a beautiful day," she laughed, even though a fine mist had begun to fall, making everyone else run for shelter.

"Let's buy up that vendor's fish from him with the money Captain Klein just so generously paid me," Nicholas said, a half-smile playing on his lips. "We shall have a feast of fish, wine, and cheese this day, to celebrate our reunion."

"Oh, yes, let's," Jennifer sighed.

"But we must hurry," Nicholas said, trying to hold his paints next to him away from the damp, falling mist.

"You go stand next to the building. I shall get the fish," Jennifer said, running to the open stall. She watched the relief in the vendor's eyes as she asked for all the fish that he had prepared. If not for her and Nicholas's sudden ravenous appetites, the vendor most surely would have ended his working day without a profit, due to the sudden downpour falling all around them.

"Many thanks to you, ma'am," the fair-skinned young man

said as he handed a box of steaming hot fish toward her. "And please do come back again."

Jennifer giggled. "I'm sure," she said, then rushed back to Nicholas's side.

"It does smell good," he said. "Come. Only a few yards and we'll be at my front doorstep."

"You do like what you're doing, don't you, Nicholas?" Jennifer asked, pulling her shawl up to cover her hair. "You look very happy and fulfilled."

"Happy? Maybe. But fulfilled? No," he said. "Only having you as mine can give me the fulfillment I am in search of."

Hope began to surge through Jennifer . . . thinking maybe Nicholas loved her enough to forgive her for what she had done with Robert. But . . . could she even forgive herself? She had behaved in such an unchristian manner. She had known she had sinned by making love that first time . . . with Nicholas. But what had made it all right in her mind was the fact that she had loved Nicholas. She did *not* love Robert Harbison. She hated him. And yet . . . she had enjoyed what they had shared together.

"Up the stairs, then you shall see my studio," Nicholas said, guiding Jennifer into a building, and on up a steep staircase.

Jennifer looked around her, noticing that the building wasn't much different from the one she had been a part of the last few days. It was just as filthy, with the same noises coming from each of the let rooms. The one difference was the added stairs. Jennifer looked upward and saw a circle of stairs that led onward, to many more floors above them. "And which floor do you live on, Nicholas?" she asked, panting, trying to keep up with the stride of his long legs.

"The very top," he laughed. "I wanted the skylight in my studio. I needed the extra lighting to paint by. You'll like it. You'll see. I even have a balcony all my own. It looks out across the streets and the bay. I spent many evenings there . . . watching . . . dreaming."

"Dreaming?"

"Of you . . . where you might be . . . what you were doing," he said. Then he quickly added, "Mostly, I worried about you. You had been so mysterious about your plans when you talked about them on the ship. It gave me much to think and worry about when I found that you had disappeared from your uncle's house."

"I'm sorry if I have worried you," she said softly, lifting the skirt of her dress to take another added step upward.

"Not only myself, but also your uncle," Nicholas grumbled.

Shadows crossed Jennifer's face. "I don't wish to speak of my uncle," she said stiffly. "Ever again."

Nicholas stopped abruptly, staring downward into her eyes. "Why the hell not?" he asked. "You were so anxious to get to San Francisco to see your uncle. What has happened to change your mind about him?"

Casting her eyes downward, Jennifer turned her head away. "I said I don't wish to speak of my uncle," she murmured, seeing him once again on the bed with Lil . . . and what Lil had been doing to him . . . and then later, seeing him with Lil out in public for all to see. He had disgraced the Brewster name.

"All right. Maybe for now," Nicholas said, moving on upward. "But damn it, Jennifer, you *will* tell me where you've been. You *will* tell. Do you hear?"

A chill surged through her, hearing the determination in his voice. Would she in the end have to tell him to secure his love . . . ? Or should she just leave as planned . . . go to Seattle . . . and forget he existed . . . as she planned to do about her uncle? But, oh, being with him had suddenly made this all the more difficult for her. She did love him so. . . .

She shook herself free from his grasp, then watched as he unlocked a door at the topmost part of this steep staircase.

"My humble abode," he laughed, entering a dimly lit room. "Come on in. Make yourself at home," he said, turning to face her as he emptied his arms of his painting equipment. "We want to have that feast before the cooked fish get too cold."

Entering, Jennifer looked slowly around her as Nicholas lit

several kerosene lamps sitting on the floor in various corners of the room. The room was bare of furniture. There wasn't even a bed. Jennifer could see a clump of blankets spread along one wall and knew that had to be Nicholas's makeshift bed.

There was a yellowed basin at one far corner and a small woodburning heating/cooking stove, but other than that, there was only the floor . . . and . . . an easel standing upright with a portrait perched on it, that had been covered neatly with a white cloth.

Something grabbed at Jennifer's heart; she knew that had to be her portrait. It brought back so many memories of her and Nicholas and the love that they had shared.

Nicholas followed her gaze. He went to the portrait and lifted the cloth from it. "Come look," he said softly. "It's as it was the last day on the ship. I haven't added one more stroke of the brush to it. It wouldn't have been the same as doing it under the spell of my subject."

Jennifer walked toward it, seeing the skylight that angled above her head and the gray light that was diffused through its stained paned glass. She stepped in front of the portrait and felt indeed strange as she saw the blue of her eyes staring back at her. "It's so real," she gasped, never having noticed before. "It's as though I'm looking into a mirror, except for my dress, Nicholas. It's truly a magnificent piece of work."

"So you see why I could never part with it," he said, pulling her into his arms. "It's you. When you're not with me, I have another you. With me at all times."

The lamps flickered all around them, creating an intimate, romantic atmosphere. The same sweet ecstasy swept through Jennifer as always when she was in Nicholas's arms, but she had to pull free. He didn't know what she had done . . . and only the night before.

"Please, Nicholas. Don't," she whispered.

"And why not?" he persisted, pulling her next to him once again. "Darling, it's been so long. Surely you can feel it also? We were meant to be together. Now. Forever."

His lips crushed down against hers, making her heart begin

to thunder wildly, then his kisses became soft, warm, like the lapping of the ocean water upon the sand, making her insides to bubble and turn to an effervescence. But when his fingers crept around to the front of her and began kneading her breast through the sheer cotton material, she pulled free and hurried to the other side of the room.

"Damn it, Jennifer," he spouted, wiping his mouth with the back of his hand. "What's the matter? You act as if I'm poison to the touch. What has happened to cause you to act this way with me?"

Jennifer looked desperately around her in search of a quick excuse. "The fish. It will be cold," she murmured, reaching down inside the box. She looked further around her for some sort of dish to place the fish upon, but found none.

Nicholas gazed toward Jennifer, no longer knowing her. Something had come between them, and he was going to find out what it was if it was the last thing he ever did. Damn. Would she ever cease to be so damn mysterious? From the first he had wondered. And he still did. But on the ship, she had given herself to him so freely. Would she ever again? "Oh, yes," he said quietly. "The feast we had planned. I have some wine and cheese over here in a cupboard above the sink, away from the roaches that seem to be forever climbing through the cracks of the skylight."

"But no dishes, Nicholas?"

"No dishes." He laughed nervously. "I didn't plan to take up housekeeping in this place forever." He urged Jennifer to sit down on the *floor* beside him next to the warm glow of the kerosene lamp. "I had hoped that one day I could buy a cottage on the side of one of San Francisco's hills and take you there as my wife," he quickly added, furrowing a brow as he popped the cork from the wine bottle. He offered her a drink from it. "I don't even have fancy wine glasses in which to serve you, my darling."

"That's all right," she said softly, taking a slight sip from the wine, feeling its warmth surging through her. She needed something to help calm her insides. She knew that she was again disappointing Nicholas, and this made her own heart ache. But she couldn't be like Lil . . . going from one man's bed . . . to another's. The aroma of the fish made her stomach growl from hunger and she accepted a piece and also a small sliver of cheese.

"Now, tell me, Jennifer," Nicholas said, chewing on both cheese and fish. "What have you been doing with yourself since I last saw you? Did you . . . accomplish . . . what you had set out to do?"

Jennifer tensed, seeing that he was trying once again to pry the truth from her. And, truly, what did it even matter? She could tell him all . . . except what had happened between Robert and herself. Couldn't telling even be a relief of sorts? Hadn't Thad already ruined the Brewster name? What harm could it do to confide in Nicholas? Maybe it would make him understand more about why she was being so distant with him. Then after telling, she could slip away and let him find another life . . . without her. She had no other choice but to do it in this way. She wasn't good enough for Nicholas. No. She just wasn't good enough. Not since Robert.

"I failed in my efforts," she said sullenly, taking another sip from the wine bottle. "I truly failed, Nicholas."

He leaned back on one elbow, stretching his feet out before him, studying her. His heartbeats quickened, knowing that he had managed to set her tongue loose. "What did you fail at?" he asked. "Are you really ready to talk about it? Maybe I can help. Yes. Maybe I can help."

"It's too late for anyone's help," she sighed, leaning back also.

"And why do you say that?"

"I'm not sure about telling you, Nicholas," she said demurely. "It's so sad . . . and parts of it are even disgusting."

"Is it to do with your Uncle Thad?"

She grew silent, biting her lower lip. Then she spoke quickly. "No. None of this has to do with my uncle."

"Then what? Why did you leave your uncle's house?"

"I had had it planned all along to leave my uncle's house,"

she answered. "Maybe not that soon . . . but I had planned to make residence in another part of the city."

"But why, Jennifer?"

"To seek my revenge."

"Revenge?" he gasped, sitting upright. Damn. He hadn't expected anything like this. But . . . what *had* he expected? None of Jennifer's actions had made any sense. None. Not even from the very beginning. And wasn't that what had attracted him to her? Hadn't he liked her because she was so different from all other women he had met? Yes. He liked this quality, still, about her . . . and always would.

"For my mother's . . . and father's death," she whispered, brushing her hands through her hair, repositioning the combs on each side. She pulled her shawl from around her shoulders and placed it on the floor beside her. The wine was fast becoming a solace for her once again. Maybe she would turn to drink . . . like her father had done . . . if nothing else could be resolved in her life.

"Your parents? How on earth could you . . . *you* . . . seek revenge for their deaths? And why would the trip to San Francisco be necessary for this revenge?"

"Because this is where Robert . . . Harbison . . . lives," she quickly blurted, surprised that she could speak his name so easily. Oh, how she had a burning hate for him. But, she had failed. Oh, how she had failed.

"Who in the hell is Robert Harbison?"

"He was my . . . mother's . . . lover," she said. "Or . . . he was the man who raped my mother. I don't know. And I guess I shall never know. Like I said, I didn't succeed at what I set out to do. It is too late now . . . and I must return to Seattle . . . to the way of life I am accustomed to."

"You . . . are . . . planning to return . . . to Seattle?"

"Yes. On the next ship that leaves, if that is at all possible."

"But, Jennifer, you must stay here with me."

"No. I cannot. It is impossible."

"Why in hell is that an impossibility? I would look after

you. You wouldn't ever have to even think of a revenge again. I would help to put it all from your mind.''

"It shall never be from my mind. Never. I had planned it for six long years . . . and I failed. I shall never forgive myself for that.''

"What had you planned to do?''

Jennifer's eyes lowered. ''That is the part that I cannot reveal to you,'' she said uneasily. ''It is something that only I can know. Forever and ever, Nicholas.''

Nicholas moved closer to her and pressed his hand in hers. ''Jennifer, whatever it is, it isn't worth ruining your life over,'' he said softly. ''You are young. You are so vital. So alive. Your parents are gone. I won't ask any further about this Robert person . . . but it is time to put all the hate aside . . . and live for your future. Your life with me . . . and the children we will have.''

Jennifer's eyes widened and her stomach felt as though butterflies were fluttering inside. ''Children?'' she gasped. ''Did you say . . . children?''

He ran a finger over the soft curve of her jaw . . . then the straight line of her nose. ''Yes. Children. Don't you think we could have beautiful children together? They would have such blue eyes . . . such straight noses . . . and beautiful lips . . . like yours are,'' he said, leaning forward to touch hers softly with his.

"Oh, Nicholas,'' she said, feeling her head swimming with sensuous desire, even though she wanted so to fight it.

"Let me show you how deeply I do care for you, darling,'' Nicholas said, taking her hand, offering to guide her toward his makeshift bed. ''As before, I will take you gently, as one should with a body as delicate and pure as yours.''

The word ''pure'' shook Jennifer from her daze. She was no longer pure . . . and she could never be again. She freed herself from Nicholas and walked to the door that led to the small outdoor balcony and hurried on out into the salty breeze that was blowing in from the bay.

Shivering from the rainy mist still falling around her, Jennifer hugged herself with her arms, tensing when she heard Nicholas move to her side.

"I cannot understand, Jennifer," he said glumly. "Nor will I question you any further. I see that you are too troubled to enjoy my caresses. What is it I can do then, to make things easier for you?"

Tears burned at the corners of her eyes as she turned to face him. "You can proceed with my portrait, if you wish," she said, so wanting to let him do whatever he pleased with her, but remembering another body next to hers . . . and only so few hours ago. She was not a whore and would not let herself be turned into one.

"My 'Portrait of Desire,' " he sighed, crossing his arms. "But there will be something lacking this time."

"My dress is different?"

"No. Your eyes."

"My eyes?"

"They are different, Jennifer."

"How, Nicholas?"

"I'm afraid much more than the desire has been erased from them."

"You . . . see this . . . when you look into my eyes?"

"Yes, darling. I see so much."

"But, Nicholas. You have already captured my eyes on the canvas. So that shouldn't . . . be a problem."

He laughed deeply. "Yes. You are quite right. There shouldn't be a problem."

"Then . . . shall I go pose for you?"

"Yes, and let's hurry before the sky gets any grayer."

"Where shall I sit?" she asked, moving back into the room.

Nicholas followed behind her and looked around the room, checking the lighting. A twinkle appeared in his eyes as he caught sight of the pile of blankets that was his bed. "For your own comfort, why don't you settle yourself over there?" he said, pointing.

Her gaze followed his. "On your bed?" she whispered.

"You remember how tired you got while posing on the ship?"

"Yes . . . I do."

"Well, then, this time, we'll make you as comfortable as we can manage in the beginning."

"I'm sure you're right," she murmured. She proceeded to straighten her dress around her as she sat down, cross-legged, onto the blankets. She watched as he arranged his paints and brushes around him.

"I wasn't sure if we'd ever be able to finish this," he said, mixing colors to match what he had already applied to the canvas. "I can't even believe that you're truly with me again. I had thought that maybe you had met with . . . uh . . . foul play."

Jennifer's eyes lowered. "But as you can see, I'm here . . . all in one piece," she said, laughing nervously.

"Yes. And now please straighten your back and tilt your chin upward. I'll see if I can succeed at capturing the rest of you as easily as I did before."

With her eyes absorbing his every flick of the wrist, Jennifer's heart raced. It was like before. Her passion for him grew with each stroke of the brush. But she couldn't let him see this in her. She had decided to flee as soon as the portrait was completed.

"Jennifer, there's one thing that *has* to be altered," he growled, placing his brush to rest on the edge of the easel's tray.

"What is it, Nicholas?" she asked, eyes wide. She could tell that he was disturbed as he moved toward her.

"It's your damn dress," he said, scowling, kneading his brow.

She looked downward, touching the thin cotton material. "My dress?" she asked, then looked toward Nicholas once again. "What about my dress?"

"You know what it is," he insisted.

"No. I truly don't know what you are speaking of."

"It's nothing like the dress you wore on the ship."

"Yes. I do know that."

"Then you must know that it . . . well . . . it covers too much of you in front."

A blush rose upward onto Jennifer's face. "Oh, I see," she whispered.

"We must do something about that," he said, reaching to unbutton the first button.

Jennifer's hand went to the button and secured it back in place. "Nicholas, you can think of a way to finish my portrait without unbuttoning my dress," she said coolly.

His lips turned downward into a pout as he persisted to unbutton the dress again. "Darling, how can I paint your cleavage if I . . . uh . . . don't . . . see it before my eyes."

"Oh, Nicholas," Jennifer said petulantly.

"It is true, Jennifer. I'm not telling you a nontruth. I cannot continue with the painting otherwise." He watched her, half amused. He knew that once she shed her dress . . . he would take care of the rest. Yes, it would be so easy . . . and she would desire him again . . . as much as he now desired her. He only hoped that she wouldn't see the erectness of his manhood pushing against the inside of his trousers. God! How he ached for her.

"How many buttons?" she asked, already working with them. She felt she owed it to him to complete the portrait. He had at one time told her that an uncompleted portrait was almost the same as having a part of his heart removed. She wondered even now if he was thinking of Lil's unfinished portrait. . . .

"I would be very happy if you could let the dress be removed to the waist," he answered hurriedly, running the words together.

"Nicholas, are you sure that's really necessary?"

"You will still have your undergarments on, though I'd like to also see you pull those straps away from your shoulders."

"I shall be almost nude," she whispered.

"Darling, I believe I've seen you nude before," he laughed. He took one more step toward her and helped to position the bodice of her dress to rest around her hips, then carefully touched the softness of her skin as he scooted the straps downward.

"Nicholas?" Jennifer said, breathless from his touch.

"Yes?" he asked thickly, smoothing his hand across her shoulder, then lower, to capture a breast to pull it free.

"Nicholas, I do desire you so," she whispered, reaching up to stroke his face, then boldly pulled his lips down to make contact with her breast. "I cannot help myself," she whispered further, feeling the slow moving ache between her thighs. "I need you. I need you now." She felt utterly wicked, but she threw her head back in a guttural moan as his teeth chewed her nipple to a stiff erectness. She freed her other breast and offered it also to him, putting her hands to his hair to pull him even closer to her. The warmth of his breath and tongue set her insides on fire and she thought to protest when his hands worked to free her of the rest of her garments.

"I truly shouldn't," she murmured.

"No more protests, darling," he said, lowering his breeches. When his manhood was set free, he caressed it for a moment, feeling its heat, then placed it between her thighs, searching, but not forgetting to continue to arouse her with his hands, readying her for their moment of gratification together.

His fingers moved over her body, touching, like the artist he was, now on the spot that aroused more lust in her, making her arch upward, meeting each stroke of his fingers, until she lay writhing, softly begging for his entrance.

"I will be gentle, Jennifer," he purred. "I will make it feel as though you're soaring . . . on a cloud . . . and you won't want to move from my side again."

His fingers dug into her hips as he entered her with one downward thrust. And as he began to move inside her all else was lost from his mind. . . .

"Nicholas. Oh, my love, Nicholas," Jennifer moaned, clutching on to him, each thrust inside her causing sensations of warmth to surge through her. She was sliding into a dizziness . . . a noncaring height of near gratification. She was alive . . .

so alive under his touch. It was an ecstasy of such intensity that she felt as though she was being fully consumed.

"I must finish. Now," he panted and surged more fiercely, to then shudder to a stop, as she did along with him.

"My God, Jennifer," he said, still caressing her inner thigh, making her tremble anew. "Don't ever leave me again. I love you so. Don't you know that?"

"And I you, Nicholas," she whispered back, kissing him softly first on the mouth, then on his closed eyes. His lovemaking differed so from Robert's. There was such a tender sweetness in every move that Nicholas made. But with the brief entrance of Robert into her thoughts, Jennifer moved away from Nicholas. Yes, her feelings of love for Nicholas still ran deep . . . but not as deep as her present feelings of shame. She had just done what she had promised herself she wouldn't. By letting Nicholas make love to her so soon after Robert . . . she indeed felt like a woman of loose morals.

Sobbing, she pushed herself upward, covering herself quickly by pulling her undergarments on to hide her nudity.

Soon Nicholas was by her side, unashamed himself of his shrunken manhood hanging limply before him. "Jennifer, why in the hell are you crying?" he asked softly. His eyes traveled over her. "Did I hurt you in some way? God, darling. I tried to be so gentle."

His soft-spoken words made Jennifer cry even harder. Her whole body shook as her eyes searched around the room for her shed, crumpled dress. But Nicholas wasn't going to give up that easily. He grabbed her by the shoulders and shook her slightly.

"Jennifer! Now damn it, get control of yourself," he ordered.

"I must leave. Now," she sobbed.

"Leave? Why?"

"I can't explain. I just must."

Nicholas threw his hands up into the air with exasperation. "Okay. If you must. Leave," he shouted, then bent to pull his trousers on. "I guess I'll never be able to understand you. Here we just made love . . . and it was beautiful . . . and you're ready to disappear on me once again. But I hope you get damned soaked to the bone if you do go.''

Jennifer wiped her eyes with the back of her hand. ''What do you mean, Nicholas?''

''The rain. Don't you see and hear the rain against the sky-light?''

''Oh, no,'' she moaned. It was raining in torrents once again. And the sky had blackened so, it appeared to be night.

Nicholas stood with his hands deep inside his front breeches pockets. ''Well? Hurry up. Get your dress on and leave. What are you waiting for?'' he said stubbornly.

''But, it *is* raining so,'' Jennifer said quietly. She knew that to leave now meant to freeze in the fast-falling rain . . . or to seek shelter in the darkened hallway of another building along the waterfront. She didn't wish to do either.

''That shouldn't make a damn bit of difference to you,'' he argued. ''It seems you have a need to always run from me. Am I so terrible a lover? Aren't I as skilled in lovemaking as I am in painting?''

His words were like arrows piercing Jennifer's heart. She rushed to him and threw her arms around his neck. ''I'm so sorry, Nicholas,'' she said, leaning her head against his chest. She could hear his heart pounding forcefully against his chest, echoing upward into her ear. It seemed to match her own racing heartbeats.

''And why are you sorry?'' he asked, sighing into the thick-ness of her dark hair. He stopped and pushed her away from him, pulling a long strand of her hair upward, studying it carefully. ''Your hair. The roots are . . . quite . . . blonde. . . .'' he said in dismay.

Feeling a blush rising, Jennifer pulled the hair from him. ''So you have discovered one of my secrets,'' she said demurely.

''Why would you feel the need to color your hair?''

''It was quite necessary . . . to carry out . . . my revenge.''

''But why, Jennifer? Only harlots use hair dye.''

A shudder passed through Jennifer. ''Nicholas,'' she gasped throatily. ''Please don't say such a thing.''

"It's true," he demanded, glaring. "Why in the hell did you do this, Jennifer? You must tell me."

She cast her eyes downward. "My mother's hair and mine were the same . . . golden . . . and I did not want to resemble my mother in this way when I came to San Francisco."

"God, Jennifer," Nicholas blurted. "You would be even more beautiful with your natural hair coloring. And why would it be so important to not look like your mother? Who in San Francisco besides your Uncle Thadeus even knew of your mother?"

"As I told you before . . . Robert Harbison," she said quietly.

Nicholas slapped his hand against his forehead. "Jesus. Now I'm beginning to see it all. Robert Harbison and your . . . mother . . . and you. . . ?"

Jennifer began to weep again. "No, Nicholas. Don't think any further about it. Please forget all of this I have told you," she pleaded.

He went to her and grasped onto her shoulders. "I need to know, Jennifer," he said darkly. "Did you and . . . this . . . Robert Harbison . . . ?" He watched her closely for a reply, then quickly added, "Tell me what I am thinking is wrong. You didn't plan the revenge I think you did . . . did . . . you. . . ?"

The web of lies continued to entangle Jennifer, so she didn't feel as though one more would hurt, especially if it meant keeping Nicholas's respect. Again with downcast eyes, she murmured, "I told you that I . . . had . . . failed."

He shook her slightly, causing her eyes to move quickly upward. "Does this mean . . . then . . . that he did not touch you in any way?"

Seeing the trust in the depths of Nicholas's blue eyes made Jennifer's burn with the need to weep even more openly. But instead, she swallowed hard and answered. "No. He did not, Nicholas," she stammered. *Oh, Father, forgive me,* she thought to herself. My *life has become one lie after another . . . and I continue to sin. But it has all been for my mother . . . and you. . . .*

"Oh, Jennifer," Nicholas crooned, wrapping his arms around her. "My dear, sweet Jennifer. Life has been cruel to you. I will make it all right. You'll see."

"And my hair . . . you don't mind that I . . . ?"

"The color will grow out," he said, laughing softly. "But there's one problem," he added, holding her at arm's length.

"What's that, Nicholas?"

"Your portrait. It seems it isn't a portrait of your true self."

"You mean because of my hair?"

"Yes."

"Then, what shall you do?"

"Leave it as it is," he said determinedly. "This portrait reflects your beauty . . . be it dark or light hair. And I could never do anything to erase those beautiful days and nights on the ship with you. When we look at this portrait in the future . . . when we are old and gray . . . we can just laugh about it . . . and even at why you felt you had to do such a thing as add dye to your long, beautiful locks of hair."

"When we are old and gray?" she whispered.

"I'm demanding that you marry me, Jennifer," he said sternly. "Tomorrow. Yes. Even tomorrow. We shall return to Seattle, if you wish . . . or we shall buy us that small cottage on the hillside after I paint a few more portraits. And don't try to say no. I won't hear of it."

"No. I won't argue with you," she said quietly. "I won't argue with you any longer. About anything," she quickly added, knowing that before morning she would be gone from him. She couldn't marry him, knowing that she had deceived him . . . and in the worst way possible. With another man.

Nicholas's eyes lit up. "Then we can be married? Tomorrow?" he shouted.

"If you wish," she answered, feeling a blush rising, hating to lie to him . . . over and over again. He was so dear . . . so sweet . . . so kind. She would never find another Nicholas.

"If it wasn't raining so hard, I would hunt up a preacher

even now," he shouted further, dancing around the room. He spied the portrait and then looked at Jennifer. "But until then, darling, shall we proceed? We have much left to be done before setting up a household. When the child is on the way . . . I want to be able to wait on you hand and foot . . . have only you to cater to. . . ."

Jennifer crept to the makeshift bed, seeing the impression they had made only moments ago, wondering now . . . could they have even already made a baby? Why hadn't she thought of such a possibility? Then terror grabbed at her heart. She thought desperately to herself that if getting with child was so easy, she could just as easily have gotten pregnant by Robert! She clutched at her throat. Hadn't her mother . . . gotten with child . . . by Robert?

Nicholas rushed to her and slumped down to her side. "God, Jennifer," he said hurriedly. "Is something the matter? You look quite ill. Has all this been a bit too much for you?"

She blinked back tears. "No, Nicholas," she said, forcing a smile and laugh. "I'm just . . . filled with happiness. That's all."

"You had me worried for a minute there," he laughed nervously, then embraced her again.

"I'm sorry," she murmured. "It seems I'm more trouble than I'm worth, Nicholas."

"Never, darling. Never," he said, then ran his hand inside her undergarment and over the flesh of her breasts. He could feel the trembling of her body as he continued to explore. "But do you know something?" he quickly added.

"What, Nicholas?" she said, closing her eyes as his lips brushed past a now exposed nipple.

"We can work on the portrait a bit later, don't you think?"

"But the light will be gone."

"I have many lamps that could be sufficient."

"But. . . ." she began to say, but was stopped by the tender, warm wetness of his lips. Suddenly he seemed to be all hands as he so expertly removed her clothes once again. Jennifer was able to forget her flight that soon would take place; she was able to forget the child that might already be forming inside her. . . . All she was aware of was his nudity moving against her . . . working . . . thrusting . . . until a gush of warmth filled not only her womb . . . but also her mind. . . .

Chapter Fifteen

Running breathlessly, Jennifer watched all around her for any sudden movements in the dark. She had waited until Nicholas had fallen into a sound sleep, then had crept from his room . . . leaving her heart with him.

The rain had stopped and all lay in shining wetness around her, emitting the fresh fragrance of after rain. Front Street seemed washed clean of all debris. But Jennifer knew that nothing could wash clean the minds of all evil men who might be lurking in the alleyways waiting to grab and attack her.

Trembling from the cold of the night and such terrible thoughts of doom, she hurried onward, and was glad to see the doorway of her building free of anyone or anything, so that she could flee inside to possible safety. A foghorn echoing from the bay startled her for a brief moment; then she found herself dashing up the stairs with key poised.

When she reached the top of the stairs, she stopped momentarily to listen. She looked toward Robert Harbison's closed door. Hatred surged through her. She hadn't wanted to return to this building. But where else could she have gone? She hadn't yet had the chance to go check on passage to Seattle. Nicholas had stood in the way of that.

"Oh, Nicholas, I already miss you," she whispered, feeling a choking sensation in her throat. "But I had to leave you. I had no other choice." Then she rushed on to her door. She stopped suddenly, alarmed to find the door already ajar. Fear grabbed at her heart. She could remember locking the door earlier in the day. She knew that she had. She would never have been so careless as to have left it open for Robert Harbison . . . or maybe even Mr. Andrews. Her eyes widened, swinging around to stare toward Mr. Andrew's door. Did he have another key? Was he the one who had opened the door . . . possibly? She swung back around, afraid to enter. Mr. Andrews might even be in there, waiting to attack her.

Backing slowly away, she stopped short when her door swung open more widely, revealing Robert Harbison and his look of utter contempt.

"Ah, I see you've returned, Jennifer," he said smoothly.

"Did . . . you call me . . . ?" she gasped, putting her hands to her throat.

"Jennifer *is* your name, isn't it, sweet thing?" he purred evilly. He moved toward her in formal evening attire, slapping white gloves against the palm of his hand. "But do you like Priscilla better? Is that why you told me your name was Priscilla? Come on, sweet thing. Tell me the truth. Why the little game? Huh?"

Jennifer continued to back away from him, trembling anew. "How did . . . you find out?" she gasped further, then stopped when she found herself leaning against Mr. Andrews's door. She quickly moved away, as though she had been shot. She was caught in the middle, between two evil men. Mr. Andrews and Robert Harbison. And who else in the building might even rescue her? Tears blurred her eyes as she began to inch her way toward the staircase. But Robert stepped in her way.

"Don't try it," he said darkly. "You just move on in the direction of your room, Jennifer. I think we will be able to talk more freely there."

Picking the skirt of her dress up into her arms, Jennifer moved slowly toward the door, watching all around her, hoping someone . . . anyone . . . besides Mr. Andrews might open their door to see her being threatened. But no one did. She was alone. She had just left the only person in the whole world, besides her Aunt Minnie, who cared anything about her. She knew that her uncle didn't truly care . . . or else why had he let himself be so degraded by the likes of Lil? Thad knew how important it was to keep the family name respectable . . . and how she would feel about his woman Lil. Yet he had flaunted Lil right in front of her.

"That's it," Robert said, moving next to Jennifer. "Let's just shut the door and be cozy. Doesn't that sound nice, Jennifer? Just the two of us? Isn't that what you came to San Francisco for? To search me out . . . just to be with me?"

"No. You are wrong," she stammered. "I just. . . ."

He laughed sarcastically. "You just what?" he mimicked. "You just dyed your hair?" he added, grabbing her by the hair, yanking it roughly, making her neck snap. "Didn't like it to be the color of Camille's? Wasn't good enough, huh? Or was that a part of this little game of yours?"

"Robert, how . . . did you . . . ?"

"I have my ways, sweet thing," he said, shoving her roughly away from him. "Thadeus Brewster has his Pinkerton men . . . and I have my own private ways."

"Then . . . you do know . . . about my uncle. . . ?"

"Your uncle . . . your mother . . . your father," he shouted. "The whole damn mess of Brewsters. I hate them all. When your mother told me about the baby . . . I laughed in her face. I had finally gotten my own little revenge on the Brewsters. After long last . . . but I had taken care of it in my own way."

"But why . . . how . . . ?"

"After seeing your reaction those two times you saw Thadeus Brewster—at People's and then at his Kinetscope Show, I began to put two and two together."

"How . . . could you . . . ?"

"Sweet thing, I don't think you look in the mirror very often.

You and Camille? You could have been twins instead of mother and daughter. I noticed your eyes that very first night, but didn't really know until I wired the church in Seattle.''

"You did what . . . ?''

"I wired the minister, asking about your whereabouts. When he told me that you had left for San Francisco . . . I knew I had found me another Brewster to manipulate.''

"But, Robert, I don't understand. I don't know what you are speaking of,'' she whispered, backing up against the bed, suddenly remembering the gun.

"You'd like to know, huh?'' he said, moving along with her to talk into her face. "And you'd even like to know why I blackmailed Thadeus Brewster all those years ago? How I came into so much money that I was able to open my Roberto's? You'd like to know all of that? Huh?''

"You . . . blackmailed . . . Thad . . . ?''

"Yes. Thad. Uncle Thadeus,'' he mocked again. "Your most respectable Uncle Thadeus who can't bed a woman now except for whores like Lil. And the one time he did bed a white, sweet thing, he got her with child. Yes. He got her with child . . . and that child's name? Do you want to hear the child's name?''

Jennifer felt a lightheadedness sweeping over her. All of this was a bit too much for her. She hadn't ever expected things to be so complicated with Robert. She had never expected *him* to reveal truths to *her*. She had wanted to reveal truths to *him*. To hurt him. Make the truth cut like a knife thrust into his heart. But instead . . . he was doing it to her. "What child are you speaking of?'' she whispered. "My uncle . . . never fathered . . . a child.''

Robert threw his head back and roared with laughter, then grew silent again as his dark eyes burned through Jennifer. "No child? My dear, *you* . . . are . . . that child,'' he blurted, watching with mocking eyes as Jennifer felt her knees slowly crumbling beneath her. But Robert wouldn't let her fall. He grabbed her and held her, laughing beneath his breath.

Jennifer's color drained from her face as she pushed at Rob-

ert, screaming, and yelling. "No. You are wrong. Uncle Thad
. . . is only that. My uncle!" she continued to yell.

"Wrong . . . wrong . . . wrong," he said flatly. "You, my
sweet thing, are Thadeus Brewster's daughter. Your father?"
Robert roared with laughter once again. "I mean the man you
thought was your father? He was so impotent, he couldn't even
get it up to get it into your mother. It took Thadeus Brewster
to satisfy your mother. Then? Later? Many others . . . and then
myself."

Jennifer tasted bitterness rising upward into her throat. She
rushed to the basin and hung her head while retching, feeling
numb, completely numb, from all that had been revealed to
her. But none of it could be true. None of it! She knew that
Robert Harbison had to be making it up. Not her mother . . .
and not her father . . . and not her Uncle Thad. *No! Please,
God,* she silently prayed. *Tell me it's all lies.* She tensed when
she felt Robert's hands on her arm.

"Weak just like all other Brewsters, aren't you?" he snarled.
"Can't take the truth without puking up your guts. Just like
Thad did when I told him that I knew about Camille . . . and
that I would tell all about it in the next morning's newspaper
if he wouldn't give me a sizable sum of money."

Jennifer wiped at her mouth, then swung around, glaring.
"You're evil. Vile. Filth," she screamed, slapping at his face.
Then she grew more frightened than angry as his eyes flashed
back at her and he raised a hand and slapped her until her ears
began to ring. "Please. Please stop," she pleaded, feeling tears
rolling down her face and into her mouth as he continued with
his assault. Then when she found herself falling, she grabbed
for the bed and reached beneath the mattress, but came to her
senses when she found the gun was gone.

"No need to search any further, Jennifer," Robert snarled.
"I think this is what you are looking for. Am I right?"

With a throbbing head and lip, Jennifer turned her face to
see her own gun pointed in her direction. She flinched as he
pulled the trigger, then went limp when he began to roar with
laughter again. He had removed the bullets. . . .

"Thought I'd give you a little scare, sweet thing," he said, tossing the gun onto the bed. "I found it while waiting for you. You see, the bed is the best place to hide things. Or have you forgotten my own little bank account I have started for myself in my bed?"

"I don't understand why you are doing any of this to me," she sobbed, brushing her hair back from her eyes. It was wet with blood from her nose and lips, and from tears that would not stop falling.

"It began a long time ago," he said, going to sit down on a chair, with legs spread wide apart.

"What do you mean . . . a long . . . time ago? Do you mean when I was born . . . ?" She had to regain her composure to possibly get control of this situation . . . if she was to leave this room alive.

"Way before that," he grumbled, lighting a cigarette.

"When then?"

"The day my mother bedded up with your grandfather Brewster," he said smoothly, flicking the burned-out match toward Jennifer.

"What . . . ?" she gasped further, suddenly seeing the name Brewster not meaning anything but evil.

"I'm also your uncle, sweet thing," he said, smirking. "Uncle Robert. Do you like the sound of that? And do you like the fact that you were screwed by your own uncle? I enjoyed it . . . and might even do it again before the night's out. Yes. I might enjoy your squirming beneath me. Could be fun. Yes. Could be fun."

Jennifer covered her face with her hands, envisioning the grandfather she had only met once . . . but how gentle and kind he had appeared. And her grandmother? So delicate and fragile. "Oh, God," she murmured. "What else shall I be told that will shatter my dreams and hopes . . . ?"

"Knowing is ugly, isn't it?" he said, puffing on his cigarette, obviously enjoying it all as far as Jennifer could tell.

She was in a state of shock. Her father wasn't her father . . . her uncle wasn't her uncle . . . she had had sex with Robert, who was in truth her uncle. And her mother? She had been a cheap . . . tramp. All those years. Oh, all those years? Had Aunt Minnie known . . . ? Had her . . . father . . . ? She swallowed hard and focused her thoughts on the present dilemma she found herself in.

"Who was . . . your . . . mother?" she quickly asked, again trying to regain her composure, to make idle conversation, while her mind was working with escape.

"She was a harlot. Lived in the room where I now live. Yes, she was a first-class harlot. But when your grandfather came along, she gave up all men but him. And then, two years later . . . I came along."

"It is a lie," Jennifer stormed. "You seem to forget the filth of this building. My grandfather wouldn't have even entered such a place. Not even for a woman."

"The age of this building? Don't you forget? It was a first-class building forty-nine years ago. In those days, only the best of people let rooms here. My mother was among that category until she found she was pregnant. Then your grandfather turned her out to pasture, so to speak . . . but kept paying her room rent . . . only forcing her to be silent by doing so . . . and even paying my way to school when I grew older. Yes. My mother was kept, in the best of fashion, until . . . she was cut by a sailor one night."

"Cut . . . ?"

"Sliced all to pieces after he was done with her. Down on the waterfront . . . in a dive . . . a crib . . . that she kept on the side, away from here. I didn't even know what a crib was . . . until my mother was found dead in one."

"What . . . is a . . . crib?"

"You are as naive as I thought," he laughed, coughing into his fist. "It seems my father's money didn't quench my mother's thirst for sex. And she couldn't flaunt it in front of me, so she established herself in a crib. And, sweet thing, a crib is where you should be. You're so good at screwing. It's where harlots take their men and push their wares. Their pussies. Yeah. You would be good at that."

Jennifer felt the nausea rising again. She swallowed hard, then whispered, "Please. Just leave me. I beg you. I plan to leave San Francisco. I shan't bother you. Ever again."

Robert laughed more harshly. "Sweet thing, I didn't get this key to your room from old Andrews just to say a farewell to you," he said, reaching into his breeches pocket to pull a key from inside it. He dangled it before him, snickering.

"You secured a key from Mr. Andrews for my room?"

"Only after making a bargain with him."

"What kind . . . of bargain?"

"I told him I'd give him a piece of the action."

Jennifer's pulse beat quickened. "What do you mean?"

"You, sweet thing. You."

"You can't mean that."

"When I get through with you, then I'll let him get a taste of you also."

Jennifer hung her head in her hands. "I didn't know there was anyone on this earth who could be so evil," she cried. The thought of Robert . . . and then the filthy, demented Mr. Andrews touching and fondling her made her want to fill her gun with bullets and kill not only them . . . but also herself.

"Not evil, niece—" he began, but was interrupted by her shoutings.

"Don't call me that," she screamed. "I'm not your niece. I'm not."

"But you are. My own blood relative. And now? My own brother will pay me well to keep my mouth shut about you and your bedding up with your own uncle."

"You would blackmail him . . . twice. . . ?"

"And again if necessary. It's a way of life for me. I told you. I'm working my way up again. I soon will be able to buy back my Roberto's and whatever else I choose."

Jennifer clung to the side of the bed, still trembling. "What do you mean it's a way of life for you? Whom else . . . have you . . . blackmailed?"

"Many," he smirked. "Many."

"You're disgusting."

"Most women wouldn't agree with you."

"Most women . . . ?"

"I can have my pick," he chuckled. "You might say I've become my mother's son."

"What does that mean?" she hissed.

"Mother was kept by men? I'm kept by women," he bragged, lighting another cigarette. "Then after I get them so crazy about me, I start my successful game of blackmail."

"That is why on two different occasions I saw women leaving your room?"

"The richest in town. Or should I say . . . their husbands are."

She shuddered. "How could they come to this place, and then even let you touch them?"

Robert arose and jerked Jennifer up to stand next to him, touching her breasts through her dress. She tried to work herself free, but he held her even tighter. "You loved it when I touched you and made love to you," he said thickly, unbuttoning her dress. "All women love it, because I do it better than anyone else. The rich bitches would go to hell's door, if it meant being with me. You see, most of their husbands just can't get it up like I can."

Jennifer groaned as he reached inside her dress and began stroking a breast.

"Tell me you hate this, Jennifer," he said, pulling her dress from her shoulders, then her undergarments, to expose her breasts. "Tell me you hate my tongue on your breasts. Yes, tell me."

Jennifer cringed as she felt his tongue circling, lingering, sucking. "I hate you. I hate what you've done to my family," she cried, kicking, trying to get free.

"Don't forget, I'm also a part of your family," he said, removing his shirt, then his jacket, and then completely disrobing her. He laughed throatily. "Thad didn't like to be told he had another brother . . . a brother who had also consorted with our other brother's wife. Yeah. Camille got around."

Jennifer finally managed to get free and lunged for him,

clawing and biting. When she felt her teeth sink into the flesh of his shoulder, she then found herself being slung against the wall, stunning her momentarily. Through bleary eyes, she could see him standing there, rubbing his shoulder and looking like the devil himself as his dark eyes smoldered.

"You'll be sorry you did that, niece," he snarled then pulled some ropes from his rear breeches pockets.

Jennifer inched her way up from the floor, forgetting her nudity momentarily, seeing him snapping the ropes as he moved toward her. "What are you going to do?" she stammered, stumbling, as she tried to stay beyond his reach.

"Tomorrow I'll contact Thad about what I know. But tonight? I'm going to let Andrews have his fun. Myself? I'm sick of your face *and* your body."

"You just can't. . . ." Jennifer cried, looking toward the door, knowing that she was only footsteps away. But looking down, seeing her naked flesh again, she knew that escape was impossible. She eyed the gun, wondering where the bullets were . . . but then began to fight again when Robert grabbed her by the wrists.

"Now, now, Jennifer," Robert mocked. "Your mother never struggled. Why, when she heard of my booming business of pleasuring women there in Seattle, she came begging for it."

"Please shut up. Just please shut up," Jennifer whined. She let out a scream when he shoved her roughly across the bed and quickly began to tie her wrists to the bed.

"Spread 'em," he shouted, slapping her thighs.

"No. I shan't" she sobbed.

"I'll do it for you," he growled, spreading her legs widely apart to secure them to the foot of the bed.

"If I *am* your kin, please think about what you're doing to me," she pleaded, wide-eyed. "I beg of you to release me. I would never tell anyone that you did this to me. Thad will more than likely pay you for your silence anyway. Why make *me* suffer so? I'm not to blame for any of your misfortunes."

"All Brewsters are responsible. Remember . . . I'm a Harbison. I was never given my rightful name. I was illegitimate. Do you hear—*illegitimate,"* he said, between clenched teeth.

"I still don't know how you heard about my mother . . . and Thad," she gulped.

"Living here so close to the harbor, one has a chance to see many things," he said, working with her wrists again, tying the final knot. He lit another cigarette and stood calmly over her, raking his eyes over her nudity. "My mother bragged quite often about who my father was and even pointed out my brothers to me when I was quite small. Then later on, many years later, I saw my brother Thad in a carriage with Camille many times. So I mounted a horse one day and followed. That's when I saw them board one of Thad's ships. A Captain Klein I believe it was kept watch while they slipped into the Captain's cabin for some hanky panky. After that, I watched it many times. Then one day when the captain wasn't watching so good, I sneaked past him and got my ears and my eyes filled."

"Captain . . . Klein?" Jennifer whispered, now remembering what Captain Klein had said about her mother. Had that only been the day before? It seemed years ago. "You are despicable," she quickly blurted, squirming until both wrists and ankles were raw.

"I was even one of the first to know of you, sweet thing," he bragged. "I heard Camille confess her pregnancy to Thad. I could have run and told my brother Frank, but I knew that the money could be better had from Thad."

"My father always thought . . . I . . . was his?"

"No. He knew quite well of his inadequacies. I heard Camille laughing and poking fun about it to Thadeus. No. Frank couldn't get it up. Not even for his beautiful wife."

"But he stayed with my mother anyway."

"He was a preacher. He couldn't divorce his wife, for fear of what it would do to his reputation. That's why he finally chose to move north. It seems Camille just couldn't satisfy her sex drive. Frank feared the news of this spreading, and when you grew older, he was afraid you might also find out. As I recall, you were quite a frequent house guest at Thad's house before leaving for Seattle.''

"My uncle . . . my mother. . . .'' she sobbed anew.

"Correction. Your mother . . . and your father, sweet thing,'' he growled, turning to pull his shirt back on. "Now I'll go tell Andrews that you're all his for the night.''

"Please don't,'' Jennifer begged. "He's so . . . filthy . . . so demented. He might do terrible things to me.''

"Do you really think I give a damn?'' he spouted with a toss of the head. "Tomorrow? I'll set you free. Then you can go where you please. But I made a bargain with Andrews and I always keep my side of a bargain.''

Jennifer watched in sheer terror as he left the room and too soon reentered with a shirtless Mr. Andrews at his side.

"There she is. Just as I promised you,'' Robert boasted, lighting another cigarette. "A bit damaged, but not the most important part of her.''

Jennifer cringed when Mr. Andrews began making his way toward her, his cheeks puffy in an awkward grin and his large stomach bouncing with each step he took. But there was something about him that was different this night. He teetered as he walked. And as he leaned down over Jennifer, she coughed as the strong aroma of alcohol circled down across her face.

"Had to tie her down, eh?'' he laughed throatily.

"Won't give you any trouble that way.''

"I likes 'em when they gives me a bit of trouble,'' Mr. Andrews drawled, leaning, as though he might fall, only to jerk himself to an upright position again.

Robert laughed and supported Mr. Andrews. "Do you think you're even able to get it up tonight, Andrews? Seems you've had a bit too much cheap whiskey this evening.''

Mr. Andrews wiped his mouth clumsily with the back of his hand, belching. "I can always get it up, Harbison,'' he said thickly. "But not with an audience. Now you jist leave me and this missus alone. Do you hear?''

"Sure. Go to it,'' Robert said darkly, then slammed the door shut as he left.

"Mr. Andrews, none of this is right," Jennifer said softly. "Please untie me. Robert Harbison is an evil man. But you're not. Surely you're not."

Mr. Andrews slipped his breeches down, then his underpants, snickering, with a hungry look in his bloodshot eyes. "You'll see just what kind of a man I am," he said, teetering once again, as he climbed on the bed beside Jennifer. She cringed when his fingers touched her flesh. "Soft. Yeah. Soft," he said, then began to rub his manhood along the outside of her leg until it became hard.

"Mr. Andrews, I beg of you once more before you do this terrible thing to me," Jennifer cried. But no words seemed to penetrate his ears. He climbed atop her and began to fondle her breasts, then covered her protests with his thick, wet lips.

Jennifer tried to scream, but couldn't, and when he made a fumbling effort to enter her from below, she felt hope for the first time. He *did* appear to be too drunk . . . to succeed in his efforts at raping her.

"Damn it all to hell," he argued with himself, positioning himself once again, panting. But before Jennifer knew what was happening, he had completely relaxed atop her and had fallen into a deep slumber.

"Mr. Andrews," she whispered. "Mr. Andrews?" she whispered again, then with one upward thrust of her body, was able to push him from atop her. He lay beside her, snoring and smacking his lips in his sleep.

"I'm saved for now," she sighed wearily. "But when he awakens . . . what then?"

Chapter Sixteen

Daybreak came with a brilliant orange sunrise, reflecting in fine misty shimmers through the rain-streaked window at Jennifer's side.

She moaned noisily, shivering from the cold of the room and the pain that was fast encompassing her body. Her legs and ankles ached from the strain in which they had been positioned, and contusions of purplish-black were quickly rising to the surface of her usually pale skin. But her wrists no longer throbbed . . . they had grown numb.

Feeling a slight twitch of the nude body next to her, Jennifer cringed. She had lain there all night listening to this man's mouth working and his loud snorings, dreading the moment that he would awaken. So far his drunken stupor had postponed what he had been given free rein to do by Robert Harbison. But Jennifer knew that he wouldn't sleep forever. . . .

Reliving in her thoughts all over again all that had been revealed to her by Robert, her tears began to flow anew. Oh, how she had loved and respected her father . . . a father who in truth had only been her uncle.

She gritted her teeth, wanting to scream out at her dead

mother: "You betrayed us all, Mother!" But instead, she whispered, "You . . . and . . . Uncle Thad . . . the both of you together. You betrayed us all."

Uncle Thad. Now that she knew, so much was falling into place. How he had always kept in close contact with her throughout the years . . . how he had always taken so much time with her as a child. And, oh, the gifts. He had showered her with gifts. But she had always thought that was just the way of uncles.

"But it was the way of a father, wasn't it, Thad?" she whispered further, hating, yet unable to forget the deep love and devotion she had felt for him all these years.

And he had never wed. Had he always loved . . . Camille . . . so much? Was that why he chose still to run with cheap tramps like Lil . . . so he wouldn't have to worry about falling in love and losing again as he had with Camille?

Yes, it *was* all falling into place, though she hated accepting the truth. And yes, she could believe that Robert Harbison was her uncle. This was a piece of the ugly puzzle that fit so well.

Nausea crept up her throat again as she remembered the unnatural attraction she had felt for Robert . . . and what intimacies they had shared together.

"Oh, God," she moaned. "I had sex with my own uncle. I *am* my mother's daughter. . . ." Then her thoughts were interrupted by another moan. Mr. Andrews began to stir beside her, rubbing his brow with his hand. She recoiled, wide-eyed, seeing the shrunken manhood flop around as Mr. Andrews tossed and turned beside her. Would he soon be lying atop her . . . forcing himself on her? She gulped back more tears as he suddenly leaned up on an elbow, looking blankly around him. When he discovered Jennifer, he stumbled from the bed.

"How'd the hell I get here?" he stammered, looking bleary-eyed toward Jennifer. Then his hand went to his throat. "Holy Jesus," he gasped. "That goddamned Robert Harbison. Did he actually . . . tie . . . you. . . ?"

Jennifer swallowed hard, seeing the alarm in his eyes. Maybe. . . . "Yes, Mr. Andrews," she murmured. "Please untie me. Please.'' She lay there, barely breathing, watching him slowly regaining his senses, as he looked down and saw his own nudity.

His eyes shot quickly upward as a hand covered his manhood. ''I didn't. Not while you were tied, did I?'' he stammered further. ''I've done some crazy damn, wild things in my day, but I've never. . . .''

Jennifer quickly reassured him, sighing with relief, knowing that he was not going to take advantage of the situation. ''No, sir. You did not,'' she said. ''But please? Untie me? Quickly? I ache so.''

He hurried beside her and began working with the ropes. ''I'll never touch the stuff again,'' he argued to himself. ''No more of that cheap whiskey. It don't only hit you in the gut, but also in the head.''

Feeling her wrists dangling free, but still numb, Jennifer scooted upward, watching as this short, paunchy man worked desperately with the ropes at her ankles. ''Oh, thank you, sir,'' she sobbed. ''You are so kind to help me.''

His eyes shot around, fear making them twitch. ''I'm not responsible for any of this, Priscilla,'' he mumbled. ''Do you hear? None. When I gave Harbison the key, I thought we were gonna have some innocent fun. Nothin' like this. You won't inform the authorities about me? Huh? I'd be hung. I'd surely be hung.''

Being so relieved to have been set free by this man, Jennifer said, ''No. I will not mention your part in this,'' she said. ''You could have done so much to me that you didn't. Sir, I'm only thankful for that.''

''I'll get Harbison for this,'' he growled, stumbling into his breeches. ''I've seen him do some damn mean, dirty tricks. But this is the lowest.''

Finally able to feel something in her arms and wrists, Jennifer scooted from the bed, quickly wrapping the bedspread around her to hide her own nudity. As she stood, she felt her head reeling, and she didn't mind his touch when Mr. Andrews guided her downward onto a chair.

"Anything I kin get for ya? Huh?" he blurted, his fat jaws bouncing.

"A glass of water please," she whispered, holding her throbbing head in her hands.

"Yeah. Sure. Sure," he mumbled and scooted his bare feet across the wood of the floor. "Damn Harbison. Damn, damn Harbison," he continued to mumble, even after handing Jennifer the glass of water. "Anything else?" he quickly added, glancing toward the door.

Jennifer smiled weakly. "No. Nothing, sir," she responded.

"Then I'll take my leave," he said, inching his way toward the door; then was gone from her sight in a flash, leaving Jennifer to sit alone, stunned, to wonder about the world . . . and its evil, evil people . . . and ways. . . .

"But then there is you, Nicholas," she said, pushing herself up from the chair. "And then there is you," she said again as she went to her bed and lifted the corner of the mattress, smiling awkwardly as she discovered one bullet that Robert had overlooked. "And then there is *you,* Robert Harbison," she said darkly. She grabbed the bullet, then went in search of the gun and found it on the floor where it had fallen when she had been scuffling with Robert, fighting for her freedom.

"One bullet is all I need to rid this earth of the likes of you," she said further, placing the bullet in the chamber, positioning it, so that one pull of the trigger would be all that was required.

Calculating in her mind just how she would do it, she slowly but deliberately dressed, even though to move at all was to move with pain.

Then with her gun hidden in the folds of her dress, Jennifer stepped out into the hallway, but stopped quickly when she heard a rush of feet up the staircase.

"Nicholas," she gasped. "How . . . did . . . ?"

He started to pull her into his arms but stopped short when he saw the contusions of her face. He grabbed her by the shoulders, frowning. "My God, Jennifer," he blurted. "What in the hell happened?"

Casting her eyes downward, she pulled the gun out before her. "Robert. I must . . . shoot Robert," she said, trembling.

Nicholas's gaze lowered, seeing the gun. His face became all shadows as he slowly lowered his hand. "Give me the gun, Jennifer," he said quietly, but firmly. "Jesus Christ. Give me the gun."

Jennifer fluttered her heavy lashes nervously as she quickly lifted her head. "But, Nicholas, I must," she murmured. "It's the only . . . the only way. He's evil. Don't you see that he's . . . evil? Possibly even the devil himself . . . ?"

"Goddamn it," he said darkly. "Yes, I can see plenty. But you must give me the gun. Let *me* take care of Harbison."

"You . . . will . . . ? For me . . . ?" she whispered, feeling the tears wetting her cheeks, then flowing like rivers of salt into her mouth.

"Yes," Nicholas answered, taking the gun gingerly from her grasp. "Your room, Jennifer. We must first get you into your room."

"Then you will go and shoot Robert for me?"

"I'll do what is needed," he said, furrowing his brow. "I will promise you that." He took her by the arm and guided her back into the room and helped her onto a chair. His gaze traveled around the room, taking in its disarray, knowing the disorder was connected to how Jennifer had become so bruised. It was quite evident that Robert had knocked her around. Then his eyes settled on the bed and the ropes that hung slack at all four corners.

He felt nausea rising as he held his face in his hands. "God," he groaned, dropping the gun on the floor. "Oh, my God. My sweet, sweet Jennifer. What has he done to you?" He slouched down onto the floor in front of Jennifer and buried his head in her lap, weeping along with her. When he felt her fingers in his hair, his heartbeats quickened, now realizing she was no longer in the state of shock she so obviously had been only moments ago.

"How did you find me, Nicholas?"

He looked up into the blue of her eyes. Oh, God. And she

was still so beautiful even after the hardships she had just been through. He clasped one of her hands tightly in his. "There's a little boy named Tommy who knows this area like the palm of his hand," he answered. "He ducks in and out of the alleys and buildings like a mouse and knows everyone's business. After I described you, he told me exactly which building and room you lived in."

Jennifer could remember vividly the messenger boy who had delivered the money to Robert that one day. Yes. It had to be the same one. "I'm so glad you came," she sighed, leaning down to kiss him on the forehead. And she was. She had just decided to never let him get away from her again. She would let his wholesomeness rub off onto her and give her faith in the human race again.

"Jennifer, what's happened here?"

"I've learned many things these past twenty-four hours."

"You . . . have . . . ?"

"Robert Harbison . . . is my uncle," she said. "Thad is my father. . . ."

Nicholas shot upward, kneading his brow as he began to pace the floor. "You're losing me, Jennifer," he mumbled. "None of what you say is making sense." He then went to the bed and lifted a rope. "And . . . do you want to . . . tell me about . . . this?"

"Robert tied me there for another man to. . . ." she began but couldn't continue. She put a hand to her mouth, gagging.

"God!" Nicholas shouted. "Oh, my God."

"But it's over now. Please take me away from here, Nicholas," she pleaded, rising to grasp onto his arm. "Before Robert returns. Please let's leave here."

"I first have to flatten the son-of-a-bitch," Nicholas growled. "Did you tell me his room is next to yours?"

"Yes. . . ."

"On which side?"

"But don't you see, Nicholas? I want to leave. I couldn't have truly shot him . . . and I couldn't have let you either. We would have burned in hell. For eternity. I only thought for a moment that I could. But now that you're here, I no longer care about what happens to Robert. All that's important is you. Me *and* you. Together.''

''I can't leave here without confronting that bastard, Jennifer,'' Nicholas insisted.

''For me? Let's just leave.'' She didn't want to reveal her fear of Robert to Nicholas. Robert didn't know anything about Nicholas . . . and in no way did she want them to meet . . . under any circumstance. For wouldn't Robert somehow conjure up a way to also make Nicholas's contented life one of misery?

''That's truly what you want? With all your heart?'' he asked, tilting her chin up to gaze more intently into her eyes.

''Yes . . . yes . . . yes,'' she whispered.

Nicholas looked around the room, at her meager belongings. ''Do you want to take anything with you, Jennifer?'' he asked. ''For once you have left this place, I shan't let you return.''

Jennifer shuddered as her gaze also traveled around the room. ''No. Nothing,'' she said. ''All I now need is you, my love.''

''Then let's go on our way before I change my mind and go bust a door down,'' he said firmly.

''I must get my shawl,'' she said, moving to the closet, stepping over the gun, shuddering once again . . . thinking how close she had come to . . . shooting a man . . . her uncle. Instead of her shawl, she pulled her cape over her shoulders, and rushed from the room with Nicholas, not even stopping to look toward Robert Harbison's closed door.

''Do you feel like walking the distance to my room, darling?'' Nicholas asked, letting her lean into his embrace as they began the walk along Front Street. ''You look so pale and worn out.'' *Except for the darkness of the bruises,* he thought to himself. One day he would murder that son-of-a-bitch.

''It isn't far, Nicholas. I can make it all right,'' she said, but kept watching all around her for any signs of Robert, who might even be out on the streets himself this early in the morning, up to even more evil, perhaps.

''I should have thought to have brought a carriage, but I had no idea I would find . . . well . . . you know,'' he stammered, leading her on past the last of the buildings on Front Street to make a turn onto the street where he lived. Even now, so early in the morning, the vendors were setting up shop. And somewhere along the walk, a lone guitarist was strumming. This had become a familiar sight to Nicholas . . . and also the hat that lay at the musician's feet waiting for coins to be tossed into it. It seemed all artists were willing to get by on a few cents to be able to demonstrate their craft to others who were less fortunate.

"Here we are, darling," he said, opening the door, and helping her on the steepness of the staircase. "Damn. Now I wish my room was at a lower level. Should I even carry you, Jennifer?"

Jennifer laughed softly, leaning against him. "No. I'm not that far gone. What would the other tenants think, if they would see you carrying me up the stairs? They would think you had captured me and were taking me against my wishes. We can't have that, can we?"

"Have I captured you, my love?" he asked, whispering into the thickness of her hair.

"Forever and ever," she said. "Maybe you can help me forget . . . all that I have been told."

"You will tell me all when you are in a better frame of mind?"

"Yes. All of it."

Nicholas swung his door open widely and led her to his makeshift bed. "Now you stretch out while I build a fire in the stove," he suggested. "The sun is bright today, but it seems the temperatures just don't want to cooperate. As soon as we have a fire going, we can pull the blankets over beside the stove and I shall hold you, and comfort you until your mind is made to rest."

"Sounds lovely," she said, moaning as she settled down onto the bed. She watched him hurry around the room, collecting papers to put into the stove. Then after he had some wood and small lumps of coal burning warmly, he helped her with the moving of the blankets.

"The warmth does feel good," she said, sighing.

"Now I must ask something," he said, settling down beside her.

"What? What can I tell you?"

"Your face. It is so bruised. Is also ... your body as bruised?"

"I fear so," she murmured, casting her eyes downward.

"I would like to apply medicine to the abrasions, darling," he said, with added hate rising inside him against Robert Harbison. "We don't want you to be as marred when we stand before the preacher. Do we?"

"The ... preacher ... ?" she gasped.

"Yes. Tomorrow. We will keep that appointment we talked about earlier."

"Nicholas, I do want so to marry you," she said, swallowing hard. "But ... could ... we possibly return to Seattle first? I do so want to leave this horrid place. I would like to be married in my ... father's. ..." She paused, feeling tears burn at the corners of her eyes ... then added quickly. "Yes, my father's church. Don't you think we could do that? Aunt Minnie could be present if we did. She is so dear to me. Please, Nicholas?"

"It does mean that much to you ... to return ... to Seattle?"

"I must. Yes, I must."

"But ... what about your Uncle Thadeus ... ?"

"I wish never to see him again," she blurted, setting her jaw firmly. "He is responsible for much of the unhappiness in the Brewster family."

"You mentioned earlier that he is ... did you say he is ... your true father?"

"Maybe by birthright, but not in my mind. My father ... my *true* father ... is ... dead."

"So you're sure about your feelings about Thad? You don't want to see him ... to talk this thing out with him?"

"No. I just couldn't."

"I won't push you into any more about this just now," he said. "One day when you feel you can talk about it, feel free to do so. I always want to be there. To help you."

"Nicholas, I should have seen earlier that you were all that was important to me. I do now, and shall never forget it. And, soon I will reveal everything about my family. But not now. I just want to forget about it."

"I have some cream that I have carried with me from my parents' farm in Illinois that I used for sunburn. I would like to soothe your body with it. Could I?"

Jennifer's fingers went to the buttons of her dress and lowered the dress and undergarments from around her, no longer ashamed to be nude in front of Nicholas. She stepped from her clothes and lay down on the blankets, relishing in Nicholas's touch as he began to apply a cooling ointment to her aching, raw flesh. Somewhere she could hear the faint strumming of a guitar, and she let it and Nicholas's fingers lull her into a half-sleep, but not deep enough for her not to be able to say, "Tomorrow, Nicholas."

"Tomorrow what?" he asked quietly.

"Can we board a ship tomorrow? I want to go home."

"Yes, darling. Tomorrow."

"Thank you, my sweet . . . Nicholas. . . ."

Chapter Seventeen

The waterfront was a hubbub of activity with ships being loaded on all sides. She watched Nicholas as he organized his few belongings around them on the pier. Among them was the portrait he had yet to finish.

"I'm sorry we can't afford to go back to Seattle in grand style, darling," he said glumly, staring toward the bleak streamer on which he had just secured passage. "This ship might not even be as clean as Captain Klein's ... and you know how dirty *it* was."

"Anything will do. Just as long as we get out of this miserable city," Jennifer said, pulling her shawl higher around her shoulders. She had arrived at San Francisco with trunks filled with the latest of fashion ... and with plans whirling in her head. She was returning empty-handed, but with her mind still awhirl ... only with much different confusions than she had begun with.

But she did have Nicholas. And when they arrived back in Seattle ... wouldn't they be able to share the wealth she had left behind? Nicholas had frowned at the idea, saying that he wanted to make their way in the world ... that he would feel "kept" under any other circumstances.

Jennifer smiled up into his dancing blue eyes. "You will be able to sell your paintings in Seattle. You will see. You know how crowded it is in the streets there now. You might be able to paint so many portraits you will be kept even too busy for your own good."

He leaned closer to her, wrapping his arm around her waist. "I shall never keep too busy to be with you, darling," he said. "Now? Shall we board this rat trap of a ship and find us a cozy corner in which to settle ourselves for the long journey ahead of us?"

A rattling of wheels on the cobblestone street drew Jennifer's attention from Nicholas. She turned and saw a carriage moving rapidly toward the pier. Then her heart skipped a few beats when she saw Lil behind the reins, slapping at the horses fiercely. "Nicholas, there's Lil," she said, stepping to hide behind Nicholas. "I mustn't let her see me. I mustn't. Maybe Pinkerton men have told my uncle that they have seen me here on the waterfront. I don't want to go to him. Please hide me."

"But, Jennifer. Lil knows me also. You know that."

"She doesn't have to know that I am with you. Please don't let her see me."

The carriage drew to a halt at the far end of the pier, then Lil jumped from it and ran toward them, panting, her dark cape flying around her. "You must come, Jennifer," she said, taking a deep breath as she reached around Nicholas to grab Jennifer's hand.

Jennifer moved from behind Nicholas, jerking free of Lil. "You must go and tell Thad that I am going back to Seattle . . . where I truly belong. You just tell him that, Lil," she said stubbornly.

"But, you don't understand, Jennifer," Lil said, wiping her dark brow with a white-gloved hand. "Thad . . . he's been . . . shot," she blurted, choking back a sob.

Jennifer's knees grew weak and her face drained of color. She looked toward Nicholas in desperation, then back to Lil. "What did you say, Lil?" she gasped.

"It's Thad. He's been asking for you, Jennifer," Lil said, grabbing Jennifer's hand once again, pulling her.

"How did he . . . get . . . shot?" Jennifer asked, standing firm and trembling. She was torn between needs. The need to escape and the need to go to the man whom she had always admired and loved. But . . . she now knew so many ugly truths about him. Could she even face him? Should she? But her heart did ache to go to him. . . .

"In a duel," Lil said, wild-eyed. "On a hillside overlooking the city."

"My God. A duel?" Nicholas said darkly. "Who with?" He wrapped his arm around Jennifer's waist, to give her moral support. He could see her eyes . . . how she was fighting her feelings.

"With that son-of-a-bitch Robert Harbison," Lil hissed, with a tilt of the head, flinging her dark, sleek hair around her shoulders.

"Robert Harbison?" Jennifer said weakly, putting her fingers to her throat.

"The swine tried to blackmail Robert again," Lil said. "You'd think once would have been enough for Thad to have reason to kill him. But, Jennifer, he tried again. Only this morning."

"You were . . . there . . . when Robert talked . . . to Thad?" Jennifer murmured.

"Yes. And I know all the details," Lil said with wavering eyes. "Jennifer, I know you hate me and have reason to, but I want you to know that I do love your . . . love your . . . love Thad with all my heart. So we mustn't linger any longer. He asked me to get you before you got on a ship."

"How did you know . . . ?"

"The same as most people on the waterfront find out anything."

"Tommy. Little Tommy," Nicholas said, laughing lightly.

"Yes. Little Tommy. I asked him to help me find you and he laughed and said that it seemed everyone was looking for you," Lil said.

"Yes. I also had to have assistance from that little mite. Only yesterday," Nicholas said. "Now, Jennifer? Do you want to go and see Thad . . . before heading back to Seattle? It's up to you. You have to make the decision. But you must make it quickly because I hear the engines starting on the ship."

Jennifer clutched her cape more closely around her shoulders, looking at the ship, then Nicholas, then Lil, then shook her head yes. "I must see him. I must," she murmured. She lifted the skirt of her dress up into her arms and followed hurriedly beside Lil. "Is he . . . going to . . . die?" she asked breathlessly, as she climbed aboard the carriage. She watched Nicholas climb aboard beside her after securing his belongings behind the seats.

"No. No need to worry about that," Lil answered. "It's a leg wound. Right below the knee. But he is bedded up with a lot of pain and can't be moved."

"Is he . . . at the Brewster House?" Jennifer asked, clinging to the seat of the carriage with one hand and Nicholas's knee with the other.

"Yes. The bullet was removed there at the house. The doctor was very encouraged by the bullet's location. If all goes well, Thad should be up and about in maybe two or three weeks," Lil said, snapping the reins, and guiding the carriage around cable cars and other carriages. People were thick along the streets this time of day and even an occasional horseless carriage chugged by, spitting out its black smoke and steam.

"Jennifer, you still must keep quiet about my relationship with Captain Klein," Lil said, directing the carriage up the steep grade of Nob Hill.

Jennifer glowered at Lil . . . remembering Lil's usual haughtiness and the way she had flaunted her relationship with the captain for her to see. "But, why did you need the captain . . . when you had Thad?" she asked. "You say you love Thad so much, but you also bedded up with Captain Klein. It doesn't make any sense."

"Jennifer, I'm young. Thad is aging. It's as simple as that," Lil said, lifting her chin up in the air as Jennifer studied her closely.

"You mean to say that Thad . . . just can't supply you with what you need?" Jennifer said hotly. "Is that what it is? That's shameful, Lil." She turned her gaze back to the street, absorbing the familiarity of it as the carriage now passed many beautiful Victorian-style houses. Thad's house was very, very close.

"I have my needs," Lil said, defending herself.

Nicholas leaned around Jennifer, clearing his throat nervously. "Not to change the subject," he said. "But you didn't say. What happened to Harbison in the duel?"

"It seems Thad was a much better shot than Robert Harbison," Lil said darkly, with a jerk of the head toward Nicholas.

Jennifer's insides quivered. "Do you mean . . . Robert is . . . dead . . . ?" she murmured. She knew that she should have felt relief, but there was something else. A feeling that brother had slain brother. In a way it was sad. And mainly sad for Robert . . . who had been born under such dreadful, unfortunate circumstances, and had never been able to speak of his true birthright . . . and be granted it.

"Yes. Quite," Lil answered. "Thad is an expert marksman."

"So Harbison is dead, huh?" Nicholas said, grinning crookedly. Now he wouldn't have to return to San Francisco at a later date to perform the ugly chore himself. It had been done for him . . . *and* Jennifer. He hugged Jennifer more tightly around the waist, wondering how she was truly feeling about it now. Surely, sheer pleasure. . . .

Jennifer felt tears welling in her eyes, seeing a blur of the white mansion towering above her as Lil swung the carriage into the narrow drive next to the house. Jennifer turned to Nicholas and clung to him. "I'm not so sure I can go in," she whispered. "I just don't know."

"Sure you can," Nicholas assured, kissing her softly on the tip of the nose. "And maybe it's best this way. If you had returned to Seattle without clearing this thing up with Thad, you wouldn't ever have been able to rest easy about it. Now chin up. I'll be by your side all the while."

"But, Thad now knows . . . that I know. . . ." she blurted feeling desperation rising inside her. How was she going to act toward Thad when confronted face to face with him? She was feeling so many things about him. But above all . . . she had to remember that he had just been wounded . . . and while fighting for her . . . and the Brewsters' honor.

"Yes. He must know that Harbison spilled the beans to you. But after all these years? Think of the relief he must be feeling. Come on, darling. Let's make the move. You will feel much better about it once it is over. You will see," Nicholas encouraged, stepping from the carriage, lifting his arms to assist her.

"He's in his room. Possibly asleep by now," Lil said, swinging her skirts around her as she stepped from the carriage. "The doctor gave him some laudanum . . . for the pain . . . and to help him to get to sleep."

"And you're sure the leg will be all right?" Jennifer asked anxiously, walking beside Lil into the main foyer of the house.

"It will be, if infection doesn't set in," Lil said, removing her gloves and cape and throwing them across the back of a chair.

"Infection?" Jennifer repeated, removing her own cape. "What if infection does set in?"

Lil lit a cigarette and walked to the hearth to stand before a roaring fire. "He could lose a leg," she said darkly.

"God," Nicholas blurted. "A leg?"

"Things look too good, though, for that to happen," Lil tried to reassure her. "The bullet came out very easily and only a small wound had to be tended to. I'm sure he will be all right."

"Nicholas? Will you please go upstairs with me?" Jennifer asked, clinging to his arms.

He leaned down into her face. "Darling, I told you I would. I will never leave your side. Not as long as you want me next to you," he said, pushing her hair back away from her eyes. Yes . . . he could see more and more golden at the roots each day. Ah, how he was anxiously waiting for her true self to be shown to him.

"Then hold on to me tightly, Nicholas," she said, securing his arm around her waist. "I do need you now. Probably more than I will ever need you again. You see . . . in a sense . . . I'm about to meet my true father . . . for the first time.''

''I know. I know,'' he said softly, glancing back toward Lil, who had hidden herself behind the back of a gilt-lined chair. All that could be seen of her was a small spiral of cigarette smoke circling upward. He wasn't sure how he felt about her now. She *did* seem genuinely concerned about Thad.

As Jennifer made her way up the staircase, she could see the library circling above her, and then when she began to walk down the hallway she felt all eyes of the Brewster ancestors following her . . . as though they also now knew of her true father. Then she was at Thad's door trembling anew from fear of that instant when their eyes would meet with the new knowledge between them.

''Shall I?'' Nicholas asked, putting his hand to the doorknob.

''Please,'' she murmured, clearing her throat as the door opened wide. She stepped on inside, seeing the dim lighting of the wall gaslights. All the drapes had been pulled closed, leaving Thad to lie in this semidarkness, which even made one think of death. . . .

Jennifer's eyes traveled to the huge bed at the far end of the room . . . and something clutched at her heart when she saw him lying there, so very, very still.

With her fingers to her throat, she crept toward the bed, watching for any sudden movement on the bed. But now that she was so close, she could see that his eyes were closed and that he was still in a drugged sleep, his head lying sideways, revealing only a portion of the face that had always so resembled Jennifer's own. When he tossed his head around, groaning in his sleep, Jennifer tensed, seeing even more clearly this resemblance . . . in the slant of the eyes. Why hadn't she thought to wonder about that earlier? But she had thought him to be her uncle?

The gaslights reflected onto his face, showing shadowed wrinkles . . . much deeper than the last time she had seen him. But maybe it was from the pain of the moment . . . or was it because he had been worrying so about her since she had disappeared? Wouldn't a true father worry so . . . about a daughter . . . ?

Jennifer quickly looked at Nicholas for reassurance, then crept even closer, until she was so close she could hear Thad's even breathing. "I do believe he is all right," she whispered, moving to pull a corner of a blanket more securely around his shoulders. Her heart palpitated. He looked so helpless. Almost like a small, innocent child.

A sudden love surged through her as she continued to watch and study him. "I couldn't have ever truly hated him, Nicholas," she whispered further. "I have loved him too long . . . to ever hate him." She leaned down and kissed him lightly on the brow, tears running down her cheeks. When one single teardrop settled on Thad's cheek, she wiped it gently away.

"Maybe we should return downstairs until he wakes up," Nicholas said, stepping to her side to take her hand.

"No. I must stay here. I want to be here when he awakens. I want him to see me here waiting for him. I want him to know that I still love him," she said, biting her lower lip as her heart pounded harder with relief. She now knew that everything was going to be all right. She knew he loved her. Now he would know she loved him. Yes, he had done wrong by his brother Frank. But he was only human . . . with manly needs. Just as Jennifer had made her own mistakes these past weeks . . . being human herself . . . with the same lusty needs as the next person. Yes. She had already forgiven him. What had happened . . . had happened twenty-one long years ago. And wouldn't she have never been a part of this earth . . . if it had not been for . . . Thadeus Brewster . . . ?

"Do you want me to leave you alone, darling?" Nicholas asked, squeezing her hand.

"Yes. Please," she said, settling down on a chair beside the bed. She wanted to take Thad's hand but felt it was a bit too soon to do that. First they would have to have a talk.

"I'll be downstairs if you need me," Nicholas said, kissing her on the cheek before he turned and left the room.

Jennifer sighed deeply, arranging the skirt of her dress more comfortably around her. Thad hadn't seen her in a simple cotton dress since she had been small. And would he notice the bruises still partly visible on her face? If so, he would be even happier about having killed Robert.

She sat stiffly erect in the chair, still watching him, wondering how he truly felt about having taken a life ... and not only just any life. It had been the life of a brother.

"But he wasn't truly your brother, Thad," Jennifer whispered, smoothing his blanket. "Brothers love one another from birth. You never ... even ... knew Robert." She choked back a lump in her throat, remembering Thad's other brother, Frank ... and how Thad had deceived him. "But it was my mother, wasn't it, Thad?" she whispered further. "She encouraged it. It wasn't you, was it, Thad?"

A noise behind her made Jennifer turn with a start. Lil had entered the room, carrying a tray. Surprising Jennifer, Lil looked quite domestic with a lace-trimmed apron tied around her middle.

"I've brought you some hot tea, Jennifer," Lil whispered as she sat the tray on a nightstand. "And I've brought a cool cloth to wipe and soothe Thad's brow."

"Why, how thoughtful," Jennifer said, accepting the cup of steaming brew. She was beginning to see just how much Lil *did* think of Thad. She watched as Lil dabbed softly across Thad's brow with a folded cloth.

"I don't believe this will awaken him," Lil further whispered. "The doctor gave him quite a dose of laudanum. He might even sleep without pain until tomorrow." She turned and eyed Jennifer. "Do you wish to see his leg?"

Jennifer shuddered. "No. I don't believe so," she answered, looking at where the legs lay beneath the layer of blankets.

"It's his right leg," Lil said, turning to go to the fireplace. "It really didn't look all that bad. I look for a full recovery." She began to add logs to the fire until an orange flame filled the room with cozy warmth. She removed her apron and smoothed the green silken folds of her dress. "Come and sit

by the fire, Jennifer,'' she encouraged. ''Let's have a talk.''
She arranged herself on a navy blue velveteen settee.

''What's there to speak of?'' Jennifer asked, rising to go
and stand with her back to the fire.

''It's about Thad . . . and . . . you,'' Lil said.

Jennifer tensed inside. She swung around and watched the
flames dancing across the logs. ''What about Thad and
myself?'' she asked, clasping her hands behind her.

''I've known all along that he was your father,'' Lil said,
pulling a cigarette from her dress pocket to light it.

Jennifer turned to face Lil again. ''You've known all along?''
she said. ''Why would Thad tell you?''

''Because he needed desperately to tell someone.''

''But . . . you . . . ?''

''I know that I am a different color than you, Jennifer,'' Lil
snapped. ''But that has never made any difference to Thad.
And the only reason I'm even speaking of this to you now is
to beg you to be kind to Thad. He's carried guilt around for
way too long now. It's time for him to enjoy life . . . and what
rewards it has offered him . . . before it is too late.''

''And, of course, you mean myself as that . . . did you say
. . . reward for him to enjoy?''

''Exactly.''

''But what do you care? What are you going to gain from
this?''

''Time.''

''What's that supposed to mean?''

''Time. More time with Thad. If he sees I've helped in his
efforts to secure your love again, he won't let me go so easily.''

''Oh, I see,'' Jennifer said. ''It's truly only yourself you're
thinking of. Not Thad *or* me.''

Lil flipped her half-smoked cigarette into the fire. ''I know
there is no lasting, secure relationship for me with Thad,'' she
said. ''I'm too young . . . and I'm black. But what I can get
from him now . . . I will gladly accept.'' She looked more
intensely into Jennifer's eyes. ''He is a unique person, Jennifer.
A man you should be proud to call father.''

Jennifer moved quickly across the room, biting her lower lip. "I can never call Thad father, Lil," she said. "I knew another father for so very long. And we had such a special relationship."

Lil moved to her side. "It would make Thad so happy, Jennifer. Can't you . . . at least while you're here?"

"While I'm here?"

"You are planning to stay until Thad is for sure out of danger of infection, aren't you?"

"Why, I never thought. . . ."

"You must."

"But . . . Nicholas . . . ?"

"The house is large."

"He can have a room here then also?"

"I'm sure Thad would approve."

"Does Thad know about Nicholas yet?"

"No. Pinkerton isn't all that they advertise to be," Lil answered. "Now shall I go and tell Carlita to prepare a room for Nicholas and also your room?"

"You might want to ask Nicholas first."

"I already have."

"You have . . . ?"

"Yes. Before bringing your tea."

"And . . . ?"

"He said he'd do whatever you wanted."

Jennifer swung the skirt of her dress around and gazed with a deep inner longing toward Thad. It would be nice to be able to stay for a while . . . yes . . . at least until he was truly well. "Please do ask Carlita to turn my bed down this evening, and I would like a bath drawn. Very soon."

"You've made a wise decision," Lil said, then hurried from the room.

Jennifer still felt torn . . . not knowing if any decision she might reach at this moment could be to her advantage. Thus far, all that she had managed to do had ended in utter chaos. Maybe life was meant to be this way for her . . . one heartache after another.

Sighing, she went back to sit beside Thad's bed. She unbuttoned the two top buttons of her dress and slouched down into the deep softness of the chair, looking around her. She had seen it so many times before . . . this room that was separate from the rest of the house, a room that was all male in design. It was a room of dark blues and grays, with its gray striped wallpapered walls and navy blue velveteen drapes at the window, with matching chairs filling the empty spaces in the room. A great mahogany bedstead was the main piece of furniture on a carpet of plush gray, and an assortment of green climbing plants stood in front of each window.

Jennifer placed an elbow on the arm of the chair and leaned into her hand. "Was that truly so long ago, Thad?" she whispered. "And weren't those the fun . . . the innocent years?" But recalling it all now, Jennifer could remember always having seen a look in Thad's eyes, a longing of sorts, a sadness. Was it because he longed to claim her as his own? Or was it because he no longer had Camille . . . ?"

Camille? Jennifer felt an inner loathing for her mother, even though she was dead. "You always appeared to be the picture of virtue," Jennifer continued to whisper. "Oh, so lovely, and even gentle when you held me in your arms and sang lullabies to me. But all along, your mind was elsewhere. On whomever you were consorting with at the time." Jennifer clenched her free hand into a tight fist onto her lap. "By betraying us all . . . you took from all Brewsters the respect of our name. . . ."

A moan of sorts from the direction of the bed drew Jennifer quickly from her troubled thoughts. She looked toward Thad and saw him licking his parched lips as his head continued to move slowly back and forth on the pillow.

Jennifer scooted to the edge of the chair, watching in a strained silence as Thad's hands began exploring everything around him. When he whispered, "Where the hell am I?", Jennifer lunged from the chair to stand over him. Her heart was thumping wildly when Thad's eyes batted open, then looked upward and settled on her.

"Jennifer? Honey? Is that you?"

Jennifer could tell that he was still heavily sedated by the thickness of his speech and the largeness of the pupils of his pale gray eyes. She swallowed back a lump in her throat and leaned down over him, touching her hand ever so lightly to his forehead. She was glad to find it cool to the touch. No temperature yet . . . which meant no complication of infection. "Yes, Thad. I'm here," she answered, almost choking on her tremulous emotions. She could remember how he had stood over her, when she, at age six, had become so ill with dysentery. She could still see the fear etched across his face and in the depths of his eyes. Oh, how he had always cared. . . .

He licked his lips again and reached for her hand. "Honey . . . did Lillian . . . tell you . . . ?"

Tears welled up in Jennifer's eyes. She leaned even closer. "Shh, Thad," she whispered. "There's no need to talk about it now."

"Then . . . she told you that . . . I . . . ?"

"That you killed Robert Harbison . . . ?" she quickly blurted. "Yes. I know it all." A tear dropped from her eye and settled on his hand that was reaching upward to touch her cheek. She could see tears also brimming his eyes.

"I'm so sorry about . . . this . . . whole damn mess," he stammered. "That damn Harbison—" he started to say further, then stopped, now able to see the discoloration on various angles of her face. *Damn it all to hell,* he thought to himself. *Did that damn Harbison do that to Jennifer?* Harbison had laughed about how Jennifer had tried to get revenge for the Brewster family in her own way . . . and that it had backfired on her. Thad would always wonder, but never be able to ask, if Harbison had forced his way on her . . . sexually.

But no. Surely not. Harbison knew that he was Jennifer's true uncle. No. He wasn't capable of incest. No. Surely not.

"Then you must also be aware of . . . ?" he finally added.

Jennifer leaned into the palm of his hand as he touched her ever so lightly. She relished his touch, now that she had been able to accept all that had been told to her. Being in Thad's presence, now that he was awake, had helped to clear her mind of the doubts that had been assailing her about whether she and Thad could ever possibly have any kind of close relationship again. She now knew that she would always love him dearly . . . no matter about the past.

"Yes," she answered softly, swallowing hard. "I know everything." She couldn't speak the word "father" to him, though, and doubted if she ever could. She had had only one father . . . and she would still respect the title her "father" had chosen to bear . . . even though he was gone from this earth.

Thad turned his eyes from her, closing them. "I've always been such a damn fool," he stammered. "Can you ever forgive me?"

She bit her lower lip. "There's . . . nothing to forgive, Thad," she whispered. "Nothing. Truly nothing at all."

He tried to move, but groaned noisily. "And now? Will I be a cripple also?" he grumbled, reaching down to touch the covered wound.

"Does it hurt much, Thad?" Jennifer crooned, trying to comfort him again by caressing his brow.

"My pride is what's damaged," he grumbled further. "My damn pride. Harbison shouldn't have had time to get a shot fired from his gun. I guess I need more practice."

Chills encompassed Jennifer, seeing how easy it was for Thad to speak of killing another human being . . . and even . . . his brother. It made clear to her the extent of the hate that Thad must have felt. A duel. It was the chosen way out . . . when hate grew to such proportions.

Remembering Robert Harbison, however, Jennifer could understand how easy it was to hate.

"We must forget that that evil man ever existed," she said, walking to stand at a window. She pulled the drapes aside and stared toward the bay. Outside these walls, all seemed well with the world. The sun was reflecting onto the San Francisco Bay water, like many jewels sparkling, and the many ships breaking through this ocean of blue made the jewels seem to shimmer even more.

She hugged herself with her arms, wondering which boat

might be the *Madrona* . . . or maybe even Thad's *Elite*. She had come so close to leaving this all behind. And couldn't she still? Wouldn't she and Nicholas be better off to escape the ugliness of the past? But Jennifer knew that she'd never be able to escape the realities of her life . . . no matter how far she traveled.

"Can you, Jennifer?" Thad asked, causing her to swing around.

Her eyes wavered as she discovered Thad watching her more closely. Had his laudanum worn off so much that he was now remembering the filthiness of Robert's words? Had Robert told Thad . . . everything . . . ?

"Can I what . . . ?" she murmured.

"Forget Harbison."

"And why should I have any problem in doing just that?"

"I see the bruises," he growled. "What the hell did he do to you?"

Jennifer's hands went to her face. She had forgotten. And Lil hadn't mentioned the bruises. Why hadn't she, if they were still so ugly? "Just a part of his own private revenge, Thad," she whispered. "He did hate us all so."

Thad pushed himself up on an elbow and attempted to climb from the bed, only to fall back in a heap, groaning. Jennifer rushed to his side.

"Is there anything I can do for you, Thad?" she asked, wringing her hands. He looked helpless, and she felt even more helpless.

"The damn laudanum has worn off completely," he groaned, clutching at his leg. He could feel the perspiration on his brow and hated being so weak that he could not bear pain . . . and especially in front of Jennifer.

"Shall I get you some more? Did the doctor leave some?"

"What I was given was supposed to knock me out damn and good," he grumbled further. "But, hell, it hasn't worked."

A rush of feet behind Jennifer made her turn with a start.

"My darling," Lil spoke suddenly from behind her. "My

darling Thad. You shouldn't be awake yet. Are you in so much pain you cannot rest?''

Jennifer stood awestruck as Lil continued to baby Thad by fussing so over him, while administering soft kisses to his brow, cheeks and lips. Jennifer now knew why Thad continued to have the young colored woman around. She didn't only treat Thad like a lover . . . but also like a small child who hungered for attention . . . love. . . .

Something grabbed at Jennifer's heart, seeing Thad so humbled by this. Wasn't Lil playing this role well? Didn't she appear to truly care?

"And did Jennifer tell you that you have a house guest?" Lil continued, as she smoothed and tucked the blankets on each side of Thad's bed.

"No," Thad answered. "She didn't." He eyed Jennifer quizzically, making her cast her eyes downward. Damn. Was that a blush? "Who is this house guest, Jennifer?" he quickly added, struggling to lean up on one elbow again.

She fluttered her heavy lashes nervously. "Nicholas. Nicholas Oglesby."

Thad's brows furrowed. "Who the hell is Nicholas Oglesby?"

Lil quickly answered with a flip of her hair, "Jennifer met him on the ship. On her voyage from San Francisco," she said, then stopped when Thad's eyes traveled from Jennifer to her.

"And how the hell do you know so much about it?" he snapped. Even though Lil's skin wasn't white, even though it was a dark brown, he damn well knew that he could see the color paling before his eyes.

Lil went to Jennifer and placed her arm around her waist, smiling weakly. "Jennifer told me all about it, didn't you, Jennifer?" she blurted.

Jennifer felt the palpitation of her heart, knowing that if there ever would be an appropriate moment to reveal to Thad the deceitful, evil ways of Lil, this would be it. And hadn't Jennifer at one time wanted to seek revenge against Lil also? But now she felt differently. It was quite apparent that Thad needed Lil.

And until he showed a change of feelings toward Lil . . . why should Jennifer be the one to interfere?

"Yes. I confided in Lil. Only today, while she was bringing me to you," she said firmly. Lies and more lies. But lies were a part of her now. One day things would be different. Surely they would!

"So you say you met him on the ship? Captain Klein's *Madrona?*"

"Yes. On my voyage from Seattle."

"And is he a . . . young man . . . the same age as yourself?"

"Yes."

"And why do you continue to be with him, if you only met while on your voyage to San Francisco?"

Jennifer cast her eyes downward again, blushing anew. "We've . . . uh . . . grown quite fond of one another."

"How fond?"

Jennifer set her jaw firmly, not liking the sudden rush of questions. "We are to be married," she suddenly blurted, with chin tilted upward, watching Thad's color draining from his face. He sank back down on the pillow and threw an arm up across his eyes.

"Damn it, Lil," he stormed, panting. "Where the hell is that laudanum?" The pain had become quite unbearable. And not only in his leg. He felt a tearing at his heart. He had just found Jennifer . . . he was finally able to claim her as his daughter, maybe even enabling them to do a bit of sharing . . . and now he found out that she'd already found someone else . . . to do this sharing with.

"I'll have to go to the kitchen to get it," Lil said nervously.

"Jesus. What are you waiting for?" he yelled.

"And Thad . . . ?" Lil said softly.

"Yes . . . ?"

"Would you want me to send Nicholas up to your room . . . so you can become acquainted . . . before the added laudanum puts you back to sleep?"

There was a strained silence, then Thad grumbled a shallow, "Yes."

"I will be only a minute," Lil said, swinging around to rush from the room once again.

Jennifer went to Thad's bedside. "Are you truly in much pain, Thad?" she asked, feeling a bit responsible now for having been so abrupt with him.

"Nothing I can't handle," he said, then stared back at her with his pale gray eyes pleading. "You are going to stay a while, aren't you, Jennifer?"

"Why do you ask, Thad?"

"You spoke of marriage. Is it to be soon?"

"When I return to Seattle. So Aunt Minnie can be a part of the special occasion."

"Then you are returning to Seattle?"

"Yes," she answered, lowering her eyes.

"But can't you stay . . . for . . . at least a little while?"

"But there's . . . Nicholas."

"He can stay also."

"You live far from the waterfront, Thad."

Thad pushed himself up on an elbow, frowning. "What the hell difference does that make?" he blurted.

"Nicholas is a painter. If we're staying here . . . he would want to be closer to the people . . . where he could work daily, painting portraits."

"It's so important to him, huh?"

"Yes."

"I could make him a gift of a special mare . . . or he could have a carriage at his disposal at all times."

Jennifer smiled weakly. Thad was trying his hardest to please her. "You will have to speak to Nicholas personally of these things. I do not speak for him."

"And even after we're married?" Nicholas said, laughing as he moved to Jennifer's side.

"Oh, Nicholas," Jennifer said, feeling her pulse beat quickening as she put her arm through his. Would he always cause her heart to act so irresponsibly? "Nicholas Oglesby, I'd like for you to meet my . . . my . . ." she began, but stopped, eyeing Thad questioningly. She knew that the word "uncle" should form so easily on her tongue . . . but that word "father" kept getting in her way.

"Thadeus Brewster," Thad hurriedly added, weakly extending a hand. He wasn't sure how much of this sticky family situation had been told to this young man . . . but Thad could tell that Nicholas was from a good stock. It was there in the set of his jaw and the look of sincerity in his blue eyes. And goddamn . . . this lad had one hell of a strong handshake, which proved many things about his character.

"I hope your wound is quick to heal," Nicholas said, releasing his handshake to thrust his one free hand inside his front breeches pocket.

"Nothing holds a Brewster down for long," Thad said, wiping the perspiration from his brow. He looked quickly toward the door, relieved to see Lil come into the room carrying a glass of liquid.

"I put the laudanum in a glass of orange juice so you couldn't taste its bitterness," she said, hurrying to the bedside.

"Thanks," he said, drinking hurriedly, licking his lips when the glass was empty. "And now a fine Cuban cigar, Lil, and I'll be ready to settle in for the night." He turned to face Nicholas once again. "Hear you're an artist," he said, fitting his hands together before himself.

"Yes, sir."

"What is your specialty?"

"Portraits."

"Portraits, you say?"

"Yes, sir."

"I've been needing my portrait done. For the outside hallway wall. Interested?"

Nicholas glanced quickly down at Jennifer. "I don't know," he said quietly.

She gazed upward at him with her large blue eyes. "Thad wants us to stay a while, Nicholas."

"Oh?"

"You could go by horseback or carriage each day to the waterfront to resume your painting. . . ." she added.

"Or stick around and work on mine," Thad interrupted. "How about it, lad?"

Nicholas leaned into Jennifer's ear. "And when would we work on yours? I thought we could finish it on our voyage back to Seattle."

"We could work on it here also. Maybe . . . evenings . . . ?" she answered hesitantly. She knew how he'd much rather be spending evenings.

"And our marriage plans?" he whispered further.

"It won't hurt to wait a bit longer, Nicholas."

"Well? How about it, lad?" Thad asked, his speech starting to thicken. The laudanum was working quickly, but he still accepted the lighted cigar from Lil. He was feeling an inner peace. He had his daughter with him. He had his Lil . . . and he was entering a state of euphoria from the laudanum. Damn. Why hadn't he tried that drug before? If it could make a person feel so peaceful? Why didn't everyone partake of it? He laughed throatily, then took a deep drag from the cigar.

"Sure. If this is what Jennifer wants. Is it, Jennifer?" Nicholas said.

"For just a little while," she encouraged. "At least until Thad shows a definite full recovery."

Thad laughed loudly again, throwing his head back against the pillow. He was drunk. That's what he was. Good and damn drunk and he hadn't had one drink of whiskey. He smacked his lips and asked, "And what'd you do before you started paintin', lad?"

"I was a farmer. In Illinois."

"A farmer boy? To hell you say. So that's how you put those muscles on you. Working the fields. That's damn good, lad," he said, as his eyes slowly closed.

"We all should leave him alone now," Lil whispered, going to take the cigar from between his lethargic fingers. "I think he's fast entering a world that won't include us. Not for some time, anyway."

"Okay," Jennifer whispered, but she stopped to kiss Thad on his shallow cheek. She giggled when a noisy snore entered her ears. It sounded like the rush of waves on an ocean. "Good night, Thad," she whispered, then strolled arm in arm with Nicholas from the room.

"What now?" Nicholas asked.

"Nicholas, I'm going to take a bath and change into something beautiful and sleek. I feel a bit washed out."

"After all you've been through? I can understand why."

"Nicholas, I'd been through so much in my thoughts before even arriving in San Francisco, it seemed nothing else could have been any worse."

"And now that you've found out?"

"Maybe a part of me always knew."

"Well, I'm glad you're taking it as well as you are," he said. "And your uncle . . . I mean. . . ."

"Yes. My uncle. He will always be an uncle to me," she answered. "And I feel he will be all right. The leg wound is uncomfortable but very small. I'm no longer concerned about it. But . . . I still would like to stay until he's on his feet."

"I agree. I think it looks good for his recovery. He seems a strong enough person."

"Which room is yours, Nicholas?"

He leaned down into her ear. "On the other side of yours. Cozy, huh?"

"Nicholas," she exclaimed, glancing around her to see if anyone had heard.

"Sorry, darling. I didn't mean to shock you. But when I'm near you, hardly anything else is on my mind."

"I have to admit, when I'm near you, my mind wanders a bit also," she said shyly. She put her hand on the doorknob. "I shan't be long, Nicholas."

"I'll be down by the fire, unless you need help," he further teased.

Jennifer fluffed his blond curls with her fingers, then rushed on into her room. She shut the door slowly behind her, turning to see the familiarity of it all. She went and touched the softness of the settee, which appeared to be of even a deeper rose as the flames from the fireplace reflected onto it.

She slipped her shoes off and buried her toes in the plush carpet, feeling so grand to be able to be in this room that was so different from what she had most recently been used to.

And the flowers? Had Thad been so sure that she would return? She cupped a pale pink rose in the bend of her hand. The fragrance of the bouquet of roses filtered upward, making her senses almost reel with delight.

"I could almost decide to stay . . . and be a part of this house, forever, Thad," she whispered, hurrying into the next room where her canopied bed sat waiting in its luxurious softness.

Laughing, she ran to it and jumped on it, rejoicing in its cleanliness. "Not like that bed I was so rudely tied to. And doesn't this room also smell so sweet?" she said, spying another arranged bouquet of roses.

Like a small child, she ran to it and pulled one free to carry with her to keep inhaling it as she opened her closet door. The dresses she had chosen in Seattle still hung there, waiting. "I shall wear this one tonight," she said, pulling free from its hanger a pale blue, low-cut velveteen dress. "And a diamond necklace. Nicholas will see me tonight as he will see me from now on. Yes. Forever and ever, my dear."

She placed the dress across the bed, then hurriedly slipped out of her dingy cotton dress and undergarments. When she entered the bathroom, she found a tub of floating bubbles waiting for her and thought to herself that Carlita knew her job quite well.

Without further hesitation, she stepped into the tub and sank down into the water. "I do feel I've made it through this crisis all right," she whispered, lifting her hair up from her shoulders. "True I have scars that are etched into my brain . . . but I'm strong, and tomorrow can only be better."

Her mind was no longer filled with revenge. Thad's gun . . . not hers . . . had finally set her free.

She closed her eyes as she moved the suds around the nipples of her breasts, making her tingle. "But tonight, Nicholas. In the comforts of *my* room, I will let you teach me further the art of making love. . . ." she thought, no longer letting herself feel guilty, even if she was in the Brewster house. She would always love only Nicholas. She would never need any other man. "I'm in *no* way my mother's daughter," she murmured. "I'm *not.*" She wiped a sudden tear from the corner of her eye.

Chapter Eighteen

"My back is unusually tired this morning, Nicholas," Jennifer sighed, stretching. She pushed herself off the chair and went to the portrait to see how much more there was to do before her posing would come to a halt.

"Just a few finishing touches, Jennifer," Nicholas said, wiping his brush on a cloth. He eyed her questioningly. Her face was drawn and lacked the usual vivacity. "You are quite pale this morning, darling. Are you ill?"

She swung the skirt of her green velveteen dress around to go relax on the settee, not wanting to tell Nicholas of the nausea she had been feeling each morning for the past week. If it persisted, she would have to seek the services of a doctor. She feared that she had contracted a disease, possibly even a parasite, while living under such horrible conditions on Thad's ship, and then in that terrible room.

She furrowed her brow. Had it truly been a full month now since the truths of the Brewster family had been revealed to her . . . since Robert had been killed by Thad . . . since Thad had been wounded by Robert . . . ? "It's Thad," she finally blurted. "I'm just terribly worried about Thad."

Nicholas placed his cleaned brush into the tin can with the many others and walked to the hearth, to rub his hands briskly next to the flames. "I've got to get out of here today, Jennifer," he said. "Thad's about to drive me crazy with his grumblings. I've never painted anyone quite as restless. There's no way to get him to look the same from moment to moment. It's almost an impossibility to continue with his portrait."

Jennifer went to Nicholas's side and placed her arm around his waist, looking up onto his face. His tan had faded. She knew that he longed to be out among the people, be a part of the crowd . . . and soak up the sunshine down on the waterfront. She knew that he was always hungering for the out doors. "I understand, Nicholas," she crooned, reaching up to push a strand of gold curls from his forehead. "You know that Thad has offered you means of transportation. You're free to go. Anytime. But can you wait just a little while this morning? At least until Doc Rose sees Thad?"

"Then you really understand my need to get away? Alone?"

"I've wondered how you've stood it *this* long."

"I kept thinking that maybe it would be the next day that we could board a ship and leave all this behind."

"Has it been so terribly bad staying here?"

He drew her into his arms. "The nights have kept me pacified. Only the nights, darling," he said, kissing her gently on the lips. He reached upward and stroked a breast, needing her even now, but he knew that even taking such liberties even at night had made her a bit uncomfortable, with her uncle—her father— only in the next room. But then Lil made nightly visits to Thad's room . . . which had made Jennifer less tense about participating in such *têtes à tête* herself. "I so long to make you my wife. That is why I eagerly await the day we can leave this house," he added.

"I know," she whispered, clinging, knowing that her heart-beats were a countdown to the day they would be exchanging their wedding vows. "But Thad. He's worsened, you know. The infection just won't leave him. I'm anxious to hear what Doc Rose has to say about it today."

"It'll be all right, darling," Nicholas soothed her, kissing her again. "It takes some people longer to heal. I guess that's how it is with Thad."

The sound of a horse's hoofbeats and the clattering of wheels from a carriage in the drive drew Jennifer and Nicholas apart. Jennifer rushed to the window and looked out, seeing a short, thinning man with a face hidden behind thick, white whiskers. He wore black, and his jacket hung loose and wrinkled, as though he might have slept in it.

Jennifer watched him secure the reins and then pull a gold pocket watch from his vest pocket to study it. He lifted his black bag from the carriage and limped, bowlegged toward the door.

"It's the doctor," she said, hurrying to the door, before the doctor even had a chance to lift the heavy brass knocker. She swung the door open and stepped aside. "Please come in, Doc Rose," she said, smelling an aroma of pipe tobacco follow after him as he walked on into the parlor.

"Damn nice day," he grumbled, checking his watch again. "But no time for dallying. See me to the patient, young missus."

She shut the door and lifted the skirt of her dress up into her arms and rushed toward the staircase, blushing, having seen the doctor staring openly at the deep cleavage of her bosom. She had forgotten about the dress that she normally wore only for posing while in this house.

She hurried on up the stairs and guided the doctor to the closed door that led to Thad's room.

"And how's he been through the night?" Doc Rose asked before entering.

"Restless. Quite restless. The laudanum seems to have lost its effectiveness," she answered quietly.

"Tsk, tsk. Brewster's abused it. Loses its strength to an individual if one exceeds the dosage. Makes one need more and more to kill the pain. Damn bad for a body. That's what it is. Damn bad."

"The infection, doctor. I'm worried about the infection."

"Now, young missus, you go on back to the parlor with that young man of yours and let me worry about the doctorin' end of things."

"All right, sir," she answered "Lil's already in the room, though. She stayed by Thad's bedside all night. The fever just wouldn't let up any."

"Like I said, young missus. Run back to your young man and warm yourself by the fire. You're not lookin' so good yourself."

"I'm fine. Just fine," she said, then clutched on to his arm, her eyes wide in silent pleading. "Please help Thad," she said, then turned and rushed down the hallway, again feeling eyes following her from the portraits on both sides of her. Brewsters. All of them Brewsters. Had they also had so many troubles as this generation continued to have?

Nicholas met her at the foot of the stairs. "Well? What does he have to say?" he asked, offering her his arm around her waist, with renewed worry about her complete paleness.

"He asked me to leave," she murmured, leaning into his embrace, having had another brief nauseous spell that had made her almost reel as she had descended the stairs. "Nicholas, I just don't like the looks of this. I'm afraid. Truly afraid for my uncle . . . for Thad. . . ."

He guided her to the settee in front of the fire and helped to ease her downward onto it. "Well, damn it," he spouted. "I don't like what I'm seeing right here." He fell to a knee in front of her, tilting her chin up so their gazes could meet. "You haven't been truthful with me, have you?"

Her lashes cast shadows over her eyes as she gave him a look of innocence. "I don't know what you're speaking of," she said, straightening her back.

"You. Damn it," he growled, standing thrusting his hands inside his rear pockets. "You know you look as pale as a ghost this morning. Why not tell me the true reason why?"

A rustling of feet into the parlor drew Jennifer to her feet. She turned and put her hands to her throat when she saw Lil standing there, crying openly.

"It's Thad," Lil murmured. "Gangrene has set in. His leg
. . . has to . . . be removed," she added, then rushed from the
room again.

"His . . . leg . . . ? Oh, no. Dear God, no," Jennifer cried,
then saw many faces of Nicholas watching her as she began
to crumple to the floor, clutching at herself, as sharp pains
suddenly began to pierce her lower abdomen. As the pain
worsened, all became as a black curtain before her eyes. . . .

Chapter Nineteen

Awakening in a haze, Jennifer licked at her dried, parched lips. She smelled the fragrance of roses close by and felt the warmth of a hand enfolding hers.

"Jennifer? Jennifer, darling," Nicholas whispered, leaning closer to her face.

"Nicholas? Where . . . am . . . I . . . ?" she stammered, still unable to quite focus on what was around her. With her free hand, she reached around her, and suddenly knew that she was in her bed, in her own room. "Why am I . . . in bed . . . ?" she further stammered, as Nicholas became clearer to her. She could see worry wrinkles at the corner of his mouth and around his eyes. She looked closer. His eyes were an ocean of blue . . . so full of fear . . . and caring . . . scaring Jennifer, making her push herself up on an elbow. But a sharp pain, up inside her, where Nicholas knew how to pleasure her so, made her recoil and slump back down onto the bed.

"Darling, are you in much pain?" Nicholas said, now lifting a dampened cloth to caress her brow.

"I don't understand," she said, now aware of the thickness of her speech. She was trying to remember what had happened prior to this moment, but could only feel a peaceful swimming of the head.

"You've been given a dose of Doc Rose's laudanum," Nicholas said, now wetting her lips with the cloth.

"But . . . why . . . ?"

"You don't remember anything?"

"Nothing," she said, closing her eyes. "I only feel . . . pain. . . ." she quickly added. "A strange kind of pain in my . . . uh . . . lower abdomen."

"You have to be told. I have to tell you, Jennifer. You've got to know. . . ."

Her eyes shot open. She searched Nicholas's face again. "I have to know what?" she asked quietly.

"It seems . . . you've . . . suffered a miscarriage. You've lost . . . a . . . baby," he stammered, watching her closely. Damn. He hated having to tell her. A baby. *Their* child. They had spoken of children. He so wanted to have many. But to lose the first child? One they hadn't even yet been aware of?

"A . . . baby . . . ?" she gasped. "I've miscarried?" An ache spread through her, settling around her heart. She hadn't even suspected. "Oh, Nicholas. I've lost a baby?" she cried, clutching onto his hand.

"Honey, didn't you even guess you might be with child?"

She turned her eyes from him, glad the tears were surfacing. They could help wash away some of her inner torment of the moment. "No," she uttered. "Why? How? How could this even happen?"

"You don't remember yet . . . about . . . Thad?" he asked cautiously, afraid to be the one to remind her of the other tragedy of this house. But she was drugged. Wouldn't it be the best time possible to tell her?

She swung her head around, wiping her nose and eyes with the back of her hand. "Thad?" she whispered. Then it all came to her in a rush. When she had been standing, waiting in the parlor with Nicholas . . . Lil had come and told them. . . .

The news had come as a shock to Jennifer, and even more than that . . . she had felt a sharp pain . . . then a blur.

Now, remembering it all so vividly, she began crying, turning her head from Nicholas. "Is he . . . alive . . . ?" she sobbed, chewing on a lower lip.

"Yes. He's gone through hell this morning, but he is alive."

"We're all being punished," Jennifer cried further. "It's God. He's punishing us all for all the wrong we've done. And to take my . . . baby . . . ?" Then shame took over. She wasn't yet wed, and she had been with child. Yes. This was surely God's way of punishing her . . . for being a loose woman.

"Please, Jennifer," Nicholas said, leaning down, to cover her, as he wrapped her in his arms. "Please quit crying. And don't think such things. God doesn't work in such ways. You, of all people, should know that."

"I want to die," she screamed. "I just want to die."

"I'll go and get Doc Rose," Nicholas said quickly. "He's staying close by here at the house, to watch Thad . . . *and* you."

Jennifer couldn't quit crying. Her body continued to be wracked with the loud sobbing. But she no longer cared. It was all *her* fault. She just knew it. Thad was made to be half a person . . . she had lost a baby . . . and all because *she* had traveled from Seattle to seek her own vengeance. "You're still succeeding at destroying us Brewsters," she shouted. "Damn you, Robert Harbison. I hope you're burning in hell."

When strange hands touched her on the brow, she tried to shake herself free but only found the rough-textured hand following her. "Jennifer, you must calm yourself," she heard Doc Rose grumbling. "This isn't goin' to help matters any. Now please. Settle down."

"But, Doc Rose, it's all so hopeless," she sobbed. "My uncle . . . and now . . . my child? Why?" She heard Doc Rose tell Nicholas to leave the room . . . that some privacy was needed. Then when she felt a glass resting against her lips, she knocked it away, then felt a cold wetness soaking through her gown, then spreading over her skin.

"Young missus, I've taken about all I'm goin' to take from a small missie like you," Doc Rose growled noisily. "Now I'm goin' to prepare another glass of liquid in which to place the laudanum and by God if I have to I'll pour it down your throat.''

Jennifer pulled the damp blanket up beneath her chin, waiting wide-eyed for his return. When he came back, glowering down at her through small slits that were supposed to be eyes, she took the glass and tipped it to her lips, gagging.

"There. Now that's a good girl," he grumbled, taking the glass from her. He sat down beside her and began speaking in a gentle, monotone voice. "Now, young lady, you have reason enough to be upset," he began. "It seems this is a gray day for this Brewster family of yours, but in a blink of an eye, it will be another year, and this will all be behind you."

"But . . . Thad . . . ?"

"If he's willin', he will walk again."

"How can he?" she said weakly. "He now has . . . only one leg."

"One and a half legs," he corrected her.

"One and . . . a . . . half . . . ?"

"I only had to take it off below the knee."

She shut her eyes and shuddered.

"And he can easily be fitted with a wooden limb," he added. "Once the wound heals."

"Do you mean it could look like and work like a real leg?"

"With lots of practice and mainly determination."

Relief washed over Jennifer. Then her hand went to her stomach. "But . . . my child?"

"A miscarriage is brought about for a reason, usually."

"What do you mean?"

"Let's say it's a way nature rids a woman of . . . maybe . . . a possible malformed child."

Jennifer put her hand to her throat, gasping loudly. "Do you mean—mine . . . ?"

"It was too early in your pregnancy to tell. This is only a theory of mine. The shock of being told about your uncle began the contractions. More than likely it if hadn't been that, something else would have eventually caused it."

"Why would my child . . . be . . . deformed . . . ?"

"There are many known reasons, but more that are less known."

"What are the . . . known . . . reasons . . . ?"

Doc Rose settled back onto the chair, furrowing his gray, thick brow. He placed his fingertips together in front of himself. "Years ago. Yes, many years ago, in newly settled colonies, where there were more men than women, cousins . . . uncles . . . nieces . . . uh, ah, hem, fornicated frequently. This is when a lot of these . . . uh . . . I guess you'd say . . . malformed children began to be born. . . ."

Jennifer clutched to the blanket and felt the spinning of her head and knew that it wasn't from the laudanum . . . but from having just heard the possible reason behind *her* miscarriage. The child had probably been . . . Robert . . . Harbison's. She turned her head in shame, now truly wanting to die. She had only been with Robert that one time . . . but one time was all that was required to get with child. And with her own blood relative . . . ?

"But you?" Doc Rose continued. "We will never know why you didn't carry your child full term. But no fear, you will be able to bear more children and these will probably be healthy young 'uns who you will even sometimes curse for even havin' been born once they keep you up at night."

Jennifer still refused to look his way, feeling a numb emptiness. She had further disgraced the family name. And . . . oh, God . . . if Nicholas was ever to find out. "I'd like to be left alone, Doc Rose," she whispered. "Please."

He laughed throatily as he pushed himself up out of the chair. "Guess you've finally calmed down. You should be able to rest now. But before leavin', I'd like to check and see if the bleedin' has slowed down a bit."

Jennifer clung to the blanket. "Must you?" she asked, suddenly trembling.

"Just let me lift the covers a mite. It'll take only a minute," he said, working quickly to pull the blankets down, revealing Jennifer in a sheer, lacy chemise. She couldn't even remember having been changed from her dress to this garment. But she knew that she was blushing as the aged, rough hands of Doc Rose scooted her chemise up and began poking gently on her stomach. "Now spread your legs a mite," he grumbled, pulling free a blood-soaked cloth. "I'll change this now," he said further, and quickly had fresh cloths pressed between her legs, her chemise pulled back in place, and the blanket tucked beneath her chin.

"I'll send Lil or your personal maid in to help you change into a dry chemise. I don't want you on your feet."

"I don't want to see anyone," she argued.

"Not even your young man?"

"No one," she replied. "And Doc Rose?"

"Yes?"

"Can I be assured that news of our misfortunes won't go any further?"

"That's a part of my service, young missus," he grumbled. "If I told all I knew about the families in good ol' San Francisco, they'd be standin' in line to take shots at *me.*"

"Then . . . no one will know . . . of my miscarriage?" she mumbled. "I am shamed . . . because I was not . . . wed."

"Young missis, you're feelin' guilty for what half the women even wed for."

"You . . . mean because . . . they're already with child?"

"More than you'd ever suspect. And mostly in the best of families . . . like the Brewsters. No sense hidin' your head over a stroke of bad luck. And remember this. Those who don't get caught outnumber those who wed before shackin' up with a fella."

"It doesn't lessen my guilt."

"It's because your pa was a minister of the Lord," he said firmly. "But if he were here today, he'd be the last to condemn you. Now you just remember *that.*"

The sweet, euphoric effect of the laudanum was now taking over. Jennifer sank back into the pillow, sighing. "I would like to see Nicholas after all," she whispered, half closing her eyes. "Could you please tell him?"

"I'm glad to see you're comin' to your senses."

"And, Doc Rose?"

"Yes . . . ?"

"Was it . . . a . . . boy . . . or girl?"

"It was too soon to tell. Too soon to tell."

She swallowed hard. "It's best that way, isn't it?" she asked, chewing on her lower lip.

"I'd think so, Young Missis," he said, then stopped to pull the drapes shut at the window, before tiptoeing out into her sitting room. He went to Nicholas and patted him on the back. "She's takin' it pretty hard, lad," he said. "She's got some mighty strange ideas racin' through that head of hers 'bout now."

"Like what?"

"Mainly guilt. She's blamin' herself."

"Yes. I do know that."

"Maybe even more than that. She needs you now. She's got to know you don't think less of her because of this."

"How in the hell could I think less of her? It was also my doing that she was with child."

"It's her that needs the convincin'. Not *me*," Doc Rose grumbled, then sauntered on out of the room.

Nicholas stood for a moment, watching the fire and kneading his brow. So much was left on his shoulders now. How could he make this all right for Jennifer? He also felt the loss of a child. But stronger still . . . the worry of possibly losing Jennifer's love. He had known of her strong moral character . . . that very first time he had tried to touch her. But damn it all to hell . . . he had persisted and had succeeded at pushing his way on her.

In his mind, he knew that it hadn't been rape . . . but if he could have only been stronger, and courted her in the proper way, she wouldn't be lying in bed guilt-ridden from all that they had shared.

Clearing his throat nervously, he moved slowly into her room, seeing her now peacefully calm, as she lay in a fetal position, like a child herself. Her dark hair was spread out on the pillow around her face, contrasting, making her appear to be even paler.

Tears burned at the corner of Nicholas's eyes as he settled down onto the chair beside her bed. Suddenly he felt like an old man as he let his shoulders slouch forward. He didn't know what to do with his hands. In his lifetime, his hands had been continuously busy . . . either working the fields in Illinois, or painting, and, only recently, caressing Jennifer's hair, face, and ah, her breasts. That was the ultimate of touches. The softness of her breasts could not even be compared to that of a rose petal.

"Nicholas? Is that you?" Jennifer suddenly asked, reaching a hand from beneath the blankets.

With a throbbing heart, Nicholas scooted to the edge of the chair and took her hand in his. He lifted it and pressed her fingers to his lips. He kissed each finger, then spoke. "Yes, darling. I'm here," he said softly, still clasping her hand as he placed it on the bed.

"I'm so sorry, Nicholas," Jennifer said, weeping quietly.

"You have nothing to be sorry for, Jennifer," he said, wiping a tear from his eye with his free hand.

"I've just messed up everything in my life, Nicholas. Don't you see that?"

"Darling, how could such a tiny person as you be responsible for all that you're blaming yourself for?" he laughed, trying to ease her mind . . . if he ever really could.

"The baby . . . Thad. . . ."

"You had no control over any of what's happened, Jennifer. You've got to quit dwelling on it. What's happened, well, it just happened. What's important is that you get well. Get back on your feet."

"I didn't even suspect I was with child," she murmured, trying to lift her head. But it felt as though it weighed a ton . . . and she knew it was because of the laudanum. She licked her lips and continued by saying, "How can . . . a woman . . . be with child . . . and not be aware of it, Nicholas?"

"Because you weren't that way . . . yet . . . long enough."

She concentrated hard through the fuzziness circling inside her head, trying to remember. "I only missed my monthly by one week," she said thickly. "I thought it was because . . . of . . . all I had recently been through."

"You have been looking poorly of late, Jennifer. I told you that only this morning."

"And . . . I do remember feeling nauseous and dizzy. Was it because of the baby?"

"Yes darling. I'm sure it was."

She turned her head from him . . . remembering even more. Had the doctor told Nicholas about the possibilities of her having aborted because of a deformed child? Would he ever suddenly recall having seen the ropes on her bed when he found her that morning . . . ? Would he think that Robert had raped her . . . and that that had caused her to be with Robert's child?

Oh, God, she thought to herself, biting down on a doubled fist, *What if Nicholas ever found out that I gave myself willingly to Robert . . . on a different night . . . than . . . that? My own uncle,* she thought further, *My own uncle's . . . child . . . ?*

Then her thoughts returned to another uncle . . . who in truth wasn't her uncle at all. She squeezed Nicholas's hand as she quickly turned her gaze back to meet his. "Thad? Is he still all right?" she gulped.

"He's going to be fine. He'll have to adjust. But physically, he should be strong as an ox once he gets back on his feet."

"But . . . his . . . leg . . . ."

"He can be fitted properly with a wooden leg. Doc Rose said so. Thad'll limp a bit, but it shouldn't hold him back too much."

"He's always been such a handsome stately man."

"And he will be again."

Does he know about the . . . child . . . ?"

"No. And he won't."

"But I can't go into his room to see him. Doc Rose said I had to stay in bed. Won't Thad get suspicious?"

"Doc Rose has already told Thad that you're ill with a slight case of dysentery . . . and that it's in Thad's best interest that you don't expose him to it.''

"And . . . Lil? Does she know?''

Nicholas laughed a bit hoarsely. "I think Lil has become one of your best friends through all this.''

"How . . . on earth . . . could she?''

"Her love for Thad, I guess," he answered. "But, darling, I must tell you. She assisted Doc Rose with both Thad and with your problems, as though she'd always been a nurse.''

"She helped . . . even . . . with me?" Jennifer gasped. "She saw . . . it . . . all?''

"You owe her a big thanks whenever you see her.''

"I'm not so sure," Jennifer stammered, licking her parched lips again.

"Why the doubts?''

"She could tell . . . so much . . . about this family.''

"But she won't.''

"And why not?''

"Her love for Thad. Even I can now see how sincere it is.''

"But she lied to Thad . . . about . . . so many things.''

"I believe that's in the past.''

"How can you be so sure?''

"Just intuition, darling. Male intuition," he said. "Just the same intuition that tells me you're going to be back on your feet and scampering around here real, real soon.''

Jennifer put her arm across her forehead, to hide her eyes. "I doubt if I'll ever feel the same about anything again," she murmured.

Nicholas's heart palpitated. He swallowed hard, then leaned up over her, removing her arm from her eyes, forcing her to look upward at him. "Your love for me? Isn't it still as strong?" he asked quietly.

Jennifer fluttered her thick lashes nervously and forced a lump to move from her throat. "Yes, my love, I shall always love you," she whispered. "But things will have to be different. Don't you now see that they must?''

"Like what, Jennifer?" he asked, applying a kiss to her cheek.

"Like our . . . making love," she stammered.

Hadn't he suspected as much? He pressed his lips against her forehead. "You will change your mind," he said hoarsely. "In time . . . you'll change your mind."

"No, I shan't," she whispered.

"But you said that you still love me, Jennifer."

"Always. Forever and ever, my love."

"Then I don't understand."

"We will have to be married before we . . . make love again, Nicholas," she said. "Don't you see? That's the only way I could ever feel right about it again."

He moved across the room, with his hands thrust deep into his rear pockets, breathing more easily. He had feared much more than this. He had feared her complete withdrawal from him. He took a deep breath and turned to gaze upon her again. "I do believe that can be arranged, darling," he laughed throatily. "Just you set the date . . . and you will have your man."

Jennifer pushed a pillow to be more fluffed beneath her head, looking downward, suddenly remembering the dampness of her chemise. She pulled it away from her body, frowning. "I simply forgot," she murmured.

"What, darling?" Nicholas asked, rushing to her side.

"I was a bit too frisky when Doc Rose was in here. I knocked the glass of water from my mouth."

Nicholas bent down to assist with the removal of the chemise, but stopped when he felt her recoil at his touch.

"No, Nicholas," she stammered. "Call for Carlita to help me." She then cast her eyes downward, fully realizing what she had done. Was it fear of what could happen again, were she to let him see her disrobed? She so longed for his touch . . . he *had* to know she did . . . But no. Not he nor any other man would stir her insides so . . . unless she was properly wed. . .

"Jennifer . . . ?" Nicholas questioned, his face all shadows.

"I'm sorry," she could only reply.

He stood upright, still beside the bed. "I'll try to under-stand," he said quietly. "But you didn't say when . . . we might . . . be wed."

"Only when we return to Seattle," she blurted.

"Then you do plan to return . . . even since Thad's misfor-tune?"

"Seattle is the only place I can think of that could help erase all this from my mind."

"Then Seattle it is—whenever you want to go."

"You do understand, Nicholas?"

"Yes, darling. Please don't worry about *me.*"

"And, Nicholas?"

"Yes . . . ?"

"Aunt Minnie? She must never know," she murmured. She still wondered how much her aunt knew of all the sordid past of the Brewsters.

"She will never be told, darling," Nicholas said, wanting so to hold and comfort Jennifer, but remembering too clearly her reaction of only moments ago. He would have to move slowly with her . . . give her time. "Now, I'll send Carlita in. It seems your bed also got a bit soiled when you showed your temper," he added, laughing softly.

"Thank you, Nicholas."

"For what?"

"For being all that represents good on this earth, my love," she whispered.

Nicholas felt a blush rising, feeling like a damn heel, if anything. *He* was responsible for her state of affairs. *He* and *only* he. "I'll get Carlita," he said, and rushed from the room, hating himself . . . but, oh, loving her so very, very much.

Chapter Twenty

Another set of eyes was being added to the upstairs hallway of the Brewster mansion on Nob Hill. But this portrait showed pale gray eyes that were more distinguishable than those of the other Brewster ancestors. These were eyes that were a bit slanted, as only one other set of eyes were in the long line of Brewsters—those of Jennifer Lynn Brewster.

Jennifer stood back away from Thad and Lil, watching Nicholas, who was working with the gilt-framed portrait of Thad, trying to get it to hang horizontal to the floor. Then her gaze settled on the portrait . . . on the eyes. It had taken five long months for Nicholas to capture the look of defeat that was so evident. It wasn't the look that Nicholas wanted to add to canvas, but being the artist he was, he painted what he saw.

It had taken Jennifer several weeks to begin accepting what had happened to her . . . but she knew that Thad still yet hadn't begun to accept *his* fate. Even though Jennifer had wanted to leave Thad's house, to get her life started anew away from the streets of San Francisco, she had agreed to stay with Thad . . . at least until his portrait was completed. But she had warned

Thad that upon its completion she and Nicholas would be on their way.

The time had arrived, and Jennifer now felt nothing but eagerness to leave, to get back with Nicholas to the familiar shores of Seattle. They would be married. They would forget Robert Harbison had ever existed. They would forget that she had miscarried a child . . . and that Thad was her father.

Thad's being her father was definitely one thing that she had refused to accept, even though she knew that it was an undisputed truth. But she had only known one father, and in her thoughts he would remain as just that. She owed him that much. When Thad had asked her to call him father, had begged her to—''Only once let me hear those words from your lips, Jennifer,'' he had said while still heavily drugged—she still had not been able to do as he bade. And he now knew that she never could. He hadn't only lost a leg . . . he had lost her . . . all over again.

''It's an amazing likeness, Thad,'' Lil purred, clinging to Thad's arm as he leaned heavily on his crutches. ''He even captured that wicked glint in your eyes. Don't you see it also?''

''No. I don't see anything of the kind. There's something about the eyes that doesn't look right,'' Thad grumbled. ''I still feel there's something lacking.''

Nicholas tensed. He was damn glad the portrait was finally complete. How he hated that Thad Brewster. Brewster was an arrogant, whimpering, son-of-a-bitch, who felt that everyone should jump and run just because he had had a leg removed. He had forgotten under what circumstances this had all came about, Nicholas thought even more angrily to himself. If Thad hadn't interfered with lives so often in the past, a duel wouldn't even have been necessary.

Yet . . . Nicholas knew, of course, that if Thad hadn't had secret liaisons with Camille those many years ago, Jennifer wouldn't even be around for Nicholas to love . . . and, now, to protect from any other evil that might be lurking to take her in its grasp.

Yes, damn it, he thought, *I'm going to get her out of this house . . . and today isn't any time too soon for us!*

He wanted to tell Brewster that what he was seeing about the eyes of the portrait that didn't look right to him was the look of self-pity. Brewster had learned the art of groveling in it quite well these past few months.

Well, damn it, Nicholas thought further, *I don't want to be around to get stuck in that mucky mire. He got himself in it . . . he can get himself out. And he's not going to pull Jennifer down into it with him, either.*

Nicholas had watched the change in Jennifer. She appeared to have come through her own misfortune unscathed. But he knew that that was because of her upbringing. She had been taught to be strong—both mentally and physically—by her father, Frank Brewster. He had succeeded. She was now her bright and cheerful self, ready to tackle the world again, and whatever it had to offer. And Nicholas was going to offer all that was good to her.

Lil looked up at Thad with her dark, flashing eyes. Her low-necked dress of orchid velvet blended in well with the velvet texture of her dark skin. "Darling, you just don't know a masterpiece when you see one," she said smoothly. "Nicholas has done himself proud, haven't you, Nicholas?" she said further, fluttering her heavy lashes as her gaze moved to the other side of the hallway.

Nicholas cleared his throat as he walked to Jennifer's side. His red plaid cotton shirt was open at the throat, revealing a crop of blonde, curly chest hairs, and his tight, pale blue breeches showed the muscles that he hadn't lost while catering to the Brewster "king." He had sneaked out most evenings and had walked the hilly streets of San Francisco . . . contemplating his and Jennifer's future. "It's one of the best I've ever done," he finally answered, setting his jaw firmly.

"Nicholas, mine will be the best when you get *it* done," Jennifer said, hugging him to her.

"Yes. And, Oglesby, now about that portrait of Jennifer,"

Thad said, shifting his weight on the crutches, groaning slightly.
"I'd like to have it. I have just the place to hang it."

Jennifer's eyes widened. She knew what that portrait meant
to Nicholas. She looked from Thad to Nicholas, then back to
Thad again, waiting for a response.

"Sorry, ol' man," Nicholas grumbled. "Nothing could be
said to get that painting from me. Nothing."

"I'd like to place it above the mantel in the parlor," Thad
persisted. "Now come on, Oglesby. You can part with it. You
can always paint another for yourself."

"No, damn it," Nicholas blurted, pulling from Jennifer's
embrace to head for the staircase. He wasn't about to let Brewster con him into giving up his "Portrait of Desire." Never.
Brewster could burn in hell first. Damn. He had to get Jennifer
away. And soon. He might punch Brewster out . . . even if he
was on crutches, he thought angrily to himself.

Jennifer swung the full skirt of her blue-flowered silk dress
around and ran to Nicholas. "Honey, you're not being yourself," she whispered. "What's wrong? Is it something . . .
maybe I even said . . . or did . . . ?"

Small wrinkles creased Nicholas's forehead as he turned to
face her. "Jennifer, you know better than that," he said. "You
know what it is."

"The portrait? Because Thad wants the portrait you painted
of me?"

"Hell, yes," Nicholas grumbled, moving on down the stairs.
He stopped once again and took Jennifer's hand in his. The
firmness of his grip reflected his inner turmoil. "Don't you
see what's beginning?"

Jennifer swallowed hard. "No. I don't guess I do," she said
softly.

"He's going to have a part of you . . . in one way or another.
He's not going to let you leave this house all that easily."

Her eyes widened. "But . . . he's not even pleaded with me
to stay. And he only . . . asked . . . for the portrait."

"Only?" Nicholas shouted. "Only? God, Jennifer. Doesn't
the portrait mean anything to you? I see it as a part of us . . .

our beginnings . . . the reflection of our love. Haven't you even studied the portrait? Seen the desire I've captured in your eyes? Don't you remember when I was even able to do that? When we first discovered our love for one another. God, Jennifer. I'll never part with that portrait,'' he stormed. ''And if I won't let him have the portrait, he will begin trying to persuade you to stay on here. You just watch. It will happen.''

Feeling a bit guilty for causing Nicholas to go into such a rage, Jennifer put her fingers to his lips and touched the softness. ''My dear, sweet Nicholas,'' she soothed. ''No need to fret. No matter what Thad's arguments are, I and the portrait will always be yours.''

''He's going to try his powers of persuasion. Will it be all that easy for you to say no?''

''Quite. Just watch,'' she said, but she couldn't help but tense inside when she heard the familiar thump thump of the crutches making contact against the stairsteps as Thad maneuvered his way downward.

''Damn, damn crutches,'' she heard him mumbling, tearing a piece of her heart away all over again. He was no longer a whole person, and again she blamed herself. Every time she heard him cursing his crutches, or his misfortune, she couldn't help but still think it was all her fault. If she hadn't left Seattle. . . .

She had to wonder if she could truly refuse everything to Thad, after all that had happened? Could she? Even though she had already promised Nicholas . . . ?

''Let's go on into the parlor,'' she said, urging Nicholas with a tug on his arm. She didn't want to have to turn around and see Thad struggling still. She had seen it too many times already . . . the way he teetered as he moved his crutches from step to step. And there was always the one pant leg that hung limply . . . empty . . . from below his right knee. Always she had seen perspiration beading his brow, and she knew that the weight of his body on the crutches made each move another task of immeasurable energy. This had aged him. What had once been rust-colored hair with a slight edging of gray . . . had become gray hair, with only a few threads of rust.

Looping her arm through Nicholas's, Jennifer went on down the stairs. She was relieved to be greeted by the cheerful colors of the parlor.

"I'll add a log on the fire," Nicholas said, then let his gaze move upward to the blank space on the wall above the mantel. He shuddered, remembering Thad's words. That's where Thad wanted to hang Jennifer's portrait. . . . *Never*, he thought to himself. *Never!* He went to the hearth and stirred the orange glowing embers on the grate, then lifted a log and placed it on top, watching its loose bark begin to smoke, then burst into flames. He swung around as Thad struggled into the room. *Damn. He is a sorry sight,* he thought. Then his gaze went to Lil . . . lovely Lil . . . faithful Lil. Yes, both he and Jennifer had misjudged Lil.

Jennifer settled down onto the settee that faced the fire. Her fingers worked with the fine white lace that bordered the not-so-revealing bodice of her dress. She watched as Carlita entered the room and began pouring wine into the tall-stemmed crystal glasses.

"Thank you, Carlita," Jennifer said, smiling as Carlita offered her a glass of the sparkling red liquid. Carlita's presence around the house was never noticed. She knew how to please without having to confer. It was all mechanical for her. She knew when to do everything, and do it to perfection. Even though she had been assigned as Jennifer's personal maid, Carlita knew how to spread her skills. Doing so meant securing her job, especially now that Thad was so suddenly helpless.

"Here, let me help you, darling," Lil said, taking the crutches from Thad as he inched himself down onto a chair. She placed them on the floor on one side of the chair, then settled herself on the floor in front of Thad, with a hand resting on his lap.

Thad pulled a half-smoked cigar from his front shirt pocket, thrust it between his lips and lit it, squinting as the smoke spiraled upward into his eyes. Then his gaze settled on the blank space above the fireplace mantel. "So you say I cannot have the portrait of Jennifer?'' he grumbled, thumping his fingers nervously on the arm of the chair.

Nicholas slouched down onto the chair, stretching his legs out in front of him. "No chance," he said.

"All right. I can understand," Thad said calmly.

Nicholas leaned forward, surprised. He had expected more of an argument than this. It wasn't like Thad to give up so easily. "You do?" he said, blinking his eyes nervously.

"Sure. I can understand," Thad said. "I can see why. You painted it for yourself." He took a deep drag from his cigar, then quickly added. "Now you can paint one for me . . . as soon as you get the first one completed."

Nicholas could feel the color draining from his face. "What . . . ?" he gasped.

"You can finish yours . . . then begin another."

Something grabbed at Jennifer's heart. Nicholas had been right. Thad had been scheming. She knew what to expect next. She sank lower into the chair, watching the anger flashing in Nicholas's eyes.

"Oh, I think I see what you're getting at," Nicholas growled.

"And what might that be, my friend?" Thad said, laughing darkly.

"This is a way to get Jennifer to stay longer. You know how long it takes to complete a portrait . . . so you know she would be around that much longer. No way, Brewster. No way."

Thad's eyes went to Jennifer, pleading in a way that he knew bothered her. He knew that she was feeling guilt about what had happened. And damn. He would try anything to have her with him longer. Once she was gone, he probably wouldn't see her again. Even though he owned many ships, he knew that Nicholas wouldn't welcome his arrival in Seattle to see Jennifer, since for her to see him would be to revive the ghosts of the past. "Jennifer? Don't you think . . . for your . . . uncle . . . ?" he said suavely.

Jennifer chewed on her lower lip, feeling torn between two people she loved. Either way she would hurt someone, and she didn't want to cause any more hurt. Enough pain had been inflicted in this family. "I . . . don't know, Thad," she said, casting her eyes downward. But even with her eyes turned from Nicholas, she could feel his eyes on her, burning. . . .

Nicholas bolted upright. "I believe Jennifer doesn't have the say so about this," he stormed. "It is I who paints . . . not Jennifer."

"Nicholas, I even thought that . . . maybe . . . you could uh . . . consider staying on, even . . . to help me with my work, now that I'm only . . . one-legged," Thad stammered, feeling a certain power, but this time from the loss of a part of his body. He had begun to find out that there were many ways to secure power. This one was a bit underhanded, but he had to try everything.

Nicholas hit his forehead with the palm of his hand, groaning. "What will you try next, Brewster?" he asked grimly. "The answer is no. A flat no."

"Lil, go and get that screen play that I've been working on," Thad said, gesturing with his hand. "We'll show Nicholas where he can fit into my plans."

Lil rose and hurried across the room to get a manila folder and carried it to Thad. She handed it to him, then positioned herself on the arm of his chair, with an arm draped around his neck.

"This venture I'm entering into not only requires writers, like myself, but artists. Here. Take a look at what I've written. Scenery is needed. You could do that for my new studio that I'm planning. You could even run the studio until I get my strength back. Here. Look at it."

Nicholas turned his back to Thad and his pleadings. "No. I'm not interested, Brewster," he said stubbornly.

"I wish you would at least consider it," Thad pleaded. "And Lil here. She needs to get back to work. She needs to get away from me, and what I've turned her into. She's not a maid. She's an actress. Only with your help can I get my production going. You could be my . . . legs. Don't you see? Think about it, Oglesby. There's much money in it for you. Moving pictures are the thing in the near future. Whoever invests now will be rich. I'm already rich. But I could see to it that you get rich in your own right.''

''I don't need you, *or* your moving picture's damn money,'' Nicholas said, turning to glare at Thad.

Thad cleared his throat nervously and took another drag from his cigar, staring squint-eyed at Nicholas. ''You mean you're marrying into another Brewster's money . . . so you don't need mine,'' he said darkly. ''Jennifer has her own. You will be marrying into that side of the family . . . so you will be rich anyway. Isn't that what you're saying, Oglesby?''

Nicholas's face turned from white to red as he went to grab Jennifer up from the chair. ''Jennifer, I'm not going to take any more of this from Thad,'' he said. ''I'm just not. Now are you coming with me . . . or do I have to leave this house alone?'' He turned with a start when he felt something tapping him lightly on the shoulder. He gasped when he saw Thad stretching one of his crutches to reach him.

''Oglesby, I apologize,'' Thad said, now lowering the crutch. ''Please go back and sit down. I see now that I have upset you greatly.''

''Oh, you do, do you?'' Nicholas snapped.

''I only wanted to try and persuade you and Jennifer to stay on. At least until I get fitted for my wooden leg. But if you must return to Seattle, you must.''

''We must,'' Nicholas stated bluntly.

''Then . . . when . . . ?''

''As soon as we can secure passage.''

''You will return on the *Elite?*''

''However Jennifer wishes to return.''

''I would encourage you to use my best ship, the *Elite,*'' Thad said, tossing his cigar stub into the fire. ''It's quite comfortable. There are many cabins below deck. All the comforts of home can be found there. Yes. If you must leave . . . please take Jennifer in the most comfortable way possible. The journey to Seattle is a long one.''

''Jennifer?'' Nicholas asked, eyeing her questioningly, hoping.

"I'll leave whenever you desire," she murmured, then looked toward Thad. His brows were furrowed and his shoulders were slouched forward. But she could no longer let her guilt stand in her way. Lil was still his faithful companion. Lil would see to it that he would come out of this depression all right. But Jennifer truly dreaded having to say a goodbye to him. She knew that it would probably be their last.

"And about that portrait," Thad said, casting his eyes downward. "Maybe once you get settled in Seattle . . . you could . . . paint one for me . . . then ship it to me? Do you think you could do that for me, Oglesby?"

Nicholas swallowed hard. He knew that he had won. So, what could this one gesture of friendship hurt? "Sure, Brewster," he said thickly, running his fingers through his hair. "Sure. Once we get settled in at Seattle, I'll get started on it right away."

"Damn nice of you, Oglesby. That'd be damn nice of you," Thad grumbled. "Lil?" he quickly added, looking up at her with heavy gray eyes.

Lil leaned down to kiss him softly on the forehead. "Yes, darling? she murmured.

"Help me back upstairs. I feel suddenly tired," he said, picking up his crutches again. "And take this . . . damn . . . screen play and toss it into the flames. It seems it will be a while before I'll be able to get into anything like this."

Tears burned at the corners of Jennifer's eyes. She wanted so to go to Thad, to tell him that she loved him, that she would stay with him forever if it meant making him feel that life was worth living. But she couldn't. She knew that to do that would be to lose Nicholas, and Nicholas was now her life. She turned her eyes away and hung her head in her hands.

"I will not," Lil said stubbornly, taking the folder and tucking it under her arm as she helped Thad up out of the chair. "I'm going to take it to your room and we are going to go over it and make corrections that are needed. And tomorrow? I shall go to your office and get things started. I'll hire someone to find an empty building for you. I'll have papers drawn up to purchase it . . . and we will get your studio organized. You'll see. I can do all that you need for now. Then when you're fitted with your new leg . . . you will take over. The moving picture industry will hear of us both. Soon. You will direct . . . I will act. It's as simple as that.''

Thad laughed nervously. ''Simple? Sure simple,'' he said. ''But, hell yes. You're right. And we might get to meet that Charlie Chaplin and his family yet. As soon as my automobile arrives, we'll head out for Los Angeles,'' he said further, laughing as he walked from the room, without saying even another word to Jennifer or Nicholas.

''Whew,'' Nicholas sighed, settling back down onto a chair, wiping his brow. ''I think he's going to be all right. Yep. I think he's going to be all right.''

''Huh?'' Jennifer asked, wide-eyed.

''It took someone to stand up to him to get him to realize that the world doesn't just turn for him and his needs.''

''But how does that make him all right?''

''Having lost the battle with me? It will just get him fighting even the harder for something else,'' Nicholas said. ''Don't you see? The next thing of importance in life to Thad is his moving pictures. Now he will have a clear mind to proceed in that direction. Yes. I'm sure he will be all right.''

Jennifer rose and rushed to Nicholas, settling down onto his lap. ''Did you do all of this on purpose?'' she purred, tracing his nose with the light touch of a finger.

Nicholas swallowed hard. He couldn't tell Jennifer of his hate for Thad . . . but he couldn't lie to her either. ''Not exactly,'' he laughed nervously. ''Not exactly.''

''Well, anyway, it does seem to have worked out.''

''Then shall we begin preparing for our departure?''

''You haven't finished my portrait, Nicholas.''

''Can you think of a better place to complete it than on the ship? It was started on a ship . . . it will be finished on a ship. Something to tell our grandchildren. Don't you think so?''

Jennifer laughed and hugged him tightly. Soon . . . soon . . . they would be home. Soon . . . all this would be behind her.

Chapter Twenty-one

Standing at the ship's railing, with her black velveteen cape blowing gently in the breeze, Jennifer took a long, last look at San Francisco. This was the way she would always remember it—the Victorian houses of different colors clinging to the sides of the hills, and, on the lower slopes, buildings that stood crowded thickly together, evidence of San Francisco's success as a thriving seaport.

Horse-drawn carriages and men on horseback had already filled the early-morning streets, competing with cable cars and even an occasional horseless carriage moving down one of the busier streets.

Jennifer shook her dark hair free from the sides of her face, sighing. Where was Nob Hill in all that confusion of buildings, houses, and traffic? she wondered, feeling a sadness, almost twisting, it seemed, at the pit of her stomach.

She had said her last goodbye to Thad in the Brewster mansion on Nob Hill. He still refused to leave its protective walls . . . not yet wanting to reveal his maimed body to those who hadn't been told.

But Jennifer had also preferred such a private goodbye. Farewells on the waterfront seemed to increase one's turmoil. Jennifer could recall so vividly another such farewell, on another waterfront. It had been so hard to leave Aunt Minnie behind. But soon . . . very soon . . . she would be embracing her again.

Jennifer's eyes searched below her, seeing the hectic confusion of the wharves. Passengers were still lined up to board this very special ship of Thad's. Jennifer and Nicholas had been luckier. They hadn't had to wait in line. They had been whisked on board and made to feel very special indeed. But that was the way it should be. Jennifer was a Brewster . . . and a Brewster owned this ship.

"Father?" she whispered, blinking back tears, having just uttered this truth for the first time ever. "Goodbye, Father," she added. "May God bless and keep you."

She wiped an eye and turned abruptly when she felt Nicholas's presence by her side. He leaned his elbow on the ship's rail, also taking in his— hopefully—last view of San Francisco.

"Regrets?" he murmured, having seen a sparkling of tears rolling down Jennifer's cheeks.

"None," she answered, setting her jaw firmly. She sniffed, then added. "Did you get my trunks and your belongings settled in cabins?"

"Yes. Two separate cabins."

"You don't mind, Nicholas?"

"I guess not."

"We will soon be married."

"Yes, soon," he said quietly, then turned to face her, needing to change the subject. "This is a damn nice ship, Jennifer. I don't think we'll even feel like we're on water, it probably moves so smoothly. This ship has been built more like a fancy hotel than any ship I ever thought could exist."

"Yes, it does tower so over the street. It seems to dwarf all the other ships around it."

Their gazes settled on the huge smokestack. Written on it in great golden letters was the name *Elite*, not even hidden as huge spirals of smoke continued to roll from the stack, settling in gray-blacks on all sides of it.

The clanking of chains at the far end of the ship made Jennifer aware that the anchor was being pulled upward, and she could now faintly feel the rumble in the floor and knew the engines were revving up.

"I'm anxious to see the deck below, Nicholas," she said, eagerly. "Please show me. It does all appear to be so grand." She didn't want Nicholas to know that, in truth, she couldn't bear to see the land move away from view once the ship began to work its way through the water. Yes, she was finally leaving behind all that had been ugly to her, she was also leaving a man whom she would always love. *Thad . . . oh . . . Thad,* she thought sadly to herself, but whirled the skirt of her dress and cape around, as she looped her arm through Nicholas's.

She looked proudly up at Nicholas who stood so tall and lean, and still so heavily muscled in both arms and legs. He had dressed smartly for the return voyage, in a black, cutaway coat and matching breeches that fit him perfectly. A ruffled white shirt that graced the front and a black bow tie made him appear to be a man of means instead of the poor artist he in truth was.

His smooth, tan skin and his wavy blond hair reflected his youthfulness and, as always, made Jennifer's heart race. She looked forward to this long voyage with him; yet there was a strain between them, and she knew that it was because of her insistence that they have two separate cabins.

"Just look at the people on this ship, Jennifer," Nicholas exclaimed as they made their way across the ship's upper deck. "There are so many." Throngs of people were standing in groups, all attired fancily in the latest fashions, some men even more decorated with diamonds than their women companions. Diamond studded-canes . . . diamond stickpins . . . diamond rings. . . .

"It's going to be quite a different experience from our previous voyage on the *Madrona,*" Jennifer giggled, leaning closer to Nicholas. "Just think. No animals sharing the same deck." She shuddered. "I'll never forget the stench of Captain Klein's filthy ship."

"Yes. How I remember, also," Nicholas laughed lightly. "The planking of this ship's floor isn't only spotlessly clean . . . but painted a sparkling white. And the cabins. They are first class. Absolutely the best."

"Then you might say I can be proud to boast of being a Brewster on this Brewster ship, Nicholas?"

"Quite," he laughed, opening a swinging door that led downward to the lower deck.

"Even carpeting?" Jennifer whispered, as they began to make their way down a long, narrow hallway that had doors on each side. The carpeting beneath their feet, in bold red, was so thick that not even a sound could be heard as they moved toward their own cabins.

Then, stopping, Nicholas pulled two keys from his pocket and held them up into the air, one in each hand. "Mine . . . yours," he gestured, then fit one into a keyhole. "This cabin is yours . . . and the cabin next to yours on the right side is mine," he said as he pushed the one door open.

Jennifer stepped into the room, sighing deeply. The walls were paneled in a highly polished veneer, and two upholstered chairs sat next to a great bed covered with a red velveteen spread. "My trunks?" she asked, seeing also delicately carved drawers that had been built into one side wall next to a gilt-lined, floor-length mirror.

"In the closet. Behind this mirror," he said, swinging a door open to reveal three trunks neatly stacked, but without enough room left above them to hang clothing for the number of days they would be on board this ship.

Jennifer removed her cape and draped it across a chair. She smoothed the front of her sleek, satin dress with her hands, still especially liking its mauve color and the way its bodice came to a point in front, emphasizing the swell of her breasts and the smallness of her waist. When she looked into a mirror, she could see no signs of having been with child. But in a sense she hadn't been, for she had never been aware of it until she had already lost it.

"And your cabin? Is it also so magnificent?" she beamed, still gazing around her.

"Also as magnificent," Nicholas laughed. He was glad to see the luster returning to her eyes. Since their definite date of departing had been set Jennifer had seemed only half alive. He had worried, thinking she would even change her mind.

"And there is enough lighting to paint by, isn't there, Nicholas?" she said, admiring the gold wall sconces that were burning brightly from wicks fueled by kerosene.

He went to her and drew her into his arms. "Yes, darling," he said. "We will finally complete your portrait. It will be finished by the time we reach Seattle."

"Thad said that he would wire Aunt Minnie. She will be so thrilled."

"And will she be as thrilled to see me?"

"She'll adore you . . . just as I do. How could she not?"

"Now . . . do you want to see my cabin?" Nicholas asked, teasing Jennifer as he held the other key before her eyes. "It also has a large, soft bed, darling," he said, leaning down to kiss her gently on the lips.

"Nicholas . . . please. . . ." she murmured, knowing what even a few kisses could do to her. She just couldn't go to bed with Nicholas, not until their wedding vows had been exchanged. She just couldn't, not after getting with child once, before having wed. To do so again would be a tragedy. . . .

He pulled away from her and ran his fingers through his hair, trying to understand. But, damn. It was so hard. After having already tasted her sweetness . . . how could he not desire her so strongly? He cleared his throat nervously and walked toward the door. "Come on, Jennifer," he said. "Let's go back up on top deck. I'll show you my cabin later."

"But, Nicholas," she stammered. "I thought. . . ."

He turned on his heel and said, "We'll see it later, Jennifer. Right now I'd rather not be alone with you in such close quarters. It . . . uh . . . has . . . would you say . . . caused urgings that you'd wish to not hear about just now."

Feeling a blush rising, Jennifer could see the increased size in the bulge beneath the buttons of his breeches. This excited her even more, making that pleasant ache grow to intensity between her thighs. She wanted him just as much as he wanted her. . . .

She tilted her chin upward, clearing her throat. "I guess we'd best join the others," she said softly. She lifted up the skirt of her dress and walked beside Nicholas until they were again mingling with others on the crowded upper deck.

As the ship pushed its way out to sea, a few seagulls persisted in following along beside it, dipping and swaying and eyeing everyone with large, black eyes. The sea breeze quickly enveloped Jennifer with its cold dampness, making her shiver. Then she forgot her chill when she saw the ship's captain approaching.

"Much different than Captain Klein, huh?" Nicholas whispered as he gently nudged Jennifer.

"Yes, quite," she also whispered, then straightened her back as Captain Thomas Adamson moved to greet them. His blue uniform was dazzling with gold braids and buttons, and his heavily tanned complexion was shining clean. Aside from his long, crooked nose and thinning hair of gray, he was handsome. He held his hands behind him as he openly admired Jennifer with a continuous sweep of his dark eyes.

"And Miss Brewster, what do you think of this ship thus far?" he asked, in a deep, resonant voice. "Does it pass the test? Your approval is of much importance to me and my crew. You see, it's not every day I have a Brewster accompanying me on a sea voyage."

Jennifer smiled widely, thinking him to be most polite. Thad had chosen well for his ship *Elite*. "Yes, it's lovely," she smiled. "I cannot imagine how Thad could associate his name with such a ship as the *Madrona* after I've boarded this one and seen its greatness."

Captain Adamson coughed into his cupped fist. "So you have also traveled on the *Madrona?*"

Jennifer cast her eyes downward, feeling a blush rising. She knew that the captain was wondering why she would have chosen the ship *Madrona* over the *Elite,* since she could always have access to both. She couldn't explain the speed with which she had made her plans to travel to San Francisco and how waiting for the *Elite's* arrival would have meant delaying her plans for revenge. "I now see that my planning has not been in my best interest," she said demurely. "Had I the opportunity to do it over again, I would most graciously wait to be a part of your *Elite.*"

A spray of sea water settled on Jennifer's face and bare arms, making her shiver again. She licked the saltiness from her lips and hugged herself with her arms.

"Are you cold, darling?" Nicholas asked, putting his arm around her waist.

She laughed awkwardly. "It seems I was foolish enough to leave my cape in my cabin."

"Miss Brewster, why don't you and your gentleman friend join me in my cabin for a glass of wine? It could warm your blood a bit."

"Sounds good to me," Nicholas said. "Jennifer? Is this what you'd also like to do?"

"Yes. Please," she said, feeling more shreds of misty sea water in the air. She could also feel the unsteadiness of her feet upon the deck as the ship began to rise and fall with the waves. She remembered Nicholas's remarks earlier . . . about probably not even being able to tell that they would be traveling by sea while on *this* ship. She laughed to herself and was glad to finally reach a brown, leather-padded door that led inside, to the captain's quarters.

"All the comforts of home," Captain Adamson laughed, as he opened the door and gestured toward two highly stuffed brown leather-covered seats. "Go ahead. Sit down while I pour the wine," he added, going to a cabinet that was attached to the wall, revealing through its glass panes shelves containing many decanters of wine and delicate-stemmed wine glasses.

Jennifer admired the room in which she now sat. Like the door that led into the room, the walls were lined with matching brown leather. A great polished desk stood against one wall, and a bunk, nothing like the bed in Jennifer's cabin, stretched out along the full length of another.

The deck was covered with plush brown carpeting, but traces of mold dotted the deepest corners, emitting a rank odor of mustiness.

"Thank you, sir," Jennifer murmured as the captain handed her a wine-filled glass. After Nicholas had been also handed his and Captain Adamson was settled in a chair behind his desk, Jennifer took a sip, glad to feel the warmth it stirred at the pit of her stomach. She then turned the glass slowly in her hands. "Captain Adamson, I am amazed by the number of people aboard this ship," she said. "Are they all truly traveling to Seattle, as Nicholas and I are doing?"

"No," he said, chuckling amusedly. "It seems most of the passengers you see are using the *Elite* only for a cruise. You see, many are from the rich communities of San Francisco. They are bored with life . . . needing an outlet. They are in search of something . . . for different ways in which to pleasure themselves. So they have chosen to escape by way of the sea . . . on my prestigious ship."

Nicholas laughed quietly. "So that accounts for all those diamonds that have set your decks to sparkling," he said.

"Afraid so," Captain Adamson answered, lighting a pipe. He then leaned back onto his chair, at peace, it seemed, with the world. "And there is another kind aboard this ship," he added.

"And who might they be?" Jennifer asked, still toying with the wine glass.

"Honeymooners," Captain Adamson said, a gleam in his dark eyes.

"Honeymooners?" Nicholas said, leaning forward, eyeing Captain Adamson . . . then Jennifer . . . then Captain Adamson again.

"The damn best place for a honeymoon, lad," Captain Adamson said, smiling broadly. "Some honeymooners have been known to never leave their cabin. We even deliver their meals to their doors. The ultimate in privacy can be found on the *Elite.*"

Nicholas cleared his throat nervously. "I've heard of captains . . . uh . . . even performing weddings on ships," he said quietly. "Have you ever . . . uh . . . done this, sir?"

Captain Adamson guffawed, almost choking on the stem of his pipe. He quickly removed it from between his lips and tapped the tobacco from it into a silver ashtray atop his desk. "Yes. I've been known to do such a pleasant deed," he said, kneading his smooth, pointed chin. "Thinking on doing it yourselves, are you?"

Jennifer felt a blush rising and took another sip of wine, glancing nervously toward Nicholas. What *did* he have brewing in that mind of his. . . . ?

"Not a bad idea," Nicholas laughed, but settled back against the chair, growing silent when he saw Jennifer's uneasiness. But damn it. It *was* a *brilliant* idea. One that he'd have to pursue. Yes, damn it. He *would.* The long sea voyage ahead of them. . . . Ah! It *could* be a romantic time. . . .

"Just have to ask once," Captain Adamson said, filling and lighting his pipe again. "Be happy to oblige. Think Thad would approve, Miss Brewster?"

Jennifer squirmed in her chair, then laughed softly. "I'm not even sure if *I* would," she said, glancing quickly toward Nicholas again. He did have something stirring inside his mind. She could see it in the depths of his blue eyes. Was he serious? Could he even consider such a wedding? Could *she?* But she *had* been wondering how she could get up enough courage to be married in her late father's church . . . after all she had been through. And when she didn't arrive at the alter in white . . . which she knew she just couldn't . . . wouldn't everyone suspect the reasons why?

Her heart began to race. Couldn't a marriage by the ship's captain be the answer to all of the embarrassment that a church wedding could cause her?

But then there was Aunt Minnie. . . .

"I have to ask you, Miss Brewster," Captain Adamson said,

interrupting her train of thought. "I heard that Thad met with an . . . an accident some months back. Is he now faring better? He usually comes and chats or takes a voyage with me occasionally. But it's been a long time between chats *and* voyages."

Jennifer's eyes shot upward in surprise. The color drained from her face as the full implications of his abrupt question made the room quickly fill with strained silence. Had word spread of Thad's duel? She straightened her back and answered him. "He's doing quite well, thank you," she said, hating herself as her voice cracked a bit.

Captain Adamson fit his fingertips together before him as he puffed on his pipe. "Damn shame it had to happen," he said, letting the pipe settle into the corner of his mouth.

"Yes. Quite," Jennifer murmured, casting her eyes downward.

"It's that damn San Francisco's hilly streets," Captain Adamson continued, chewing on the stem of the pipe.

Again Jennifer's eyes shot upward. "What did you say, sir?" she murmured.

"I said it's those damn streets. The hills," he answered. "I knew that one day I'd hear of a carriage getting away from a driver. Damn shame it had to be Thad."

Jennifer's heart began to race. Had she heard right? Who had protected the Brewsters' name by fabricating such a story as she had now heard only portions of? She had to find out exactly what *had* been said. And she had to be prudent with her questioning. "But, Thad does plan to mingle among his friends and employees soon," she said. "A small accident like he has encountered couldn't keep *him* down for long."

"Small accident, did you say?" Captain Adamson said, leaning forward. He removed his pipe from between his lips, looking questioningly in her direction. "You'd call being thrown from a runaway carriage into the path of a cable car . . . a . . . small accident?" he said darkly.

Jennifer smiled to herself. So *that* was the story being spread. She now knew of only one person who could invent such a tale. Lil. Lil had done her homework quite well. "Well, I . . . didn't mean to say. . . ." she began, but was interrupted.

"When a man loses part of a leg, he loses his soul," Captain Adamson said, grumbling. "Makes me shudder all over again to think such a thing could happen. But I don't only curse those hills . . . I've known all along those damn cars on tracks could be dangerous as hell. The only safe way to travel . . . *ever* . . . *is* by ship."

"I'm sure you're right," Jennifer said, amused at how well this had all come about. She would have to wire Thad of this. Soon. It could make Thad feel more comfortable about leaving his house . . . if he knew the word "duel" wasn't even being spoken. Would Lil ever cease to amaze Jennifer?

Jennifer sighed to herself. If Lil was only white. Couldn't she be a perfect wife for Thad? The age barrier no longer seemed to matter. But the color of one's skin . . . would always remain . . . a barrier. . . .

"And now," Captain Adamson said, rising. "I must see to my crew. But before doing so, is there anything else I can help you with, Miss Brewster?"

Jennifer glanced over at Nicholas, blushing, thinking "marriage," but then turned her gaze back to the captain as she placed her wine glass on a table beside her. "No. Everything seems to be in order," she murmured, pushing herself out of the chair.

"I believe you will enjoy all meals served on this ship," Captain Adamson said. "The noon meal should be within the hour. I shall look forward to having you and your young man seated at my table."

"That's very kind, sir," she said, straightening the skirt of her dress. "Nicholas?" she then added. "Shall we?"

"Until later, Captain," Nicholas said, half saluting the captain, then securing his arm around Jennifer's waist as they stepped out onto the open deck.

The sun had disappeared behind low, rolling gray clouds and a fine mist had begun to fall, which had caused the deck to empty of people.

"We must hurry before you catch pneumonia," Nicholas said, leaning against the brisk, ocean breeze.

"Can I now see your cabin, Nicholas?" she asked, trying to protect her hair with her free right hand. "I'm anxious to see where you've placed your easel. You know that only a few strokes of the brush should have the portrait completed."

"If it hadn't been for Brewster and his damn persistence about his own portrait, I'd have had yours finished long ago," Nicholas grumbled.

"But you should be so proud that Thad wanted you to paint his portrait."

"Think so, huh?"

"You've immortalized another Brewster to hang on the wall of the Brewster ancestors."

"You *are* proud of the name, aren't you?"

She tensed inside, remembering so much, then blurted, "Shouldn't I be?"

"Yes, you should be, darling. Just as I am to be an Oglesby."

"But you never speak of your family."

"It's not because I don't miss them."

"You do, then?"

"Like hell," he grumbled, opening the door that led to the lower deck. "I've written my mom and dad. Many times."

"You . . . have . . . ?" she asked, shaking the wetness from her dress, suddenly realizing how little she *did* know of Nicholas. But this had never seemed important . . . as even now it still wasn't. She knew enough about him to know that she could never love another.

"I'm the only child."

"Then I'm sure they miss you terribly."

"Would you want to travel to Illinois sometime with me to meet them?"

Jennifer grabbed his hand anxiously. "I'd love it," she beamed.

"All right, then. After we have grandchildren to show them, we shall return. We'll return in grand style. We'll return by train."

"You . . . said . . . grandchildren . . . ?" Jennifer mumbled, tensing. Would she even be able to have children, since her one miscarriage? It would always haunt her.

Nicholas threw his head back and laughed heartily. "No. I was only teasing," he said. "Grandchildren? God. Who can look that far into the future?" He fit the key in the lock. "But, darling? I do want to begin a family. Right away. And I want to have several children. There will be no child raised alone in *our* house."

"Children are that important to you, Nicholas?" she asked demurely.

"Aren't they also to you?" He swung the door open widely and stepped aside, letting her enter before him.

"Yes, I'm sure," she answered, wondering if he had put the miscarried child from his mind so quickly. He never mentioned it. Never. But maybe he was trying to save her pain by not doing so.

She looked quickly around the cabin, sighing. It was as grand as her own, with the same furnishings and the same red velveteen accessories. But one thing *had* been added: Nicholas's easel, which had been set up in the middle of the room. And already placed on it was the portrait that had been carried from place to place . . . but showed no signs of wear and tear.

She went to it and studied it, remembering quite vividly where each stroke of the brush had taken place. The memories set her face to flaming, since intimate caresses had followed most of her sessions of posing.

She studied the eyes. Ah! Hadn't he so captured the desire she had been feeling for him at the time? A desire that set her heart to racing even now? If he was to begin the portrait anew, at this very moment, she knew that he would see the same thing . . . all over again. . . .

As she felt his hand touching her cheek, a slow melting began inside her, causing her to tremble.

"You are so very beautiful, darling," he said softly. "Never could I find anyone as beautiful to paint. Never."

When his hand moved from her cheek, to her shoulders, the

familiar tingling began to ripple through her, making her grow even a bit dizzy. She turned to face him, whispering, "Nicholas. . . ." His mouth sealed her lips. His lips were warm . . . persuasive . . . as his hands moved down to her breasts, massaging them through the dress that lay between them and the passion that was building.

Jennifer felt her breath coming in rasps . . . knowing that they shouldn't. But his mouth and hands were once again performing magic on her body. Her nipples had become taut and stiff, throbbing from the need to be set free so his lips could stimulate her even more.

"We mustn't, Nicholas," she murmured, yet she couldn't help but let her own hands wander to touch his swollen hardness beneath the buttons of his breeches.

"We can be married. Even today, Jennifer," Nicholas said thickly, now reaching to unsnap the back of the dress. "It will be all right, darling. Please believe me."

He now kissed her long and deeply, causing her blood to surge in wild ecstasy. She no longer cared. All that her mind could now comprehend was the pulsating need between her thighs. It had been way too long.

"Shall I?" Nicholas asked, teasing her as his hands still proceeded to unfasten her dress.

She threw her head back in frenzied pleasure. "Yes, yes," she sighed. She ached with a tormented need. She moaned when his lips moved to the hollow of the throat, then on downward to capture a nipple between his teeth as her dress and undergarments fell to the floor. She reached downward and began to caress herself as she now waited for him to undress, then flushed scarlet when a tapping on the closed door made her suddenly aware of what she had been doing.

"Nicholas . . . I. . . ." she stammered, moving her hand away from her body. "I've never done that before," she quickly added. The persistent knocking on the door made her grab her clothes and quickly pull them upward.

"Mr. Oglesby," a voice spoke from the hallway. "It is I, the ship's steward. Captain Adamson wanted me to inform you that he is waiting at his table in the dining hall. Lunch is now about to be served.''

Nicholas clenched his fists at his side. He had been waiting so long for Jennifer to be responsive to his touches again . . . and now . . . when she had just begun . . . a damn ship's steward had interrupted. ''You can tell Captain Adamson that I will be there shortly,'' he grumbled, reaching down to pull his breeches back in place.

''And also Miss Brewster?'' the ship's steward persisted. ''If you know of her whereabouts, will you also inform her?''

''Yes. I shall,'' Nicholas answered, gazing toward Jennifer, who had managed to become fully clothed once again. He eyed her wearily. Would it all be lost to them again? He had to make it not so. He tucked his shirt inside his breeches and moved to her side. ''Jennifer?'' he mumbled, watching her smooth her dark hair back in place. There were the roots, more gold as each day passed.

She cast her eyes downward. ''Yes, Nicholas?''

''We must be wed. Today,'' he said determinedly.

''Today?'' she murmured, as she rose her head to let their gazes meet. Her heartbeats filled her body.

''Yes. It is foolish to wait any longer. You heard the captain. He could marry us. Right on this ship.''

''Is that truly what you desire, Nicholas?''

He swooped her into his arms and held her tightly, feeling the heat rising anew beneath the tight confines of his breeches. He tilted her chin upward to kiss her ever so lightly on the lips. ''It is *you* I desire, my darling,'' he said. ''I can wait no longer. And neither can you. You must know this.''

Tears came to her eyes. ''Since I was a child, I've dreamed of being wed in my father's church . . . in a beautiful, flowing white gown that would be trimmed with the most delicate of lace—''

He interrupted her with a long, sweet kiss on her lips. Then he pulled away and said, ''This is our hideaway. I am your love,'' he whispered. ''We need no church. You need no fancy wedding gown. All you need is me and what I will always offer you. My love. And my deepest devotion.''

She blinked back more tears and swallowed hard. "But . . . Aunt . . . Minnie . . . ?''

"She would only want you to do what would make you the happiest."

"Yes. I know," she said, fluttering her lashes.

"Then we will ask the captain to perform a ceremony? Today . . . ?''

"But where, Nicholas?"

"In the privacy of your cabin."

"You really want this badly, don't you?"

"Yes. And it must be," he answered flatly. "Seattle is many days away by sea. We would be foolish not to take advantage of this opportunity to be alone."

"Yes. I do agree," she said, trembling.

"Then we shall now go inform the captain?"

"Yes. Let's," Jennifer sighed, then formed her body into his as he crushed his mouth to hers. She could feel his heartbeats in unison with her own.

Everything had finally fallen into place. If it had not been for her setting out to seek revenge . . . she would have never met Nicholas.

Robert Harbison, I have something to thank you for after all, she thought as she threw her head back in ecstasy, while Nicholas's lips moved to the swell of her bosom.

Chapter Twenty-two

The timbers of the ship creaked as the water slapped against its side, and only a faint rumbling of the boilers could be heard as Nicholas was helping to ease Jennifer down onto the bed. He was showering her with kisses, all the while watching the glow of her skin in the golden light of the kerosene lamps.

"I didn't know it was so easy to become man and wife," Jennifer sighed, knowing that, now, everything and anything that she and Nicholas chose to do together was quite legal. There would no longer be the dread of getting with child. She now looked forward to it. Getting pregnant again could possibly help erase the first time from her memory.

"Only a few words are ever required," Nicholas said, still admiring her nudity. He arranged her on the bed, as though she were a rag doll, and began touching and exploring every part of her body. His blood surged as her fingers circled his throbbing manhood.

"A few beautiful words," she added, now unashamedly working her hand up and down as she had seen Nicholas do to himself so often in preparing himself for his entrance into her innermost part. Her heart raced with anticipation, but she could tell that he was savoring each moment . . . each touch . . . as she was also doing. This time, their union would be the ultimate of all unions.

He now moved next to her, turning her to face him, fitting his body into the curve of hers, molding her to him, while his fingers sought entrance between them, pressing urgently into her breasts. His mouth found hers. He kissed her long and deeply, flooding her with bone-weakening desire.

Then in one quick movement he was atop Jennifer, letting his hands travel again, but this time down across her stomach, stopping when he had found her pulsating love mound.

Moaning, she pushed her body up to meet his caresses. Had it ever been this beautiful before? If so, she couldn't remember when. Her breath began coming in short rasps as she continued to be more stimulated, and when his mouth covered a breast, sucking and teasing its nipple to a sharp peak, she felt her body grow limp. She sighed with another moan of ecstasy. Her mind was leaving her, it seemed, as delicious shivers began to soar through her body.

"I do love you so, Jennifer," Nicholas whispered, kissing her again, this time more urgently.

"And . . . I . . . you . . ." she whispered, reaching down to touch his manhood again, as it lay throbbing against her. The ache between her thighs was becoming intense . . . needing that release of the liquid warmth that she could remember so vividly from their other times together. . . .

When Nicholas's hands positioned themselves beneath her, guiding her body upward to meet his first thrust, guiding her to the ultimate pleasure shared between man and woman, Jennifer spread her legs in waves of desirous anticipation. When he pressed deeply inside her, she moaned again from the intense pleasure of the moment, and met his thrusts, as their bodies slapped together noisily.

"Ride me, darling," Nicholas said thickly, closing his eyes, throwing his head back, feeling the moment of glorious release so ever, ever close. God! Had she ever been so good before? She was like a tigress set free for the very first time. The heat of his semen was building . . . boiling . . . ready to spill over inside her. "Aw, God," he moaned, then plunged even more deeply as they rose to a crescendo of climaxes together. . . .

"It's always as though different colors are set free inside my head," she giggled afterwards, still clinging. "Is it the same for you, Nicholas? Is it always so beautiful?" She was still feeling the vibrations of her vaginal walls, and a desire to begin the lovemaking anew. Her hands traced his body, feeling the wetness from their combined perspiration. When she touched his limp manhood, it seemed suddenly to spring to life all over again.

"Too beautiful to even describe," he said, closing his eyes as her fingers succeeded at arousing him again. He stiffened his body, concentrating only on the moment, feeling the heat building inside, sending tidal waves of pleasure soaring upward to his brain.

"Can we truly . . . again . . . so soon?" she asked, positioning herself so he could return the caresses. She tremored slightly and shut her eyes as his fingers circled a breast, then cupped it as he turned to now be above her, spreading light kisses from her stomach, then down lower until he gently spread her legs, enabling his lips to explore where no other mouth had been before.

Jennifer tensed. "What . . . are . . . you doing, Nicholas?" she asked quietly, feeling a slight swimming of the head from the sudden touch of his wet tongue circling and wetting her where she had felt such intense pleasure only moments earlier.

"Just enjoy it, darling," he said, reaching up with a hand to capture a breast.

"But, Nicholas," she began, wanting to protest. What he was doing seemed most wicked . . . indecent . . . but she couldn't ask him to stop. Her mind was becoming an explosion of effervescence . . . suddenly all pale colors of blues and lilacs . . . when Nicholas moved his body upward to mount her.

With three crashing thrusts inward, they rode waves again together until they lay completely spent in each other's arms.

"It didn't hurt, did it, Jennifer?" he asked, touching her gently on her flushed cheek.

"Why would you think it might?"

"This is the first time since the miscarriage," he said. "I was worried that having lost the child might be cause for having pain while having sex."

She leaned her face more into his hand, not able to get enough of him. "I told you . . . only moments ago . . . how beautiful it had been for me, Nicholas," she whispered. "Please let's not mention anything about the loss of the child . . . ever again. Let's let tonight be a new beginning for us. Let's please put San Francisco . . . all that ever happened there, behind us."

Nicholas threw his arms beneath his head and rested against them, staring at the ceiling. "You really do believe that's possible, Jennifer? Now do you really?"

She turned on her side and leaned up on one elbow. "I must," she answered. "Don't you see? I must."

"And . . . Thadeus Brewster?"

"Thad? I'm sure we'll keep in touch. Just as before."

"You don't think he'll ever make any more demands on you?"

"None. Except for the one commitment that we've already made."

Nicholas turned his gaze to her. His face had suddenly become all shadows. "The portrait?" he said, barely audible.

"Yes. You did promise."

Nicholas arose and pulled his breeches on. "I guess that's not a big problem," he said. "But I've been doing some serious thinking about something else."

Jennifer climbed from the bed and slipped into a sheer, lacy nightgown in which she could proudly reveal her magnificent breasts and the dark vee between her thighs. The silken folds of the gown rustled around her as she settled herself deeply onto a chair. "And what are you speaking of, Nicholas?" she asked, taking long strokes through her hair with a brush.

"It's a remark that Brewster made that set my mind to worrying," Nicholas said, kneading his brow.

"What kind of remark, Nicholas?"

He sat down opposite Jennifer, slouching, with his legs spread out in front of him. "It was what he said about my marrying into the Brewster money," he grumbled.

She placed her brush on the nightstand and leaned forward. "But, Nicholas, you and I know that isn't so," she said softly.

"I don't like thinking that anyone might think that I married you only for your money."

"I'm sure no one will."

"I won't give them a chance to."

"What are you planning to do?"

"It's a decision we must reach together, darling," he said, leaning forward, eyeing her questioningly.

"Whatever is it that you're speaking of, Nicholas?"

He arose and began pacing the floor. "I've decided that we'd be happier if we didn't live in Seattle," he said.

Jennifer pushed herself up from the chair and went to him and took his hand. "Nicholas, will you please quit your pacing and tell me what you mean? Where else but Seattle could we live?"

He turned and took her by the shoulders. "We could live on a farm. Outside of Seattle. You know . . . purchase some property . . . maybe even where we can see that beautiful Mount Rainier every morning when we arise," he said hurriedly. "I've enough money to purchase a small strip of land. I could even build the house. And by farming the land, I would feel as though I'm making my own way in the world. Darling, what do you think?"

Jennifer's mind was awhirl. She hadn't thought about Nicholas and his insecurities. She had only thought of her own . . . and her eagerness to get back to the familiar walls of the Brewsters' Seattle home. It hadn't occurred to her that Nicholas would ever want to live anywhere else. "I just . . . don't know," she stammered.

"Please say yes, Jennifer," he said thickly, furrowing his brows. "It's very important to me."

"And your painting? When could you do that? There would be no people to paint on a farm."

He moved from her and pulled a shirt on, slowly buttoning it. "I've thought about that," he said. "I could travel to the city maybe once or twice a month. Or I could change my format entirely. Start painting nature scenes. God. Think of all the beauty I could capture on canvas if we lived near that beautiful mountain."

She went to him and touched him lightly on the cheek. She leaned up and touched her lips to his. "Nicholas, I will go wherever you want me to go," she said. "I will be happy . . . no matter where . . . as long as I am with you."

He drew her to him and buried his nose in the thickness of her hair. "What if I had never found you, darling?" he said. "How could life have ever meant anything, if I hadn't met you?"

His hand moved along her back and then circled around to capture a breast, making her breath catch in her throat. "You looked so cute that first time I saw you, Nicholas," she purred, as his hands were working the same magic against her skin.

"Cute?" he laughed hoarsely.

"In that stocking hat," she laughed.

"And you? You looked so damn mysterious in that black, hooded cape, flitting to and from that room. I knew that first time I saw you that I had to find out what made you tick."

His hand had lowered and was caressing her between the thighs. The silk texture of the evening gown being rubbed against her seemed to arouse her even more. "And, my love, do you know now what makes me tick?" she laughed throatily.

"I sure as hell do," he said. He scooped her up into his arms and carried her to the bed.

"But, Nicholas. You've only just dressed," she teased.

He lowered his breeches and positioned himself above her. "The hell I have," he said, groaning as he made contact inside her.

Part Three

Seattle

Chapter Twenty-three

To the east of the ship, Mount Rainier's snow-clad peak of white rose into thickening clouds, with streaks of blue-black ridges on its lower slopes. Jennifer thought it to be so splendid that it was like a mirage . . . something that couldn't be real.

As the *Elite* moved closer to Seattle's harbor on Puget Sound, Jennifer clung to her bonnet with one hand and Nicholas's arm with the other. "Isn't the mountain hauntingly beautiful, Nicholas?" She sighed. "The clouds that are swirling so restlessly in and around it remind me of what ghosts might truly look like."

"Now you see why I feel it appropriate to build our house so that our parlor window looks out on that mountain," he answered. "I plan to capture Mount Rainier's many moods on canvas. It might prove to be even more challenging than painting a certain Mrs. Nicholas Oglesby that I . . . uh . . . know," he teased further.

"Mrs. Nicholas Oglesby," Jennifer repeated. "I still can't believe it. I am so happy, Nicholas."

"Happiness is all that lies ahead of us, darling," Nicholas said, drawing her next to him. "You'll see. You'll see." Since their wedding night, he had seen the difference in Jennifer. She was now full of laughter and as carefree as a young child. Nicholas felt that the past was just that now. And didn't Jennifer look radiantly beautiful this day in her pale blue velveteen bonnet, tied beneath her chin? It made her eyes appear to be wider and bluer beneath the thickness of her lashes. And the slant to her eyes seemed less prominent to him now, since her cloak of mystery had been lifted and left behind as a part of her past.

Her matching blue velveteen cape blowing in the wind had a way of wrapping itself around her, clinging, revealing her magnificent bosom even beneath the heaviness of the layer of clothing pressing against her flesh. Even now, Nicholas felt the heat rising in his loins. Would it always be this way for him?

He ran his finger around the tightness of his stiffly starched white collar, anxious to rid of himself of such attire. A flannel shirt and denim breeches were all he ever desired to wear . . . not the fancy suit and tie required on this prestigious ship of Thadeus Brewster's.

"But there is a certain sadness that I'm feeling, Nicholas," Jennifer said, lifting her gaze to meet his.

"A sadness? How could you? You just revealed to me how happy you were."

"I'm saddened because the portrait is now finished," she sighed. "It seemed to have become a part of us . . . the sharing . . . while you were painting it."

"So you felt it also?"

"Yes, my darling."

"Then there's no need to feel saddened."

"And why not, Nicholas?"

"The portrait will always be a part of us. It will be a symbol of our love. We shall look back on it when we are maybe even grandparents and still be able to see the look of desire in your eyes that guided my brush on the canvas."

A rustling of feet and quiet utterings from voices around her urged Jennifer to look and see what the attraction was at the ship's railing. Then she saw it herself. The first she had seen of Seattle since she had left those many months ago. Her heart palpitated . . . remembering so much. Seattle had been where her nightmares had begun . . . where she had heard the rogue Robert Harbison's name spoken for that very first time.

She trembled. If she had been able to have looked into the future and seen the havoc that seeking him out was going to create, would she even have made that first attempt? But feeling the strength in the arm now around her waist . . . and Nicholas's closeness . . . made Jennifer know that . . . yes . . . if she had it to do all over again, she would. Because had she not taken that room across from Harbison's Pawnshop, she and Nicholas would have never met.

"Are you all right, darling?" Nicholas asked, leaning closer to her face. "I felt you tremble. Is the sea breeze too cool? If so, we can return to our cabin until the ship is moored."

"No. I'm fine, Nicholas," she murmured. Her anxiety to see Aunt Minnie was quickly brushing aside all previous doubts. Aunt Minnie represented all that was good in the world. And wouldn't Nicholas and Aunt Minnie get along just fine together? It seemed to Jennifer that they had been made from the same mold.

Nicholas looked toward the land, seeing a city clinging to the sides of the hills, just like San Francisco. But this city didn't have the cheerful, welcoming atmosphere that he remembered San Francisco having upon his first arrival there.

"Does Seattle always have such a gray cloud hanging over it?" he grumbled. "The short time I was there, after arriving from Illinois, I remember it raining almost every day."

Jennifer laughed as she captured the tail of her cape in her arms, to straighten it. "It might be damp and rainy in Seattle quite often," she replied. "But this city *can* boast of displaying bright red roses on its hillsides even on Christmas day." She peered upward at Nicholas, blue eyes twinkling. "Now, Nicholas, can your state of Illinois brag of anything like that?"

He bent and kissed her lightly on the tip of her nose. "No, my darling. Not quite," he laughed. "On Christmas day in

Illinois, one can usually expect ten feet of snow, with possibly even an ice storm to boot.''

Her eyes widened. ''Really, Nicholas?'' she gasped. ''How on earth does anyone survive?''

''Many don't. That's why the California sunshine has become so inviting. Many Illinoisians have traveled by wagon train seeking the gold of the sunshine, as they did years ago seeking gold in the hills.''

''But you chose Seattle.''

''I sought the excitement of the time. And that was the talk of the Yukon.''

''And you're not sorry that you got sidetracked?''

He pulled her next to him and devoured her with his eyes. ''Do you even have to ask such a question?''

''The answer is always there in the depth of your blue eyes, Nicholas,'' she said softly, tiptoeing to kiss him on the warmth of his lips. ''My darling, my darling. Oh, how I love you.'' She wrapped her arms around him and clung to him, placing her head on his chest. She smiled when she could hear the racing of his heartbeat.

''Jennifer, look. Out in the water,'' Nicholas exclaimed, pointing.

''What is it?'' she asked, turning swiftly, then sighed when she saw several seals bobbing up and down in the water, close to a bluff. ''I'd heard my father speak of these little sea creatures, but I've never seen any. Aren't they so cute, Nicholas?''

''I would have thought the heavy traffic of ships would have scared them off.''

''And the starfish!'' Jennifer exclaimed. ''See how many there are clinging to those rocks?''

Then a full view of the wharves drew her steady gaze. Never had she seen so many ships moored in Puget Sound's waters. This meant that the city was thriving even more than when she had left it. She inhaled deeply. The winds weren't only sharp with salt water, but sweet as well with the scent of red cedar. ''It seems the sawmills are still doing quite well,'' she added, seeing logs stacked along the waterfront in the vicinity of what had so long ago been named Yessler's wharf, which had been built to accommodate the largest sawmill in Seattle.

Then her gaze moved to the houses that lined the streets on the hills. Her pulse beat quickened when she was able to make out the large Brewster house, and the church that sat even higher up on the hill. Her childhood memories were there . . . drawing her home once again. And wouldn't it always be that way? Her childhood had been one of innocence . . . happiness . . . love. . . .

"Do you see her yet, Jennifer?"

"What? Who?" Jennifer asked, jolted to the present, suddenly looking more closely around her.

"Your Aunt Minnie," Nicholas said, looking into the vastness of the crowd moving about on the wharves. It was a mass of hectic confusion. Even more so, it seemed, than what they had left behind at San Francisco.

Jennifer stepped closer to the ship's railing, clasping her hands together. "There are so many people," she said, furrowing her brow. "I see no one familiar to me. Absolutely no one."

Captain Adamson moved briskly toward them and stepped between Nicholas and Jennifer, swinging his arms around each of their shoulders. He pulled them both to him. "And I do hope your trip was pleasant enough," he said, winking.

Jennifer cast her eyes downward, feeling a blush rising. She knew what was on the captain's mind. She and Nicholas had hardly left their cabin after their marriage vows had been exchanged. Their cabin had been turned into a honeymoon suite . . . supplied steadily with the best of wines and tastiest of foods. "Yes. Thad's ship is one of extreme luxury," she said. Then she lifted her gaze to meet the captain's. "And you, kind sir, are the best captain a ship could have."

He chuckled deeply. "And I shall see that your trunks and painting equipment are safely delivered to your doorstep, Mrs. Oglesby," he said.

"The portrait" Nicholas said quickly. "You must make sure

that the portrait among my possessions isn't damaged in any way.''

''No fret, lad. I think I understand the importance of such a piece of art,'' Captain Adamson answered, now moving on away, toward his cabin. ''And you two? Come aboard again sometime. I always welcome a member of the Brewster household on the ship I command,'' he quickly added with the toss of his head.

''That we might, sir,'' Nicholas yelled after him, half saluting. ''That we might.''

Jennifer's heart skipped a beat, now seeing a familiar carriage and a woman completely hidden beneath a black velveteen hooded cape standing next to it. ''There she is,'' she shouted, motioning, waving. ''There's my Aunt Minnie, Nicholas.'' Jennifer had to laugh a bit over what her aunt wore. Hardly an inch of her face was showing to the crowd. ''No place for a Christian woman to be,'' her aunt had grumbled, while waiting with Jennifer on the pier, before Jennifer had boarded the *Madrona* for her trip to San Francisco.

''I do hope she approves of me,'' Nicholas said, straightening his jacket and standing more tall and erect.

''She will. She will,'' Jennifer encouraged. She moved nervously from one foot to the other, waiting for the anchor to be dropped, and for the crowd to disperse, so she would be free to run from the ship, to fall into her aunt's embrace. . . .

Then she was. Running, feeling tears streaking down her cheeks, pushing her way through the crowded pier . . . until familiar arms reached out and captured her.

''Oh, Auntie. Auntie,'' she sobbed, clinging. ''It's so good to be home.''

''There, there. Aunt Minnie's here. I'll always be here. You know that.''

Jennifer pulled away a bit, wiping her eyes with the back of her hand, seeing that nothing had changed about her aunt. She looked no older . . . and no prettier, with her broad nose and pointed, stubble-covered chin. She *was* the same. The ever-caring aunt, whom Jennifer could always rely on. ''And, Auntie, you do look as though things are going fine for you," she said, sniffling.

"Just a touch more arthritis," Aunt Minnie said, rubbing a wrist. "And you?" she asked, studying Jennifer's eyes and feeling a deep relief. The restlessness . . . the sadness, were no longer there. And her complexion. How soft and radiant. Yes. Things had worked out for Jennifer. *But I'll never ask about Robert Harbison,* she thought. *Never. I don't even want to know what happened. He was evil . . . the devil himself. And he wouldn't have ever revealed the complete truths to Jennifer. Never. The truth that Thad . . . was her . . . father . . . instead of Frank.* Even though Robert Harbison was the devil . . . he couldn't have been *that* evil.

It still felt like knives piercing her heart when she would let herself remember it all. Her Camille . . . and how twisted Camille had become when she had discovered the intense pleasuring of sex. It had sickened Camille . . . absolutely sickened her.

"I'm gloriously happy, Auntie," Jennifer sighed, stepping back to tuck her arm through Nicholas's. "And here is my reason why." She looked upward onto Nicholas's weather-tanned face and piercing blue eyes and could see a nervous half-smile playing on his lips as Aunt Minnie's eyes settled on him. "This is my Nicholas," Jennifer quickly added, smiling warmly. "And, Nicholas, this is my Aunt Minnie."

"It's so nice to finally be meeting you, ma'am," Nicholas said, extending his free hand.

Jennifer's insides warmed even more when Aunt Minnie covered his hand with both of hers. "Young man, you just don't know the pleasure I'm receiving from this moment," Aunt Minnie said, now patting his hand fondly. "Jennifer is like my own daughter . . . and how I welcome a son into our midst."

Jennifer giggled. "Then shall we go home? I'm so anxious to see what you've done. Do you have many elderly housed there? Is it all going as well as we had hoped . . . ?"

Aunt Minnie laughed throatily. "Now hold on there Jennifer Lynn," she said. "You're getting way ahead of yourself with your questions. Just climb aboard this carriage and I'll take you and show you the happiness I shelter beneath the Brewster roof.''

''Then my plans did succeed?'' Jennifer asked, letting Nicholas assist her onto the carriage. She then watched as he hurried to the other side to also help her aunt. Then when he climbed beside her, she scooted closer to him and took his hand to place with hers on her lap. She couldn't be happier. She just couldn't.

''Land sakes, child,'' her aunt said, snapping the reins and clucking to the sleek black horse that Jennifer had commanded so often herself. ''The church gladly accepted the parsonage to be used as just that. It saved them having to spend money building another. And the elderly that we now house couldn't find anywhere else in Seattle that could give them such warmth and kindness as our house provides for them.''

''I'm so glad,'' Jennifer said. Then she remembered her one night on Market Street in San Francisco. ''Auntie, have you ever heard of the Salvation Army?'' she blurted.

''Only recently, Jennifer,'' she answered. ''Why do you ask?

''I saw some Salvation Army workers in San Francisco. They were actually uniformed. They seemed to be quite persuasive in preaching the ways of the Lord.''

''We've had a few street corner musicians here in Seattle,'' Aunt Minnie said. ''It seems to be a good movement. A group of sincere people. I haven't had a chance to see for myself, but I've heard that this group has bought a large house on Skid Road.''

''Skid Road?'' Jennifer gasped. Skid Road was the street lining the waterfront, similar to Front Street in San Francisco where she had had that dreadful room. ''Why would they choose Skid Road, Auntie?''

''Because that's where most of the poor and hungry are. I've heard that the Salvation Army plans to provide shelter and clothing to the needy, as we are also doing, plus administer to the spirit by bringing religion to many whom churches never reach. They are supposed to even help rebuild character for those men who have lost themselves in the bottle.''

"That is exactly how I'd like to add to our services also," Jennifer said, now taking in all the activity around her. As the carriage moved across the newly installed cobblestones on the streets, she was amazed at how much Seattle had begun to resemble San Francisco. In each city many well-dressed men and women filled the sidewalks, all absorbed, it seemed in their own little worlds of "self" as they hurried along, the women clutching on to their fancy bonnets and the men on to their derby hats.

The tall buildings that lined the main thoroughfare teased the eyes with their wares so invitingly arranged behind the pane-glass windows, and even an occasional vendor could be seen shouting his advertisements into the wind.

The streets were a steady clatter of carriage wheels and the clip-clopping of horse's hooves. There seemed to be much competition for the centermost part of the street, making Jennifer laugh to herself. Now if Seattle had cable cars and even horseless carriages to add to this mass of confusion . . . what a turmoil these drivers' minds would be in!

Then Jennifer felt the strain of the carriage as Aunt Minnie guided the horse left and upward onto Union Avenue. With a skipped heartbeat, Jennifer let her gaze wander and settle onto a window of a store that held unpleasant memories for her. She slowly read "Harbison's Pawnshop" . . . remembering it all over again. She turned her head away and squeezed her eyes tightly together. She had hoped that the new owner would have changed the name to his own. She didn't want this reminder. Not on the same street as the Brewster house. When she felt Nicholas tighten his grip on her hand, she suddenly realized that he had also seen the name.

"I've left your room untouched, Jennifer," Aunt Minnie said, snapping the reins again. "You and Nicholas can now redecorate it . . . to make it more suitable for man and wife."

Jennifer and Nicholas exchanged quick glances. They hadn't yet had a chance to tell Aunt Minnie of their decision to live away from Seattle. Now Jennifer dreaded it. She had seen the happiness that her arrival back home had brought to her aunt.

"Auntie?" she said softly, reaching to touch her aunt on a cheek. "Nicholas and I . . . well . . . we've come to a decision about something."

"What about, Jennifer? You do sound so serious."

"Auntie, Nicholas is originally from Illinois, where he was a farmer," Jennifer began, stopping to clear her throat nervously.

"Yes, dear? That's nice. But what else are you wanting to say?"

"Nicholas wants to live . . . on . . . a farm . . . somewhere outside Seattle," Jennifer stammered, watching her aunt closely for her reaction. She could see her aunt's face paling and the wavering of her pale gray eyes.

"You're saying . . . you don't want to share the Brewster house . . . and all the love that's there?"

"We can. For a while," Jennifer quickly answered.

"Until Nicholas builds your own house," Aunt Minnie said flatly. "That's what you mean. Isn't it?"

"Well . . . yes. . . ." Jennifer said softly, casting her eyes downward. An ache circled her heart. She didn't like disappointing Aunt Minnie, but Jennifer felt it quite imperative that she and Nicholas get a house of their own, to begin their new life together away from *all* remembrances of the past . . . no matter how much she also loved the Brewster house on Union Avenue.

"I will try to understand, Jennifer Lynn," Aunt Minnie sighed. You and your young man. I'm sure you need to be alone. And it *could* be an ideal place to raise children."

Jennifer's insides tightened, with the mention of children on her aunt's lips. What would Aunt Minnie think, if she knew of her first child . . . and the loss of its life? A tremor crept down her spine. But there was *no* way that her aunt could ever find out. Even Thad didn't know. . . .

"And Thad? Is he as well as he stated in his latest wire to me?" Aunt Minnie asked.

Another skipped heartbeat on Jennifer's part. So many truths were being kept from Aunt Minnie. "Yes. Thad is doing quite well," she murmured, knowing that Aunt Minnie hadn't been told of a "duel" . . . hadn't been told that Jennifer knew that

Thad was in truth her father and that Robert Harbison was in truth a Brewster.

"I've worried myself about the carriages on these Seattle hills," Aunt Minnie said, guiding the horse and carriage into the narrow drive next to the two-storied white frame house.

Jennifer's heart raced, seeing its familiar Victorian design, with its bristling turrets and bay windows, and its rich, gingerbread moldings. "It is nice to be home," she said softly, glad when Nicholas jumped from the now stopped carriage to assist her from it.

"But, darling, you must remember. It's for only a short time," he whispered, feeling the need to remind her. He could see something unsettling in her eyes as she kept looking toward the house.

Chapter Twenty-four

San Francisco, Wednesday, April 18, 1906

The skies had just begun to show a small trace of dusk through the shimmering layers of fog, while most of the city of San Francisco still lay in a deep, peaceful sleep. . . .

Thad pulled on his breeches, then his shirt, watching Lil pin a hat atop her thick clusters of curls. "Damn," he grumbled, stretching his arms above his head lazily. "I had hoped you would take an interest in my newest theater project, but I never counted on this kind of devotion. Do you have any idea what time it is, Lil?"

Lil swung the skirt of her maroon-colored velveteen dress around and smiled warmly toward him, showing no traces of having arisen so early. Her eyes were alive . . . vibrant . . . revealing her eagerness to move into another day of the exciting rewards of the theater. "Thad, doing this means so much to me," she said. "I feel as though I've elevated myself a bit above those snobbish bores who have looked down their noses at me for having a different colored skin. I feel I've arrived. Playing the lead role in "Graceful Gains" has done this for me."

"But, Lil. Rehearsals so early? God. Even I don't expect this much from my actors."

Lil set her jaw firmly, placing her hands on her hips. "But I do, Thadeus Brewster," she argued. "The earlier we rehearse, the fresher we are by earlier afternoon . . . when you plan to arrive to see what we have accomplished."

He went to her and pulled her into his embrace, kissing the tip of her pert nose. "Well, if you must, you must."

"Yes, I must," she said, kissing him in return, but only faintly, brushing her lips against his. She couldn't be happier . . . not even if they were wed. He treated her as his wife. To her that was all that truly mattered. And who cared what the gossip spreaders had to say?

"Tonight we'll go somewhere special. To make up for all your hard work, Lil."

"I like my quiet evenings with you, Thad."

"Then we'll go out for steaks and champagne and then come back here and celebrate in our own private corner of the world."

"Sounds marvelous, darling," she purred. She stepped back away from him and went to the window and stopped to look across the city. "It is a magnificent place in which to live," she whispered.

Thad went to stand beside her, also looking outward, seeing the bay . . . his ships . . . and then toward the city and at its tallest, newest buildings. "Progress," he said. "That's what it is. I'm sure you couldn't find theaters or hotels to compare in any other city."

Lil grew silent, suddenly studying the sky. Thad noticed this also, feeling slight waves of apprehension bubbling through him.

"The sky," Lil said. "Only moments ago, it was beautiful, with pinkish casts. Now it's a dirty color of gray. Do you think we're going to have one of those dreadful spring storms?"

Thad suddenly remembered the whispering of the transients on the waterfront the previous day. They had commented about its having been a muggy, breezeless afternoon. "Earthquake weather" they had called it.

But Thad had scoffed at this, knowing that these sailors had fun building tales to such ungodly proportions. ''I'm sure it's nothing to worry about, Lil,'' he finally answered. ''It's probably just something the sea breeze has blown in. It will probably blow away again just as quickly.''

Lil lifted the skirt of her dress and rushed for the bedroom door. ''Well, I hope so, darling,'' she sighed. ''I would at least like to make it to the theater's door before a nasty rain begins to fall.''

Thad followed her down the stairs and to the front door. He grabbed her hands and pulled her next to him, feeling the need to have her lips next to his again. It was as though he would never see her again. It was a foreboding . . . one he didn't understand. His fingers moved to the front of her and caressed a breast. ''Now you take care of yourself, Lil,'' he said thickly. ''You're my girl. Forever and ever. You know that, don't you?''

Lil laughed nervously, looking upward into his eyes. ''Darling, you're acting as strangely as the weather,'' she said. ''In fact, you're making me a bit afraid.''

He pulled away from her and opened the door, inhaling the fresh fragrance of early morning. He reached outward and plucked a red rose from a trellis and offered it to her. ''You just don't pay any attention to me,'' he said. ''Be on your way and enjoy what you do best.''

She eyed him warily. ''You'll be all right?''

''Hell yes,'' he laughed.

She blew him a kiss and rushed down the steps and on around to the livery stable. Thad continued to watch until her black carriage began to move down Nob Hill and onward, until it made a turn at Fifth Avenue.

Again his gaze moved slowly around him. His brows furrowed. It was too damn quiet. Even the neighborhood dogs had ceased to bark. A slight rumbling noise in the distance made him tense. His eyes grew wide with fear as he saw the newly installed telephone lines outside his house begin to sway slowly back and forth, then come to a halt once again.

Shivers engulfed Thad, making him rush back into the

warmth of his house. He went to stand before the fire, glad that a servant had chosen to get one started so early in the morning for him.

He wiped his brow with the back of his hand. "Damn. I sure feel spooked," he mumbled, then grew quiet again when the chandelier hanging from the center of the parlor ceiling began to make slight tinkling noises. Thad swung around and stared upward, but found that even that noise ceased as quickly as it had begun.

"What the hell's going on here?" he thought, turning to face the fire once again. His eyes shifted upward, noticing that Jennifer's portrait had slid to an off angle. Fear truly began to grip him then, and when he heard the thuds of books falling from his bookcases, he knew what was happening.

He took a step forward, reaching up to rescue Jennifer's portrait before the earthquake surely hit with full force. But he was too late. The outer wall collapsed before his eyes. Now all he could hear was the deafening sound of rumbles and roars, and when he looked out onto the street, he saw the street rippling likes waves on an ocean.

"God, what can I do?" he shouted, trying to steady himself. The chandelier crashed behind him and he could now feel the floor swaying beneath his feet.

He rushed to the door that hung open at an awkward angle and continued on down the steps. A shower of fire fell around him, as though from a large Fourth of July sparkler. Everywhere he looked, walls were collapsing, and the torn streets were becoming heaps of tangled rubble and smoking ashes.

Struggling to run uphill, Thad feared the worst. His thoughts lay heavily on Lil and what had become of her. It was impossible for him to go and try to find her in all the destruction.

Breathless, he stopped and turned, gasping loudly at what he saw. Hundreds of brick chimneys had been snapped off at the rooflines. Interior walls and floors of many buildings were rudely exposed because the outer walls had crumbled and fallen away. Electric wires were dangling, sizzling at the tips. . . .

Where there wasn't fire ravaging the city there were billowing clouds of smoke where the fire had just begun.

Thad covered his eyes and hung his head. Sobs tore through him, as he heard the frantic cries of terror from all around him. He was only one among the hundreds who were seeking refuge at the top of Nob Hill. He was only one among the hundreds who had just lost everything. . . .

Two weeks later
Seattle

"Mother, should I set the table yet?" five-year-old Carolyn Ann asked, as she slipped her golden curls around her shoulders.

Jennifer tasted the stew, smelling its aroma of garden vegetables and beef circling upward. Nicholas had proven himself as a farmer. Their small family of four never lacked for food. The garden Nicholas seemed to toil in both day and night consistently thrived with fresh vegetables and fruit . . . the cattle provided them with all the meat, butter, and milk that they ever would desire . . . and the chickens kept their cellar filled with fresh eggs.

Placing the lid back on the pot, Jennifer turned and eyed her daughter warmly. "Yes, dear. You can, if you wish," she answered, wiping her hands on her lace-trimmed apron.

"I'm going to grow up to be a perfect wife just like you are, Mother," Carolyn Ann said, folding and placing linen napkins next to each plate on the table. She batted her thick lashes nervously as she stopped to look out the dining room window. "I shan't be like my sister, Martha Elaine." She shuddered visibly. "I just shan't. How *can* she stand to get her hands in the dirt? She's disgusting. She's always in the garden with father. Does she think she was born a boy . . . or what?"

Jennifer pulled the skirt of her cotton dress up into her arms and moved also to the window. She gazed with pride toward the garden where six-year-old Martha Elaine Oglesby was working alongside her father, dropping corn into furrowed mounds. Yes, it seemed that somewhere along the line a mistake had been made. Martha Elaine had the willowy limbs of a boy and the desire to act as one, even though she had been given the delicate, hidden traits of a female.

"See, Mother?" Carolyn Ann stormed, stomping a foot. "Isn't it just too disgraceful?"

Jennifer bent down to be at eye level with Carolyn Ann, holding her by the waist. Looking into her slanted, piercing blue eyes, Jennifer was again aware of the possibilities of a stormy future ahead for her daughter. She had all the Brewster traits . . . the determination . . . the haughtiness . . . and the restlessness. And vain as Jennifer was, she recognized the beauty that this child also possessed.

She smoothed Carolyn Ann's hair back from her forehead. "Darling, we all are born with different needs," she began. "You mustn't be constantly judging your sister. If she likes to be outdoors with her father, be that as it may. When the time is proper, she will become as a lady must. Now will you please quit fretting about such a small thing as dirt beneath your sister's fingernails?"

"But the picture books we've been taught to read never show a girl doing boy things."

"Well, maybe I'd better buy you some different picture books," Jennifer said flatly. "Now if you wish to set the table, please get to it. But I do ask that you leave your sister be. Do you hear me, Carolyn Ann?"

Carolyn Ann's lips drew into a tight pout. "Yes, Mother," she murmured.

Jennifer turned and playfully smacked Carolyn Ann on her small behind and said, "Okay, then. What are you waiting for?"

When Carolyn Ann was all absorbed in getting each piece of china, silverware and glass set perfectly in place, Jennifer strolled on into the parlor, feeling at peace with the world.

Each room in the house spoke of comfort. Not the kind of comfort found in either the Brewster home in San Francisco or in Seattle. But this house had a cozy comfort, radiating from the simple line of mahogany tables and upholstered, thickly cushioned chairs. The walls were papered in delicate prints, and the hardwood floors glistened from a fresh coat of wax.

Ruffled curtains hung at each window and intimate family portraits had been placed in clusters along the staircase wall that led upward.

Jennifer sat down on a brightly flowered, upholstered sofa in front of a blazing fire on the hearth. She and Nicholas had spent many romantic nights in this very room, on this very sofa . . . while their two daughters slept soundly in their separate rooms on the second floor of this house that Nicholas had built with his own hands.

After they had moved in with Aunt Minnie those seven long years ago, it had taken Nicholas longer than he had planned to build this house in the country, and Jennifer had soon fallen into a set pattern at the Brewster house. She had loved catering to the elderly people, all the while not realizing that, while doing so, she had neglected the one of more importance to her . . . her beloved Nicholas.

But once the house had been completed and Jennifer and Nicholas were finally on their own, she had soon found herself to be with child. And soon after Martha Elaine's birth, she was pregnant again. And now? They were hoping that the child she was now carrying would be the son that Nicholas had been so hoping and praying for.

Her gaze shifted upward. The ''Portrait of Desire,'' hung above the mantelpiece. Jennifer's hands went to her hair, frowning, thinking about the many times her daughters had questioned her about the dark hair of the portrait. Their mother's hair was as golden and soft as golden spun silk.

''This was painted in your mother's daring, carefree days,'' Nicholas had laughed. But Jennifer could never laugh about it. She knew the story behind the dyed hair and hated the reminder of the ugly past of the Brewsters.

The sound of carriage wheels against the graveled path that led up the narrow lane to the house drew Jennifer's attention. She pushed herself up from the sofa and removed her apron.

She sucked in her belly, smiling, glad that she hadn't yet begun to swell in front. But she would. And soon. She was at least three months along now. Hopefully Nicholas Junior would be born during the summer months.

The carriage drawing nearer made her brows tilt in wonder. Nicholas hadn't mentioned expecting company. And neighbors lived too far apart on this quiet, empty strip of country to just casually drop in on one another.

"Mother?"

Jennifer looked around as Martha Elaine ran into the room, tracking garden dirt in with each step.

Exasperated, Jennifer hurried to her. "Would you look at the mess you're making, Martha Elaine?" she scolded, guiding her daughter toward the front door. "Now you get yourself right out that door and clean yourself off before entering this house again."

Martha Elaine tossed her rust-colored pigtails around as she set her jaw firmly. Her pale gray eyes danced as she openly defied her mother. "But, Mother," she said, "Father sent me in to tell you that he believes that's Aunt Minnie's carriage coming toward the house."

Jennifer's eyes widened and heart began to thump nervously. "Why didn't you tell me sooner?" she said, rushing toward the door. It had been at least six months now since she had seen her aunt. Aunt Minnie kept so involved with the elderly and Jennifer was so busy with her family and household chores that neither took the time that they should have to be in one another's company.

"But, Mother, I tried," Martha Elaine said, following close behind. "If you hadn't been so worried about a little bit of dirt. . . ." she began to add, but was interrupted.

"Just hush about the dirt, Martha Elaine," Jennifer scolded. "Just hush." She pushed the door open just in time to see Aunt Minnie tying the horse's reins to a hitching post at the foot of the front porch steps. Then Jennifer's heart jolted, making her head begin to spin when she saw another familiar figure climbing from the carriage. Her hand went to her mouth as she gasped loudly.

Martha Elaine pushed next to her, clinging to her skirt. ''Who is that with Aunt Minnie?'' she asked, seeing a tall, thin man, who was limping and leaning heavily onto a cane as he moved toward the house. She had never seen such sadness expressed in eyes before. And . . . weren't his eyes shaped like her mother's and her sister Carolyn Ann's . . . and the color of pale gray like her very own?

''Thad?'' Jennifer whispered, not believing what the past seven years had done to him. He no longer looked the successful businessman. He walked instead like a man who had lost everything. Where was his restlessness . . . that had helped keep his interest in life soaring . . . no matter what happened to him?

''Mother? Who *is* that?'' Martha Elaine persisted, as she tugged harder on her mother's dress.

''That's your . . . Uncle Thadeus, darling,'' Jennifer said softly, full of wonder now as to what was behind Thad's arrival. When the goodbyes had been exchanged in San Francisco, Jennifer had thought them to be the last.

But now? What hurts were going to be revived . . . ?

''Jennifer?'' Thad said cautiously as he stood at the porch steps looking upward.

Jennifer swallowed back a lump in her throat and inched her way to the edge of the porch, wishing that she could keep the trembling from showing in her hands and voice. ''Thad, how nice to see you,'' she said, extending a hand as Thad began to maneuver his wooden leg up the steps. Jennifer wanted to look away from him, seeing now the deep furrows of his face and the grayness of his thinning hair. And, oh, how he was struggling with each step!

''I wired Minnie of my arrival,'' Thad said, clasping onto Jennifer's hand. ''She only informed me today that you didn't know I was on my way.''

Jennifer felt the boniness of his hand as she now clung to it. ''We don't have means of communication out here in the shadow of Mount Rainier,'' she said, laughing nervously. ''We're lucky if we even get mail delivered once a month.''

''And you like it that way?'' Thad asked. ''What if you or your . . . children . . . were to get suddenly ill?''

''We have a doctor friend who lives up the road apiece,'' Jennifer said, now seeing Thad staring openly at Martha Elaine. Tears burned at the corner of Jennifer's eyes, knowing what had to be in Thad's thoughts . . . that he was seeing one of his . . . granddaughters . . . for the very first time.

''Martha Elaine, come stand beside me,'' Jennifer urged, surprised at her daughter's sudden shyness. Martha Elaine was usually quite forward. And, oh, if she had only at least scrubbed her face and shaken the garden dirt from her gathered cotton dress. . . .

''Yes, Mother?'' Martha Elaine said demurely.

''This is your Uncle Thadeus. I've spoken of him so often to you. Now you're finally getting to meet him.''

Martha Elaine smiled weakly and extended a hand. ''It's grand to get to meet you, sir,'' she said most politely, again surprising Jennifer. But, oh, those fingernails. They were indeed black with the field dirt.

''The pleasure is all mine,'' Thad said, clasping her hand tightly. ''Yes, the pleasure is *all* mine.''

Jennifer bit her lower lip, filled with the deep, hurtful emotions of the moment.

Aunt Minnie moved up the steps and to Jennifer's side, attired in her usual black velveteen hooded cape. ''I hope our visit isn't an imposition on your family,'' she whispered. ''But it was a trip that was needed.''

''But why didn't you let me know, Auntie?'' Jennifer whispered back.

''I didn't want you worrying your fool head off about it. That's why,'' Minnie answered.

''Tell me what's happened, Auntie. Thad didn't come all the way to Washington State just to see us . . . and he looks so . . . bedraggled. Tell me what's happened.''

''After we get settled by the fire and Nicholas and Carolyn

Ann are also present," Aunt Minnie said, glancing back to Thad.

"Then let's hurry on inside now," Jennifer said. "Nicholas saw your arrival. I'm sure he's inside washing up."

Aunt Minnie turned to Thad and held out a hand. "Thadeus, let's go see the inside of Jennifer's house," she said quietly, as though she was urging a mindless child onward.

Jennifer looked toward Mount Rainier and shivered. Somehow it seemed foreboding this late afternoon. The sun was lost from its peak, and low, swirling clouds circled and fell, creating a slow falling mist at its base.

With arms hugging herself, Jennifer hurried on inside the house after Aunt Minnie, Thad, and Martha Elaine, dreading to hear the reasons behind Thad's visit. She had succeeded at pushing the knowledge of his being her true father from her mind . . . till now. But now? He appeared so helpless. Unloved. And . . . where was Lil? Hadn't Lil truly loved him as much as she had professed? Or had he grown too old and feeble for the likes of Lil . . . ?

Chapter Twenty-five

The coffee was poured and served, and everyone was filled with the evening meal of beef stew and fresh apple pie. It was a family reunion of sorts. They were all arranged around the cozy flames burning on the hearth in the parlor.

"Cigar, Brewster?" Nicholas asked, offering one to Thad, sticking the tip of one in his own mouth. Damn. He would never have put bets on the arrival of Brewster at his house. Thad should have known just how unwelcome he'd be.

"Thanks," Thad mumbled, seeing the utter contempt that Oglesby still held him in. Damn it. Didn't Oglesby know that he wouldn't have shown up without a hell of a good reason; he thought harshly to himself. Then he had to truly wonder if he really should have pulled Jennifer and her family into his own personal tragedy? But he had to. Damn it. He just had to.

"Auntie, you and Thad will want to spend the night," Jennifer said. "You wouldn't want to travel in the dark by horse and carriage clear back to Seattle."

"You have the room, do you?" Aunt Minnie asked, pushing some loose strands of hair into the tight bun on her head.

"The girls can share a room tonight. One of theirs will be

available. And I have a spare bedroom besides that,'' Jennifer said, drawing some ''Oh, nos'' from both her daughters. They had never liked sharing a bedroom . . . the same as they never liked sharing anything of one another's. They were two separate individuals . . . so obviously opposites.

Nicholas settled down onto his favorite overstuffed chair and laughed to himself as his daughters settled on the floor in front of him, each choosing a separate knee to rest their arms upon. He patted first one head and then the other . . . then eyed Thad questioningly.

''Okay, Brewster,'' he began, furrowing his brow. ''We've had supper, our coffee, and idle chat. Now, let's find out what the true reason is behind this visit. Should I ask the girls to leave the room?''

Thad leaned forward with his full weight on his cane. ''No. The girls can hear what I've got to say,'' he said. ''In fact, what's happened will be in the history books for as long as there's people interested in reading about tragedies of the past.''

Jennifer's eyes widened. She scooted to the edge of her chair, working nervously with the gathers of her dress. ''What *are* you talking about, Thad?'' she asked.

''Then you haven't heard about what happened in San Francisco?''

Nicholas glared toward Thad. ''Good God, man, will you get on with it?'' he said irritably.

''There was an earthquake,'' Thad said, stopping to puff nervously on his cigar.

''An earthquake?'' Jennifer gasped. ''When? How . . . bad . . . ? And . . . how were you affected personally, Thad?''

Thad settled back against the chair with his thin, narrow shoulders slumped. ''When?'' he said. ''Two weeks ago. How bad? The worst. Four hundred fifty-two people died. I was a lucky one. I at least got out alive.''

''Brewster, how terrible,'' Nicholas said, unable to envision any tragedy besides war that could cause so many deaths at once. ''Tell us more about the details.''

''The damn fire caused by broken gas pipes caused far more

damage than the shock of the earthquake,'' Thad said sullenly.
''The firefighting equipment could not be counted on to help
because the streets were stacked so with fallen debris from the
buildings.''

''Thad, this is all so terrible,'' Jennifer gasped further. ''And
. . . the . . . Brewster house?''

''Destroyed. Gutted by fire,'' he answered. ''In fact, everything I owned . . . all lost in smoke and flames.''

''Everything?'' Nicholas asked, remembering the house, and
Thad's many buildings that housed his business.

''Everything. All that was left were my ships, and they were
at sea. And even those I've just sold.''

Jennifer rose and went to stand closer to the fire. A chill had
filled her. A chill that was circling and settling around her
heart. ''You've sold . . . your . . . ships?'' she asked quietly.

''Everything else was gone in the fire, so I felt that I had
nothing else left.'' His face became all shadows. ''You see . . .
even Lil . . . was lost in the fire.''

''Lil . . . ?'' Jennifer said, feeling her head spinning from
the shock of this all being revealed to her.

''She was in one of my buildings, rehearsing for a stage
play. She didn't . . . have . . . a chance.''

''I'm sorry, Brewster,'' Nicholas mumbled. ''And now.
What are your plans?''

''I've moved in with Minnie,'' Thad said hurriedly.

Jennifer's gaze shot toward Minnie then back to Thad. ''You
. . . and . . . Minnie . . . ?''

Thad laughed hoarsely. ''It's not what you think, Jennifer,''
he said, flipping ashes from his cigar into an ashtray. Then his
brows tilted upward. ''But . . . it's an idea. . . .''

''Then you are planning to live in Seattle?'' Jennifer said
softly, turning to face the fire. She knew that she shouldn't be
thinking of her own self at such a time as this. Thad had lost
everything . . . except for his daughter, his granddaughters, and
his sister-in-law. . . .

But could he live so close to his granddaughters without
revealing his true identity to them?

"Would it be so terribly wrong if I did, Jennifer?" Thad said, pushing himself up from the chair to go to her side. His gaze went to the portrait. "And even all the Brewster portraits were lost in the fire ... along with the one special one you painted for me, Oglesby."

A warning shot through Jennifer as her gaze traveled to Martha Elaine and Carolyn Ann. Their eyes were wide and their ears were even larger. They had a way of absorbing things that they shouldn't yet hear ... at their young ages. "Girls, please go on and prepare for bed," she urged. "I'll be up directly and tuck you both in."

"Oh, Mother, please," Carolyn Ann begged.

"I don't want to sleep with Carolyn Ann," Martha Elaine blurted.

"Both you girls heard your mother. To bed with the both of you," Nicholas said firmly.

"Oh, all right," the girls said in unison, then arose and took turns kissing everyone good night, except for Thad.

Carolyn Ann was the first to approach Thad. She looked up at him, with her hands clasped tightly behind her. "Would you want me to kiss you good night, Uncle Thadeus?" she asked demurely.

Martha Elaine pushed her way in front of Carolyn Ann. "And me too?" she said eagerly. "I've never been kissed by an uncle before. Would you want to kiss me, Uncle Thadeus? Huh?"

Jennifer's heartbeats filled her as she watched Thad bend and kiss each girl on the cheek. Then as they rushed, squealing, up the stairs, Jennifer watched Thad's expression of sheer delight.

"And now, Brewster," Nicholas said, rising to go to Jennifer. He placed his arm around her waist, drawing her to him. "What does all of this mean?"

"It seems I've aged a bit, Oglesby," Thad grumbled, leaning his weight against his cane. "I'm ready to retire and felt it should be done in a more serene setting than California. I've heard many speak highly of this paradise in the northwest country, and I knew that Minnie had this retirement home of hers going. I didn't care to live alone any longer. It gets lonesome on the top . . . and even more lonesome when one is suddenly thrown to the bottom.''

"Then you have lost everything . . . all your wealth, because of the earthquake?'' Nicholas prodded.

"All but what I will receive from the sale of my ships.''

Aunt Minnie arose and went to Jennifer's side. "Honey, all Thad's asking is that you'll say his being in Seattle won't create problems for you.''

"But, Auntie . . . you just . . . don't. . . .''

"Yes. I do. I know it all.''

"Everything?'' Jennifer gasped. "Who . . . ?''

"I've known all along,'' Aunt Minnie said. "But I didn't know that *you* knew until Thad confided in me. That Robert Harbison. He *was* the devil. Most surely the devil himself.''

"But I'd never want Carolyn Ann or Martha Elaine to know . . . *any* of this,'' Jennifer said, chewing nervously on her lower lip.

"I'd never let them know my true identity,'' Thad said softly, glancing quickly toward the staircase. "But I would like to have the opportunity of seeing them occasionally.''

"I thought you were going to get so involved in moving pictures,'' Nicholas said.

"Like I said. *All* lost in the fire. And along with it . . . also went my spirit. It's hard to explain how one's ambitions can suddenly be gone in the blink of an eye. But that's how it is with me, Oglesby.''

"Jennifer, what do you think?'' Nicholas asked, taking her by the shoulders.

"It's not only my decision,'' she murmured.

"But he is asking for your approval.''

"Then I must say yes to whatever he wishes.''

"Jennifer, are you sure?''

"Nicholas . . . he . . . *is* . . . my . . . father,'' she said, casting her eyes downward. A sudden warmth surged through her, realizing what she had just said. She looked quickly up at Thad

. . . and saw that he had also heard. It showed in the wetness of his eyes as tears began to trickle down his cheeks.

"It is truly all right with me, Thad," she murmured. "I'd be glad to share my family with you. Truly I would."

She crept slowly into his arms and hugged him.

Even though Thad was now an old man, he was even more that small child that she had discovered in him after his duel with Robert Harbison.

Yes, Thad hungered for attention and love, and she would gladly share all that she had been so blessed with herself. He *was* . . . her father . . . wasn't he?

Chapter Twenty-six

The sunrise was like a half-orange resting against the horizon, and the moisture in the air were sprays of sweetness from it.

The swaying of the carriage moving along the dirt road made Jennifer cling more tightly to the seat. She inhaled deeply. She loved these early mornings in the country, and dreaded spending necessary time required to have her baby in the busy pace of Seattle.

She reached up and patted her swollen abdomen, feeling stirrings of her unborn child. She longed for a boy . . . as did Nicholas . . . but a third daughter born to her would be welcome enough.

She sighed deeply. She was just anxious to lose the added burdensome weight and become someone Nicholas could desire . . . hold . . . and make love to once again. She had so missed his most intimate of caresses these past several weeks. But the complications she had developed had become cause to change all of their lives.

Loud bouts of throaty squeals startled Jennifer, making her turn with a start to look behind her. Her brow furrowed when she found Carolyn Ann and Martha Elaine pushing at one another, instead of sitting quietly, as prim and proper as girls were supposed to do.

"What's the matter now?" Jennifer sighed, looking from one daughter to the other. They were constant rivals. Would it always be that way? But maybe a new baby in the house would change even this.

"Martha won't scoot over and give me more room on the seat," Carolyn pouted, sucking in her lower lip.

"You appear to have enough room, Carolyn Ann," Jennifer scolded, breathing hard when a sudden pain shot through her abdomen. She clutched at herself, hoping Nicholas wouldn't notice. The pains had come and gone now for way too many days. The country doctor had suddenly seemed inadequate.

Jennifer's gaze went to Martha. "And Martha," she blurted, "will you please quit sucking on the tip of your pigtail? That's a very nasty habit you have recently acquired."

Martha's eyes cast downward. "Yes, Mother," she replied, but now fidgeting nervously with the fringe that hung, wiggling and swaying, from the carriage top.

"Honey. . . ." Jennifer heard Nicholas say from close beside her.

She held on to her abdomen and tried to straighten her back, to look as though nothing was wrong. The pain would subside. It always did. It would probably be days yet before the baby was born. She forced a smile when she looked toward Nicholas. "Yes, dear?" she purred mechanically.

Nicholas flicked the reins and clucked to the team of sleek black horses. When his gaze met Jennifer's, she could see the concern in the depths of the blue. "You mustn't excite yourself," he said, with the firmness that he used when speaking to the children. "The girls will be girls. Just let them be. We shall reach Seattle soon. Then all will be all right. You'll see."

Jennifer grabbed at the seat when the carriage wheels fell into a pothole and bounced roughly out again. "But the girls do always argue so," she grumbled. "I grow so weary of it, Nicholas."

"Then we have made the right decision to go to Thad's

house for a while. Maybe his female house servants can take charge. It can do us all some good.''

''Maybe it would have been best if we had decided on Aunt Minnie's house,'' Jennifer said softly. ''I still worry a bit about . . . well . . . you know. . . .''

''Shhh, Jennifer,'' Nicholas scolded. ''The girls. Always remember the big ears. . . .''

Glancing over her shoulder, Jennifer could see that the girls had not heard. They were once again fussing at one another. ''Please, Carolyn Ann?'' she scolded. ''Your father's paintings are right beside your feet. One kick and a week's hard labor would be destroyed. Do you hear me?''

A loud sigh emerged, along with a quick blink of the eyes. ''Yes, Mother,'' she said sullenly. ''I hear you.''

''All right then. I hope I don't have to tell you again.'' A warm hand fell across Jennifer's, enfolding it. She looked toward Nicholas once again and smiled weakly. She knew that the tensions of the past several weeks had kept him from painting at his best. She had seen it in the strokes of the brush in the evenings as he had sat painting . . . when she had tried to look busy knitting. But soon . . . very soon . . . it would surely be over.

''And also, honey,'' Nicholas said. ''The elderly people at Aunt Minnie's. So many aren't capable of taking care of themselves. Aunt Minnie just doesn't need two frisky girls disturbing all those people who take naps at all hours of the day.''

''Yes, I know,'' Jennifer agreed. It warmed her heart seeing the change in Nicholas toward Thad. It had come slowly, but it had come. But she had known all along that this would be, for all who knew Thad *had* to like him. His personality had always been jovial. Only immediately after the earthquake had she seen a change. But now he seemed to be his old self . . . ready to meet and challenge the world.

The skyline of Seattle came into view, almost hidden by a low-lying foggy haze. But the closer the carriage moved toward it, the more Jennifer could see. It was a city of means, now. The population had tripled since the Yukon gold rush. And the buildings reached into the sky, almost resembling the mountains in the distance. It amazed Jennifer how they could build such tall structures of brick and concrete. But she had seen it also in San Francisco. The two cities had so resembled each other with their streets climbing up such steep grades and their bays always filled with ships. Yes, to be in Seattle had almost been the same as being in San Francisco.

But now? Whenever she thought of San Francisco and how it had been leveled by the earthquake, an ache crept around her heart. In San Francisco, she had learned many things. Some she would rather forget, and others she stored inside the deepest recesses of her mind. San Francisco was where her and Nicholas's love and faith in one another had grown into what they still shared today.

"Do you really think you'll be all right while I try and sell some of my art work?" Nicholas said, interrupting Jennifer's train of thought.

Readjusting the hat atop her head and placing the hatpin through the thin layer of straw and into a thicker wad of hair that lay beneath the hat, Jennifer tried to reassure Nicholas. She knew the importance to him of selling some of his paintings. Not so much for the money . . . but for Nicholas's self-esteem. "I shall be fine, Nicholas," she said, thrusting her chin proudly up into the air, yet hating the extra layer of fat that had circled beneath it, making her appear almost double-chinned. She only hoped that once the baby was born she could be assured of being just as lovely as the portrait of her that hung in her parlor.

"And you do want me to drop you and the girls off at Thad's new theater?" he asked. "Are you sure he'll be there?"

Jennifer laughed softly. "Yes, dear. Isn't he always?"

"But so early in the day?"

"I wrote him of my arrival. When he telephoned, he said that I could find him there. That he was anxious to show off what he had accomplished."

"I don't like the fact that Thad took it upon himself to call the telephone company and have that telephone contraption installed in our house," Nicholas grumbled. "We have the money to take care of our own needs."

"He only was worried about my welfare, Nicholas."

"And I'm not?" he stormed.

"Please, Nicholas," Jennifer said softly. "Every once in a while, you sound as though you are renewing your hate for Thad. Please don't. I thought you had changed your mind about him. Completely. I don't think I could bear to go through all that hatred all over again."

Nicholas slackened his hold on the reins and leaned an elbow on a knee when he thrust his foot to rest against the front of the carriage. "It's a fact that I like Thad," he said thickly. "But I just don't want charity. Not from anyone. You know how I feel about that."

"But aren't you glad that Thad has come out of the shell he built around himself after that tragic earthquake took all he owned in San Francisco?"

"Yeah. Sure."

"Just look at what he's done for himself. He took the money he received from the sale of his ships and invested it in a beautiful home, and then even was able to buy that old opera building. Why, I bet he's fixed it up to be beautiful. I bet it's a showplace to outshine all other theaters in Seattle."

"I guess that's better than wasting away like he had planned," Nicholas said. "But I sure don't see why he would choose the theater again. You know he sure isn't any spring chicken. I wonder how long he thinks he can keep up the rat race he chooses to run?"

"I'm sure he's perfectly capable of taking care of himself, Nicholas."

"Yeah. Sure. And who else? Didn't you say he had another wench to cling onto his arm? Damn. I sure wouldn't have believed it. When he first arrived from San Francisco, he looked like he was at death's door. I guess it's the Brewster in him. Just strong-willed and determined . . . like someone else I know?"

Jennifer laughed and scooted closer to Nicholas. She wrapped her arm around his waist and leaned into him. "I'm a bit tamed now, don't you think?'' she purred, looking sheepishly up into his eyes. She tried not to wince when another sharp pain shot downward, into her lower abdomen, then seemed to rock her vaginal walls. Darn. When would she know when it was for real? All pains were the same now. When the doctor had said that the baby might be lying wrong inside her, her fears had begun to mount. But surely the well-known doctors of Seattle could help her and her unborn child. She so wanted this baby . . . as well as many more if at all possible. She loved being a mother . . . a wife.

"And who tamed you? Huh?'' Nicholas boasted, winking.

"The one and only Nicholas Oglesby. That's who,'' Jennifer teased. She began to wonder about what Nicholas had said about Thad's having another woman as a companion. That was the only thing disturbing her now about having agreed to stay at Thad's house until the baby was born.

What if Thad had chosen another black woman to share his bed? How could Martha Elaine and Carolyn Ann understand anything like that? They hadn't even seen any Negroes yet. Living in the country had kept them too sheltered, it seemed.

But. No. Surely not. Surely Thad had chosen to look more respectable in his later years. Mixed relationships were very much frowned upon in Seattle. Seattle was not as loose in morals as San Francisco had been. She only hoped that he hadn't taken from the Brewster name by being so darn foolish.

As they approached the city the houses at the side of the road were closer and closer together. Jennifer became all eyes. It had been months since she had been to Seattle and she always marveled at what changes she discovered each time she returned. New houses seemed to be springing up from the soil just like trees. They were very nicely built in neat wooden brown squares, and most all were painted neatly and had yards decorated with flower beds or flowering bushes. The aromas of lilacs and roses continued to cling to Jennifer like rare perfumes as Nicholas turned the carriage onto Market Street and began to move toward the busiest thoroughfares of the city.

Vendors were busy setting up their stalls, some already chanting to people in carriages and on horseback who moved on the street in front of them. The shine of the apples represented the best picked from Seattle's own trees and reminded Jennifer of the orchard that she was told that she could look down upon from Thad's newly purchased mansion on Seventh Avenue.

A vendor holding a swollen bouquet of gold roses caught Jennifer's eye. She hadn't been to the graveyard to visit her mother and father's graves for some time now. How she would love to place a bouquet on each grave and even whisper a silent prayer for them to possibly hear. But Nicholas moved the carriage on past and stopped before a towering red brick building.

Jennifer stared all around her, seeing billboards covering the front of the building, advertising the stage play that was performed there each evening of the week. A tremble passed through her, knowing that Thad's dreams had once again come true. He owned another theater . . . and this one was more respectable than the last, visited, he had said, by only the richest of clientele.

"Isn't it something, Nicholas?" she whispered, seeing the fresh shine of the door that led inside. Its red enamel was reflected in the huge brass handles, and gaslights flickered on each side of it, even though it was day, and even though the electric lightbulb was now the most fashionable way to light one's establishment.

Thad had told Jennifer that he had had this new invention installed in his new house. She was anxious to see the lighted rooms. She had heard that the lightbulbs made crystal sparkle even more than candles.

Nicholas secured the reins and jumped from the carriage, walking to Jennifer's side. "I'm going in with you, honey," he said, lifting his arms, offering to help her from the carriage. "No way am I going to rush off without seeing that you are safe and sound with Thad. At least I will know that if those pains get to doing what they should to bring our baby to us, Thad will take you by his carriage to the hospital."

Jennifer tossed her head, tsk tsking. "Oh, how you fret so, my darling," she sighed. She inched across the seat, then held arms out to him, groaning when she stepped down onto the cobblestones of the street. It always seemed to send a tearing sensation clear through her whenever she moved too much at one time. Bed rest. That's what the doctor had said. But Jennifer had had enough of lying flat on her back to last for a lifetime ... unless Nicholas was stretched out beside her, touching her making her come to life. . . .

"I don't think I should even go and sell my paintings on a street corner today, Jennifer," he grumbled further, circling her waist with an arm to steady her as she teetered. "You know I'm only doing it because you've insisted."

Jennifer wiped her brow with the back of a hand, breathing hard. "I wouldn't be happy if you didn't, Nicholas," she said. She tried to straighten her back and waddled away from him, putting her hand to her side, pushing into it when the baby gave a quick kick from inside her. She eyed Nicholas with heavy lids. "Now will you go on? I'm sure Thad is here. Your daughters will have the time of their lives in this magnificent building."

Nicholas set his jaw firmly, again circling her waist. "Let's all go inside," he said. "I guess I must admit, I'm a bit anxious to see it all, too. And I'd like to shake hands with Thad, for bettering himself. Damn proud of that man, I am."

Jennifer closed her eyes, and leaned into him. "Oh, darling, you make me the happiest. Did you know that?"

"I certainly hope so," he chuckled, then turned his eyes to the back seat of the carriage. "Come on, daughters. Let's go see your Uncle Thadeus." His eyes settled on the many paintings he had placed against the back seat. "But I can only stay for a brief moment," he quickly added. "I can't take a chance that someone will steal my masterpieces while we're inside the theater." He chuckled again and gladly accepted the hands of his daughters as they ran to him. The family of four and one-half made their way toward the door.

The first step inside took Jennifer into semidarkness. When

her eyes adjusted she could see a figure walking toward her. From the slow gait, she knew that it was Thad. Her heart palpitated. She hadn't seen him since that day he had surprised them . . . the day he had looked at least a hundred years old because of the hardships he had encountered. She was almost afraid to see him again. Had he aged even more? If he had, she knew that seeing him would tear at her heart.

Thad stopped to flip a switch, then watched in admiration as his theater was flooded with bright lights from all sides. He looked toward Jennifer and ached for what he still felt for the past . . . for Camille . . . and now for his daughter . . . that he couldn't shout to the world was his. Then his eyes shifted downward, seeing his two grandchildren. He couldn't even be allowed to claim them . . . and weren't they a delight? He could hardly wait to have them as a part of his house. Wouldn't it take him back a few years? To when Jennifer had been a child and had made her brief visits to his house . . . to sit by the fire and talk. . . . How he had enjoyed telling her ghost stories. He now could even recall some of these to tell his . . . grandchildren.

One on each . . . knee. No. He knew that this was impossible. The damn leg. Oh, how it ached and ached. It was as though none of it had even been removed. Even the empty socket seemed to ache as much as the rest of the leg that was intact. Strange. Strange as hell.

His eyes moved back to Jennifer. She was almost ready to give birth to her child. His heart swelled with pride, knowing that he was going to have the opportunity to have a big part in this. Maybe he would even see the new grandchild seconds after it was born. And hadn't Jennifer mentioned that she might name the child Frank Thadeus . . . ? This way, she had said, she could remember both fathers in the best way imaginable. He was damn glad that Nicholas had decided against having a Nicholas Junior running around the house. If he had, the name Thadeus would possibly have been forgotten forever . . . unless . . . yes . . . unless. . . . His thoughts went to home and the surprise he had waiting for Jennifer. . . .

He moved on toward the cluster of family that he could

silently call his own . . . glad at least that Nicholas had finally decided to like him.

Jennifer's eyes sparkled like the crystal chandeliers hanging above her. She had never seen such a beautiful interior in her life. And the electric lightbulbs did reflect so onto everything. Even the red velvet seats and wide stage curtain appeared to be more plush . . . looking as smooth as the petals of a prize-winning rose. Then when Thad reached her, she turned and stared in disbelief toward him. The lines had smoothed a bit around his eyes and mouth, and his hair had been dyed a jet black and smoothed neatly with pomade.

Why, he was his old self, it seemed. It was hard to even believe that he wore an artificial leg, he walked so smoothly and so straight-backed. His black frock coat fit snugly along his shoulders and he was wearing his usual silk cravat, displaying a diamond stickpin. Yes. He was the man she remembered from San Francisco. He had somehow left behind him the old man she had seen only a few months before.

She moved as quickly as her heaviness would allow and hugged him to her. "Thad. Oh, Thad," she sighed. "It's so good to see you." She pulled away and stood at arm's length from him, still studying him. His pale gray eyes were twinkling and his cheeks were rosy from his own anxiety. She was glad to see that he had gained back some of his former weight. "And don't you look content? Is this new theater of yours the reason? Or is it this new female interest you've only barely hinted at?" she quickly added.

"A bit of both," Thad said, smiling. His gaze moved past Jennifer, to Nicholas. "And how have you been faring, Oglesby?" he asked, offering a hand of friendship.

Nicholas stepped forward and offered a firm grip in return. "Just fine, Brewster," he answered. "A bit impatient, though, where the newest member of my family is concerned. I don't think the baby is ever going to decide to show its face to us."

Thad pulled Nicholas aside and whispered, "Is there any true dangers . . . of . . . uh . . . the baby causing Jennifer's . . . death . . . ?"

"God, Thad," Nicholas grumbled. "Don't even think along those lines."

"Had to ask," Thad said, clearing his throat nervously. "I've been damned worried myself. Surely you know that."

"Well, now that she's here so close to the hospital, we can maybe quit some of that worrying."

Thad forced a smile and went to stand between his two granddaughters. He placed a hand on each head, feeling hair that reminded him of pure silk. "And would you girls like to go exploring in my fantasy land?" he asked, winking.

Martha squealed, bouncing her pigtails from her shoulders as she began to jump up and down. "Can we, Uncle Thad? Can we?"

Thad looked more intensely at Martha. Her pale gray eyes matched his own. And her willowy limbs showed that her future height would be in proportion to what his had once been. Yes, she was a granddaughter after his heart. "Go have a ball," he laughed, then gestured toward the balcony that hung low overhead. "And even run up there if you like. You can get a bird's eye view from there."

Carolyn Ann looked upward at Thad through blue, slanted eyes, causing a chill of sorts to race through Thad's blood. "And may we even go on your fine stage, Uncle Thad?" she asked, so very politely. She batted her heavy lashes nervously and said further, "You see, I would like to be an actress one day."

Thad's eyes widened as he glanced quickly at Jennifer, then Nicholas, then back at Carolyn Ann. His pulse was racing. He bent and placed his hands on Carolyn's shoulders. "You truly wish to be an actress?" he asked, barely audible.

"Even on your stage some day, Uncle Thadeus," she said proudly, realizing she had suddenly become the center of attention. Martha had managed to get the most attention until now by her way of acting like a boy; now Carolyn had found that her own secret world was something to be recognized for.

"Then, yes. Rush up on the stage. See the beautiful curtain and the way the electric lights shine on it?" He straightened his back and gestured toward the stage, beaming. "Just imagine yourself on the stage, with curtain drawn, and an audience applauding you!"

Jennifer's face became flushed. She didn't want this sort of future for her daughter . . . for *any* daughter. "Thadeus," she gasped, interrupting him.

Thad's eyes held a deep hurt as he turned to face Jennifer.

"I don't want you encouraging her childish dream, Thad," Jennifer said, trembling a bit.

"But, why Mother?" Carolyn whined, turning her lips into a brooding pout.

"We'll talk about it later," Jennifer snapped. "And if there's any exploring to be done, you'd best get along with it. I don't believe we'll be here long, will we, Thad? I'm also anxious to see your new house." She couldn't tell him that she felt a desperation rising inside her, feeling that possibly Carolyn Ann was serious . . . that she had perhaps been dreaming about a future of being the queen of some movie house, even. No. She had to get her daughter away from this place. Immediately, if at all possible.

Nicholas moved forward, checking his pocket watch. "I'm the one who has to rush," he said, watching his daughters running up and down the aisles of the theater, and in between the seats. "And you will see to my wife's safety? You have your carriage handy just in case the stork decides to come calling?"

"The finest carriage available," Thad boasted. "And one day soon, when my theater shows some profit, I plan to place an order for another automobile. Damn if the earth didn't just open up and swallow my other automobile whole."

"Damn shame, Thad," Nicholas commiserated.

"It's in the past," Thad said, patting Nicholas on the back. "Now you just go on. The paintings should sell fast. Seems the townspeople are buying more frills these days."

Nicholas pulled a small slip of paper from his front breeches pocket, checking what was written on it. "It says here 201 East

Seventh Avenue,'' he said, then thrust it back inside his pocket. ''I should be able to find your house easy enough.''

Thad placed his arm around Nicholas's shoulder. ''Glad you brought your family, Oglesby,'' he said thickly. ''You know how I appreciate it.''

''The girls are a handful, Brewster,'' Nicholas chuckled. ''The day might come you'll regret your invitation. Just hope your house is bigger than ours so they can spread out their fun a bit.''

''It's big enough, Oglesby. You'll soon see.''

Nicholas went to Jennifer and pulled her into his arms . . . as close as humanly possible. ''If you feel the time for the baby is upon you, be sure and get to the hospital first and then send a messenger boy to fetch me,'' he said kissing her gently on the lips.

''I will,'' she whispered, taking his hand, squeezing it.

''Then I must run, hon.''

''I hope you sell all you've painted this time. Give you an incentive to paint even more.''

Nicholas laughed. ''Do I need more incentive?''

''I truly doubt it,'' she answered.

A final soft kiss and another fast handshake and Nicholas was gone. When he climbed aboard the carriage, his heart raced. He loved to mingle with the people on the streets. It made him feel free . . . soaring. . . .

But he was always anxious to return to Jennifer . . . knowing there would always be a next time . . . and a next . . . and a next to return to the eagerness of people wanting to purchase his works.

He gave the reins a slap and turned the buggy into the thickness of traffic of other horse-drawn carriages and even an occasional shiny automobile. He grumbled to himself, ''Those things'll never last. Just junk. The horse and carriage will always be much more dependable.''

His eyes lit up when he saw a crowd of people mulling around the vendors' outdoor stands. His heart hammered out the minutes that it would take him to line his pictures up along the sidewalk. He couldn't wait to see the look of admiration in the people's eyes when they began to pick up and study his paintings.

The sound of footsteps racing around overhead made Jennifer tense. She looked in seriousness toward Thad. "Can Martha Elaine and Carolyn Ann fall from the balcony?"

Thad pulled a cigar from inside his jacket pocket and wet its tip with the swirl of his tongue. "No need to worry, Jennifer," he said, lighting the cigar. He walked to a large ashtray and flipped the burned-out match into it. He fitted his hands into his front breeches pockets, staring admiringly around him. "And do you really like it, Jennifer? Is my theater an eye catcher or isn't it?"

Once again Jennifer took it all in. The theater appeared to be made all of red velvets. The many overhead chandeliers tinkled as an unseen breeze blew gently against them.

Even though she wanted to be sure Carolyn had no part in this theater's future, she couldn't keep from thinking about maybe being in the audience one day. Maybe after the baby was born and all was well. "It's too beautiful," she said. "And I have to ask. Is your new lady friend an aspiring actress like Lil was?"

Shadows fell across Thad's face with the mention of Lil. He chewed on the cigar, then answered. "I've got a surprise for you, Jennifer," he said. "Get the girls and let me take you to my home."

"But your lady friend," she said softly. "When shall I meet her?"

Thad puffed eagerly on his cigar as he walked away from her. He glanced over his shoulders and said, "Get the girls. Come and see my surprise."

Jennifer looked after him in wonder. She went to the steps, then yelled as gracefully as possible, "Martha Elaine, Carolyn Ann! We're going to Uncle Thad's house!"

Chapter Twenty-seven

Stepping up into Thad's carriage, Jennifer was reminded of another time; oh, so long ago it seemed. The night of her arrival in San Francisco from Seattle had been one of a swirling, rolling damp mist. If she closed her eyes, she could remember it all so vividly . . . Nicholas rushing away from her . . . leaving her to stand alone on the ship's deck . . . then herself hurrying to Thad's carriage with its flickering lamps flanking the perch on each side. . . .

"Are you all right, Mother?" Carolyn asked, scooting next to Jennifer in the carriage.

Jennifer blinked her eyes and looked quickly around her. It had been so easy to let herself drift back into the past . . . but this was now . . . the present. She had it all. But, oh, what struggles she had been through to get her to this point in her life. She laughed nervously, making room for Martha to scoot onto the seat on the other side of her. "I'm fine, sweetheart," she said. "Just fine."

"You did look a bit funny, mother," Martha said, chewing on the tip of a pigtail. "I thought maybe it was the baby. Oh, when shall you ever have that baby?"

Jennifer pulled the pigtail from between Martha's lips. "The baby will come . . . when it comes," she said, then smiled toward Thad as he moved onto the seat across from her. "This is such a lovely carriage, Thad," she said, feeling the comfort of the thickly stuffed cushion beneath her. The seats, as well as the fringe-edged curtains at the two windows, were made of green velvet. Oh, so rich-appearing. Brass rings glistened on pale-colored shades beneath the curtains and one lone gaslight glowed warmly at the far end, next to where Thad sat.

"I've once again learned how to live luxuriously," he boasted. "When I saw how much money I made from the sale of my ships, nothing could keep me at Minnie's."

Feeling the jolt of the carriage as the horses began to draw it along the cobblestone streets, Jennifer clutched at her abdomen. Sudden jolts always caused added pains to begin. She felt cold sweat beading her brow, but pretended otherwise. She laughed nervously. "So you and Aunt Minnie didn't hit it off so good, huh?"

Thad lit a fresh cigar and filled the carriage interior with a fragrance similar to baked apples. "She's too set in her ways," he grumbled, frowning.

"And you're not, Thad?"

"Now I didn't say that," he said. "But, Jennifer, if I'd have stayed around all those old folk any longer, I'd be in my grave now. Damn. It was so depressing at Minnie's. I had to get away."

"Your house. Is it as grand as the one you had in San Francisco?"

"Yes, you might say that," Thad chuckled. "You just might say that."

The loud shouts from street vendors grabbed Jennifer's attention. She leaned as best she could toward the window, hoping to see Nicholas. Disappointment sent a sad pang around her heart, then she found herself studying the vendor who was offering roses to her. Again she was reminded of her parents' graves. Her gaze shot to Thad. Would he . . . ?

"What is it, Jennifer?" he asked, seeing the questioning in her eyes.

"I'd like some of those roses the vendor is offering," she said softly.

Thad tapped on the window that separated him from his private coachman. This was always an order to stop the carriage. "Then roses it shall be," he said, scooting to open the door. He leaned his head out and ordered one bouquet.

"Make it two please," Jennifer said, blushing a bit. "And gold ones, please."

Thad's eyebrows tilted, but he reached into his pocket and pulled enough crisp green bills from it to cover the cost of two separate bouquets. He offered them to Jennifer, smiling amusedly.

"Thank you, Thad," she said, pressing her nose into the softness, inhaling the heady sweetness.

Thad closed the door and tapped on the window for the carriage to resume its journey. "And now, may I ask . . . why two?" he questioned her, puffing on his cigar again.

Jennifer's lashes blinked nervously. "I'm going to ask one more thing of you, Thad," she said quietly.

"Anything you want, I'll give. You know that."

"I'd like to go to the cemetery," she blurted, casting her eyes downward. She knew how he would react. They had never gone to the cemetery together to see the graves of mother . . . lover . . . brother . . . father. . . . She didn't know if he had ever even gone in private. Camille had been so many things to him . . . as she had been to Jennifer.

But now Jennifer felt the need to bring past and present together and seal the two together for eternity. In this way, life could be made easier for the Brewsters who remained alive. . . .

"The . . . cemetery . . . ?" he gasped, growing ashen. He suddenly looked a bit older to Jennifer. His facial lines were deeper and there was a strain around his lips.

"I haven't been for so long, Thad."

"But why . . . now . . . ?"

''It's just something I feel. I have the need to see my parents' graves.''

''Yes . . . your parents. . . .'' he said, looking away from her.

She wanted to reach out to him with her heart, tell him of her deep love and affection for him . . . to reassure him. But two sets of eyes had widened . . . silently watching. . . .

''Then we can go, Thad?'' she pleaded, reaching over to take his hand.

His eyes shot around, the pale gray almost empty. ''It's so important?''

''Yes, it is.''

''We shall go then,'' he said, tapping on the window again. When the coachman slid the window aside, to inquire, Thad instructed him, then grew silent with crossed arms and furrowed brow.

It wasn't long until Jennifer felt the familiar strain of the carriage, and she knew that the horses were moving uphill. The cemetery would soon be reached . . . and then what? How would Thad react when he saw his beloved Camille's grave? How would Jennifer feel?

''Mother?'' Carolyn whispered.

''Yes, darling?''

''May I hold one bouquet of roses?''

Jennifer smiled and placed the bouquet in her arms.

Not wanting to be outdone, Martha nudged her mother's arm.

''Yes, Martha?''

''May I hold the other?''

Jennifer placed it on Martha's lap. Tears formed at the corner of her eyes, knowing how much her father would have loved his granddaughters. Then her gaze shot toward Thad . . . her father . . . and she thought: *No. I must remember. They are Thad's granddaughters. And isn't he so proud?*

''Why did you have Uncle Thadeus buy the flowers, Mother?'' Carolyn questioned.

Jennifer placed an arm around each daughter.

They had been at the cemetery, but only once. They had

been too small to ask questions then. A child of two or three just romps and plays atop graves ... not realizing what lies beneath. But children the ages of her daughters? They had to know it all, or die of curiosity. "They are for your grandmother and grandfather's graves," she finally answered, evading Thad's look of despair.

"Do you mean your own mother and father?" Martha asked, rolling the petal of a rose between her fingers.

Jennifer brushed her daughter's hand away, frowning at her. Such a nervous, fidgety child. Surely she would grow out of it. "Yes, my mother and father," she answered sullenly.

"Was your mother pretty like you?" Carolyn questioned, moving her face closer to Jennifer's.

A quick glance from Thad made Jennifer grow tense, causing pains to circle her abdomen again. She looked away, chewing on her lower lip. Suddenly she doubted the wisdom of her intentions. Maybe deep wounds would only be made wider from a visit to the cemetery. But she had only to remember her first idea. That, somehow, this could make some of the rights wrong. By facing up to the past ... surely something good could come from it. "Yes, my mother was very pretty," she sighed. Then she lifted a finger to trace Carolyn's facial features, seeing so much of herself *and* Camille in her. "Just like you, sweetheart."

Martha nudged Jennifer again. "And just like me?" she said loudly.

Jennifer laughed softly, reaching to hug Martha. "And, yes, just like you also, my sweet."

The carriage came to a halt. When Jennifer leaned forward to see through the side window, many gravestones made of marble and some of cheaper stone met her eyes. Now she knew that Thad had made his own visits to the cemetery. How else would the coachman know where to stop? He had carried them almost exactly to the spot. . . .

Jennifer's eyes burned with the need to cry freely as the past swirled all around her. She swallowed hard, watching Thad, so aware of the efforts it took for him to move from the carriage.

His artificial leg made him a bit clumsy, making even more of the past move to the front of Jennifer's mind.

Jennifer waited until she was the only one left in the carriage, then scooted, groaning, until Thad had her by the elbow and helped her down onto the ground.

Her eyes searched for the familiar twin marble gravestones. When she saw them, a slow, aching pain circled her heart. Camille's had been recently visited. Fresh, long-stemmed red roses had opened to the rays of the sun, still standing in the statuesque vase that had been inserted into the ground on Camille's own private mound of ground.

Jennifer and Thad exchanged quick glances and it was evident who had been at the grave, possibly even earlier this morning. . . .

"Shall we?" Thad said, offering an arm.

"Thank you," Jennifer answered, then lifted her skirt and began to walk through ankle-high grass, avoiding other mounds of dirt, where fresh graves had been dug.

When Jennifer saw the fading photographs of her mother and father beneath glass on the front of the gravestones, she couldn't keep the tears from burning her cheeks. She accepted a handkerchief from Thad, avoiding his eyes. It had been Aunt Minnie's idea to place the photographs into the marble. Now it only made the hurt worse. Her mother's perfect face was the face of an angel, the truth of what she really had been tore at Jennifer's heart.

And then looking at her father's face and the sadness stored in the depth of his eyes for the rest of eternity made her turn her head away, only to sob even more loudly.

"Mother?"

The voice from the present was welcomed. Jennifer cleared her throat and wiped her eyes free as she stepped between her daughters. "This is where your grandmother lies," she whispered, coughing into a cupped hand. "Martha Elaine, please lay the bouquet you have up next to the gravestone . . . next to those . . . that are already there." She glanced quickly toward Thad once again, then cast her eyes downward when he looked quickly away from her.

In silence, Martha did so. . . .

"Now this other gravestone shows where your grandfather lies," Jennifer said, glancing toward Thad once again, aching for him. "Carolyn Ann, please place your bouquet there."

"Yes, Mother," Carolyn said, then stopped and paused long enough to study the portrait, then very reverently placed the flowers on the ground.

"Grandmother was beautiful," Martha sighed, studying the photograph. Then she went to Thad and took a hand in hers. "Uncle Thadeus, did you ever know my grandmother?"

Thad tossed his half-smoked cigar over his shoulder, looking suddenly tired. "Yes, I knew your grandmother," he answered. "You see, she was my sister-in-law. Your granddaddy's wife."

"Why did she die, Mother?" Carolyn blurted. "She looks so young. Even as young as you."

It was as though arrows were piercing Jennifer's heart. She hadn't expected such a question. With her eyes she pleaded with Thad for a quick, safe answer.

He walked over to stand next to Carolyn and grabbed her hand, now having both granddaughters next to him. "Because God asked her to come to Heaven to be with him," he answered. "Just as he did your . . . your . . . grandfather."

Jennifer's hands went to her throat, choked with emotion. She had never expected Thad . . . her Uncle Thad . . . to speak of . . . God. She had never known him to even enter a house of the Lord . . . not even when his own brother preached a weekly sermon. She now knew that Thad hadn't only found renewed success in Seattle . . . but a spiritual happiness as well. She suddenly felt that things were indeed going to be all right. It appeared that Thad had accepted the past as best he could, and was ready to move onward, which meant that Jennifer could feel more relaxed whenever she spoke of Camille . . . or Frank.

"So they are happy?" Martha said.

"Yes, quite," Thad answered.

"Just like you and me?" Martha persisted.

Thad's coloring returned and he smiled warmly toward Jennifer. "Yes. Just like you, me, your sister, mother and father," he boasted, holding his head high. "We are all very happy."

A lump dissolved in Jennifer's throat. She went to Thad and touched him tenderly on the cheek.

"Now then. What say we head for my house. I still have a surprise waiting there," he laughed.

"Surprise?" the small girls yelled in unison. "We love surprises." They both took off running toward the carriage, leaving Thad and Jennifer standing alone before the graves.

Jennifer was the first to speak. "Is it all behind us now . . . Father?" she asked, swallowing hard.

Thad hugged her to him, knowing that this was a new beginning. "Yes," he said thickly.

"But you know, I can only call you Father when we're alone."

"Yes, I know."

"Shall we go? I also love surprises."

Jennifer knew now that it hadn't been only the spiritual awakening that had caused Thad's sudden change, but the innocence of her children . . . their questions . . . that had helped mend the inner wounds. Jennifer cringed when even a sharper pain shot through her, but smiled, eager to bring this other child of hers into this world.

Chapter Twenty-eight

Leaning heavily into Thad's embrace, Jennifer puffed and wheezed as he helped her up the steep steps of his house. She looked upward at the cantilevered windows and the gingerbread ornamentation that lined the roof of this very Victorian house. "I still can't get over it, Thad," she said. "You have had a house built that is the exact duplicate of the San Francisco Brewster house. I find that most amazing."

Thad chuckled. "If you are amazed by the outside, just you wait until you see what I've done inside."

Jennifer's eyes widened. "You didn't. . . ." she gasped.

Thad reached for the front door and opened it, stepping aside for Jennifer to enter, then his granddaughters after her. . . .

The breath caught in Jennifer's throat when she walked from the foyer on into the parlor, staring wide-eyed as she took in the familiarity of this all now surrounding her. It was as though she had stepped into the past . . . the Brewster past that had tumbled to piles and dust and rubble when the earthquake had taken its revenge on all the sordid past deeds of the Brewsters.

"It is the same. . . ." she whispered, beginning to walk around the room, touching the thickly cushioned, gilt-trimmed chairs and the smoothness of the redwood furniture. Thad had duplicated his house, even to the flower-bedecked wall coverings and fabrics. And when her eyes traveled upward, she discovered, yes, he had even duplicated the gallery, with a similar brass railing overlooking the living room. Above her also, the magnificent chandelier's electric lights sparkled as hundreds of rare diamonds would. And the wall sconces burned brightly, each with its individual lightbulb inside it.

The electric lights were the only difference, it seemed, in this house that only a Brewster could be the owner of.

Thad moved next to Jennifer, knitting his brow, speaking as though he had just read her thoughts. "The only things that are missing are the family portraits and my collection of books that I had filled my library with," he said sorrowfully. "But in time . . . maybe those can be replaced . . . by this generation of Brewsters."

By an elbow, Thad guided Jennifer further into the parlor. An oriental rug lay in its splendor in front of a huge fireplace that had a fire smoldering on its hearth, and above this fireplace there was an empty space on the wall, where, it was obvious, Thad had plans to request another portrait painted by Nicholas.

Jennifer touched her forehead, feeling suddenly light-headed. She moved toward a chair and slowly settled down onto it. "May I have a drink of water, Thad?" she whispered, seeing things spinning a bit before her eyes.

Thad's concern lined his face. "What's wrong, Jennifer?"

"Oh, the usual," she complained. "All that goes with my ninth month of being with child."

"Maybe a glass of sherry . . .?"

"No, Thad. Just water. I've been too afraid to partake of spirits during this particular pregnancy." She tried to compose herself when her daughters fell at her feet, eyeing her wonderingly. She knew what was probably on their minds. The baby had been the prime subject of their thoughts for way too long now. She reached up and touched them both on the cheeks, smiling. "You girls relax now," she said. "Mother is just having one of her weak spells. That's all. Nothing to worry about.''

''Then can we go and explore this magnificent house?'' Carolyn asked.

''And also the grounds, Mother?'' Martha piped in.

''Yes. I think that is a very good idea,'' Jennifer said, then thanked Thad when he handed her a goblet filled with sparkling, clear water. She took several fast swallows, then closed her eyes and sucked in a deep gulp of air. Then she smiled as she pushed herself up from the chair. ''I do feel a bit foolish, Thad,'' she said. ''Here I am a house guest and suddenly causing alarm.''

''But you are all right?'' Thad asked, circling her waist with an arm.

''Yes, Thad,'' she answered, seeing her daughters still standing, waiting for Thad's permission to take a grand tour of his house. ''And, Thad, is it all right if Martha and Carolyn go exploring? I'm sure they wouldn't leave any fingerprints on your lovely polished furniture, or on your freshly painted walls.''

Thad laughed and went and gave the girls a quick swat on their behinds. ''Now get along with you girls,'' he said. ''This house is now yours, as well as mine. Always remember that.''

Giggling trailed along behind Martha and Carolyn as they dashed up the steep staircase and disappeared from sight.

''I think they forgot about the surprise you mentioned,'' Jennifer said, smiling. Her eyes twinkled. ''But I haven't, Thad.'' She began to look around her once again, seeing that possibly this house alone was the surprise that he had spoken of. It was indeed a surprise to her. But she felt there was something else to Thad's surprise. It showed in the depth of his eyes. A silent amusement. A silent pride. . . .

''I shall return in only a matter of moments with my surprise,'' he said, turning on a heel to hurry from the room, only to be slowed by the stairs.

It pained Jennifer still to see him struggle with climbing with his artificial limb. But she could remember when he had almost given up even trying. It was quite a relief to see this changed man. The future seemed so bright for him . . . for them all. . . .

A quick, driving pain sent Jennifer back to a chair. She clutched at her abdomen, panting heavily. ''Oh, God,'' she said aloud. ''I think . . . maybe . . . my time has for sure arrived now.'' Perspiration trickled down her cheeks, wetting the tips of her hair that circled her face.

''Thad?'' she whispered, wishing he would return . . . and quickly. She had to get to the hospital. God. She hadn't expected this to come on her so quickly.

The bearing-down pressure inside her felt as though the . . . baby . . . was trying . . . to release itself from her body. . . .

Another searing pain made a muffled scream erupt from between her lips and the lightheadedness returned. She clasped onto the arms of the chair, spreading her legs, praying that what was happening . . . wasn't. When a wetness flooded from inside her and wet the skirt of her dress and made a pool in the chair beneath her . . . she knew that her water had just broken . . . and that the baby wasn't far behind.

''Thad!'' she screamed, trying to push herself upward. ''Oh, God, Thad!'' she screamed, then closed her eyes when another pain wracked her body into a million throbbing pinpricks.

A rushing of feet made Jennifer turn, only causing her more pain. She closed her eyes and felt soft, warm hands caressing her brow. Then when a woman's voice spoke, Jennifer looked upward onto a face of gentleness and warmth. . . .

''We'll need plenty of hot water and some blankets,'' Gloria said, stooping to hold Jennifer, to calm her.

''Who . . . are . . . you . . . ?'' Jennifer gasped, seeing that this woman was pregnant, but by only a few months.

Gloria laughed softly. ''I believe I'm the surprise Thad told you about,'' she said, smoothing some hair from Jennifer's brow.

Jennifer's eyes traveled over this woman. She appeared to be in her late twenties, with a full, rounded face, dark eyes shaded by thick lashes, and a kind smile. Her dress was one of full pleats, rust, to match the coloring of the hair that was piled high on her head, circled in a tight bun. "You're . . . the . . . surprise . . . ?" Jennifer said throatily.

"I'm Thad's wife," Gloria whispered, looking anxious as Jennifer strained with more pains. "Gloria. I'm Gloria."

Jennifer clamped her lips together tightly, then whispered, "My baby . . . I . . . think . . . it's coming. . . ."

"I know, I know," Gloria said, glad to see servants assisting Thad with bringing blankets and other necessary objects for the birthing of a child into the room. "Make a thick pallet on the floor in front of the fire. Add even more wood to get the room warmer. Jennifer shouldn't be allowed to take a chill . . . nor the baby . . . when it arrives."

"On . . . the floor . . . ?" Thad gasped.

"We must. Now," Gloria commanded.

Fear gripped Jennifer even more than pain. Her eyes widened. "You mean . . . I'm . . . going to have to have the baby here?" she said, almost frantic.

"My dear, you don't have much time," Gloria said, examining Jennifer's abdomen with deft fingers.

"Before marrying Thad . . . I was a nurse," she said. "Now, my dear, you must move to the pallet. I need to make a thorough examination, to see how the baby is positioned."

Tears swelled in Jennifer's eyes. She hadn't expected anything like this to happen. She had thought to be in the safety of a hospital, with only experts around her. But now? To have the baby in Thad's house? Be assisted by his . . . wife . . . ? God. His wife! And a wife so obviously with child herself? Why hadn't Thad told her? Why had he kept it a secret?

"Come on, my dear," Gloria reassured. "You will be in good hands. I have aided in many deliveries. "

Thad moved to help Jennifer, helping her to spread out onto the pallet. Jennifer looked upward at him, puzzled still by what she had found out. But it was giving her more to worry about than the pains . . . the birth. . . .

Then she remembered. The country doctor had said that the baby was turned wrong. "The baby," she said groaning when a fresh pain caused her to stop and bite her lip.

Gloria moved to the floor and covered Jennifer to her waist with a blanket, then searched beneath the blanket with her hands, removing Jennifer's underpants. With skilled fingers, she probed and pushed, then slowly inserted her fingers into Jennifer's outspread vaginal lips. "Yes, just as I suspected," she said quietly. Her eyes turned upward, seeing Thad watching with all the fear that a father would feel for a daughter. "You can assist, Thad?" she whispered.

"What . . . must . . . I do . . . ?"

"Anything that I might suddenly ask of you," she blurted, knowing the pain that he must be feeling at this moment. Thank God he had told her all. She knew now how to cope with both daughter and father.

He knitted his brow, seeing Jennifer in such pain, and his wife on her knees, also with child . . . but ready to help with the birthing of another. He tried to push doubt from his mind, but couldn't. "Can't we have time to take her to the hospital?" he asked.

"No. I say that this child is only moments away."

"My girls . . ." Jennifer suddenly cried. "Please see that they are kept from this room."

"I have already seen to that," Thad said, maneuvering his way down, to be by her side, taking her hands in his. He set his jaw firmly, then said, "Go on, Gloria. Let's get this thing over with. My Jennifer is about to have her baby in her father's house."

"Okay . . . now. . . ." Gloria said patiently. "Jennifer, I am going to reach up inside you as you have your next pain. Then, when you get ready to push, I will assist in turning the baby to the right position. Do you understand?"

"Can . . . you . . . truly . . . do that . . . ?"

"I've midwifed many times before. Please trust me."

Jennifer threw her head back and moaned loudly when the next pain engulfed her. She squeezed mercifully onto Thad's hands, then pushed down with all her might . . . as soft, gentle hands reached up inside her and gave the baby a quick turn. Then, as the hand was released, so was the baby.

Gloria squealed like a teenager. "It's a girl, Jennifer," she shouted. "It's . . . a girl!"

"A . . . girl . . . ?" Jennifer thrilled. Now she had three daughters. Fleeting disappointment passed through her . . . that Nicholas hadn't been present when the child was born . . . and that she hadn't given him the son she knew he had silently prayed for. But he would love this daughter as he loved the two before this one. She knew this to be true. She knew Nicholas . . . sweet . . . sweet . . . Nicholas.

"Another granddaughter," Thad sighed. He watched his wife expertly cut and tie the umbilical cord, then lift the baby to Jennifer's arms. "And what will you call this daughter, Jennifer?" he asked proudly.

"I don't know," she whispered. "You know that Nicholas and I had been expecting a boy." She studied the baby's tiny facial features. She just couldn't have been as proud with her other births. She just couldn't. The feelings of fulfillment were flooding her senses with warm splashes of joy. Her heart throbbed anxiously as the baby opened her eyes and seemed to look at her, squinting. This child was its own individual person. It didn't resemble any Oglesby . . . or Brewster. Could she name her child . . . ? She closed her eyes as a tremble shook her body.

Thad touched her free hand, feeling its iciness. "Good Lord," he exclaimed. "We must get you upstairs. To a bed. We *can* move her now, can't we, Gloria?"

"Yes, dear," Gloria said, taking the baby to clean it and wrap it in a blanket of its own.

"Gloria?" Jennifer said.

Gloria smiled as she fussed with the baby. "Yes?" she said.

"Thank you. I shall always be grateful."

"So you approve of my surprise?" Thad asked, tilting an eyebrow.

Jennifer managed a soft laugh. "She's more than I could have ever expected," she said.

"Didn't think this old man had it in him, did you?"

"I'm very happy for you. So very, very happy for you, Thad."

"You don't look to me as a dirty ol' man?" he asked. "By marrying someone so much younger . . . and getting her with child so quickly?"

Jennifer pushed herself up on an elbow. "You could never be called a dirty old man," she said. "Please don't say that."

"Respectable is the title I choose to be labeled with. Nothing more. Nothing less."

Gloria moved next to him, showing him his tiny grand-daughter. Only the baby's face showed from beneath the wrapped blanket. "And soon we shall have a baby of our own," she said. "Won't it be nice to have two small ones in the Brewster family at the same time? Think of the alliance the two can establish."

"Yes. Think of it," Thad said, then glanced quickly at Jennifer again, remembering how cold she had felt to him. He began to walk away, talking over his shoulder. "I must get some servants to assist in lifting Jennifer upstairs. I won't be a minute."

Gloria settled down onto a chair, still admiring the bundle in her arms. "Thad is so proud, Jennifer," she sighed.

"Yes, I . . . know. . . ."

"And has a name come to you yet?"

Jennifer's eyes lowered. "Yes. I believe so."

"Oh, I am so anxious to hear what you'll be naming this dear."

"I must first see what Nicholas thinks of my choice. Then if he approves, I shall share it with everyone else."

"It must be a special name to give to such a special child," Gloria whispered.

"It is a special name," Jennifer said. "It . . . truly is. . . ."

The sun filtered across the bed in gold velvet streamers. The baby slept soundly in the bed next to Jennifer. Jennifer lay content, looking around her, liking what Thad had done with the spare bedroom. The wallpaper was of a delicate pattern of wild violets, dotted with pale orchids, and orchid-colored satin draperies hung at the windows to match, and the furnishings were of solid red oak.

Jennifer listened to footsteps approaching and watched the door anxiously, hoping it was Nicholas. Thad had sent for him as soon as he had seen her settled comfortably in bed. When the door swung widely open and Nicholas rushed to Jennifer's side, the familiar racing of her heart filled her with a special warmth.

"Darling," Nicholas said, taking her hand in his. "When the messenger boy told me that a girl child had been born to me, all I could think about was you. Your safety. You are all right, aren't you?"

Jennifer lifted her fingers to his lips. "Shh, my love," she said. "Can't you see? And also our daughter. She came through this with all fingers and toes intact."

Nicholas leaned down and lifted a corner of the blanket, pride swelling his head. He had wanted a son . . . but damn it . . . who could regret having fathered such a tiny . . . sweet baby girl? "She is perfect, Jennifer," he said thickly. His gaze moved to Jennifer. "But we do have us a problem, don't we?"

Jennifer's heart skipped a beat. "A . . . problem?" she asked quietly, wondering if he really was too disappointed.

"A name. Have you come up with another name for a girl?" he blurted. "One that can fit in well enough with Martha and Carolyn?"

Relief flooded her senses. She exhaled deeply, then said, "You have none in mind yourself, Nicholas?"

"A girl's name should be chosen by its mother," Nicholas said firmly.

"Then whatever I choose will be approved by you?"

He straightened his back and placed his hands in his rear breeches pockets. "Most certainly," he boomed.

Jennifer's gaze went to the baby. She now felt free to call this child what she had ached to call Carolyn Ann until Jennifer had seen the slant to Carolyn Ann's eyes. The resemblance to Thad was too strong—the association between herself, her child and Thad would have been too apparent.

But now that Jennifer had another daughter, one who so far resembled no one but her own self, and now that all past feelings had been put to rest, she felt free to call this daughter ... Camille. . . .

Her thoughts went to Thad. He had begun a new life for himself, with a new wife, a wife who was young enough to bear him a son ... a son to possibly carry the Brewster name on into a future of even more Brewsters. Surely he had so much going for him ... he wouldn't be too upset by another Camille in the family.

She looked up at Nicholas. "I just hope Thad won't mind. . . ." she blurted.

"Mind about what, Jennifer?"

"About the name I have chosen. . . ."

"And why would he? What have you chosen?"

"Camille," she whispered. "I will name this daughter ... Camille."

The color rushed from Nicholas's face. "Camille?" he stammered. "Did you say . . .?"

"Yes. Camille," Jennifer said firmly, knowing that no one would change her mind. No one. It was as though by giving this daughter the name Camille ... it was as though she was giving her mother another lease on life.

Yes, this Camille would be a woman of morals ... of purity. . . .

Books by Bestselling Author
Fern Michaels

___The Jury	0-8217-7878-1	$6.99US/$9.99CAN
___Sweet Revenge	0-8217-7879-X	$6.99US/$9.99CAN
___Lethal Justice	0-8217-7880-3	$6.99US/$9.99CAN
___Free Fall	0-8217-7881-1	$6.99US/$9.99CAN
___Fool Me Once	0-8217-8071-9	$7.99US/$10.99CAN
___Vegas Rich	0-8217-8112-X	$7.99US/$10.99CAN
___Hide and Seek	1-4201-0184-6	$6.99US/$9.99CAN
___Hokus Pokus	1-4201-0185-4	$6.99US/$9.99CAN
___Fast Track	1-4201-0186-2	$6.99US/$9.99CAN
___Collateral Damage	1-4201-0187-0	$6.99US/$9.99CAN
___Final Justice	1-4201-0188-9	$6.99US/$9.99CAN
___Up Close and Personal	0-8217-7956-7	$7.99US/$9.99CAN
___Under the Radar	1-4201-0683-X	$6.99US/$9.99CAN
___Razor Sharp	1-4201-0684-8	$7.99US/$10.99CAN
___Yesterday	1-4201-1494-8	$5.99US/$6.99CAN
___Vanishing Act	1-4201-0685-6	$7.99US/$10.99CAN
___Sara's Song	1-4201-1493-X	$5.99US/$6.99CAN
___Deadly Deals	1-4201-0686-4	$7.99US/$10.99CAN
___Game Over	1-4201-0687-2	$7.99US/$10.99CAN
___Sins of Omission	1-4201-1153-1	$7.99US/$10.99CAN
___Sins of the Flesh	1-4201-1154-X	$7.99US/$10.99CAN
___Cross Roads	1-4201-1192-2	$7.99US/$10.99CAN

Available Wherever Books Are Sold!
Check out our website at **www.kensingtonbooks.com**

Romantic Suspense from
Lisa Jackson

See How She Dies	0-8217-7605-3	$6.99US/$9.99CAN
Final Scream	0-8217-7712-2	$7.99US/$10.99CAN
Wishes	0-8217-6309-1	$5.99US/$7.99CAN
Whispers	0-8217-7603-7	$6.99US/$9.99CAN
Twice Kissed	0-8217-6038-6	$5.99US/$7.99CAN
Unspoken	0-8217-6402-0	$6.50US/$8.50CAN
If She Only Knew	0-8217-6708-9	$6.50US/$8.50CAN
Hot Blooded	0-8217-6841-7	$6.99US/$9.99CAN
Cold Blooded	0-8217-6934-0	$6.99US/$9.99CAN
The Night Before	0-8217-6936-7	$6.99US/$9.99CAN
The Morning After	0-8217-7295-3	$6.99US/$9.99CAN
Deep Freeze	0-8217-7296-1	$7.99US/$10.99CAN
Fatal Burn	0-8217-7577-4	$7.99US/$10.99CAN
Shiver	0-8217-7578-2	$7.99US/$10.99CAN
Most Likely to Die	0-8217-7576-6	$7.99US/$10.99CAN
Absolute Fear	0-8217-7936-2	$7.99US/$9.49CAN
Almost Dead	0-8217-7579-0	$7.99US/$10.99CAN
Lost Souls	0-8217-7938-9	$7.99US/$10.99CAN
Left to Die	1-4201-0276-1	$7.99US/$10.99CAN
Wicked Game	1-4201-0338-5	$7.99US/$9.99CAN
Malice	0-8217-7940-0	$7.99US/$9.49CAN

Available Wherever Books Are Sold!
Visit our website at **www.kensingtonbooks.com**

More by Bestselling Author
Hannah Howell

__Highland Angel	978-1-4201-0864-4	$6.99US/$8.99CAN
__If He's Sinful	978-1-4201-0461-5	$6.99US/$8.99CAN
__Wild Conquest	978-1-4201-0464-6	$6.99US/$8.99CAN
__If He's Wicked	978-1-4201-0460-8	$6.99US/$8.49CAN
__My Lady Captor	978-0-8217-7430-4	$6.99US/$8.49CAN
__Highland Sinner	978-0-8217-8001-5	$6.99US/$8.49CAN
__Highland Captive	978-0-8217-8003-9	$6.99US/$8.49CAN
__Nature of the Beast	978-1-4201-0435-6	$6.99US/$8.49CAN
__Highland Fire	978-0-8217-7429-8	$6.99US/$8.49CAN
__Silver Flame	978-1-4201-0107-2	$6.99US/$8.49CAN
__Highland Wolf	978-0-8217-8000-8	$6.99US/$9.99CAN
__Highland Wedding	978-0-8217-8002-2	$4.99US/$6.99CAN
__Highland Destiny	978-1-4201-0259-8	$4.99US/$6.99CAN
__Only for You	978-0-8217-8151-7	$6.99US/$8.99CAN
__Highland Promise	978-1-4201-0261-1	$4.99US/$6.99CAN
__Highland Vow	978-1-4201-0260-4	$4.99US/$6.99CAN
__Highland Savage	978-0-8217-7999-6	$6.99US/$9.99CAN
__Beauty and the Beast	978-0-8217-8004-6	$4.99US/$6.99CAN
__Unconquered	978-0-8217-8088-6	$4.99US/$6.99CAN
__Highland Barbarian	978-0-8217-7998-9	$6.99US/$9.99CAN
__Highland Conqueror	978-0-8217-8148-7	$6.99US/$9.99CAN
__Conqueror's Kiss	978-0-8217-8005-3	$4.99US/$6.99CAN
__A Stockingful of Joy	978-1-4201-0018-1	$4.99US/$6.99CAN
__Highland Bride	978-0-8217-7995-8	$4.99US/$6.99CAN
__Highland Lover	978-0-8217-7759-6	$6.99US/$9.99CAN

Available Wherever Books Are Sold!

Check out our website at
http://www.kensingtonbooks.com